Stronghand
Or, The Noble Revenge

by

Gustave Aimard

Double 9
BOOKS

Stronghand
Or, The Noble Revenge
by Gustave Aimard

ISBN: 978-93-67141-21-2

Published by

DOUBLE 9 BOOKS

2/13-B, Ansari Road
Daryaganj, New Delhi – 110002
info@double9books.com
www.double9books.com
Tel. 011-40042856

ABOUT THE AUTHOR

Gustave Aimard (13 September 1818 - 20 June 1883) wrote several novels about Latin America and the American frontier. Oliver Aimard was born in Paris. As he previously stated, he was the offspring of two married individuals, "but not to each other". His father, François Sébastiani de la Porta (1775-1851), was a commander in Napoleon's army and a representative of the Louis Philippe government. Sébastiani was married to the Duchess of Coigny. In 1806, the couple had a daughter, Alatrice-Rosalba Fanny. The mother died shortly after she was born. Fanny was reared by her grandmother, Duchess of Coigny. According to the July 9, 1883 edition of the New York Times, Aimard's mother was named Madame.

CONTENTS

CHAPTER I
AN EXCHANGE OF SHOTS

The country extending between the Sierra de San Saba and the Rio Puerco, or Dirty River, is one of the most mournful and melancholy regions imaginable.

This accursed savannah, on which bleach unrecognized skeletons, which the wind and sun strive to convert into dust, is an immense desert, broadcast with grey rocks, beneath which snakes and wild beasts have, from time immemorial, formed their lurking-place, and which only produces black shrubs and stunted larches that rise from distance to distance above the desert.

White or Indian travellers rarely and most unwillingly venture to cross this frightful solitude, and at the risk of lengthening their journey they prefer making a detour and following the border, where they are certain of finding shade and water—those delights of tropical countries and indispensable necessities for a long trip on the western prairies.

Towards the second half of June—which the Navajo Indians call the "strawberry moon" in their harmonious language—and in the Year of Grace 1843, a horseman suddenly emerged from a thick clump of oaks, sumachs, and mahogany trees, entered the savannah at a gallop, and, instead of following the usual travellers' track, which was distinctly traced on the edge of the sand, he began without any hesitation crossing the desert in a straight line.

This resolution was a mark of great folly, or a proof of extraordinary daring on the part of a solitary man, however brave he might be; or else some imperious reasons compelled him to lay aside all prudence in order to reach his journey's end more speedily.

However, whatever the motives that might determine the traveller, he continued his journey rapidly, and buried himself deeper and deeper in the desert, without seeming to notice the gloomy and desolate aspect the landscape around him constantly assumed.

As this person is destined to play an important part in our story, we will draw his portrait in a few words. He was a man of from twenty-five to thirty years of age—belonging to the pure Mexican race, of average height, and possessed of elegant manners; while his every gesture, graceful though it was, revealed a far from ordinary strength. His face, with its regular features and bright hue, evidenced frankness, bravery, and kindliness; his black eyes, haughty and well open, had a straight and penetrating glance; his well cut mouth, adorned with dazzling white teeth, was half concealed beneath a long brown moustache; his chin, of too marked an outline perhaps, denoted a great firmness of character; in short, his whole appearance aroused interest and attracted sympathy.

As for his dress, it was the Mexico costume in all its picturesque richness. His broad-brimmed Vicuna skin hat, decorated with a double gold and silver *golilla*, was carelessly set on his right ear, and allowed curls of luxurious black hair to fall in disorder on his shoulders. He wore a jacket of green velvet, magnificently embroidered with gold, under which could be seen a worked linen shirt. An Indian handkerchief was fastened round his neck by a diamond ring. His *calzoneras*, also of green velvet, held round his hips by a red silk gold-fringed *faja* were embroidered and slashed like a jacket, while two rows of pearl-set gold buttons ran along the opening that extends from the boot to the knee. His vaquero boots, embroidered with pretty designs in red thread, were fastened to his legs by silk and gold garters, from one of which emerged the admirably carved hilt of a long knife. His zarapé, of Indian fabric and showy colours, was folded on the back of his horse, an animal full of fire, with fine legs, small head, and flashing eye. It was a true prairie mustang; and its master had decorated it with the coquettish elegance peculiar to Mexican horsemen.

In addition to the knife we referred to, and which the horseman wore in his right boot, he had also a long American rifle laid across his saddle-bow, two six-shot revolvers in his girdle, a machete, or species of straight sabre, which was passed, unsheathed, through an iron ring on his left side; and, lastly, a reata of plaited leather, rolled up and fastened to the saddle.

Thus armed, the man we have just described was able—on the admission that his determined appearance was not deceitful—to make head against several adversaries at once, without any serious disadvantage. This was a consideration not at all to be despised in a country where a traveller ever runs the risk of encountering an enemy, whether man or beast, and, at times both together.

While galloping, the horseman carelessly smoked a husk cigarette, only taking an absent and disdainful glance at the coveys of birds that rose on his approach, or the herds of deer and packs of foxes which fled in terror on hearing the horse's gallop.

The savannah, however, was already beginning to assume a more gloomy tinge; the sun, now level with the ground, only appeared on the horizon as a red unheated ball, and night was soon about to cover the earth with its dense gloom. The horseman drew up the bridle of his steed to check its speed, though not entirely stopping it, and, casting an investigating glance around him, seemed to be seeking a suitable spot for his night halt.

After a few seconds of this search, the traveller's determination was formed. He turned slightly to the left, and proceeded to a half dried up stream that ran along a short distance off, and on whose banks grew a few prickly shrubs and a clump of some dozen larches, forming a precarious shelter against the curiosity of those mysterious denizens of the desert that prowl about in search of prey during the darkness.

On drawing nearer, the traveller perceived to his delight that this spot, perfectly hidden from prying glances, by the conformation of the ground and a few blocks of stone scattered here and there among the trees and shrubs, offered him an almost certain shelter.

The journey had been tiring; and both man and horse felt themselves worn with fatigue. Both, before proceeding further, imperiously required a few hours' rest.

The horseman, as an experienced traveller, first attended to his steed, which he unsaddled and led to drink at the stream; then, after hobbling the animal for fear it might stray and become the prey of wild beasts, he stretched his zarapé on the ground, threw a few handfuls of Indian corn upon it, and when he was assured that his horse, in spite of its fatigue, was eating its provender willingly, he thought about himself.

Mexicans, when travelling, carry behind their saddle two canvas bags, called *alforjas*, intended to convey food, which it is impossible to procure in the desert; and these, with two jars filled with drinking water, form the sole baggage with which they cover enormous distances, and endure privations and fatigue, the mere enumeration of which would terrify Europeans, who are accustomed to enjoy all the conveniences supplied by an advanced stage of civilization.

The horseman opened his alforjas, sat down on the ground with his back against a rock, and, while careful that his weapons were within reach, for fear of being attacked unawares, he began supping philosophically on a piece of tasajo, some maize tortillas, and goat's cheese as hard as a flint, the whole being washed down with the pure water of the stream.

This repast, which was more than frugal, was soon terminated. The horseman, after cleaning his teeth with an elegant gold toothpick, rolled a pajilla, smoked it with that conscientious beatitude peculiar to the Hispano-Americans, and then wrapped himself in his zarapé, shut his eyes, and fell asleep.

Several hours passed; and it is probable that the traveller's sleep would have been prolonged for some time, had not two shots, fired a short distance from him, suddenly aroused him from his lethargy. The general rule on the prairie is, that when you hear a shot, it is rare for it not to have been preceded by the whistle of a bullet past your ear—in other words, there are ninety-nine reasons in a hundred that the lonely man has been unconsciously converted into the target of an assassin.

The traveller, thus unpleasantly aroused, seized his weapons, concealed himself behind a rock, and waited. Then, as after the expiration of a moment, the attack was not renewed, he rose softly, and carefully looked around him.

Not a sound disturbed the majestic solitude of the desert. But this sudden tranquillity after the two shots, instead of re-assuring the traveller, only augmented his anxiety, by revealing to him the approach of a certain danger, though it was impossible for him to divine the cause or the magnitude.

The night was clear, and, so to speak, transparent; the sky, of a deep blue, was studded with a profusion of sparkling stars, and the moon shed a white and melancholy light, that allowed the country to be surveyed for a long distance.

At all hazards he saddled his horse; then, after concealing it in a rocky cavity, he lay down, placed his ear to the ground, and listened. Then he fancied he could hear a long distance off a sound, at first almost imperceptible, but which rapidly approached; and he soon recognized in it the wild galloping of several horses.

It was a hunt, or a pursuit. But who would dream of hunting in the middle of the night? The Indians would not venture it, while white and half-bred trappers only rarely visited these deserted regions, which they abandoned to the savages and border ruffians; utter villains, who, expelled from the towns and pueblos, have no other shelter than the desert.

Were the galloping horsemen pirates of the prairie, then?

The situation was becoming painful to the traveller when, all at once, the noise ceased, and all became silent.

The traveller rose from the ground.

Suddenly, the shrieks of a woman or girl burst forth on the night, with an expression of terror and agony impossible to depict.

The stranger, leaving his horse in the shelter he had selected for it, dashed forward in the direction whence the cry came, leaping from rock to rock and clearing shrubs, at the risk of hurting himself, with the feverish speed of the brave man who believes himself suddenly called by Providence to save a fellow being in danger.

Still, prudence did not desert him in his hazardous enterprise; and, before risking himself on the plain, he stopped behind a fringe of larch trees, in order to try and find out what was going on, and act in accordance.

This is what he saw:—two men, who from their appearance he at once recognized as belonging to the worst species of prairie runners, were madly pursuing a young girl. But, thanks to her juvenile agility—an agility doubtless doubled by the profound terror the bandits inspired her with—this maiden bounded like a startled fawn across the prairie, leaping ravines, clearing every obstacle, and gaining at each moment a greater advance on her pursuers, who were impeded by their vaquero boots and heavy rifles.

A few minutes later, and the maiden reached the belt of trees behind which the traveller had concealed himself. The latter was about to rush to her assistance, when suddenly one of the bandits raised his rifle and pulled the trigger.

The girl fell, and the horseman seemed to change his mind—for instead of advancing, he drew himself back and stood motionless, with his finger on the trigger, ready to fire.

The pirates rapidly approached, talking together in that medley of English, French, Spanish and Indian which is employed throughout the Far West.

"Hum!" said a hoarse and panting voice; "What a gazelle! At one moment I really thought she would escape us."

"Yes, yes," the other answered, shaking his head and tapping the barrel of his rifle with his right hand; "but I always felt certain of bringing her down when I thought proper."

"Yes, and you did not miss her, *caray!* Although it was a long shot, and your hand must have trembled after such a chase."

"Habit, compadre! Habit!" the bandit answered, with a modest smile.

While talking thus, the two bandits had reached the spot where the body of the girl lay. One of them knelt down, doubtless to assure himself of the death of their victim; while the other, the one who had fired, looked on carelessly, leaning on his rifle.

The traveller then drew himself up, raised his piece, and fired. The bandit, struck in the centre of the breast, sank down like a sack, and did not stir. He was dead.

His companion had started and laid his hand on his *machete*; but not leaving him time to employ it, the traveller rushed on him, and with a powerful blow of the butt end on his head, sent him to join his comrade on the ground, where he rolled, half killed.

The traveller, taking the bandit's reata, then firmly bound his hands and feet; and, easy in mind on this point, he eagerly approached the maiden. The poor girl gave no sign of life, but, for all that, was not dead; her wound, indeed, was slight, as the pirate's bullet had merely grazed her arm. Terror alone had produced her fainting fit.

The stranger carefully bandaged the wound, slightly moistened her lips and temples, and, after a comparatively short period, had the satisfaction of seeing her open her eyes again.

"Oh!" she murmured, in a voice soft and melodious as a bird's song, "Those men—those demons! Oh! Heaven! Protect me!"

"Reassure yourself, Señorita," the traveller answered; "you have nothing further to fear from those villains."

The maiden started at the sound of this strange voice; she fixed her eyes on the stranger without giving him any answer, and made an instinctive movement to rise. She doubtless took the man who had spoken for one of her pursuers. The latter smiled mournfully, and pointed to the two bandits lying on the ground.

"Look, Señorita," he said to her; "you have only a friend here."

At this sight an expression of unbounded gratitude illumined the wounded girl's face, and a sickly smile appeared on her lips; but almost immediately her features grew saddened again. She sprang up, and raising herself on the tips of her small feet, she stretched out her right arm toward a point on the horizon, and exclaimed in a voice broken by terror—

"There, there! Look!"

The stranger turned to the indicated direction. A party of horsemen were coming up at full speed, preceded about a rifle shot distance by another horseman, evidently better mounted than they, and whom they appeared to be pursuing. The stranger then remembered the furious galloping he had heard a few moments previously.

"Oh!" the girl exclaimed, clasping her hands in entreaty, "Save him, Señor! Save him!"

"I will try, Señorita," he replied, gently; "all that a man can do, I swear to do."

"Thank you," she said, offering him her pretty little hand; "you are a noble-hearted man, and Heaven will aid you."

"You must not remain here exposed to the insults of these men, who are evidently the comrades of those from whom you have just escaped."

"That is true," she said; "but what can I do? Where shall I seek shelter?"

"Follow me behind these trees; we have not a moment to lose."

"Come," she said, resolutely. "But you will save him! Will you not?"

"At least I will try. I have only my life to offer the person in whom you take an interest; and believe me, Señorita, I shall not hesitate to make the sacrifice."

The maiden looked down with a blush, and silently followed her guide. They soon reached the thicket in which the stranger had established his quarters for the night.

"Whatever happens," he said, while reloading his rifle, "remain here, Señorita. You are in safety in this hollow rock, where no one will dream of seeking you. For my part, I am going to help your friend."

"Go," she said, as she knelt down on the ground; "while you are fighting I will pray for you—and Heaven will grant my prayer."

"Yes," the stranger answered, mournfully, "God listens gladly to the voice of angels, so let us hope for the best."

He leaped on his horse; and after giving a parting glance at the maiden, who was praying fervently, he dashed at full speed in the direction of the newcomers. There were seven in number—bandits with stern faces and dangerous aspect, who dashed up brandishing their weapons and uttering horrible yells.

The pursued horseman, on seeing a man emerge so unexpectedly from the thicket, and come towards him at full speed, rifle in hand, naturally supposed that assistance was arriving for his foes, and dashed on one side to avoid a man whom he assumed, with some show of reason, to be an adversary the more. But the bandits were not mistaken when they saw the stranger not only let their prey escape, but stop in front of them and cock his rifle.

Two shots were fired at the same moment, one by a bandit the other by the stranger, with the difference, however, that the bandit's shot, being fired haphazard was harmless; while the stranger's, being deliberately aimed, struck exactly in the mass of his serried foes.

A few seconds later, one of them let go his bridle, beat the air with his arms, fell back on his horse, and at length on the ground, tearing with his huge spurs the sides of his steed, which reared, kicked, and started off like an arrow.

A war so frankly declared could not have a sudden termination: four shots succeeding each other with extreme rapidity on either side were a sufficient proof of this. But the stranger's position was growing critical: his rifle was discharged, and he had only his revolvers left.

The revolver, by the way, is a weapon more convenient than useful in a fight, for if you wish to hit your man, you must fire at him almost point blank, otherwise the bullets have a tendency to stray. This is a sufficient explanation why, in spite of the immoderate use the North Americans make of this weapon, the number of murders among them is proportionately limited.

The stranger was, therefore, somewhat embarrassed, and was preparing in his emergency for a hand-to-hand fight, when help he had been far from calculating on suddenly reached him.

The pursued horseman, on hearing the firing, and yet finding no bullets whizzed past him, understood that something unusual was taking place, and that some strange incident must have occurred in his favour. Hence he turned back, and saw one of his enemies fall. Recognising his mistake, he made up his mind at once: though only armed with a *machete*, he wheeled his horse round and bravely drew up alongside his defender.

Then the two men, without exchanging a word, resolutely dashed at the bandits. The contest was short—the success unhoped for. Moreover, the sides were nearly equal, for of the seven pirates only four were now alive.

The attack was so sudden, that the pirates had not time to reload. Two were killed with revolver shots. The third fell with his head severed by a *machete* blow from the horseman, who was burning to take an exemplary vengeance; while the fourth, finding himself alone leaped his horse over the corpses of his comrades, and fled at full speed without attempting to continue longer a combat which could not but be fatal to him.

The two men consequently remained masters of the battlefield.

CHAPTER II
ON THE PRAIRIE

When the last bandit had disappeared in the darkness, the horseman turned to his generous defender, in order to thank him; but the latter was no longer by his side, and he saw him galloping some distance off on the plain.

The horseman knew not to what he should attribute this sudden departure—(for the stranger was following a direction diametrically opposite to that on which the pirate had fled)—till he saw him return, leading another horse by the bridle.

The stranger had thought of the young lady he had so miraculously saved; and on seeing the horses of the killed bandits galloping about, he resolved at once to capture the best of them, in order to enable her to continue her journey more comfortably; and when the animal was lassoed, he returned slowly towards the man to whom he had rendered so great a service.

"Señor," the horseman said, as soon as they met again, "all is not over yet; I have a further service to ask of you."

"Speak, Caballero," the stranger replied, starting at the sound of the voice, which he fancied he recognised. "Speak, I am listening to you."

"A woman, an unhappy girl—my sister, in a word, is lost in this horrible desert. Some of the scoundrels started in pursuit of her, and I know not what may have happened to her. I am in mortal agony, and must rejoin her at all risks; hence do not leave the good action you have so well begun unfinished; help me to find my sister's track,—join with me in seeking her."

"It is useless," the stranger answered, coldly.

"What, useless!" the horseman exclaimed with horror; "Has any misfortune happened to her? Ah! I remember now; I fancied, while I was flying, that I heard several shots. Oh, Heaven, Heaven!" he added, writhing his hands in despair, "My poor sister, my poor Marianita!"

"Reassure yourself, Caballero," the stranger continued in the same cold deliberate accent; "your sister is in safety, temporarily at least, and has nothing to fear. Heaven permitted that I should cross her path."

"Are you stating truth?" he exclaimed, joyfully. "Oh, bless you, Señor, for the happy news! Where is she? Let me see her! Let me press her to my heart. Alas! How shall I ever acquit my debt to you?"

"You owe me nothing," the stranger answered in a rough voice; "it was chance, or God, if you prefer it, that did everything, and I was only the instrument. My conduct would have been the same to any other person; so keep your gratitude—which I do not ask of you. Who knows," he added ironically, "whether you may not some day repent of having contracted any obligations toward me?"

The horseman felt internally pained at the way in which his advances were received by a man who scarce five minutes previously had saved his life. Not knowing to what he should attribute this sudden change of temper, he pretended not to notice anything offensive the words might contain, and said, with exquisite politeness—

"The spot is badly chosen for a lengthened conversation, Caballero. We are still, if not strangers, at least unknown to each other. I trust that ere long all coldness and misunderstanding will cease between us, and make room for perfect confidence."

The other smiled bitterly.

"Come," he said, "your sister is near here, and must be impatient to see you."

The horseman followed him without replying; but asking himself mentally who this singular man could be, who risked his life to defend him, and yet appeared anxious to treat him as an enemy.

All the sounds of the combat had reached the maiden's ear: she had heard them while kneeling on the ground, half dead with terror, and searching her troubled memory in vain for a prayer to address to Heaven.

Then the firing had ceased: a mournful silence again spread over the desert—a silence more terrifying a thousandfold than the terrible sounds of the fight, and she remained crouching in a corner and suffering from nameless agony, alone, far from all human help, not daring to retain a single hope, and fearing at each moment to see a frightful death awaiting her. The poor girl could not have said how long she remained thus crushed beneath the weight of her terror. A person must really have suffered, to know of how many centuries a minute is composed when life or death is awaited.

Suddenly she started: her strong nerves relaxed, a fugitive flush tinged her cheek, she fancied she had heard a few words uttered in a low voice not far from her. Were her enemies again pursuing her? Or was her saviour returning to her side?

She remained anxious and motionless, not daring to make a movement or utter a cry to ask for help; for a movement might reveal her presence, a cry hopelessly ruin her.

But, ere long, the bushes were parted by a powerful hand; and two horsemen appeared at the base of the rock. The maiden stretched out her hands to them with an exclamation of delight; and, too weak to support this last emotion, she fainted.

She had recognised in the men, who arrived side by side, her brother and the stranger to whom she owed her life.

When she regained her senses, she was lying on furs in front of a large fire. The two men were sitting on her right and left; while in the rock cave, three horses were eating their provender of alfalfa.

Somewhat in the shadow a few paces from her, the maiden perceived a mass, whose form it was impossible for her to distinguish at the first glance, but which a more attentive examination enabled her to recognise as a bound man lying on the ground.

The maiden was anxious to speak and thank her liberator; but the shock she had received was so rude, the emotion so powerful, that it was impossible for her to utter a word—so weak did she feel. She could only give him a glance full of all the gratitude she felt, and then fell back into a state of feverish exhaustion and morbid apathy, which almost completely deprived her of the power of thinking and feeling, and which rendered her involuntarily ignorant of all that was going on around her.

"It is well," said the stranger, as he carefully closed a gold mounted flask and concealed it in his bosom. "Now, Caballero, there is nothing more to fear for the Señorita; the draught I have administered to her, by procuring her a calm and healthy sleep, will restore her strength sufficiently for her to be able to continue her journey at sunrise, should it be necessary."

"Caballero," the stranger answered, "you are really performing the part of Providence towards me and my sister, I know not, in truth, how to express to you the lively gratitude I feel for a procedure which is the more generous as I am a perfect stranger to you."

"Do you think so?" he answered sarcastically.

"The more I examine your face, the more convinced I am that I have met you tonight for the first time."

"You would not venture to affirm it?"

"Yes, I would. Your features are too remarkable for me not to remember them if I had seen you before; but I repeat, if you fancy you know me, you are mistaken, and an accidental resemblance to some other person is the cause of your error."

There was a momentary silence, and then the stranger spoke again, with a politeness too affected for the irony it concealed not to be seen—

"Be it so, Caballero," he answered, with a bow; "perhaps I am mistaken. Be good enough, therefore, if you have no objection, to tell me who you are, and by what fortuitous concourse of circumstances I have been enabled to render you what you are kind enough to call a great service?"

"And it is an immense one, in truth, Caballero," the stranger interrupted with warmth.

"I will not discuss that subject any longer with you, Caballero; I am awaiting your pleasure."

"Señor, I will not abuse your patience for long. My name is Don Ruiz de Moguer, and I reside with my father at a hacienda in the vicinity of Arispe. For reasons too lengthy to explain to you, and which would but slightly interest you, the presence of my sister (who has been at school for some years at the Convent of the Conception at El Rosario) became indispensable at the hacienda. By my father's orders I set out for El Rosario a few months ago, in order to bring my sister back to her family. I was anxious to rejoin my father; and hence, in spite of the observations made to me by persons acquainted with the dangers attending so long a journey through a desert country, I resolved to take no escort, but start for home merely accompanied by two peons, on whose courage and fidelity I could rely."

"My sister who had been separated from her family for several years, was as eager as myself to quit the convent; and hence we soon set out. For the first few days all went well; our journey was performed under the most favourable auspices, and my sister and I laughed at the anxiety and apprehensions of our friends, for we had begun to believe ourselves safe from any dangerous encounter."

"But yesterday at sunset, just as we were preparing our camp for the night, we were suddenly attacked by a party of bandits, who seemed to emerge from the ground in front of us, so unforeseen was their apparition. Our poor brave peons were killed while defending us; and my sister's horse, struck by a bullet in the head, threw her. But the brave girl, far from surrendering to the bandits, who rushed forward to seize her, began flying across the savannah. Then I tried to lead the aggressors off the scent, and induce them to pursue me. You know the rest, Caballero; and had it not been for your providential interference, it would have been all over with us."

There was a silence, which Don Ruiz was the first to break.

"Caballero," he said, "now that you know who I am, tell me the name of my saviour?"

"What good is that?" the stranger answered, sadly. "We have come together for a moment by chance, and shall separate tomorrow never to meet again. Gratitude is a heavy burden. Not knowing who I am, you will soon have forgotten me. Believe me, Señor Don Ruiz, it is better that it should be so. Who knows if you may not regret some day knowing me?"

"It is the second time you have said that, Caballero. Your words breathe a bitterness that pains me. You must have suffered very grievously for your thoughts to be so sad and your heart so disenchanted at an age when the future ordinarily appears so full of promise."

The stranger raised his head, and bent on his questioner a glance that seemed trying to read to the bottom of his soul: the latter continued, however, with some degree of vivacity—

"Oh! Do not mistake the meaning I attach to my words, Caballero. I have no intention to take your confidence by surprise, or encroach on your secrets. Every man's life belongs to himself—his actions concern himself alone; and I recognise no claim to a confidence which I neither expect nor desire. The only thing I ask of you is to tell me your name, that my sister and myself may retain it in our hearts."

"Why insist on so frivolous a matter?"

"I will answer—What reason have you to be so obstinate in remaining unknown?"

"Then you insist on my telling you my name?"

"Oh, Caballero, I have no right to insist; I only ask it."

"Very good," said the stranger, "you shall know my name; but I warn you that it will teach you nothing."

"Pardon me, Caballero," Don Ruiz remarked, with a touch of exquisite delicacy, "this name, repeated by me to my father, will tell him every hour in the day that it is to the man who bears it that he owes the life of his children, and a whole family will bless you."

In spite of himself, the stranger felt affected. By an instinctive movement he offered his hand to the young man, which the latter pressed affectionately. But, as if suddenly reproaching himself for yielding to his feelings, this strange man sharply drew back his hand, and reassuming the expression of sternness, which had for a moment departed from him, said, with a roughness in his voice that astonished and saddened the young Mexican, "You shall be satisfied."

We have said that Doña Marianita, in looking round her, fancied she saw the body of a man stretched on the ground a few paces from the fire. The maiden was not mistaken; it was really a man she saw, carefully gagged and bound. It was in a word, one of the two bandits who had pursued her so long, and the one whom the stranger had almost killed with a blow of his rifle butt.

After recommending Don Ruiz to be patient by a wave of his hand, the stranger rose, walked straight up to the bandit, threw him on his shoulders, and laid him at the feet of the young Mexican, perhaps rather roughly—for the pirate, in spite of the thorough Indian stoicism he affected, could not suppress a stifled yell of pain.

"Who is this man, and what do you purpose doing with him?" Don Ruiz asked, with some anxiety.

"This scoundrel," the stranger answered, harshly, "was one of the band that attacked you; we are going to try him."

"Try him?" the young gentleman objected; "We?"

"Of course," the stranger said, as he removed the bandit's gag, and unfastened the rope that bound his limbs. "Do you fancy that we are going to trouble ourselves with the scoundrel till we find a prison in which to place him, without counting the fact that, if we were so simple as to do so, the odds are about fifty to one that he would escape from us during the journey, and slip through our fingers like an opossum, to attack us a few hours later at the head of a fresh band of pirates of his own breed. No, no; that would be madness. When the snake is dead, the venom is dead, too; it is better to try him."

"But by what right can we constitute ourselves the judges of this man?"

"By what right?" the stranger exclaimed, in amazement. "The Border law, which says, 'Eye for eye; tooth for tooth.' Lynch law authorizes us to try this bandit, and when the sentence is pronounced, to execute it ourselves."

Don Ruiz reflected for a moment, during which the stranger looked at him aside with the most serious attention.

"That is possible," the young man at length answered; "perhaps you are right in speaking thus. This man is guilty—he is evidently a miserable assassin covered with blood; and, had my sister and myself fallen into his hands, he would not have hesitated to stab us, or blow out our brains."

"Well?" the stranger remarked.

"Well," the young man continued, with generous animation in his voice; "this certainly does not authorize us in taking justice into our own hands; besides, my sister is saved."

"Then it is your opinion—"

"That as we cannot hand this man over to the police, we are bound to set him at liberty, after taking all proper precautions that he cannot injure us."

"You have, doubtless, carefully reflected on the consequences of the deed you advise?"

"My conscience orders me to act as I am doing."

"Your will be done!" and, addressing the bandit, who throughout the conversation had remained gloomy and silent, though his eyes constantly wandered from one to the other of the speakers, he said to him, "Get up!"

The pirate rose.

"Look at me," the stranger continued; "do you recognise me?"

"No," the bandit said.

The stranger seized a lighted brand, and held it up near his face.

"Look at me more carefully, Kidd," he said, in a sharp, imperious voice.

The scoundrel, who had bent forward, drew himself back with a start of fear.

"Stronghand!" he exclaimed, in a voice choked by dread.

"Ah!" the horseman said, with a sardonic smile; "I see that you recognise me now."

"Yes," the bandit muttered. "What are your orders?"

"I have none. You heard all we have been saying, I suppose?"

"All."

"What do you think of it?"

The pirate did not answer.

"Speak, and be frank! I insist."

"Hum!" he said, with a side-glance.

"Will you speak? I tell you I insist."

"Well!" he answered, in a rather humbling voice, but yet with a tinge of irony easy to notice; "I think that when you hold your enemy, you ought to kill him."

"That is really your opinion?"

"Yes."

"What do you say to that?" the stranger asked, turning to Don Ruiz.

"I say," he replied, simply, "that as this man is not my enemy, I cannot and ought not to take any vengeance on him."

"Hence?"

"Hence, justice alone has the right to make him account for his conduct. As for me, I decline."

"And that is truly the expression of your thoughts?"

"On my honour, Caballero. During the fight I should not have felt the slightest hesitation in killing him—for in that case I was defending the life he tried to take; but now that he is a prisoner, and unarmed, I have no longer aught to do with him."

In spite of the mask of indifference the stranger wore on his face, he could not completely hide the joy he experienced at hearing these noble sentiments so simply expressed.

There was a moment's silence, during which the three men seemed questioning each other's faces. At length Stronghand spoke again, and addressed the bandit, who remained motionless, and apparently indifferent to what was being said—

"Go! You are free!" he said, as he cut the last bonds that held him. "But remember, Kidd, that if it has pleased this Caballero to forget your offences, I have not pardoned them. You know me, so do your best to keep out of my way, or you will not escape, so easily as this day, the just punishment you have deserved. Begone!"

"All right, Stronghand, I will remember," the bandit said, with a covert threat.

And at once gliding into the bushes, he disappeared, without taking further leave of the persons who had given him his life.

CHAPTER III
THE BIVOUAC

For some moments the bandit's hurried footsteps were audible, and then all became silent once again.

"You wished it," Stronghand then said, looking at Don Ruiz from under his bent brows. "Now, be certain that you have at least one implacable enemy on the prairie; for you are not so simple, I assume, as to believe in the gratitude of such a man?"

"I pity him, if he hates me for the good I have done him in return for the harm he wished to do me, but honour ordered me to let him escape."

"Yours will be a short life, Señor, if you are obstinate in carrying out such philanthropic precepts in our unhappy country."

"My ancestors had a motto to which they never proved false."

"And pray what may that motto be, Caballero?"

"Everything for honour, no matter what may happen," the young man said, simply.

"Yes," Stronghand answered, with a harsh laugh; "the maxim is noble, and Heaven grant it prove of service to =you; but," he continued, after looking round him, "the darkness is beginning to grow less thick, the night is on the wane, and within an hour the sun will be up. You know my name, which, as I told you beforehand, has not helped you much."

"You are mistaken, Caballero," Don Ruiz interrupted him, eagerly; "for I have frequently heard the name mentioned, of which you fancied me ignorant."

Stronghand bent a piercing glance on the young man.

"Ah!" he said, with a slight tremor in his voice; "And doubtless, each time you heard that name uttered, it was accompanied by far from flattering epithets, which gave you but a poor opinion of the man who bears it."

"Here again you are mistaken, Señor; it has been uttered in my presence as the name of a brave man, with a powerful heart and vast intellect, whom unknown and secret sorrow has urged to lead a strange life, to fly the society of his fellow men, and to wander constantly about the deserts; but who, under all circumstances, even spite of the examples that daily surrounded him, managed to keep his honour intact and retain a spotless reputation, which even the bandits, with whom the incidents of an adventurous life too often bring him into contact, are forced to admire. That, Señor, is what this name, which you supposed I was ignorant of, recalls to my mind, and the way in which I have ever heard the man who bears it spoken of."

Stronghand smiled bitterly.

"Can the world really be less wicked and unjust than I supposed it?" he muttered, in self-colloquy.

"Do not doubt it," the young man said, eagerly. "God, who has allowed the good and the bad to dwell side by side on this earth, has yet willed that the amount of good should exceed that of bad, so that, sooner or later, each should be requited according to his works and merits."

"Such words," he answered, ironically, "would be more appropriate in the mouth of a priest or missionary, whose hair has been blanched, and back bowed by the weight of the incessant struggles of his apostolic mission, than in that of a young man who has scarce reached the dawn of life, whom no tempest has yet assailed, and who has only tasted the honey of life. But no matter; your intention is good, and I thank you. But we have far more serious matters to attend to than losing our time in philosophical discussions which would not convince either of us."

"I was wrong, Caballero, I allow," Don Ruiz answered; "it does not become me, who am as yet but a child, to make such remarks to you; so, pray pardon me."

"I have nothing to pardon you, Señor," Stronghand replied with a smile; "on the contrary, I thank you. Now let us attend to the most pressing affair—that is to say, what you purpose doing to get out of your present situation."

"I confess to you that I am greatly alarmed," Don Ruiz replied, with a slight tinge of sadness, as he looked at the girl, who was still sleeping. "What has happened to me, the terrible danger I have incurred, and from which I only escaped, thanks to your generous help—"

"Not a word more on that subject," Stronghand interrupted him quickly. "You will disoblige me by pressing it further."

The young man bowed.

"Were I alone," he said, "I should not hesitate to continue my journey. A brave man, and I believe myself one, nearly always succeeds in escaping the perils that threaten him, if he confront them: but I have my sister with me—my sister, whose energy the terrible scene of this night has broken, and who, in the event of a second attack from the pirates of the prairies, would become an easy prey to the villains—the more so because, too weak to save her, I could only die with her."

Stronghand turned away, murmuring to himself compassionately.

"That is true, poor child;" then he said to Don Ruiz, "Still, you must make up your mind."

"Unfortunately I have no choice; there is only one thing to be done: whatever may happen, I shall continue my journey at sunrise, if my sister be in a condition to follow me."

"That need not trouble you. When she awakes, her strength will be sufficiently recovered for her to keep on horseback without excessive fatigue; but from here to Arispe the road is very long."

"I know it: and it is that which frightens me for my poor sister."

"Listen to me. Perhaps there is a way for you to get out of the scrape, and avoid up to a certain point the dangers that threaten you. Two days' journey from here there is a military post, placed like an advanced sentry to watch the frontier, and prevent the incursions of the Indios bravos, and other bandits of every description and colour, who infest these regions. The main point for you is to reach this post, when it will be easy for you to obtain from the Commandant an escort to protect you from any insult for the rest of your journey."

"Yes; but, as you remark, I must reach the post."

"Well?"

"I do not know this country: one of the two peons who accompanied me acted as guide; and now he is dead, it is utterly impossible for me to find my way. I am in the position of a sailor, lost without a compass on an unknown sea."

Stronghand looked at him with surprise mingled with compassion.

"Oh!" he exclaimed, "How improvident is youth! What! Imprudent boy! You dared to risk yourself in the desert, and entrust to a peon your sister's precious life?" But, recollecting himself immediately, he continued, "Pardon me; reproaches are ill suited at this moment; the great thing is to get you out of the danger in which you are."

He let his head fall on his hands, and plunged into serious reflections, while Don Ruiz looked at him with mingled apprehension and hope. The young man did not deceive himself as to his position: the reproaches which Stronghand spared him, he had already made himself, cursing his improvident temerity; for things had reached such a point, that if the man to whom he owed his life, refused to afford him his omnipotent protection, he and his sister were irremediably lost.

Stronghand, after a few minutes, which seemed to last an age, rose, seized his rifle, went up to his horse, saddled it, mounted, and said to Don Ruiz, who followed all his movements with anxious curiosity—

"Wait for me, however long my absence may be; do not stir from here till I return."

Then, without waiting for the young man's answer, he bent lightly over his horse's neck, and started at a gallop. Don Ruiz watched the black outline, as it disappeared in the gloom; he listened to the horse's footfalls so long as he could hear them, and then turned back and seated himself pensively at the fire, and looked with tearful eyes at his sleeping sister.

"Poor Marianita!" he murmured, with a heart-rending outburst of pity.

He bowed his head on his chest, and with pale and gloomy face awaited the return of Stronghand—a return which, in his heart, he doubted, although, with the obstinacy of desperate men, who try to deceive themselves by making excuses whose falsehood they know, he sought to prove its certainty.

We will take advantage of this delay in our narrative to trace rapidly the portraits of Don Ruiz de Moguer and his sister Marianita. We will begin with the young lady, through politeness.

Doña Mariana—or rather Marianita, as she was generally called at the convent, and by her family—was a charming girl scarce sixteen, graceful in her movements, and with black lustrous eyes. Her hair had the bluish tinge of the raven's wing; her skin, the warm and gilded hues of the sun of her country; her glance, half veiled by her long brown eyelashes, was ardent; her straight nose, with its pink flexible nostrils, was delicious; her laughing mouth, with its bright red lips, gave her face an expression of simple, ignorant candour. Her movements, soft and indolent, had that indescribable languor and serpentine undulation alone possessed in so eminent a degree by the women of Lima and Mexico, those daughters of the sun in whose veins flows the molten lava of the volcanoes, instead of blood. In a word, she was a Spanish girl from head to foot—but Andalusian before all. Hers was an ardent, wild, jealous, passionate, and excessively superstitious nature. But this lovely, splendid statue still wanted the divine spark. Doña Mariana did not know herself; her heart had not yet spoken; she was as yet but a delicious child, whom the fiery breath of love would convert into an adorable woman.

Physically, Don Ruiz was, as a man, the same his sister was a woman. He was a thorough gentleman, and scarce four years older than Doña Mariana. He was tall and well built; but his elegant and aristocratic form denoted great personal strength. His regular features—too regular perhaps, for a man—bore an unmistakable stamp of distinction; his black eye had a frank and confident look; his mouth, which was rather large, but adorned with splendid teeth, and fringed by a fine brown moustache, coquettishly turned up, still retained the joyous, careless smile of youth; his face displayed loyalty, gentleness, and bravery carried to temerity;—in a word, all his features offered the most perfect type of a true-blooded gentleman.

Brother and sister, who, with the exception of a few almost imperceptible variations, had the most perfect physical likeness, also resembled each other morally. Both were equally ignorant of things of the world. With their pure and innocent hearts they loved each other with the holiest of all loves, fraternal affection, and only lived through and for each other.

Hence, Doña Mariana had felt a great delight and great impatience to quit the convent, when Don Ruiz, in obedience to his father's commands, came to fetch her from the Rosario. This impatience obliged Don Ruiz not to consent to wait for an escort on his homeward journey, for fear of vexing his sister. It was an imprudence that caused the misfortunes we have already described, and for which, now they had arrived, Don Ruiz reproached himself bitterly. He cursed the weakness that had made him yield to the whims of a girl, and accused himself of being, through his weakness, the sole cause of the frightful dangers from which she had only escaped by a miracle, and of those no less terrible, which, doubtless, still threatened her on the hundred and odd leagues they had still to go before reaching the hacienda del Toro, where dwelt her father, Don Hernando de Moguer.

Still the hours, which never stop, continued to follow each other slowly. The sun had risen; and, through its presence on the horizon, immediately dissipated the darkness and heated the ground, which was chilled by the abundant and icy dew of morning.

Doña Marianita, aroused by the singing of the thousands of birds concealed beneath the foliage, opened her eyes with a smile. The calm sleep she had enjoyed for several hours restored not only her strength, which was exhausted by the struggles of the previous evening, but also her courage and gaiety. The girl's first glance was for her brother, who, anxious and uneasy, was attentively watching her slumbers, and impatiently awaiting the moment for her to awake.

"Oh, Ruiz," she said, in her melodious voice, and offering her hand and cheek simultaneously to the young man, "what a glorious sleep I have had."

"Really, sister," he exclaimed, kissing her, gladly, "you have slept well."

"That is to say," she continued, with a smile, "that at the convent I never passed so delicious a night, accompanied by such charming dreams; but it is true there were two of you to watch over my slumbers—two kind and devoted hearts, in whom I could trust with perfect confidence."

"Yes, sister; there were two of us."

"What?" she asked in surprise mingled with anxiety. "You were—What do you mean, Ruiz?"

"What I say; nothing else, dear sister."

"But I do not see the caballero to whom we have incurred so great an obligation. Where is he?"

"I cannot tell you, little sister. About two hours ago he mounted his horse and left me, telling me not to stir from here till his return."

"Oh, in that case I am quite easy. His absence alarmed me; but now that I know he will return—"

"Do you believe so?" he interrupted.

"Why should I doubt it?" she continued with some animation in her voice; "Did he not promise to return?"

"Certainly."

"Well! A caballero never breaks his pledged word. He said he would come, and he will come."

"Heaven grant it!" Don Ruiz muttered.

And he shook his head sadly, and gave a profound sigh. The maiden felt herself involuntarily assailed by anxiety. This persistency undoubtedly terrified her.

"Come, Ruiz," she said, turning very pale, "explain yourself. What has happened between this caballero and yourself?"

"Nothing beyond what you know, sister. Still, in spite of the man's promise, I know not why, but I fear. He is a strange, incomprehensible being—at one moment kind, at another cruel—changing his character, and almost his face, momentarily. He frightens and repels, and yet attracts and interests me. I am afraid he will abandon us, and fear that he will return. A secret foreboding seems to warn me that this man will have a great influence over your future and mine. Perhaps it is our misfortune that we have met him."

"I do not understand you, Ruiz. What means this confusion in your ideas? Why this stern and strange judgment of a man whom you do not know, and who has only done you kindness?"

At the moment when Don Ruiz was preparing to answer, the gallop of a horse became audible in the distance.

"Silence, brother!" she exclaimed, with an emotion she could not repress; "Silence, here he comes!"

The young man looked at his sister in amazement.

"How do you know it?" he asked her.

"I have recognised him," she stammered, with a deep blush. "Stay— Look!"

In fact, at this moment the shrubs parted, and Stronghand appeared in the open space. Don Ruiz, though surprised at the singular remark which had escaped his sister, had not time to ask her for an explanation. Without dismounting, Stronghand, after bowing courteously to the young lady, said, hurriedly—

"To horse!—To horse! Make haste! Time presses!"

Don Ruiz at once saddled his own horse and his sister's, and a few minutes later the two young people were riding by the hunter's side.

"Let us start!" the latter continued. "*Cuerpo de Cristo*, Caballero, I warned you that you were doing an imprudent action in liberating that villain. If we do not take care, we shall have him at our heels within an hour."

These words sufficed to give the fugitives wings, and they started at full gallop after the bold wood ranger. An hour elapsed ere a word was exchanged between the three persons; bent over the necks of their steeds they devoured the space—looking back anxiously from time to time, and only thinking how to escape the unknown dangers by which they felt themselves surrounded. About eight o'clock in the morning, Stronghand checked his horse, and made his companions a sign to follow his example.

"Now," he said, "we have nothing more to fear. When we have crossed that wood, which stretches out in front of us like a curtain of verdure, we shall see the Port of San Miguel, whose walls will offer us a certain shelter against the attacks of all the bandits of the desert, were there ten thousand of them."

"Last night I fancy that you spoke to me of a more distant post," Don Ruiz said.

"Yes; for I fancied San Miguel abandoned, if not in ruins. Before I gave you what might prove a fallacious hope, I wished to assure myself of the truth of the case."

"Do you believe that the Commandant will consent to receive us?" the young lady asked.

"Certainly, Señorita, for a thousand reasons. In the first place, the frontier posts are only established for the purpose of watching over the safety of travellers; and then, again, San Miguel is commanded by one of your relations—or, at any rate, an intimate friend of your family."

The young people looked at each other in surprise.

"Do you know this Commandant's name?" Don Ruiz asked.

"I was told it: he is Don Marcos de Niza."

"Oh!" Doña Mariana exclaimed, joyfully; "I should think we do know him: Don Marcos is a cousin of ours."

"In that case, all is for the best," the hunter answered, coldly. "Let us continue our journey; for there is a cloud of dust behind us that forebodes us no good, if it reaches us before we have entered the post."

The young people, without answering, resumed their gallop, crossed the wood, and entered the little fort.

"Look!" Stronghand said to Don Ruiz and his sister, the moment the gate closed upon them. They turned back. A numerous band of horsemen issued from the wood at this moment, and galloped up at full speed, uttering ferocious yells.

"This is the second time you have saved our lives, Caballero," Doña Mariana said to the partizan, with a look of gratitude.

"Why count them, Señorita?" he replied, with a sadness mingled with bitterness. "Do I do so?"

The maiden gave him a look of undefinable meaning, turned her head away with a blush, and silently followed her brother.

The Spaniards, whatever may be the opinion the Utopians of the old world express about their mode of civilization, and the way in which they treated the Indians of America, understood very well how to enhance the prosperity of the countries they had been endowed with by the strong arms of those heroic adventurers who were called Cortez, Pizarro, Bilboa, Alvadaro, &c., and whose descendants, if any by chance exist, are now in the most frightful wretchedness, although their ancestors gave a whole world and incalculable riches to their ungrateful country.

When the Spanish rule was established in America, the first care of the conquerors—after driving back the Indians who refused to accept their iron yoke into frightful deserts, where they hoped want would put an end to them—was to secure their frontiers, and prevent those indomitable hordes, impelled by hunger and despair, from entering the newly conquered country and plundering the towns and the haciendas. For this purpose they established along the desert line a cordon of presidios and military posts, which were all connected together, and could, in case of need, assist each other, not so much through their proximity—for they were a great distance apart, and scattered over a great space—but by means of numerous patrols of lanceros, who constantly proceeded from one post to the other.

At present, since the declaration of independence, owing to the neglect of the governments which have succeeded each other in this unhappy country, most of the presidios and forts no longer exist. Some have been burned by the Indians, who became invaders in their turn, and are gradually regaining the territory the Europeans took from them; while others have been abandoned, or so badly kept up, that they are for the most part in ruins. Still, here and there you find a few, which exceptionable circumstances have compelled the inhabitants to repair and defend.

As these forts were built in all the colonies on the same plan, in describing the post of San Miguel, which still exists, and which we have visited, the reader will easily form an idea of the simple and yet effective defence adopted by the Europeans to protect them from the surprises of their implacable and crafty foes.

The post of San Miguel is composed of four square pavilions, connected together by covered ways, the inner walls of which surround a courtyard planted with lemon trees, peach trees, and algarrobas. On this court opens the room intended for travellers, the barracks, &c. The outer walls have only one issue, and are provided with loopholes, which can only be reached by mounting a platform eight feet high and three wide. All the masonry is constructed of *adobes*, or large blocks of earth stamped and baked in the sun.

Twenty feet beyond this wall is another, formed of cactuses, planted very closely together, and having their branches intertwined. This vegetable wall, if we may be allowed the use of the expression, is naturally very thick, and protected by formidable prickles, which render it impenetrable for the half-clad and generally badly-armed Indians. The only entrance to it is a heavy gate, supported by posts securely bedded in the ground. The soldiers, standing at the loopholes of the second wall, fire in perfect shelter, and command the space above the cactuses.

On the approach of the Indians, when the Mexican Moon is at hand—that is to say, the invariable season of their invasions—the sparse dwellers on the border seek refuge inside San Miguel, and there in complete safety wait till their enemies are weary of a siege which can have no result for them, or till they are put to flight by soldiers sent from a town frequently fifty leagues off.

Don Marcos de Niza was a man of about forty, short and plump, but withal active and quick. His regular features displayed a simplicity of character, marked with intelligence and decision. He was one of those educated honest professional officers, of whom the Mexican army unfortunately counts too few in its ranks. Hence, as he thoroughly attended to his duties, and had never tried to secure promotion by intrigue and party manoeuvres, he had remained a captain for ten years past, without hope of promotion, in spite of his qualifications (which were recognised and appreciated by all) and his irreproachable conduct. The post he occupied at this moment as Commandant of the Blockhouse of San Miguel proved the value the Governor of the province set upon him; for the frontier posts, constantly exposed to the attacks of the Redskins, can only be given to sure men, who have long been accustomed to Indian warfare.

CHAPTER IV
THE POST OF SAN MIGUEL

As the dangerous honour of commanding one of the border forts like San Miguel is not at all coveted by the brilliant officers accustomed to clatter their sabres on the stones of the Palace in Mexico, it is generally only given to brave soldiers who have no prospect of promotion left to them.

Informed by a cabo, or corporal, of the names of the guests who thus suddenly arrived, the Captain rose to meet them with open arms and a smile on his lips.

"Oh, oh," he exclaimed, gleefully; "this is a charming surprise! Children, I am delighted to see you."

"Do not thank us, Don Marcos," Doña Mariana answered, smilingly. "We are not paying you a visit, but have come to ask shelter and protection of you."

"You have them already. ¡Rayo de Dios! Are we not relations, and very close ones, too?"

"Without doubt, cousin," Don Ruiz said; "hence, in our misfortune, it is a great happiness for us to come across you."

"Hilloh! You have something serious to tell me," the Captain continued, his face growing gloomy.

"So serious," the young man said, with a bow to the partizan, who stood motionless by his side, "that had it not been for the help of this caballero, in all probability we should be lying dead in the desert."

"Oh, oh; my poor children! Come, dismount and follow me; you must need rest and refreshment after such an alarm. Cabo Hernandez, take charge of the horses."

The corporal took the horses, which he led to the corral; and the young people followed the Captain, after having been kissed and hugged by him several times. Don Marcos pressed the hunter's hand, and made him a sign to follow them.

"There," he said, after introducing his guests into a room modestly furnished with a few butacas; "sit down, children; and when you have rested, we will talk."

Refreshments had been prepared on the table. While the young people enjoyed them, the Captain quitted them, and went with the hunter into another room. So soon as they were alone, the two men became serious, and the joy that illumined the Captain's face was suddenly extinguished.

"Well," he asked Stronghand, after making him a sign to sit down, "what news?"

"Bad," he answered, distinctly.

"I expected it," the officer muttered, with a sad toss of the head; "we must put on our harness again, and push out into the savannah, in order to prove to these bandits that we are able to punish them."

The hunter shook his head several times, but said nothing. The Captain looked at him attentively for some minutes.

"What is the matter, my friend?" he at length asked him, with growing anxiety; "I never saw you so sad and gloomy before."

"The reason is," he answered, "because circumstances have never been so serious."

"Explain yourself, my friend; I confess to you that you are really beginning to alarm me. With the exception of a few insignificant marauders, the borders have never appeared to me more quiet."

"It is a deceitful calm, Don Marcos, which contains the tempest in its bosom—and a terrible tempest, I, assure you."

"And yet our spies are all agreed in assuring us that the Indians are not at all thinking of an expedition."

"It proves that your spies betray you, that's all."

"Possibly so; but still, I should like some proof or sign."

"I ask for nothing better; I am enabled to give you the most positive information."

"Very good; that is the way to speak. I am listening to you."

"Before all, is your garrison strong?"

"I consider it large enough."

"Perhaps so: how many men have you?"

"Sixty or seventy, about."

"That is not enough."

"What! Not enough? The garrisons of blockhouses are never more numerous."

"In a time of peace, it may be so; but under present circumstances, I repeat to you, that they are not enough, and you will soon agree with me on that score. You must send off a courier, without the loss of a moment, to ask for a reinforcement of from one hundred and fifty to two hundred men. Do not deceive yourself, Captain; you will be the first attacked, and the attack will be a rude one. I warn you."

"Thanks for the hint. Still, my good friend, you will permit me not to follow it till you have proved to me that there are urgent reasons for doing so."

"As you please, Captain; you are the commandant of the post, and your responsibility must urge you to prudence. I will therefore abstain from making any farther observations on the subject which only concerns me very indirectly."

"You are annoyed, and wrongly so, my friend; the responsibility to which you refer demands that I should not let myself be led by vague rumours to take measures I might have cause to regret. Give me the explanation I expect of you; and, probably, when I know the imminence of the danger that threatens me, I shall follow your advice."

"I wish for nothing more than to satisfy you; so listen to me. What I have to tell you will not take long."

At this moment the room door opened and Corporal Hernandez appeared. The Captain, annoyed at being thus inopportunely disturbed, turned sharply round and angrily addressed the man—

"Well Corporal," he said, "what the fiend do you want now?"

"Excuse me, Captain," the poor fellow said, astounded at this rough greeting, "but the Lieutenant sent me."

"Well, what does the Lieutenant want? Speak! But be brief, if that is possible."

"Captain, the sentry has seen a large party of horsemen coming at full gallop towards the fort, and the Lieutenant ordered me to warn you."

"Eh," said the Captain, looking uneasily at the hunter, "were you in the right? and is this troop the vanguard of the enemy you threaten us with?"

"This troop," the hunter answered, with an equivocal smile, "has been following Don Ruiz and myself since the morning. I do not believe that these horsemen are Indians."

"What's the Lieutenant's opinion about these scamps?" the Captain asked the corporal.

"They are too far off yet, and too hidden by the dust they raise, Captain, for it to be possible to recognise them," the non-commissioned officer replied with a bow.

"That is true. We had better, I believe, go and look for ourselves. Will you come?"

"I should think so," the hunter said, as he seized his rifle, which he had deposited in a corner of the room; and they went out.

Don Ruiz and his sister were talking together, while doing ample justice to the refreshment placed at their disposal. On seeing the Captain, the young man rose and walked up to him.

"Cousin," he said to him, with a bow, "I hear that you are on the point of being attacked; and as it is to some extent my cause you are going to defend, for the bandits who threaten you at this moment are allies of those with whom I had a fight last night, pray allow me to fire a shot by your side."

"¡Viva Dios! Most heartily, my dear cousin," the Captain answered, gaily: "although these scoundrels are not worth the trouble. Come along!"

"That's a fine fellow!" the Captain whispered in the hunter's ear.

The latter made no answer. He contented himself with shrugging his shoulders, and turned away.

"Oh," Doña Mariana exclaimed, "Ruiz, what are you going to do? Stay with me, I implore you, brother!"

"Impossible, sister," the young man answered, as he kissed her; "what would our cousin think of me were I to skulk here when fighting was going on?"

"Fear nothing, Niña; I am answerable for your brother," the Captain said with a smile.

The girl sat down again sadly on the butaca from which she had risen, and the four men then left the room, and proceeded to the patio, or court. Here everybody was busy. The Lieutenant, an old experienced soldier, with a grey moustache and face furrowed by sabre cuts, and whose whole life had been spent on the borders, had not lost his time. While, by his order, Corporal Hernandez warned the Captain, he had ordered the "fall-in" to be beaten, had placed the best shots at the loopholes, and made all arrangements to avoid a surprise and give a warm reception to the enemy who advanced so daringly against the fort.

When the Captain set foot in the court, he stopped, embraced at a glance the wise and intelligent arrangements made by his Lieutenant, and a smile of satisfaction spread over his features.

"And now," he said to the hunter, "let us go and see who the enemy is with whom we have to deal."

"It is unnecessary; for I can tell you, Captain," the other replied; "they are the pirates."

"Pirates!" Don Marcos exclaimed in amazement. "What! Those villains would dare—"

"Alone, certainly not," Stronghand quickly interrupted him; "but with the certainty of being supported by the Indians, of whom they are only the vanguard, they will not hesitate to do so. However, unless I am greatly mistaken, their attack will not be serious; and their object is probably to discover in what state of defence the post is. Receive them, then, in such a way as to leave them no doubt on this head, and prove to them that you are perfectly on your guard; and this demonstration will without doubt be sufficient to send them flying."

"You are right," said the Captain. "Viva Dios! They shall have their answer, I promise you."

He then gave the Corporal an order in a low voice; the latter bowed, and went off hurriedly. For some minutes a deep silence prevailed in the fort. The moments that precede a contest bring with them something solemn, which causes the bravest men to reflect, and prepare for the struggle, either by a powerful effort of the will, or by mentally addressing a last and fervent prayer to Heaven.

All at once, horrible yells were heard, mingled with the furious galloping of many horses; and then the enemy appeared, leaning over the necks of their steeds, and brandishing their weapons with an air of defiance. When they came within pistol shot, the word to fire was given from the walls, and a general discharge burst forth like a clap of thunder.

The horsemen fell into confusion, and turned back precipitately and in the greatest disorder, followed by the Mexican bullets, which, directed by strong arms and sure eyes, made great ravages in their ranks at every step. Still, they had not fled so fast but that they could be recognised for what they really were—that is, pirates of the prairies. Half naked for the most part, and without saddles, they brandished their rifles and long lances, and excited their horses by terrific yells.

Two or three individuals, probably chiefs, with their heads covered by a species of turban, were noticeable through their ragged uniforms, doubtless torn off murdered soldiers; their repulsive dirt and ferocious appearance inspired the deepest disgust. No doubt was possible: these wretches were certainly whites and half-breeds. What a difference between these sinister bandits and the Apaches, Comanches, and Arapahoes—those magnificent children of nature, so careful in the choice of their weapons—so noble in their demeanour.

After a rather long race, they stopped to hold counsel, out of range of the firearms. They were at this moment joined by a second band, whose leader began speaking and gesticulating with the utmost excitement, pointing to the fort each moment with his rifle. The two bands, united, might possibly amount to one hundred and fifty horsemen.

After a rather long discussion, the pirates started again, and stopped at the very foot of the walls. Captain Niza, wishing to inflict a severe chastisement on them, had given orders not to fire, but to let them do as they pleased. Hidden by the thick cactus hedge, the bandits had suddenly become invisible; but the Mexicans, confiding in the strength of their position and the solidity of the posts and gates, felt no fear.

Reassured by the silence of the garrison, some thirty pirates, among whom were several of their chiefs, escaladed the great gate in turn, and rushed toward the second wall. Unluckily for the success of their plan, the wall was too lofty to be cleared in the same way; hence they scattered. Some sought stones and posts to beat in the second gate; while others tried, though in vain, to open the one they had so easily scaled.

The Mexicans could distinctly hear the pirates in the second *enceinte* explaining to their comrades the difficulty they experienced in penetrating into the fort, and they must force the gate, in order to allow a passage for those who remained outside. The latter then threw their *reatas,* which, caught upon the posts, were tightened by the combined efforts of the men and horses, and seemed on the point of pulling the gate off its hinges; but the posts held firmly, and were not even shaken by this supreme effort.

"What are you waiting for, Captain?" Don Ruiz whispered in the Commandant's ear. "Why do you not kill these vermin?"

"There are not enough yet in the trap," he answered, with a cunning look; "let them come."

In fact, as if the bandits had wished to obey the old soldier, some twenty more clambered over the gale, so that there were fifty of the pirates between the cactus and the stone wall. Encouraged by their numbers, which momentarily increased, they made a general assault. But, all at once, every loophole was lit up by a sinister flash, and the bullets began showering uninterruptedly on the wretches, who, through their own position, found it impossible to answer the plunging fire of the Mexicans. Recognising the fault they had committed, and the trap they had so stupidly entered, the pirates became demoralized, fear seized upon them, and they only thought of flight.

Then they dashed at the outer gate, to clamber over it and reach the plain; there the bullets dashed them down again—suffering from a desperation which was the greater because they had no help to hope for from their friends outside, whom, at the first check, they had heard start off at full speed; and consequently they felt they were lost.

The Mexicans, pitiless in their vengeance, fired incessantly on the wretches, some of whom, by crawling on their hands and knees, succeeded in reaching the foot of the wall below the loopholes—a position in which they could not be attacked, unless the Mexicans exposed themselves, and ran the risk of being killed or wounded. Of fifty bandits who had scaled the gate, fourteen still lived; the others were dead, and not one had succeeded in making his escape.

"Ha! Ha!" said the Captain, rubbing his hands gleefully. "I fancy that the lesson will be useful, though it may have been a trifle rough."

But, on the reiterated entreaties of Don Ruiz, the worthy Commandant, who in his heart was not cruel, consented to ask the survivors if they were willing to surrender, a proposition which the pirates greeted with yells of rage and defiance. These fourteen men, though their rifles were discharged, were not enemies to despise, armed as they were with long and heavy *machetes,* and resolved to die. The Mexicans were acquainted with them, and knew that in a hand-to-hand fight they would prove tough customers.

Still there must be an end to it. At an order from the Captain the gate of the second wall was suddenly opened, and some twenty horsemen charged at full gallop the bandits, who, far from recoiling, awaited them with a firm foot. The *mêlée* was terrible, but short. Three Mexicans were killed, and five others seriously wounded; but the pirates, after an obstinate resistance, fell never to rise again.

Only one of them—profiting by the disorder and the attention which the soldiers remaining at the loopholes paid to the fight—succeeded by a miracle of resolution and strength in scaling the wall and flying. This pirate, the only one who escaped the massacre, was Kidd. On reaching the plain he stopped for a second, turned to the fort with a gesture of menace and defiance, and, leaping on a riderless horse, went off amid a shower of bullets, not one of which struck him.

CHAPTER V
THE STAY IN THE FOREST

When the fight was over, and order restored at the post, the Captain bade his Lieutenant have the bodies lying on the battlefield picked up and hung by the feet to the trees on the plain, so that they might become the prey of wild beasts, though not until they had been decapitated. The heads were to remain exposed on the walls of the forts, and act as an object of terror to the bandits, who, after this act of summary justice, would not venture to approach the neighbourhood of the post.

Then, when all these orders had been given, the Commandant returned to his residence, where Don Ruiz had already preceded him in order to re-assure his sister as to the result of the fight. Don Marcos was radiant: he had gained a great advantage—at least he thought so—over the border ruffians; he had inflicted on them an exemplary punishment at the expense of an insignificant loss, and supposed that for a long time no one would venture to attack the post entrusted to him.

Unfortunately, the wood ranger was not of the same opinion: each time the Captain smiled and rubbed his hands at the recollection of some episode in the fight, Stronghand shook his head sadly, and frowned anxiously. This was done so frequently, that at last the worthy Commandant was compelled to take notice of it.

"What's the matter with you now?" he asked him, with an air half vexed, half pleased. "You are, on my soul, the most extraordinary man I know. Nothing satisfies you; you are always in a bad temper. Hang it! I do not know how to treat you. Did we not give those scoundrels a remarkable thrashing, eh? Come, answer!"

"I allow it," the hunter replied laconically.

"Hum! It is lucky you allow so much. And yet they fought bravely, I fancy."

"Yes; and it is that which frightens me."

"I do not understand you."

"Was I not giving you important information when we were interrupted by the Cabo Hernandez?"

"That is to say, you were going to give it me."

"Yes; and with your permission, now that we have no fear of being interrupted for a while, I will impart the news to you."

"I ask nothing better; although I suppose that the defeat the pirates have experienced must deprive the news of much of its importance."

"The pirates play but a very small part in what I have to tell you."

"Speak, then! I know that you are too earnest a man to try and amuse yourself at my expense by inspiring me with ridiculous alarm."

"You shall judge for yourself the perils of the situation in which you may find yourself at any moment, if you do not employ the greatest precaution and the most excessive prudence."

The two men seated themselves on butacas, and the Commandant, who was more excited than he wished to show by this startling preamble, made the hunter a sign to commence his revelations.

"About two months ago," the latter began, "I was at the Presidio of San Estevan, whither certain personal matters had called me. This Presidio, which, as you know, is about two days' journey from here, is very important, and serves to some extent in connecting all the posts scattered along the Indian border."

The Captain gave a nod of assent.

"I am," the hunter continued, "on rather intimate terms with Don Gregorio Ochova, the Colonel commanding the Presidio, and during my last stay at San Estevan I had opportunities for seeing him rather frequently. You know the savageness of my character, and the species of instinctive repulsion with which anything resembling a town inspires me; hence, I need hardly say, that no sooner was my business ended than I made preparations to depart, and, according to my custom, intended to leave the Presidio at a very early hour. I did not like to go away without saying good-bye to the Colonel and shaking hands with him; so I went to his house for the purpose of taking leave. I found him in a state of extreme agitation, walking up and down, and apparently affected by a violent passion or great anxiety. On seeing me, he uttered an exclamation of delight, and ran up to me, exclaiming—"

"'Oh, Stronghand! Where on earth have you been hiding? I have been seeking you everywhere for the last two hours, and have put a dozen soldiers on your heels, who could not possibly find you.'"

"I looked at the Colonel in surprise."

"'You were seeking for me, Don Gregorio? I assure you that I was close to you, and very easy to find.'"

"'It seems not. But here you are—that is the main point; and I care little where you were, or what you were doing. Do you think about making any lengthened stay at San Estevan?'"

"'No, Colonel,' I answered at once, 'my affairs are settled; I intend to start at an early hour tomorrow, and I have just come to say good-bye, and thank you for the hospitality you have shown me during my stay at the Presidio.'"

"'Good!' he said eagerly, 'that is all for the best but,' he added, recollecting himself, and taking my hand in a kindly way, 'do not suppose that it is my desire to see you depart that makes me speak thus.'"

"'I am convinced of the contrary,' I remarked with a bow."

"He continued,—'You can, Stronghand, do me a great service, if you will.'"

"'I am at your command.'"

"'This is the matter,' he said, at once entering on the business. 'For some days past, the most alarming reports have been spreading through the Presidio, though it is impossible to find out their origin.'"

"'And what may they be?' I asked."

"'It is said—(notice, I say it is said, and affirm nothing, as I know nothing positive)—it is said, then, that a general uprising against us is preparing— that the Indians, laying aside for a moment their private hatreds, and forgetting their clannish quarrels to think only of the hereditary hatred they entertain for us, are combining to attempt a general attack on the posts, which they purpose to destroy, in order to devastate our borders more freely. Their object is said to be, not only the destruction of the posts, but also the invasion of several States, such as Sonora and Sinaloa, in which they intend to establish themselves permanently after expelling us.'"

"'The reports are serious,' I remarked, 'but nothing has as yet happened to confirm their truth.'"

"'That is true; but you know that there is always a certain amount of truth in every vague rumour, and it is that truth I should like to know.'"

"'Is no nation mentioned by name among those which are to take up arms?'"

"'Yes; more particularly the Papayos—that is to say, the grand league of the Apaches, Axuas, Gilenos, Comanches, Mayos, and Opatas. But the more serious thing is, always according to the report, that the white and half-bred marauders on the border are leagued with them, and mean to help them in their expedition against us.'"

"'That is really serious,' I answered; 'but, pardon me for questioning you, Colonel; what do you purpose doing to make head against the imminent danger that threatens you?'"

"'That is exactly why I want you, my friend; and you would do me a real service by assisting me in this affair.'"

"'I am ready to do anything that depends on myself to oblige you.'"

"'I was certain of that answer, my friend. This is the matter, then. You understand that I cannot remain thus surrounded by vague rumours and terrors that have no apparent cause, but still carry trouble into families and cause perturbation in trade. During the last few weeks, especially, various serious events have given a certain consistency to these rumours—travellers have been murdered, and several valuable waggon trains plundered, almost at the gates of the Presidio. It is time for this state of things to cease, and for us to know definitively the truth or falsehood of the rumours; for this purpose I require a brave, devoted man, thoroughly acquainted with Indian manners and customs, who would consent—'"

"I interrupted him quickly."

"'I understand what you want, Colonel; seek no further, for I am the man you stand in need of. Tomorrow at sunrise I will start: and within two months I pledge myself to give you the most explicit information, and tell you what you may have to fear, and what truth there is in all that is being said around you.'"

"The Colonel thanked me warmly, and the next morning I set out on my tour of investigation, as we had arranged."

"Well," the Captain exclaimed, who had followed this long story with ever increasing interest, "and what information have you picked up?"

"This information," the hunter answered, "is of a nature far more serious than even public report had said. The situation is most critical, and not a moment must be lost in preparing for defence. I was going to San Estevan, where Colonel Don Gregorio must be awaiting my return with the utmost impatience, when I thought of seeing whether the Post of San Miguel, which had been so long unoccupied, had received a garrison. That is how chance, my dear Captain, made us meet here when I thought I should see you at the Presidio."

The Captain shook his head thoughtfully. "A month ago," he said, "Don Gregorio ordered me to come here and hold my ground, though he did not inform me of the motives that compelled him so suddenly to place San Miguel in a state of defence."

"Well; now you know the reasons."

"Yes; and I thank you for having told me. But, between ourselves, are matters so serious as you lead me to suppose?"

"A hundred times more so. I have traversed the desert in all directions; I have been present at the meetings of the chiefs—in a word, I know the most private details of the expedition that is preparing."

"¡Viva Dios! I will not let myself be surprised—be at your ease about that; but you were right in advising me to ask for help, as my garrison is too weak to resist a well-arranged assault. This morning's attack has made me reflect; so I will immediately—"

"Do not take the trouble," the hunter interrupted him; "I will act as your express."

"What! Are you going to leave us at once?"

"I must, my dear Captain; for I have to give Don Gregorio an account of the mission he confided to me. Reflect what mortal anxiety he must feel at not seeing me return."

"That is true. In spite of the lively pleasure I should feel in keeping you by me, I am compelled to let you go. When do you start?"

"This moment."

"Already?"

"My horse has rested; there are still five or six hours of daylight left, and I will take advantage of them?" He made a movement to leave the room.

"You have not said good-bye to Don Ruiz and his sister," the Captain observed.

The hunter stopped, his brows contracted, and he seemed to be reflecting.

"No," he said, ere long, "it would make me lose precious time. You will make my apologies to them, Captain. Moreover," he added with a bitter smile, "our acquaintance is not sufficiently long, I fancy, for Don Ruiz and his sister to attach any great importance to my movements, so for the last time, good-bye."

"I will not press you," the Captain answered; "do as you please. Still, it would have perhaps been more polite to take leave."

"Nonsense," he said, ironically; "am I not a savage? Why should I employ that refinement of politeness which is only customary among civilized people?"

The Captain contented himself with shrugging his shoulders as an answer, and they went out. Five minutes later the hunter was mounted.

"Do not fail to report to the Colonel," Don Marcos said, "what happened here today; and, above all, ask him for assistance."

"All right, Captain; and do not you go to sleep."

"*Caray*—I shall feel no inclination. So now, good-bye, and good luck!"

"Good-bye, and many thanks."

They exchanged a last shake of the hand, the hunter galloped out into the plain, and the Captain returned to his house, muttering to himself.

"What a strange man! Is he good or bad? Who can say?"

When the supper hour arrived, the two young people, astonished at the hunter's absence, asked after him of the captain. When the latter told them of his departure, they felt grieved and hurt at his having gone without bidding them farewell; and Doña Mariana especially was offended at such unaccountable behaviour on the part of a caballero; for which, in her desire to excuse him, she in vain sought a reason. Still they did not show their feelings, and the evening passed very pleasantly.

At the hour for retiring, Don Ruiz, more than ever eager to rejoin his father, reminded the Captain of the offer of service he had made him, and asked for an escort, in order to continue his journey on the morrow; but Don Marcos answered with a peremptory refusal, that not only would he give no escort, but he insisted on his relations remaining temporarily under his guard.

Don Ruiz naturally asked an explanation of his cousin; which he did not hesitate to give, by telling them of the conversation between himself and the hunter. Don Ruiz and his sister had been too near death to expose themselves again to the hazards of a long journey in the desert alone, and unable to offer any effectual defence against such persons as thought proper to attack them; still the young man, annoyed at this new delay, asked the Captain at what period they might hope to regain their liberty.

"Oh! Your seclusion will not be long," the latter replied with a smile; "so soon as I have received the reinforcements I expect from San Estevan—

that is to say, in seven or eight days at the most—I will pick you out an escort, and you can be off."

Don Ruiz, forced to satisfy himself with this promise, thanked him warmly; and the young people made their arrangements to pass the week in the least wearisome way possible. But life is very dull at a frontier post, especially when you are expecting a probable attack from the Indians, and when, consequently, all the gates are kept shut, when sentries are stationed all around, and the only amusement is to look out on the plain through the loopholes.

The Captain, justly alarmed by the news the hunter had given him, had made the best arrangements his limited resources allowed to resist any attack from the Indians, if they appeared before the succour arrived from San Estevan. By his orders all the rancheros and small landowners established within a radius of fifteen leagues had been warned of an approaching invasion, and received an invitation to take shelter within the post.

The majority, recognising the gravity of this communication, hastened to pack up their furniture and most valuable articles; and driving before them their horses and cattle, hurried from all sides at once to the fort, with a precipitation which proved the profound terror the Indians inspired them with. In this way, the interior of San Miguel was soon encumbered with young men and old men, women, and children, and cattle—most of whom, unable to find lodgings in the houses, were forced to bivouac in the yards; which, however, was but a trifling inconvenience to them in a country where it hardly ever rains, and where the nights are not cold enough to render sleeping in the open air unpleasant.

The Captain organized this heterogeneous colony to the best of his ability. The women, children, and old men were sheltered under tents or *jacales* made of branches, to protect them from the copious morning dew, while all the men capable of bearing arms were exercised, so as in case of attack to assist in the common defence.

But this enormous increase of population required an enormous stock of provisions; and hence the Captain sent out numerous patrols for the purpose of procuring the required corn and cattle. Don Ruiz took advantage of this to make excursions in the vicinity; while his sister, in the company of young girls of her own age, of whom several had entered the fort with their families, tried to forget, or rather cheat, the weariness of their seclusion.

The appearance of the post had completely changed; and, thanks to the Captain's intelligence, ten days after the hunter's departure San Miguel had become a really formidable fortress. Large trenches had been dug, and barricades erected; but, unfortunately, the garrison, though numerous enough to resist a sudden attack, was too weak to sustain a long siege.

One morning, at sunrise, the sentries signalized a thick cloud of dust advancing towards the post with the headlong speed of a whirlwind. The alarm was immediately given; the walls were lined with soldiers; and preparations were made to resist these men, who, though invisible, were supposed to be enemies.

Suddenly, on coming within gunshot, the horsemen halted, the dust dispersed, and the garrison perceived with delight that all these men wore the Mexican uniform. A quarter of an hour later, eighty lanceros, each carrying an infantry man behind him, entered the fort, amid the deafening shouts of the garrison and the farmers who had sought refuge behind the walls. It was the succour requested by the Captain, and sent off from San Estevan by Colonel Don Gregorio.

CHAPTER VI
A GLANCE AT THE PAST

In Spanish America, and especially in Peru and Mexico, all the Creoles of the pure white breed pretend to be descended in a straight line from the first Conquistadors. We have no need to discuss this claim, whose falsehood is visible to any man at all conversant with the sanguinary history of the numberless civil wars—a species of organized massacre—which followed the establishment of the Spaniards in these rich countries.

Still there are in America some families, very few in number it is true, which can justly boast of this glorious origin. Most of these families live on the estates conceded to their ancestors—they only marry among themselves, and only interfere against the grain in the political events of the day. With their eyes turned to the past, which is so full of great memories for them, they have kept up the old traditions of the chivalrous loyalty of the time of Charles V., which are forgotten everywhere else. They maintain the national honour unsullied, and those patriarchal virtues of the old time which they alone still practise with a proud and simple majesty.

The Creoles, half-breeds, and Indians, in spite of the hatred they affect for their old masters, and the principles of so-called republican equality which they profess with such absurd emphasis in the presence of strangers, feel for these families a respect bordering on veneration; for they seem to understand inwardly the superiority of these powerful natures, which no political convulsion has been able to level or even bind, over their own vicious decrepit natures, which have grown old without ever having been young.

A few leagues from Arispe, the old capital of the Intendancy of Sonora, but now greatly fallen, and only a second-class city, there stands like an eagle's nest, on the summit of an abrupt rock, a magnificent showy mansion, whose strong and haughty walls are crowned with *Almenas*, which at the time of the Spanish conquest were only permitted to families of the old and pure nobility, and they alone had the right to have battlements on their houses.

This fortress-palace—which dates from the first days of the conquest, and whose antiquity is written on its walls, which have seen so many bullets flatten, so many arrows break against them, but which time, that grand destroyer of the most solid things, is gradually crumbling away by a continuous effort, under the triple influences of the air, the sun, and rain—has never changed masters since the day of its construction, and the chiefs of the same family, on dying, have ever left it to their descendants.

This family is one of those to which we just now referred, whose origin dates back to the first conquerors, and whose name is Tobar de Moguer—(Moguer was added at a later date, doubtless in memory of the Spanish town whence the chief of the family came.)

In 1541, Don Antonio de Mendoza, Viceroy of New Spain, organized the expedition to Cibola, a mysterious country, visited a few years previously by Alvaro Núñez Cabeza de Vaca, and about which the most marvellous and extraordinary reports were spread, all the better suited to inflame the avarice and unextinguishable thirst for gold by which the Spanish adventurers were devoured.

The expedition, consisting of 300 Spaniards and 800 Indian allies, started from Compostela, the capital of New Galicia, on April 17, 1541, under the orders of Don Francisco Vásquez de Coronado. The officers nominated by the Viceroy were all gentlemen of distinction; among them as standard bearer was Don Pedro de Tobar, whose father, Don Fernando de Tobar, had been Majordomo-Major in the reign of Jane the Mad, mother of the Emperor Charles V.

We will only say a few words about this expedition, the preparations for which were immense; and which would have doubtless furnished better results, and proved to the advantage of all, had the chief thought less of the immense fortune he left behind in New Spain, and more of the immense responsibility weighing upon him.

After innumerable fatigues, the expedition reached Cibola, which, instead of being the rich and magnificent city they expected to see, was only a wretched insignificant village, built on a rock, and which the Spaniards seized after an hour's fighting. Still, the Indians defended themselves bravely, and several Spaniards were wounded. The General himself, hurled down by a stone, would have been infallibly killed, had it not been for the devotion of Don Pedro de Tobar and another officer, who threw themselves before him, and gave their chief time to rise and withdraw from the fight.

The Spaniards, half discouraged by the extraordinary fatigue they were forced to endure, and the continual deceptions that awaited them at every step, but still urged on by that spirit of adventure which never deserted them, resolved after the capture of Cibola to push further on and try their fortunes once again. Thus they reached, with extreme difficulty, the last country visited by Cabeza de Vaca, to which he had given the name of the Land of Hearts (Tierra de los Corazones)—not, as might be supposed, because the inhabitants had seemed so gentle and amiable, but solely because, at the period of his passing, the only food they offered him had been stags' hearts.

On reaching this place the Spaniards halted. Don Tristán de Arellano, who had taken the command of the army in place of Don Francisco Coronado, who was ailing from the wound received at Cibola, seeing the rich and fertile appearance of this country, resolved to found a town, which he called San Hieronima de los Corazones. This town was, however, almost immediately abandoned by the Spaniards, who carried the various elements further, and started a new town, to which they gave the name of Señora, afterwards corrupted into Sonora, which eventually became the name of the province.

During this long expedition Don Pedro de Tobar distinguished himself on several occasions. At the head of seventeen horsemen, four foot soldiers, and a Franciscan monk of the name of Fray Juan de Padella who in his youth had been a soldier, Don Pedro de Tobar discovered the province of Tutaliaco, which contained several towns, the houses being of several storeys. All these towns, or rather villages, were carried by storm by Don Pedro, and the province was subjugated in a few days.

When, twenty years after, the Viceroy wishing to recompense Don Pedro's services, offered him estates, the latter, who held Señora in pleasant recollection, asked that land should be granted him in this province, which reminded him of the prowess of his youth, and to which he was attached by the very fatigues he had undergone and the dangers he had incurred. During the twenty years that had elapsed since Coronado's expedition, Don Pedro had married the daughter of Don Rodrigo Maldonado, brother-in-law of the Duke of Infantado, and one of his old comrades in arms. As Don Rodrigo had settled in Sonora, Don Pedro, in order to be near him, took up his abode on the site of Cibola, which had long been destroyed and abandoned, and built on the crest of the rock the magnificent Hacienda del Toro, which, as we have said, remained for centuries in the family, with the immense estates dependent on it.

Like all first-class haciendas in Mexico, El Toro was rather a town than a simple habitation, according to the idea formed in Europe of private estates. It comprised all the old territory of Cibola. On all sides its lofty walls, built on the extremity of the rock, hung over the abyss. It contained princely apartments for the owners, a chapel, workshops of every description, storehouses, barracks, quarters for the pious, and corrals for the horses and cattle, with an immense *huerta*, planted with the finest trees and the most fragrant flowers. In a word, it was, and probably still is, one of those gigantic abodes which appear built for Titans, and of which the finest feudal châteaux in the Old World offer but an imperfect idea.

The fact is, that at the time when the conquerors built these vast residences, inhabitants were sparse in these countries, as is indeed the case now. The owners having their elbows at liberty, could take what land they liked, and hence each ultimately became, without creating any surprise, possessors of a territory equal in size to one of our counties.

It was in 1811, twenty-nine years before the period when our story begins, at the dawn of that glorious Mexican revolution the first cry of which had been raised on the night of September 16, 1810, by Hidalgo—at that time a simple parish priest in the wretched town of Dolores, and whose success, sixteen months later, was so compromised by the disastrous battle of Calderón, in which countless bands of fantastic Indians were broken by the discipline of the old Spanish troops—that the most sensible men regarded it as an unimportant insurrection—a fatal error which caused the ruin of the Spanish domination.

But on November 25, 1811, the day on which we begin this narrative, the insurgents had not yet been conquered at Calderón; on the contrary, their first steps had been marked by successes; from all sides Indians came to range themselves beneath their banner, and their army, badly disciplined, it is true, but full of enthusiasm, amounted to 80,000 men. Already master of several important towns, Hidalgo assembled all his forces with the evident design of dealing a great blow, and generalizing the insurrection, which had hitherto been confined to two provinces.

About two in the afternoon, that is to say, the time when in these climes the heat is most oppressive, a horseman, mounted on a magnificent mustang, was following at a gallop the banks of a small stream, half dried up by the torrid heat of the southern sun, and by whose side a few sickly cottonwood trees were withering.

The dust, reduced to impalpable atoms, formed a dense cloud round the horseman, who, plunged into sad and gloomy thought, with pale forehead and brows contracted till they touched, continued his journey without noticing the desolate aspect of the country he was traversing, and the depressing calm that prevailed around him. In fact, an utter silence brooded over this desert: the birds had hidden themselves gasping under the foliage, and no other sound could be heard save the shrill, harsh cry of the grasshoppers, which occupied in countless myriads the calcine grass that bordered the road, or rather the track, the traveller was following.

This rider appeared to be about twenty-five years of age; his features were handsome, his glance proud, and the expression of his face haughty, although marked with kindness and courtesy. He was tall and well built; his gestures, which were pleasing, though not stiff, indicated a man who, through his position in the world, was accustomed to a certain deference, and to win the respect of those who surrounded him. His dress had nothing remarkable about it: it was that usually worn by wealthy Spaniards when travelling; still, a short sword in a silver sheath and with a curiously carved hilt, the only weapon he openly carried, showed him to be a gentleman; besides, his complexion, clearer than that of the Creoles, left no doubt as to his Spanish origin.

This horseman, who had left Arispe at sunrise, had been travelling, up to the moment we join him, without stopping or appearing to notice the stifling heat that made the perspiration run down his cheek—so deep was he in thought. On reaching a spot where the track he was following turned sharply to the left, his horse suddenly stopped. The rider, thus aroused from his reverie, raised his head and looked before him, with grief, almost despair, in his glance.

He was at the foot of the rock on the summit of which stands the Hacienda del Toro in all its gloomy majesty. For some minutes he gazed with an expression of regret and sorrow at these frowning buildings, which doubtless recalled happy memories. He shook his head several times, a sigh escaped from his overburdened chest, and, seemed to form a supreme resolution, he said, in a choking voice, "I will go;" and letting his horse feel the spur, he began slowly scaling the narrow path that led to the summit of the rock and the hacienda gate. A violent contest seemed to be going on in his mind: his flexible face changed each moment, and reflected the various feelings that agitated him; several times his clenched hand drew up the bridle, as if he wished to check his horse and turn back. But each time his will was the more powerful; he constantly overcame the instinctive repugnance that seemed to govern him, and he continued his ascent, with his eyes constantly looking ahead, as if he expected to see someone whose presence he feared come round an angle of the track. But he did not see a soul the whole way.

When he reached the hacienda gate, it was open, and the drawbridge lowered; but though he was evidently expected, there was no one to bid him welcome.

"It must be so," he murmured sadly. "I return to my paternal roof, not as a master, but as a stranger, a fugitive—an accursed man, perhaps."

He crossed the drawbridge, the planks of which re-echoed his horse's footfall, and entered the first courtyard. Here, too, there was no one to greet him. He dismounted; but instead of throwing the bridle on his horse's neck, he held it in his hand and fastened it to a ring in the wall, saying, in a low, concentrated voice—"Wait for me, my poor Bravo; you, too, are regarded as an accursed one: be patient; we shall doubtless soon set out again."

The noble animal as if understanding its master's words and sharing in his grief, turned its delicate, intelligent head toward him, and gave a soft and plaintive whine. The young man after giving a parting glance at his steed, crossed the first yard with a firm and resolute step, and entered a second one considerably larger. At the end of this court two men were standing motionless on the first step of a magnificent marble staircase, apparently leading to the apartments of the master of the hacienda.

On seeing these two men, the young horseman drew himself up; his face assumed a gloomy and ironical expression, and he walked rapidly toward them. They still remained motionless and stiff, with their eyes fixed on him. When he was but a few paces from them, they uncovered by an automatic movement, and bowed ceremoniously.

"The Marquis is waiting for you, Señor Conde," one of them said.

"Very good," the strange visitor answered; "one of you can announce my arrival to his lordship my father, while the other will guide me to the apartment where I am expected."

The two men bowed a second time, and with heads still uncovered, preceded the young man, who followed with a firm and measured tread. On reaching the top of the steps, one of the servants hurried forward, while the second, slightly checking his speed, continued to guide the horseman. When the footsteps of the first man died out in the immense corridors, the face of the second one suddenly lost its indifferent expression, and he turned round, his eyes full of tears.

"Oh, my young master!" he said, in a voice broken by emotion, "What a misfortune! Oh, Heavens! What a misfortune!"

"What?" the young man asked anxiously; "Has anything happened to the marquis? Or is my lady mother ill?"

The old servant shook his head sadly. "No," he answered; "Heaven be blessed! Both are in good health: but why did you leave the paternal mansion, your lordship? Alas! Now the misfortune is irremediable."

A cloud of dissatisfaction flitted across the young man's forehead.

"What has happened so terrible during my absence, Perote?"

"Does not your Excellency know?" the servant asked in amazement.

"How should I know, my friend?" he answered, mildly. "Have you forgotten that I have been absent from the hacienda for two years?"

"That is true, Excellency;—forgive me, I had forgotten it. Alas! Since the misfortune has burst upon us, my poor head has been so bad."

"Recover yourself, my good fellow," the young man said, kindly. "I know how much you love me. You have not forgotten," he added, with a bitter sorrow, "that your wife, poor Juana, nourished me with her milk. I know nothing; am even ignorant why my father ordered me so suddenly to come hither. The servant who handed me the letter was doubtless unable to tell anything, and, indeed, I should not have liked to question him."

"Alas! Excellency," the old servant continued, "I am myself ignorant why you have been summoned to the hacienda; but Hernando, he may know."

"Ah!" said the young man, with a nervous start, "My brother is here, then?"

"Did you not know it?"

"Have I not already told you that I am utterly ignorant of everything connected with this house?"

"Yes, yes, Excellency. Don Hernando is here, and has been here a long time. Heaven guard me from saying anything against my master's son; but perhaps it would have been better had he remained at Guadalajara, for all has greatly changed since his arrival. Take care, Sir, for Don Hernando does not love you."

"What do I care for my brother's hatred?" the young man answered haughtily. "Am I not the elder son?"

"Yes, yes," the old servant repeated, sadly, "you are the elder son; and yet your brother commands here as master. Since his arrival, it seems as if everything belonged to him already."

The young man let his head sink on his chest, and remained for some minutes crushed; but he soon drew himself up, with flashing eye, and gently laid his hand on the old servant's shoulder.

"Perote," he said to him affectionately, "what is the motto of my family?"

"What do you mean, Excellency?" the manservant asked, startled at the singular question his master asked him.

"You do not remember it," the young man continued, with a smile, as he pointed to an escutcheon over a door. "Well; look, what do you read there?"

"What does your Excellency want?"

"Read—read, I tell you."

"You know that motto better than I do, as it was given to one of your ancestors by King Don Ferdinand of Castile himself."

"Yes, Perote, I know it," he replied, in a firm voice; "and since you will not read it, I will repeat it to you. The motto is: 'Everything for honour, no matter what may happen.' That motto dictates my conduct to me; and be assured, Perote, that I will not fail in what it orders me."

"Oh, your Excellency, once again take care. I am only a poor servant of your family, but I saw you born, and I tremble as to what may happen in the coming interview."

"Do not be anxious, my old friend," he answered, with an expression of haughty pride, full of nobleness. "Whatever may happen, I will remember not only what I owe to the memory of my ancestors, but also what I owe to myself; and, without going beyond the limits of that obedience and respect those who gave me birth have a right to, I shall be able to defend myself against the accusations which will doubtless be brought against me."

"Heaven grant, Sir, that you may succeed in dissipating the unjust suspicions so long gathering in the minds of your noble parents, and carefully kept up by the man who, during your lifetime, dares to look with an eye of covetousness on your rich inheritance."

"What do I care for this inheritance?" the young man exclaimed, passionately. "I would gladly abandon it entirely to my brother, if he would cease to rob me of a more precious property, which I esteem a hundred times higher—the love of my father and my mother."

Old Perote only answered with a sigh.

"But," the young man continued, "let us not delay any longer. His lordship must be informed of my arrival; and the slight eagerness I seem to display in proceeding to him and obeying his orders will probably be interpreted to my injury by the man who has for so many years conspired my ruin."

"Yes, you are right: we have delayed too long as it is; come, follow me."

"Where are you taking me?" the young man remarked. "My father's apartments are not situated in this part of the hacienda."

"I am not leading your Excellency to them," he answered, sorrowfully.

"Where to, then?" he asked, stopping in surprise.

"To the Red Room," the old servant remarked in a low voice.

"Oh!" the young man muttered; "Then my condemnation is about to be pronounced."

Perote only answered by a sigh; and his young master, after a moment's hesitation, made him a sign to go on; and he silently followed him, with a slow step that had something almost solemn in it.

CHAPTER VII
THE FAMILY TRIBUNAL

The Hacienda del Toro, like many feudal mansions, contained one room which remained constantly closed, and was only opened on solemn occasions. The head of the family was conveyed there to die, and remained on a bed of state till the day of his funeral: and the wife was confined there. There, too, marriage contracts were signed. In a word, all the great acts of life were performed in this room, which inspired the inhabitants of the hacienda with a respect greatly resembling terror; for on the few occasions on which the Marquises de Tobar found themselves compelled to punish any member of their family, it served as the tribunal where the culprit was tried and sentence pronounced.

This room, situated at the end of the hacienda, was a large hall of oblong shape, paved with alternate large black and white slabs, and lighted by four lofty windows, which only allowed a gloomy and doubtful light to penetrate.

Tapestry, dating from the fourteenth century, and representing with all the simplicity of the age the different episodes of the mournful battle of Xeres—which delivered Spain to the Moors, and in which Don Rodrigo, the last Gothic king, was killed—covered the walls, and imprinted an indescribable character of sepulchral majesty on this cold and mournful hall, which was probably called the "Red Room" from the prevalence of that colour in the tapestry work.

The young Count de Tobar had never entered this room since the day of his birth; and, however far back his thoughts reverted in childhood, he never remembered to have seen it open. Hence, in spite of all his courage, and the firmness with which he had thought it wise to arm himself for this decisive interview with his father, he could not restrain a slight start of fear on learning that his parents were prepared to receive him there.

The folding doors were open, and on reaching the threshold the young man took in the room at a single glance. At one end, on a dais covered with a petate, the Marquis and Marchioness of Tobar were seated, gloomy and silent, beneath a canopy of black velvet with gold fringe and tassels. Candles, lit in tall, many-branched candelabra, in order to overcome the habitual gloom of the room, threw their flickering light on the aged couple, and imparted to their faces an expression of sternness and harshness that probably did not belong to them.

At the foot of the dais, and almost touching it, stood a young man of three or four-and-twenty, with handsome and distinguished features, whose elegant attire contrasted with the simple dress of the aged couple: this gentleman was Don Hernando de Tobar, younger son of the Marquis. A footman, the same who had preceded the Count in order to announce his arrival to his master, took a step forward on perceiving the young man.

"El Señor Conde, Don Rodolfo de Tobar y Moguer," he said, in a loud and marked voice.

"Show in the Count," the Marquis said, in a voice which, though broken, was still powerful.

The manservant discreetly retired, and the door closed upon him. The Count walked up to the foot of the dais: on reaching it, he bowed a second time, then drew himself up, and respectfully awaited till it pleased his father to address him.

So profound a silence prevailed for some minutes in the room, that the hearts of the four persons might have been heard beating in their bosoms. Don Hernando took cunning side-glances at his brother, whom the aged couple examined with a mixture of sadness and severity.

The young Count, as we said, was standing motionless in front of the dais. His posture was full of nobility, without being in any way provocative: with his right foot in front, his hand on his sword guard, and the other holding his hat, whose long feather swept the ground, and his head slightly thrown back, he looked straight before him, without any display of arrogance or disdain. He waited, with a brow rather pale, it is true, owing to the internal emotions he felt; but the expression of his features, far from being that of a culprit, was, on the contrary, that of a man convinced of his innocence, and who expects to see his conduct approved rather than blamed.

"You have arrived, then, Señor Conde," the Marquis at length said, sharply.

The young man bowed, but did not answer.

"You did not display any great eagerness in obeying my invitation."

"My lord, I only received very late last night the letter you did me the honour to send me," the Count answered, gently. "This morning before sunrise I mounted my horse, and rode twenty leagues without stopping, so anxious was I to obey you."

"Yes," the Marquis said, ironically, "I know that; for you are a most obedient son—in words, if not otherwise."

"Excuse me, my lord," he replied, respectfully, "but I do not understand to what you deign to allude at this moment."

The old gentleman bit his lips angrily. "It is because we probably no longer speak the same language, Señor Conde," he said, drily; "but I will try to make myself better understood."

There was a silence, during which the Marquis seemed to be reflecting.

"You are the elder son of the family, sir," he presently continued, "and, as such, responsible for its honour, which your ancestors handed down to you unsullied. You are aware of this, I presume?"

"I am, my lord."

"Since your birth your sainted mother and myself have striven to place before you only examples of loyalty; during your childhood we took pleasure in training you in all the chivalrous virtues which for a long succession of centuries have been the dearest appanage of the race of worthies from whom you are descended. We continuously kept before your eyes the noble motto of our family, of which it is so justly proud. How is it, then, sir, that, suddenly forgetting what you owe to our care and the lessons you received from us, you suddenly, without your mother's permission or mine, abandoned without any plausible motive the paternal roof, and that, deaf to the remonstrances and tearful entreaties of your mother, and rebellious against my orders, you have so completely separated your life from ours, that, with the exception of the name you continue to bear, you have become a perfect stranger?"

"My lord!" the young man stammered.

"It is not an accusation I bring against you, Don Rodolfo," the Marquis continued, quickly; "but I expect a frank and honourable explanation of your conduct. But, take care; the explanation must be clear and unreserved."

"My lord," the Count answered, throwing up his head proudly, "my heart reproaches me with nothing: my conduct has been ever worthy of the name I have the honour to bear. My object, in obeying your orders so eagerly, has not been to justify myself, as I am not guilty of any fault, but to assure you of my respect and obedience."

An incredulous smile played round Don Hernando's mouth, and the Marquis continued with the same tone of frigid sternness—

"I expected another answer from you, sir. I hoped to find you eagerly seize the opportunity my kindness offered you to justify yourself in my sight."

"My lord," the young man replied, respectfully but firmly, "in order that the justification you demand may be possible, I must know the charges brought against me."

"I will not press this subject for the present, sir; but since, as you say, you profess such great respect for my orders, I wish to give you an immediate opportunity to prove your obedience to me."

"Oh, speak, father!" the Count exclaimed, warmly; "Whatever you may ask of me—"

"Do not be overhasty in pledging yourself, sir," the Marquis coldly interrupted him, "before you know what I am about to ask of you."

"I shall be so happy to prove to you how far from my heart are the intentions attributed to me."

"Be it so, sir. I thank you for those excellent feelings; hence I will not delay in telling you what you must do to reinstate yourself in my good graces."

"Speak,—speak, my lord!"

The old man, cold and impassive, still regarded his son with the same stern look. The Marchioness, restrained by her husband's presence, fixed on the young man's eyes filled with tears, without daring, poor mother, to interfere on his behalf. Don Hernando smiled cunningly aside. As for Don Rodolfo, his father's last words had filled him with fear; and in spite of the pleasure he affected, he trembled inwardly, for he instinctively suspected a snare beneath this pretended kindness.

"My son," the Marquis continued, with a slight tinge of sadness in his voice, "your mother and I are growing old. Years count double at our age, and each step brings us nearer the tomb, which will soon open for us."

"Oh, father!" Don Rodolfo exclaimed.

"Do not interrupt me, my son," the Marquis continued, with a commanding gesture. "You are our firstborn, the hope of our name and race; you are four-and-twenty years of age; you are handsome, well built, instructed by us in all the duties of a gentleman; in short, you are an accomplished cavalier, of whom we have just reason to be proud."

The Marquis paused for a little while. Don Rodolfo felt himself growing more and more pale. His eyes turned wildly to his mother, who sorrowfully bowed her head, in order that his anxious glance might not meet hers. He was beginning to understand what sacrifice his father was about to demand of his filial obedience, and he trembled with terror and despair. The old man continued, in a firm and more marked voice—

"Your mother and I, my son, may be called away soon to appear before the Lord; but as I do not wish to repose in the tomb without having the satisfaction of knowing that our name will not die with us, but be continued in our grandchildren—this desire, which I have several times made known to you, my son, the moment has now arrived to realise; and by marrying, you can secure the tranquillity of the few days still left us to spend on this earth."

"Father—"

"Oh, re-assure yourself, Count," the old gentleman continued, pretending to misunderstand his son's meaning. "I do not intend to force on you one of those marriages in which a couple, united against their wish, only too soon hate one another through the instinctive aversion they feel. No; the wife I intend for you has been chosen by your mother and myself with the greatest care. She is young, lovely, rich, and of a nobility almost equal to ours;—in a word, she combines all the qualities necessary not only to render you happy, but also to revive the brilliancy of our house and impart a fresh lustre to it."

"Father!" Don Rodolfo stammered again.

"My son!" the Marquis continued, with a proud intonation in his voice, as if the name he was about to utter must remove all scruples; "my son, be happy, for you are about to marry Doña Aurelia de la Torre Azul, cousin in the fifth degree to the Marquis del Valle."

"Oh, my son!" the Marchioness added entreatingly "this alliance, which your father so dearly desires, will soothe my last days."

The young man was of livid pallor. He tottered, his eyes wandered hesitatingly around, and his hand, powerfully pressed to his heart, seemed trying to stifle its beating.

"You know my will, sir," the Marquis continued, not appearing to perceive his unhappy son's condition. "I hope that you will soon conform to it: and now, as you must be fatigued after a long ride in the great heat of the day, withdraw to your apartments. Tomorrow, when you have rested, we will consult as to the means of introducing you to your future wife as soon as possible."

After uttering these words, in the same cold and peremptory tone he employed during the whole interview, the Marquis prepared to rise.

By an effort over himself the young count succeeded in repressing the storm that was raging in his heart. Affecting a tranquillity he was far from feeling, he took a step forward, and bowed respectfully to the Marquis.

"Pardon me, my lord," he said, in a voice which emotion involuntarily caused to tremble, "but may I say a few words now?"

The old gentleman frowned.

"Did I not say tomorrow, sir?" he answered drily.

"Yes, my lord," the young man answered, sadly; "but, alas! If you do not consent to listen to me today, tomorrow may be too late."

"Ah!" said the Marquis, biting his lips with a passion that was beginning to break out, "And for what reason, sir?"

"Because, father," the young man said, firmly, "tomorrow I shall have left this house never to reenter it."

The Marquis gave him a thundering look from under his grey eyelashes.

"Ah, ah!" he exclaimed, "Then I was not deceived; what I have been told is really true."

"What have you been told?"

"Do you wish to know?" the old gentleman exclaimed, furiously. "After all, you are right; it is time that this pitiable farce should end."

"Sir,—sir!" the Marchioness said, with deep grief, "remember that he is your son—your firstborn!"

"Silence, madam!" the old man said, harshly; "This rebellious son has played with us long enough; the hour of punishment has pealed, and, by Heaven! It shall be terrible and exemplary."

"In God's name, sir," the Marchioness continued, "do not be inexorable to your child. Let me speak to him; perhaps you are too harsh with him, although you love him. I am his mother; I will convince him, and induce him to carry out your wishes: a mother can find words in her heart to soften her son, and make him understand that he ought not to reject his father's orders."

The old man seemed to hesitate for a moment, but immediately recovered.

"Why should I consent to what you ask, madam?" he replied, with a roughness mingled with pity; "Do you not know that the sole quality, or rather the sole vice, of his race which this rebellious son has retained is obstinacy? You will get nothing from him."

"Oh, permit me to say, sir," the old lady continued, in a suppliant voice, "he is my son as well as yours. In the name of that love and that unswerving obedience you have ever found in me, I beseech you to let me make a final attempt to break his resistance, and lead him penitent to your feet."

"And then, my lord," Don Hernando, who had hitherto remained an apparent stranger to all that was taking place, remarked in a mocking voice, "perhaps we are mistaken; do not condemn my brother without hearing him; he is too good a gentleman, and of too old a family, to have committed the faults of which he is accused."

"That is well, Hernando; I am delighted thus to hear you undertake your brother's defence," said the old lady, smiling through her tears, and deceived by his words.

"Certainly, mother; I love my brother too dearly," the young man said ironically, "to let him be accused without proof. That Rodolfo has seduced the daughter of the principal Cacique of the Opatas and made her his mistress is evident, and known to all the world as true, but it is of very little consequence. But what I will never believe until it is proved to me is, that he has married this creature, any more than I will put faith in the calumnies that represent him not only as one of the intimate friends of the Curate Hidalgo, but also as one of his most active and influential partisans in this province. No; a thousand times No! A gentleman of the name and blood of Tobar knows too well what honour demands to commit such infamy! Acting so would be utter apostasy, and complete forgetfulness of all that a noble Castilian owes to himself, his ancestors, and that honour of which he is only the holder. Come, Rodolfo; come, my brother, raise your head: confound the calumniators: give a solemn denial to those who have dared to sully your reputation! One word from you, but one that proves your perfect innocence, and the storm unjustly aroused against you will be dispersed; my father will open his arms to you, and all will be forgotten."

During this speech, whose deep perfidy the Count recognised, he was suffering from extreme emotion. At the first words his brother uttered, he started as if he felt the sting of a viper; but gradually his anger had made way for contempt in his heart; and it was with a smile of crushing disdain that he listened to the emphatic and mocking conclusion.

"Well, my son," the marquis said, "you see everybody defends you here, while I alone accuse you! What will you answer to prove your innocence to me?"

"Nothing, father!" the young man said, coolly.

"Nothing?" the old gentleman repeated, angrily.

"No, father!" he continued; "because, if I attempted to justify myself, you would not listen to me; and that, supposing you consented to listen to me, you would not comprehend me. Oh! Do not mistake my meaning," he said, on seeing the Marquis about to speak; "you would not understand me, father, not through want of intellect, but through pride. Proud of your name and the privileges it gives, you are accustomed to judge men and things from a peculiar point of view, and understand honour in your own fashion."

"Are there two sorts of honour, then?" the Marquis exclaimed, involuntarily.

"No, father," Don Rodolfo answered, calmly, "there is only one; but there are two ways of comprehending it: and my brother, who a moment back told you without incurring your disapproval that a gentleman had the right to abuse the love of a maiden and make her his mistress, but that the honour of his name would forbid him marrying her, seems to me to have studied the point thoroughly, and is better able than I to discuss it. As you said yourself, father, we must come to an end. Well, be it so. I will not attempt to continue an impossible struggle with you. When I received orders to come to you, I knew I was condemned beforehand, and yet I obediently attended your summons; it was because my resolution was irrevocably formed. What am I reproached with? Having married the daughter of an Indian Cacique? It is true; I avow openly that I have done so: her birth is perhaps as good as mine, but most certainly her heart is greater. What is the next charge—that I am a friend of the Curate Hidalgo, and one of his firmest adherents? That is also true; and I am happy and proud of this friendship: I glory in these aspirations for liberty with which you reproach me as a crime. Descendants of the first conquerors of Mexico, this land, discovered and subjugated by our fathers, has become our country; for the last three centuries we have not been Spaniards, but Mexicans. The hour has at length arrived for us to shake off the yoke of this self-called country, which has so long been battening on our blood and tears, and enriching itself with our gold. In speaking thus to you, my venerated father, my heart is broken, for Heaven is my witness that I have a profound respect and love for you. I know that I am invoking on my head all the weight of your anger, and that anger will be terrible! But, in my sorrow, one sublime hope is left to me. Faithful to the motto of our ancestors, I have done everything for honour; my conscience is calm; and some day—soon, perhaps—you will forgive me, for you will see that I have not failed in fealty."

"Never!" the Marquis shouted in a voice the more terrible because the constraint he had been forced to place on himself, in order to hear his son's speech to the end, had been so great. "Begone! I no longer know you! You are no longer my son! Begone!—villain! I give you my—"

"Oh!" the Marchioness shrieked, as she threw herself into his arms, "Do not curse him, sir! Do not add that punishment to the one you have inflicted on him. The unhappy boy is already sufficiently punished. No one has the right to curse him; a father less than any other—for in that case it is God who avenges."

The Marquis stood for a moment silent and gloomy, then stretched out his arms to his son, and shook his head sadly.

"Begone!" he said in a hollow voice. "May God watch over you—for henceforth you have no family. Farewell!"

The young man pale and trembling, bent beneath the weight of this sentence; then rose and tottered out of the room without saying a word.

"My son!—My son!" the Marchioness exclaimed in a heart-rending voice.

The implacable old man quickly stopped her at the moment when, half-mad with grief, she was rushing from the dais, and pointed to Don Hernando, who was bowing hypocritically to her.

"You have only one son, madam," he said, in a harsh voice, "and that son is here."

The Marchioness uttered a cry of despair, and, crushed with grief, fell senseless at her husband's feet; who, also overcome in this fearful struggle of pride of race against paternal love, sank into a chair and buried his face in his hands, while a mighty sob escaped from his bosom.

Don Hernando had rushed after his brother, not for the purpose of consoling or bringing him back, but solely not to let the joy be seen which covered his face at this mournful scene, all the fearful incidents in which he had been so long preparing with feline patience.

CHAPTER VIII
THE TWO BROTHERS

After quitting the Red Room, Don Rodolfo, under the weight of the condemnation pronounced against him, with broken heart and burning head had rushed onwards, flying the paternal anger, and resolved to leave the hacienda as quickly as possible, never to return to it. His horse was still in the first yard, where he had tied it up. The young man went up to it, seized the bridle, and placed his foot in the stirrup. At the same moment a hand was laid on his shoulder—Don Rodolfo turned as if seared with a hot iron. His brother was standing before him.

A feverish redness suffused his face; his hands closed, and his eyes flashed lightning; but at once extinguishing the fire of his glance and affecting a forced calmness, he said, in a firm voice—

"What do you want brother?"

"To press your hand before your departure, Rodolfo," the young man said, with a whining voice.

Rodolfo looked at him for a moment with an expression of profound disdain, then unhooking the sword that hung at his side, he handed it to his brother.

"There, Hernando," he said, ironically, "it is only right that, since you will henceforth bear the name and honour of our family, this sword should revert to you. You desired my inheritance, and success has crowned your efforts."

"Brother," the young man stammered.

"I am not reproaching you," Don Rodolfo continued, haughtily. "Enjoy in peace those estates you have torn from me. May Heaven grant that the burden may not appear to you some day too heavy, and that the recollection of the deed you have done may not poison your last years. Henceforth we shall never meet again on this earth. Farewell!" And letting the sword he had offered his brother fall on the ground, he leaped on his horse and went off at full speed, without even giving a parting glance at those walls which had seen his birth, and from which he was now eternally banished. Don Hernando stood for a moment with hanging head and pale face, crushed by the shame and consciousness of the bad action he had not feared to commit. Already remorse was beginning to prey on him. At length, when the galloping of the horse had died away in the distance, he raised his eyes, wiped away the perspiration that inundated his face, and picked up the sword lying at his feet.

"Poor Rodolfo!" he muttered, stifling a sigh; "I am very guilty."

And he slowly returned to the hacienda. Count Don Rodolfo de Moguer kept the word he had given his brother: he never reappeared. Nothing was ever heard of him, and his intimate friends never saw him again after his journey to the hacienda, nor knew what had become of him. The next year, a few Indians who escaped from the massacre at the bridge of Calderón, when Hidalgo was defeated by the Spanish General Calleja, spread the report that Don Rodolfo, who during the whole action kept by Hidalgo's side, was killed in a desperate charge he made into the heart of the Spanish lines, in the hope of restoring the fortunes of the day; but this rumour was not confirmed. In spite of all the measures taken by the Marquis, the young man's body was not found among the dead, and his fate remained a mystery for the family.

In the meanwhile, Don Hernando, by his father's orders, had succeeded to his brother's title, and almost immediately married Doña Aurelia de la Torre Azul, originally destined for Don Rodolfo. The Marquis and Marchioness lived some few years longer. They died a few days after one another, bearing with them a poisoned sting of remorse for having banished their firstborn son from their presence.

But, inflexible up to his dying hour, the Marquis never once made a complaint, and died without mentioning his son's name. However, the Marquis's hopes were realized ere he descended to the grave, for he had the supreme consolation of seeing his family continued in his grandchildren.

At the funeral, a man was noticed in the crowd wrapped up in a wide cloak, and his features concealed by the broad brim of his hat being pulled over them. No one was able to say who this man was, although one old servant declared he had recognised Don Rodolfo. Was it really the banished son who had come for the last time to pay homage to his father and weep on his tomb? The arrival of the stranger was so unexpected, and his departure so sudden, that it was impossible to get at the truth of the statement.

Then, time passed away, important events succeeded each other, and Don Rodolfo, of whom nothing was heard, was considered dead by his family and friends, and then forgotten; and Don Hernando inherited without dispute the title and estates.

The Marquis de Moguer, in spite of the light under which we have shown him to our readers, was not a wicked man, as might be supposed; but as a younger son, with no other hope than the tonsure, devoured by ambition, and freely enjoying life, he internally rebelled against the harsh and unjust law which exiled him from the pleasures of the world, and condemned him to the solitude of the cloister. Assuredly, had his brother frankly accepted his position as firstborn, and consented to undertake its duties, Don Hernando would never have thought for a moment of defrauding him of his rights. But when he saw Don Rodolfo despise the old tradition of his race—forget what he owed to his honour as a gentleman, so far as to marry an Indian girl and make common cause with the partisans of the Revolution, he eagerly seized the opportunity chance so providentially offered him to seize the power lost by his brother, and quietly put himself in his place. He thought that, in acting thus he was not committing a bad action, but almost asserting a right by substituting himself for a man who seemed to care very little for titles and fortune.

Don Hernando, while whitewashing himself in this way, only obeyed that law of justice and injustice which God has placed in the heart of man, and which impels him, when he does any dishonourable deed, to seek excuses in order to prove to himself that he was bound to act as he had done. Still, the Marquis did not dare to confess to himself that the chance by which he profited he had helped by all his power, by envenoming by his speeches and continual insinuations his brother's actions, ruining him gradually in his father's mind, and preparing, long beforehand, the condemnation eventually uttered in the Red Room against the unfortunate Rodolfo.

And yet strange contradiction of the human heart, Don Hernando dearly loved his brother; he pitied him—he would like to hold him back on the verge of the precipice down which he thrust him, as it were. Once master of the estates and head of the family, he would have liked to find his brother again, in order to share with him this badly-acquired fortune, and gain pardon for his usurpation.

Unfortunately these reflections came too late—Don Rodolfo had disappeared without leaving a trace, and hence the Marquis was compelled to restrict himself to sterile regrets. At times, tortured with the ever-present memory of the last scene at the hacienda, he asked himself whether it would not have been better for him to have had a frank explanation with his brother, after which Don Rodolfo, whose simple tastes agreed but badly with the exigencies of a great name, would have amicably renounced in his favour the rights which his position as elder brother gave him.

But now to continue our narrative, which we have too long interrupted.

At the beginning of 1822, on a day of madness which was to be expiated by years of disaster, the definitive separation took place between Spain and Mexico, and the era of *pronunciamientos* set in. After the ephemeral reign of the Emperor Iturbide, Mexico reverted to a republic, or, more correctly, to a military government. Under the pressure of an army of 20,000 soldiers, which had 24,000 officers, the Presidents succeeded each other with headlong speed, burying the nation deeper and deeper in the mire, in which it is now struggling, and which will eventually swallow it up.

By *pronunciamiento* on *pronunciamiento* Mexico had reached the period when this story begins; but her wealth had been swallowed up in the tornado—her commerce was annihilated, her cities were falling in ruins, and New Spain had only retained of her old splendours fugitive recollections and piles of ruins. The Spaniards had suffered greatly during the War of Independence, as had their partisans, whose property had been burned and plundered by the revolutionists. The fatal decree of 1827, pronouncing the expulsion of the Spaniards, dealt the final and most terrible blow to their fortunes.

The Marquis de Moguer was one of the persons most affected by this measure, although, during the entire War of Independence and the different governments that succeeded each other, he had taken the greatest care not to mix himself up at all in politics, and remained neutral between all parties. This position, which it was difficult and almost impossible to maintain for any length of time, had compelled him to make concessions painful to his pride: unfortunately, his fortune consisted of land and mines, and if he left Mexico he would be a ruined man.

His friends advised him frankly to join the Mexican government, and give up his Spanish nationality. The Marquis, forced by circumstances, followed their advice; and, thanks to the credit some persons enjoyed with the President of the Republic, Don Hernando was not only not disturbed, but authorized to remain in the country, where he was naturalized as a Mexican.

But things had greatly changed with the Marquis. His immense fortune had vanished with the Spanish government. During the ten years of the War of Independence, his estates had lain fallow, and his mines, deserted by the workmen he formerly employed, had gradually become filled with water. They could not be put in working order again except by enormous and most expensive works. The situation was critical, especially for a man reared in luxury and accustomed to sow his money broadcast. He was now compelled to calculate every outlay with the utmost care, if he did not wish to see the hideous spectre of want rise implacable before him.

The pride of the Marquis was broken in this struggle against poverty; his love for his children restored his failing courage, and he bravely resolved to make head against the storm. Like the ruined gentleman who tilled the soil, with their sword by their side, as a proof of their nobility, he openly became hacendero and miner,—that is to say, he cultivated his estates on a large scale, and bred cattle and horses, while trying to pump out the water which had taken possession of his mines. Unfortunately, he was deficient in two important things for the proper execution of his plans: the necessary knowledge to assist the different operations he meditated: and, above all, money, without which nothing was possible. The Marquis was therefore compelled to engage a majordomo, and borrow on mortgage. For the first few years all went well, or appeared to do so. The majordomo, Don José Paredes, to whom we shall have occasion to refer more fully hereafter, was one of those men so valuable in haciendas, whose life is spent on horseback, whose attention nothing escapes, who thoroughly understand the cultivation of the soil, and know what it ought to produce, almost to an arroba.

But if the estates of the Marquis were beginning to regain their value under the skilful direction of the bailiff, it was not the same with the mines. Taking advantage of the convulsions in which Mexico was writhing, the independent Indians, no longer held in subjection by the fear of the powerful military organization of the Spaniards, had crossed the frontiers and regained a certain portion of their territory. They had permanently settled upon it, and would not allow white men to encroach on it. Most of the Marquis's mines being situated in the very country now occupied by the Indians, were consequently lost to him. The others, almost entirely inundated, in spite of the incessant labour bestowed on them, did not yet hold out any hopes of becoming productive again.

What Don Hernando gained on one side he lost on the other; and his position, in spite of his efforts, became worse and worse, and the abyss of debt gradually enlarged. The Marquis saw with terror the moment before him when it would be impossible for him to continue the struggle. Sad and aged by sorrow rather than years, the Marquis no longer dared to regard the future, which daily became more gloomy for him. He watched in mournful resignation the downfall of his house—the decay of his race; seeking in vain, like the man without a compass on the mighty ocean, from what point of the horizon the vessel that would save him from shipwreck would arrive.

But, alas! Days succeeded days without bringing any other change in the position of the Marquis, save greater poverty, and more nearly impending ruin. In proportion as the misfortune came nearer, the Marquis had seen his relations and friends keep aloof from him; all abandoned him, with that selfish indifference which seems a fundamental law of every organized society, when the precept, "Each man for himself," is put in practice, with all the brutal force of the *vae victis*.

Hence Don Hernando resided alone, with his son, at the Hacienda del Toro; for he had lost his wife several years before, and his daughter was being educated in a convent at the town of Rosario; with that noble pride which so admirably becomes men of well-tempered minds, the Marquis had accepted without a murmur the ostracism passed upon him. Far from indulging in useless recriminations with men, the majority of whom had, in other days, received obligations from him, he had made his son a partner in his labours, and, aided by him, redoubled his efforts and his courage.

Some months before the period when our story begins, ill fortune had seemed, not to grow weary of persecuting the Marquis, but desirous of granting him a truce—this is how a gleam of sunshine penetrated the gloomy atmosphere of the hacienda. One morning, a stranger, who appeared to have come a great distance, stopped at the gate, leading a mule loaded with two bales. This man, on reaching the first courtyard, threw the mule's bridle to a peon, with the simple remark,—"For Signor Don Hernando de Moguer—" and, without awaiting an answer, he started down the rocky road at a gallop and was lost in the windings of the path ere the peon had recovered from the surprise caused by the strange visit. The Marquis, at once warned, had the mule unloaded, and the bales conveyed to his study. They each contained twenty-five thousand piastres in gold, or nearly eleven thousand pounds of our money: on a folded paper was written one word—Restitution.

It was in vain that the Marquis ordered the most minute researches; the strange messenger could not be found. Don Hernando was therefore compelled to keep this large sum, which arrived so opportunely to extricate him from a difficult position, for he had a considerable payment to make on the morrow. Still, it was only on the repeated assurances of Don Ruiz and the majordomo, that the money was really his, that he consented to use it.

Cheered by this change of fortune, Don Hernando at length consented that Don Ruiz should go and fetch his sister, and bring her back to the hacienda, where her presence had been long desired; though there had been an obstacle, in the dangers of such a journey.

We will now resume our narrative, begging the reader to forgive this long digression, which was indispensable for the due comprehension of what is about to follow, and lead him to the Hacienda del Toro, a few hours before the arrival of Don Ruiz and his sister; that is to say, about three weeks since we left them at the post of San Miguel.

CHAPTER IX
A NEW CHARACTER

Although, owing to its position on the shores of the Pacific, Sonora enjoys the blessings of the sea breeze, whose moisture at intervals refreshes the heated atmosphere; still, for three hours in the afternoon, the earth incessantly heated by the torrid sunbeams produces a crushing heat. At such times the country assumes a really desolate aspect beneath the cloudless sky, which seems an immense plate of red-hot iron. The birds suddenly cease their songs, and languidly hide themselves beneath the thick foliage of the trees, which bow their proud crests towards the ground. Men and domestic animals hasten to seek shelter in the houses, raising in their hurried progress a white, impalpable, and calcined dust, which enters mouth and nostrils. For some hours Sonora is converted into a vast desert from which every appearance of life and movement has disappeared.

Everybody is asleep, or at least reclining in the most shady rooms, with closed eyes, and with the body abandoned to that species of somnolency which is neither sleeping nor waking, and which from that very fact is filled with such sweet and voluptuous reveries—inhaling at deep draughts the artificial breeze produced by artfully contrived currents of air, and in a word indulging in what is generally called in the torrid zones a siesta.

These are hours full of enjoyment, of those sweet and beneficent influence on body and mind we busy, active Englishmen are ignorant, but which people nearer the sun revel in. The Italians call this state the *dolce far niente*, and the Turks, that essentially sensual race, *keff*.

Like that city in the "Arabian Nights," the inhabitants of which the wicked enchanter suddenly changed into statues by waving his wand, life seemed suddenly arrested at the Hacienda del Toro, for the silence was so profound: peons, vaqueros, craidos, everybody in fact, were enjoying their siesta. It was about three in the afternoon; but that indistinct though significant buzz which announces the awakening of the hour that precedes the resumption of labour was audible. Two gentlemen alone had not yielded to sleep, in spite of the crushing midday heat; but seated in an elegantly furnished *cuarto*, they had spent the hours usually devoted to slumber in conversation. The cause for this deviation from the ordinary custom must have been most serious. The Hispano-American, and especially the Mexican, does not lightly sacrifice those hours of repose during which, according to a Spanish proverb, only dogs and Frenchmen are to be seen in the sun.

Of these two gentlemen, one, Don Hernando de Moguer, is already known to us. Years, while stooping his back, had furrowed some wrinkles on his forehead, and mingled many silver threads with his hair; but the expression of his face, with the exception of a tinge of melancholy spread over his features by lengthened misfortunes, had remained nearly the same, that is to say, gentle and timid, although clever; slightly sarcastic and eminently crafty.

As for the person with whom Don Hernando was conversing at this moment, he deserves a detailed description, physically at least, for the reader will soon be enabled to appreciate his moral character. He was a short, plump man, with a rubicund face and apoplectic look, though hardly forty years of age. Still his hair, which was almost white, his deeply wrinkled forehead, and his grey eyes buried beneath bushy whiskers, gave him a senile appearance, harmonizing but little with the sharp gesticulation and youthful manner he affected. His long, thin, violet nose was bent like a parrot's beak over a wide mouth filled with dazzling white teeth; and his prominent cheekbones, covered with blue veins, completed a strange countenance, the expression of which bore a striking likeness to that of an owl.

This species of nutcracker, with his prominent stomach and short ill-hung limbs, whose whole appearance was most disagreeable, had such a mobility of face as rendered it impossible to read his thoughts on his features, in the event of this fat man's carcase containing a thought. His cold blue eyes were ever pertinaciously fixed on the person addressing him, and did not reveal the slightest emotion; in short, this man produced at the first contact that invariable antipathy which is felt on the approach of reptiles, and which, after nearer acquaintance, is converted into disgust and contempt.

He was a certain Don Rufino Contreras, one of the richest landowners in Sonora, and a year previously had been elected senator to the Mexican Congress for the province.

At the moment when we enter the *cuarto*, Don Hernando, with arms folded at his back and frowning brow, is walking up and down, while Don Rufino, seated on a butaca, with his body thrown back, is following his movements with a crafty smile on his lips while striving to scratch off an invisible spot on his knee. For some minutes, the hacendero continued his walk, and then stopped before Don Rufino, who bent on him a mocking, inquiring glance.

"Then," he said, in a voice whose anxious expression he sought in vain to conceal, "you must positively have the entire sum within a week?"

"Yes," the fat man replied, still smiling.

"Why, if that is the case, did you not warn me sooner?"

"It was through delicacy, my dear sir."

"What—through delicacy?" Don Hernando repeated, with a start of surprise.

"You shall judge for yourself."

"I shall be glad to do so."

"I believe you do me the justice of allowing that I am your friend?"

"You have said you are, at least."

"I fancy I have proved it to you."

"No matter; but let us pass over that."

"Very well. Knowing that you were in a critical position at the moment, I tried to procure the sum by all possible means, as I did not wish to have recourse to you, except in the last extremity. You see, my dear Don Hernando, how delicate and truly friendly my calculations were. Unfortunately, at the present time it is very difficult to get money in, owing to the stagnation of trade produced by the new conflict which threatens to break out between the President of the Republic and the Southern States. It was therefore literally impossible for me to obtain the smallest sum. In such a perplexing position, I leave you to judge what I was obliged to do. The money I must have; you have owed it for a long time, and I applied to you—what else could I do?"

"I do not know. Still, I think you might have sent a peon to warn me, before you left Sonora."

"No, my dear sir, that is exactly what I should not do. I have not come direct to you: in pursuance of the line of conduct I laid down I hoped to collect the required sum on my road, and not be obliged to come all the way to your hacienda."

Don Hernando made no reply. He began his walk again after giving the speaker a glance which would have given him cause for thought, had he noticed it; but the latter gentleman had begun rubbing the invisible spot again with more obstinacy than before. In the meanwhile the sunbeams had become more and more oblique; the hacienda had woke up to its ordinary life; outside the shouts of the vaqueros pricking the oxen or urging on the horses could be heard mingled with the lowing and neighing of the draught cattle. Don Hernando walked up to a window, the shutters of which he threw open, and a refreshing breeze entered the *cuarto*. Don Rufino gave a sigh of relief and sat up in his *butaca*.

"Ouf," he said, with an expression of comfort, "I was very tired; not through the long ride I was compelled to make this morning, so much as through the stifling heat."

Don Hernando started at this insinuation, as if he had been stung by a serpent; he had neglected all the laws of Mexican hospitality; for Don Rufino's visit had so disagreeably surprised him, and made him forget all else before the sudden obligation of satisfying the claims of a merciless creditor. But at Don Rufino's remarks he understood how unusual his conduct must have seemed to a weary traveller, hence he rang a bell, and a peon at once came in.

"Refreshment," he said.

The peon bowed, and left the room.

"You will excuse me, Caballero," the hacendero continued, frankly, "but your visit so surprised me, that at the moment I did not think of offering the refreshment which a tired traveller requires so much. Your room is prepared, rest yourself tonight, and tomorrow we will resume our conversation, and arrive at a solution I trust mutually satisfactory."

"I hope so, my dear sir. Heaven is my witness that it is my greatest desire," Don Rufino answered, as he raised to his lips the glass of orangeade brought by the peon. "Unhappily I fear that, with the best will in the world, we cannot come to a settlement unless—"

"Unless!" Don Hernando sharply interrupted. Don Rufino quietly sipped his orangeade, placed the glass on the table, and said, as he threw himself back on the *butaca*, and rolled a cigarette—

"Unless you pay me in full what you owe me, which, from what you have said, appears to me to be difficult, I confess."

"Ah!" Don Hernando remarked with an air of constraint, "What makes you suppose that?"

"I beg your pardon, my dear sir, I suppose nothing: you told me just now that you were hardly pressed."

"Well, and what conclusion do you derive from that?" the hacendero asked impatiently.

"A very simple thing—that seventy thousand piastres form a rather round sum, and that however rich a man may be, he does not always have it in his hands, especially when he is pressed."

"I can make sacrifices."

"Believe me, I shall be sincerely sorry."

"But can you not wait a few days longer?"

"Impossible, I repeat: let us understand our respective positions, in order to avoid any business misunderstanding, which should always be prevented between honourable gentlemen holding a certain position. I lent you that sum, and only stipulated for small interest, I believe."

"I allow it, Señor, and thank you for it."

"It is not really worth the trouble; I was anxious to oblige you. I did so, and let us say no more about it; but remember that I made one condition which you accepted."

"Yes," Don Hernando said, with an impatient start, "and I was wrong."

"Perhaps so; but that is not the question. This condition which you accepted was to the effect that you should repay me the sum I advanced upon demand."

"Have I said the contrary?"

"Far from it; but now that I want the money, I ask you for it, and that is natural: I have in no way infringed the conditions. You ought to have expected what is happening today, and taken your precautions accordingly."

"Hence, if I ask a month to collect the money you claim?"

"I should be heartbroken, but should refuse; for I want the money, not in a month, but in a week. I can quite put myself in your position, and comprehend how disagreeable the matter must be; but unluckily so it is."

What most hurt Don Hernando was not the recall of the loan, painful as it was to him, so much as the way in which the demand was made; the show of false good nature employed by his creditor, and the insulting pity he displayed. Carried away involuntarily by the rage that filled his heart, he was about to give Don Rufino an answer which would have broken off all friendly relations between them for ever, when a great noise was heard in the hacienda, mingled with shouts of joy and the stamping of horses. Don Hernando eagerly leant out of the window, and at the expiration of a moment turned round to Don Rufino, who was sucking his cigarette with an air of beatitude.

"Here are my children, Caballero," he said; "not a word of this affair before them, I entreat."

"I know too well what I owe you, my dear Señor," the other replied, as he prepared to rise. "With your permission, however, I will withdraw, in order to allow you entire liberty for your family joy."

"No, no!" Don Hernando added, "I had better introduce you at once to my son and daughter."

"As you please, my dear sir. I shall be flattered to form the acquaintance of your charming family."

The door opened, and Don José Parades appeared. The majordomo was a half-breed of about forty years of age, tall and powerfully built, with bow legs and round shoulders that denoted his capacity as a horseman; in fact, the worthy man's life was spent in the saddle, galloping about the country. He took a side-glance at Don Rufino, bowed to his master, and lowering his usual rough tone, said—

"Señor amo, the niño and niña have arrived in good health, thanks to Our Lady of Carnerno."

"Thanks, Don José," Don Hernando replied; "let them come in. I shall be delighted to see them."

The majordomo gave a signal outside, and the two young people rushed into the room. With one bound they were in their father's arms, who for a moment pressed them to his heart; but then he pushed them away, remarking that a stranger was present. The young couple bowed respectfully.

"Señor Don Rufino," the Marquis said, "I present to you my son, Don Ruiz de Moguer, and my daughter, Doña Marianita: my children, this is Señor Don Rufino Contreras, one of my best friends."

"A title of which I am proud," Don Rufino replied, with a bow, while giving the young lady a cold searching glance, which made her look down involuntarily and blush.

"Are the apartments ready, Don José?" Don Hernando continued.

"Yes, Excellency," the majordomo said, who was contemplating the young people with a radiant face.

"If Señor Don Rufino will permit it, you can go and lie down, my children," the hacendero said. "You must be tired."

"You will also allow me to rest, Don Hernando?" the Senator then said. The hacendero bowed.

"We will resume our conversation at a more favourable moment," he continued, as he took a side-glance at Donna Marianita, who was just leaving the room with her brother. "However, my dear Señor, do not feel too anxious about my visit; for I believe I have discovered a way of arranging matters without inconveniencing you too much."

And, bowing to his knees to the Marquis, who was astounded at this conduct, which he was so far from expecting, Don Rufino left the room, smiling with an air of protection.

CHAPTER X
DON JOSÉ PAREDES

Several days had elapsed since the return of Don Ruiz and his sister to the hacienda, and Don Rufino had not said a word about the money which occasioned his visit. The hacendero, while employing all the means in his power to procure the necessary sum to pay his debt, had been careful not to allude to the conversation he had held with his creditor on the first day; the more so because Don Rufino seemed to have forgotten the pressing want of money he had at first given as his excuse for not granting any delay.

At the hacienda everything had returned to its old condition. Don Ruiz went out on horseback in the morning with José Paredes, in order to watch the peons and vaqueros, leaving to his father and sister the care of doing the honours to Don Rufino. For the first two or three days Doña Marianita had been considerably embarrassed by their guest's obsequious smiles and passionate glances; but she soon made up her mind, and only laughed at the craving look and absurd postures of the stout gentleman. The latter, while perceiving the effect he produced on the young lady, appeared to take no heed of it, and conscientiously continued his manoeuvres with the tenacity that formed the basis of his character. Probably in acting thus, and by openly paying his court to Doña Marianita, in the presence of her father and brother, Don Rufino was carrying out a pre-arranged plan, in order to gain an end which may be easily guessed.

It was evident to everybody that Don Rufino was seeking to obtain the hand of Doña Marianita. Don Hernando, in spite of the secret annoyance this pursuit caused him, for this man was the last he would have desired as his son-in-law, did not dare, however, let his vexation be seen, owing to his delicate position, and the sword of Damocles which Don Rufino held in suspense over his head. He contented himself with watching him closely, while leaving him free to act, hoping everything from him, and striving to collect all his resources in order to pay him off as speedily as possible; and once liberty was regained, to dismiss him. Unfortunately, money was difficult to obtain. Most of Don Hernando's debtors failed in meeting their engagements; and it was with great difficulty he obtained at the end of a fortnight one quarter the sum he owed Don Rufino, and this sum even could not be employed in liquidating the debt, for it was indispensable for the continuation of the works at the hacienda.

Since his arrival at the hacienda, Don Rufino had sent off messengers in several directions, and received letters. One morning he entered Don Hernando's study with an easy air, where the latter passed nearly the day, engaged in the most abstruse calculations. The hacendero raised his head with amazement on seeing the Senator; it was the first time the latter had come to seek him in this room. He suffered a heart pang; but he succeeded in hiding his emotion, and good-humouredly invited his visitor to take a seat.

"My dear Señor," Don Rufino began, as he comfortably stretched himself out upon a butaca, "excuse me for pursuing you into your last entrenchments, but I want to talk seriously with you, and so I frankly knocked at this door."

"You have done well," Don Hernando answered, with ill-dissembled agony: "you know that I am entirely at your disposal. How can I be of any service to you?"

"I will not trouble you long: I am not fond of lengthy conversations, and have merely come to terminate the affair which we began on the day when I arrived at the hacienda."

The hacendero felt a cold perspiration stand on his temples at this brutally frank avowal.

"I had not forgotten you," he replied: "at this very moment I was making arrangements which, I trust, will enable me to discharge the debt in a few days."

"That is not the point," Don Rufino remarked, airily: "I do not want the money, and request you to hold it for me as long as you possibly can."

Don Hernando looked at him in amazement. "That surprises you," the Senator continued, "and yet the affair is very simple. I was anxious to prove to you that you had in me not a pressing creditor, but a truly devoted friend. When I saw that it would greatly embarrass you to repay me this trifle, and as you are a gentleman I am anxious to oblige, I turned to another quarter."

"Still," Don Hernando, who feared a snare, objected: "you said to me—"

"I believed it," Don Rufino interrupted him. "Fortunately it was not so, as I have recently acquired the proof: not only have I been able to meet my payment, but I have a considerable sum left in my hands which I do not know what to do with, and which I should feel much obliged by your taking; for I do not know a more honourable gentleman than yourself, and I wish to get rid of the money, which is useless to me at the moment."

Don Hernando, confounded by this overture, which he had been so far from expecting from a man who had at first been so harsh with him, was silent, for he knew not what to answer, or to what he should attribute this so sudden and extraordinary change.

"Good gracious!" continued Don Rufino, with a smile; "During the few days I have been with you, my dear Señor, I have been enabled to appreciate the intelligent way in which you manage your immense estate; and it is evident to me that you must realize enormous profits. Unfortunately for you, you are in the position of all men who undertake great things with limited resources. You are short of capital just at the moment when it is most necessary; but as this is a common case, you cannot complain. You have made sacrifices, and will have to make more before obtaining real results. The money you want I have, and I offer it to you. I trust you will not insult me by doubting my friendship, or my desire to be of service to you."

"Certainly, Caballero. Still," Don Hernando stammered, "I am already your debtor to a heavy amount."

"Well, what matter? You will be my debtor for a larger amount, that is all."

"I understand all the delicacy and kindness of your conduct, but I fear—"

"What?—That I may demand repayment at an inconvenient moment?"

"I will not conceal from you—"

"You are wrong, Don Hernando. I wish to deal with you as a friend, and do you a real service. You owe me seventy thousand piastres, I believe?"

"Alas, yes!"

"Why that 'alas?'" the senator asked, with a smile. "Seventy thousand piastres, and fifty thousand more I am going to hand you directly, in six bills payable at sight, drawn on Wilson and Co., Bankers, at Hermosillo, will form a round sum, for which you will give me your acceptance payable— come, what date will suit you best?"

Don Hernando hesitated. Evidently Don Rufino, in making him so strange a proposal, had an object; but that object he could not see. The Senator's love for his daughter could not impel him to do such a generous act: this unexpected kindness evidently concealed a snare; but what was the snare? Don Rufino carefully followed the different feelings that were reflected on Don Hernando's face.

"You hesitate," he said to him, "and you are wrong. Let us talk candidly. You cannot possibly hope to realize any profit within eight months, so it will be impossible for you to pay me so large a sum before that period." Then, opening his pocketbook and taking out the six bills, which he laid on the table, he continued: "Here are the fifty thousand piastres; give me an acceptance for one hundred and twenty thousand, payable at twelve months' date. You see that I give you all necessary latitude to turn yourself round. Well, supposing—which is not probable—that you are unable to pay me when the bill falls due; we will renew it, that is all. *¡Cuerpo de Cristo!* I am not a harsh creditor. Come, is the matter settled, or must I take the bills back?"

Money, under whatever shape it presents itself, has an irresistible attraction in the eyes of the speculator and embarrassed man. Don Hernando, in spite of all his efforts—in spite of all the numerous sacrifices he had made, felt himself rapidly going down the incline of ruin, on which it is impossible for a man to stop; but time might save him. Don Rufino, whatever his wishes might be, rendered him an immense service by giving him, not only time, but also the money he required, and which he despaired of obtaining elsewhere. Any longer hesitation on his part would therefore have been unjustifiable; hence he took the bills, and gave his acceptance.

"That's settled," Don Rufino said, as he folded the document and carefully placed it in his pocketbook. "My dear Señor, you are really a singular man. There is more difficulty in getting you to accept money than there would be in getting another to pay it."

"I really do not know how to thank you, Don Rufino, for the service you have rendered me, and which I am now free to confess has arrived very opportunely."

"Money is always opportune," the Senator replied, with a laugh; "but let us say no more about that. If you happen to have a safe man, send him off at once to cash these bills at Hermosillo, for money is too scarce to be allowed to lie idle."

"This very day my majordomo, Don José Paredes, shall set out for the *ciudad*."

"Very good. Now I have one request to make of you."

"Speak, speak! I shall be delighted to prove to you how grateful I am."

"This is the matter: now that I am, temporarily at least, no longer your creditor, I have no decent pretext for remaining at the hacienda."

"Well, what does that matter?"

"It matters a great deal to me. I should like to remain here a few days longer, in order to enjoy your agreeable society."

"Are you jesting, Don Rufino? The longer you remain at the hacienda, the greater honour you will do us; we shall be delighted to keep you, not for a few days, but for all the time you may be pleased to grant us."

"Very good; that is what I desired. Now, I shall go away and leave you to your business."

When the majordomo returned to the hacienda at about eleven o'clock in the morning, Don Hernando sent for him. Without taking the time to pull off his vaquero boots or unbuckle his heavy spurs, José Parades hurried to his master.

"Have you a good horse?" the hacendero asked, so soon as the majordomo entered the study.

"I have several, Excellency," he answered.

"I mean by a good horse, one capable of going a long distance."

"Certainly, mi amo; I have a mustang on which I could ride to Hermosillo and back without giving it any further rest than that of the camping hours."

"I want to send you to Hermosillo."

"Very good, Excellency; when must I start?"

"Why, as soon as possible after you have rested."

"Rested from what?"

"The ride you have taken this morning."

The majordomo shrugged his shoulders with a smile. "I am never tired, Excellency; in half an hour I shall have lassoed my horse, saddled it, and mounted, unless you wish me to defer my journey."

"The hours for the siesta will soon be here, and the heat will be insufferable."

"You are aware, Excellency, that we half-Indians are children of the sun; its heat does not affect us."

"You have an answer for everything, Don José."

"For you, Excellency, I feel myself capable of performing impossibilities."

"I know that you are devoted to my house."

"Is it not just, Excellency? For two centuries my family has eaten the bread of yours; and, if I acted otherwise than I am doing, I should be unworthy of those from whom I am descended."

"I thank you, my friend; you know the esteem and affection I have for you. I am about to intrust an important commission to you."

"Be assured that I shall perform it, Excellency."

"Very good. You will start at once for Hermosillo, where you will cash these bills for fifty thousand piastres, at the bank of Wilson and Co."

"Fifty thousand piastres!" the majordomo repeated, with surprise.

"It surprises you, my friend, to whom I have confided my most secret affairs, that I have so large a sum to receive. You ask yourself, doubtless, in what way I managed to obtain it."

"I ask nothing, Excellency; it does not concern me. I am here to carry out your orders, and not permit myself improper observations."

"This money has been lent me by a friend whose kindness is inexhaustible."

"Heaven grant that you are not mistaken, Excellency; and that the man from whom you have this money is really a friend."

"What do you mean, Don José? To what are you alluding?"

"I make no allusion, mi amo; I merely think that friends who lend fifty thousand piastres from hand to hand—pardon my frankness, Excellency—to a man whose affairs are in such a condition as yours, are very rare at present; and that, before forming a definite judgment about them, it would be wiser to wait and learn the cause of such singular generosity."

Don Hernando sighed. He shared his majordomo's opinions, though he would not allow it. Following the tactics of all men who have not good reasons to allege, he suddenly turned the conversation.

"You can take three or four persons with you," he said.

"What to do, Excellency?"

"Why, to act as escort on your return."

The majordomo began laughing.

"What use is an escort, Excellency? You want your money here? I will buy a mule at Hermosillo, and load the money on it, and it will take a very clever fellow to rob me, I assure you."

"Still, it would be, perhaps, better to have an escort."

"Permit me to remark, Excellency, that it would be the best way of setting robbers on my track."

"¡*Viva Dios!* I should be curious to know how you arrive at that conclusion."

"You will easily understand me, mi amo. A single man is certain to pass unnoticed, especially when, as at this moment, the roads are infested with bandits of every description and every colour."

"Hum! what you are saying is not re-assuring, Don José, do you know that?" Don Hernando remarked, with a smile, for his majordomo's reasoning amused him.

"On the contrary, the bandits to whom I am referring, Excellency, are clever, too clever, and it is that which ruins them; they will never imagine that a poor devil of a half-breed, leading a sorry mule, can be carrying fifty thousand piastres. Deceived by my appearance, they will let me pass, without even pretending to see; while if I take persons with me, it will arouse their suspicions, they will want to know why I am guarded, and I shall be plundered."

"You may really be right, Don José."

"I am certain I am, Excellency."

"Well, I will not argue any longer; do what you think proper."

"All right, Excellency; I will deliver the money to you, without the loss of a real, I promise you."

"May Heaven grant it: here are the bills, and now—you can start whenever you please."

"I shall be gone within an hour, Excellency," the majordomo answered.

He took up the bills, hid them in his bosom, and, after bowing to his master, left the study. José Paredes went straight to the corral, where in a few minutes he had lassoed a mustang with small head and flashing eye, which he began saddling, after he had carefully rubbed it down. Then he inspected his weapons, laid in a stock of powder and ball, placed some provisions in his alforjas, and mounted. But, instead of leaving the hacienda, he proceeded to a separate building, and twice gently tapped a window before which he pulled up. The window opened, and Don Ruiz appeared.

"Ah! Is that you, Paredes; going back to the plantations already?" he said; "Well, wait a minute, and I will be with you."

The majordomo shook his head.

"Do not disturb yourself, Niño," he said. "I am not going to the plantations, but on a journey."

"A journey?" the young man asked, in surprise.

"Yes; but only for a few days. The Marquis has sent me, and I shall soon be back."

"Can you tell me the reason why you are going, and whither?"

"The master will tell you himself, Niño."

"Good! But I suppose you have some other motive for coming to wish me good-bye?"

"Yes, Niño; I wished to give you a piece of advice before leaving the hacienda."

"Advice?"

"Yes; and of a serious nature. Niño, during my absence, watch carefully the man who is here!"

"Whom do you mean, Paredes?"

"The Senator, Don Rufino Contreras."

"For what reason?"

"Watch him, Niño, watch him! And now, good-bye for the present."

And without awaiting the question the young man was about to ask him, the majordomo dug his spurs into his horse's flanks, and left the hacienda at a gallop.

CHAPTER XI
ON THE ROAD

Mexico, considering its size, is one of the least populated countries in the world. With but few exceptions, the old Spanish colonies, since they have proclaimed their independence and become free republics, having been constantly engaged in war with each other, or in overthrowing the government they themselves elected, have seen all the ties attaching families to the soil broken in turn. Foreigners, no longer finding the necessary safety for their speculations in countries incessantly troubled by revolutions, have gone away. Trade has been annihilated; commerce has fallen into a state of atrophy; and the population has frightfully decreased, with such rapidity, that sensible men, who sought a remedy for this incurable evil, called emigration to the help of these states, which nothing can galvanise, and which only possess a factitious existence.

Unfortunately, the Hispano-American race is essentially haughty and jealous. Poor fellows, who let themselves be seduced by the brilliant promises made them, and who consented to cross the sea to settle in this country, found, on their arrival, and especially in Mexico, an ill-disguised hatred and contempt, which was displayed in all classes of society by ill will and aversion. Hence, being disgusted by their reception, and recognising the slight trust they could place in the promises of the men who had summoned them, they hastened to leave a country in which they had only found unjust prejudices and deplorable ill faith, and went to ask of the United States the protection refused them by those who had so pressingly summoned them.

Mexico, in spite of a certain varnish of civilization, the last reminiscence of the Spanish occupation, which may still be found in the large cities and their environs, is, therefore, in reality plunged into a state of barbarism relatively greater than it was fifty years ago. The Pacific States, especially, being less frequently visited by strangers, and left, as it were, to themselves, have retained a peculiar physiognomy, whose picturesque savageness and rough manners would cause the tourist's heart to beat with joy, if ever a tourist ventured into these countries; but which inspire an involuntary fear, justified, however, by everything the traveller, forced to visit this land on business, witnesses.

In Europe and all civilized countries, the means of transport are numerous and convenient, but in Mexico only one is known—the horse. In the Central States, and those which run along the Atlantic seaboard, some towns possess diligences, which change horses at the *tambos*, a species of inn, where the travellers stop to pass the night. But these *tambos* and *mesones*, which possess a great resemblance to the Sicilian hostelries and Spanish ventas, supply absolutely nothing to the guests they shelter, excepting a roof, reduced to its simplest expression; that is to say, the traveller is compelled to take his bed with him, in addition to provisions, if he does not wish to sleep wrapped up in his cloak.

In spite of the numberless disagreements which the uncomfortable mode of progressing from one place to another entails, the traveller derives one advantage from it—that of not being exposed, in a fickle atmosphere like that of Mexico, where after burning days the nights are chilly, to the attacks of the climate. In the Pacific States, matters are no longer thus; the traveller who proceeds from one town to another is forced to do so on horseback, without any hope of finding for a distance of sixty or eighty leagues the smallest inn, or even most wretched rancho, where he can shelter himself from wind and rain at nightfall. At sunset he camps where he is in the open air, and begins his journey again on the morrow Still, as Providence has been in its wisdom careful to give an equal amount of good and evil, the robbers, salteadores, and brigands of every description, who infest all the roads in the interior, on which they reign as masters, plundering travellers in open day and assassinating them with the most perfect impunity, are rarely found in Sonora. In this country the roads in this respect enjoy a relatively complete security, except when the Indians have risen, or a fresh *pronunciamiento* has let bands of revolted soldiers loose on the country. These fellows have no scruple about imitating professional robbers, and killing and plundering people, whose unlucky stars have exposed them to their tender mercies.

José Paredes, though he had in reality only fifty leagues to go, a distance which in most European countries is comfortably performed in a railway carriage in a few hours, was obliged, on account of the bad state of the roads, and the indispensable precautions he had to take, to remain at least four days on the road before reaching Hermosillo. This journey, which would have been very painful to any man accustomed to the ease and luxuries of life, was only a pleasure trip for the worthy majordomo, a real Centaur, whose life was spent on horseback—who slept more frequently in the open air than under a roof, and whose powerful constitution rendered him insensible to the annoyances inseparable from a journey made under such conditions. The Mexicans have two expressions which admirably depict the class of men to whom the majordomo belonged; they call them *Jinetes* and *Hombres de a Caballo*.

José Paredes, then, rode along jauntily on his horse, at one moment carelessly smoking a husk cigarette, at another humming a *jarabe* or a *seguedilla*, while keeping his eye and ear on the watch, and his finger prudently laid on the trigger of his gun, which was placed across his saddle-bow. His second day's ride was drawing to a close; he had left Arispe far behind him, which town he had passed through without stopping longer than he required to lay in fresh provisions and forage for his horse.

The sun was rapidly declining on the horizon; a rather powerful wind blew in gusts, raising clouds of dust, which blinded the horseman and formed a thick fog round him, in the midst of which he almost entirely disappeared. Although, as we have said, the day was drawing to a close, the heat was stifling, the sky had assumed a livid appearance; yellow clouds gradually collected in the horizon and were rapidly brought up by the wind. The birds whirled in the air, uttering shrill and discordant cries; sharp noises and shrill whistlings rose from among the rocks that on both sides flanked the narrow ravine the majordomo was now following, and large drops of rain fell on the calcined soil, which easily imbibed them. The horse pricked its ears, shook its head, and snorted in terror. All presaged one of those storms which it is only possible to witness in these regions—veritable cataclysms which rend and uproot the largest trees, force streams from their beds, and overthrow the soil, as if the earth were struggling wildly beneath the grasp of those horrible convulsions of Nature, which completely change within a few hours the aspect of the country over which they have swept with the fury of the African simoom.

"Hum!" José Paredes muttered to himself, as he took an anxious glance along the road; "If I am not greatly mistaken, within an hour we shall have one of the most tremendous *cordonazos* that has been seen for some time. That will be most agreeable for me, and my position will not fail to be most amusing. Confound the temporal! Why could it not have waited for another eight-and-forty hours?"

The majordomo lost no time in vain lamentation. The situation in which he found himself was really critical: he knew that if the temporal surprised him on this ravine, he would have enormous difficulties to overcome in escaping its violence. He therefore resolved at all hazards to attempt the greatest efforts in getting out of the scrape. Minutes were precious; hesitation was impossible, and he must form a decision at once. José Paredes was a resolute man, long accustomed only to reckon on his courage, strength, and energy, to get him out of difficult situations; he therefore carefully wrapped himself in his zarapé, pulled his hat down over his forehead, and, bending over his horse's neck, dug his spurs, while crying, sharply, one word: "Santiago!" a cry employed in this country to excite horses. The noble animal, astonished that its master should deem it necessary to employ spurs to give it ardour, gave a snort of passion, and started at a headlong pace.

In the meanwhile the clouds had completely covered the blue sky; the atmosphere was gradually growing darker; the sunbeams had lost their heat; the horse still dashed on, rendered furious by the incessant prick of the spurs, which the majordomo dug into his panting flanks. At length Paredes uttered a cry of joy, for he had reached the end of the ravine, and before him extended a vast plain, bordered by tall mountains in the horizon. These mountains the majordomo wanted to reach, for there alone had he chance of safety. Although his position had greatly improved after leaving the ravine, it was still extremely difficult, if the storm were to burst before he had succeeded in crossing the plains, which afforded him no shelter to brave the tornado. Hence, the traveller, after exploring the neighbourhood with a rapid glance, and assuring himself that he had no hope of escaping the tempest, and the barren sandy plain which was only traversed by a few streams, repeated his cry of "Santiago," and set out on his mad ride once more.

As always happens, and as anyone who has studied the admirable instinct of the horse can certify, the noble animal the majordomo rode seemed to have identified itself with its master. Through the effort of that magnetic current, whose power is no longer doubted, it appeared to understand that their common safety depended on its efforts; and it literally devoured the space, darting across the plain with the fantastic rapidity of the spectre steed of the German ballad.

All at once a vivid flash broke through the clouds, followed by a tremendous thunderclap. The horse gave a start of terror, but quickly checked by its rider, started again through the torrents of rain which were beginning to fall. Night bad suddenly set in; the sun, veiled by the clouds, had become invisible, and it was in condemned obscurity that the majordomo was compelled to attempt the supreme efforts on which life or death depended. Still, Paredes was not discouraged, and his will seemed to grow fearless in the struggle; while sitting firmly in the saddle, like a granite statue, with contracted brows and eyes looking ahead, as if constantly trying to pierce the gloom, and exciting his horse with spur and voice, his features were as calm and impassive as if he were merely in one of the thousand ordinary accidents of his adventurous life in the desert. In the meanwhile the tempest had changed into a fearful hurricane, and raged with extreme fury. The unchained winds whistled violently, dashing the rain, and upraising masses of mud, which flew along the ground.

An ill-omened swashing made the unhappy traveller, who was surprised by the tornado, understand that the streams were beginning to overflow and inundate the plain. By the vivid flashes which uninterruptedly followed each other, the majordomo could see all around large grey pools of water, which constantly widened and enclosed him in an incessantly contracting circle; distant sounds borne by the breeze heightened his apprehensions. An hour more, he felt, and the plains would only form one vast lake, in the midst of which he would infallibly perish. Warned by that instinct which never deceives them, the wild beasts had left their lairs, and were flying madly, while uttering hoarse roars of terror. When a flash lit up the horizon, Paredes could see indistinct forms pass by his side, which were no other than the dangerous denizens of the prairie. All was overthrown and confounded. The swash of the water was mingled with the artillery of the thunder and the howling of the wind. But the horse still galloped on straight ahead, sustained by the very terror which maddened it and spurred it on better than the sharpest knife could have done.

Suddenly the majordomo uttered a cry of terror and anger, drew himself up, and pulled bridle with such strength that the horse stopped short on his trembling legs. He fancied he had heard the distant sound of a bell. When an inundation comes, the hacenderos have all their bells rung, in order to warn straggling travellers and tell them of a place of refuge. The majordomo listened; in a few seconds a sound, faint as a sigh, reached the ear. The practised hunter was not mistaken; it was really the expiring sound of a bell that reached him, and the sound, came from a direction diametrically opposite to the one he was following. In the darkness he had left his track; he was lost in the midst of an entirely submerged country without chance of help. In spite of his indomitable bravery the majordomo felt an internal horror; an icy perspiration stood on his forehead, and he shook all over. At this supreme moment the man had but one terrible thought that he would bear with him to the tomb the fortune entrusted to him by his master, and on which the future of his children perhaps depended. Paredes felt burning tears start from his eyes, and a choking sob from his bosom. He cared little for life; he would gladly have sacrificed it for his master; but the thought of dying thus, and completing his master's ruin, caused him indescribable grief. For some minutes this lion-hearted man, this bold wood ranger, who had faced without blenching the most terrible dangers, felt weaker than a child. But this prostration only lasted a short time, and a reaction quickly took place; ashamed of the passing despondency to which he had yielded, the majordomo became the firmer when all seemed to abandon him, and resolved to sustain the insensate struggle till he drew his last breath.

Rendered stronger by his energetic resolution, the majordomo, whose arteries were beating as if about to burst, passed the back of his band over his eyes, addressed to Heaven that mental prayer which the most intrepid men find in their hearts at the supreme moment when life or death only hangs by a thread; and, instead of going on, he waited for a flash, by which he could examine his position, and decide the new course he had to take. He had not to wait long; almost immediately a flash shot athwart the sky. Paredes uttered a cry of joy and surprise: he had seen, a few paces from him on his right, a rather tall hill, on the top of which he fancied he noticed a horseman, motionless and upright as an equestrian statue.

With that coolness which powerful men alone possess in critical circumstances, the majordomo, although he felt that the water was rapidly encircling him, and was almost up to his horse's girths, would not leave anything to chance. Fearing he had been deceived by one of those optical illusions, so frequent when the senses are overexcited, he resolved to wait for a second flash, and kept his eyes fixed on the spot where the hill must be, which he fancied he must have seen as in a dream. All at once, at the moment when the desired flash lit up the darkness, a voice, that overpowered the roar of the tempest, reached his ear:

"Courage! Keep straight on," he heard.

The majordomo uttered a cry of delight, which resembled a yell; and, lifting his horse with his bridle and knees, he dashed toward the hill, pursued by the seething waters which were powerless to arrest him; and, after an ascent that lasted scarce ten minutes, he fell fainting into the arms of the man whose summons had saved him. From this moment he had nothing to fear: an inundation could not reach the top of the hill where he had found such a providential refuge.

CHAPTER XII
A CONVERSATION BY NIGHT

The majordomo's fainting fit, caused rather by the moral struggle he had sustained than by the physical fatigue he had endured, was not of any duration: when he re-opened his eyes, he was alone on the top of the hill. He threw off the furs and blankets laid over him, to protect him, doubtless from the icy cold of the night, and looked curiously round him. The tempest was still raging, but it had lost a great deal of its violence. The rain had ceased: the deep blue sky was gradually becoming studded with twinkling stars, which shed an uncertain light, and gave the landscape an aspect of strange and desolate wildness. The wind blew furiously, and formed waves on the seething top of the waters, which had now almost risen to the spot where the majordomo lay. A few yards from its master, his horse was quietly grazing; it was eating the young tree shoots, and the tall close grass that covered the ground like a thick carpet of verdure. Another horse was browsing close by.

"Good!" Paredes muttered to himself, "My saviour has not gone away; I hope he is not far off, and that I shall see him soon. Where can he be? At his own business, of course, though I cannot guess the nature of his occupation at such a moment. Well, the best plan will be to wait for him."

The Mexican had scarce ended his soliloquy, ere a shadow stood out in the gloom, and the man of whom he was speaking appeared.

"Ah, ah!" he said, gaily, "You are all right again, I see: all the better; I would sooner have you in that position than the one you were in just now."

"Thanks," the majordomo cordially answered. "I fancy I must have looked very pitiable, stretched out like a half-throttled *novillo*. Is it not disgraceful for a strong man to faint like a child or a feeble woman?"

"Not the least in the world, *compañero*," the other said, frankly. "Accident decreed that I should be for a long time the involuntary witness of the contest you waged, though it was impossible to help you, and *¡Viva Dios!* I declare that you are a tough combatant; you sustained the shock bravely, and many others in your place—I the first, perhaps—would not have got out of the scrape so well."

This answer completely broke the ice, and made the two men comparatively friends at once.

"I confess," Paredes remarked, as he offered his hand to his new friend, "that for a moment I believed myself lost, and had it not been for you I should have been so."

"Nonsense," the other replied, as he pressed the hand offered him. "You owe me nothing, for, by Jove! You saved yourself all alone. But let us not dwell on this point any longer. Although we are in relative safety, as the water cannot reach us here, our position is not the most agreeable; and I fancy it would be the best for us to try and get out of it as quickly as possible."

"That is my opinion, too; but, unluckily, the means at our disposal are very limited."

"Perhaps so; at any rate, with your consent, we will hold an Indian council."

"That is the best thing we can do at this moment. However," he added, as he looked up to the sky, "day will not break for three hours."

"We have time before us, in that case."

Daring this short conversation the storm had entirely ceased, and the wind only blew in gusts.

"Before all," the majordomo said, "let us light a fire; now that the tempest has ceased, the wild beasts, whose instinct is infallible, will seek the shelter of this hill, swarm round us, and, if we do not take care, carry our position by assault."

"Excellently argued; I see that you are a hunter."

"I was one for some time," Paredes replied, with a sigh of regret, "but now it is all over; my adventures in the desert are ended."

"I pity you sincerely," the stranger said, with an accent of sincerity; "for no existence is comparable with it."

"The finest years of my life were those I spent in the desert."

While conversing thus, the two men had dug a hole with their machetes at the foot of an enormous larch tree, to act as a hearth. In this hole they piled up all the resinous wood they were able to procure, lit it with some gunpowder rolled up in leaves, and in a few minutes a long jet of flame sprung up and joyously ascended to the sky, while the wood crackled and emitted millions of sparks. Fire has an immense influence upon the human mind; among other benefits, it has the faculty of restoring joy and hope;

and while warming a man with its reviving heat, it often makes him forget perils incurred and fatigues endured. The two men, who were as wet as if they had been in a river, dried themselves for a considerable time, enjoying the pleasant sensations which the heat made them experience, in proportion as it penetrated into the pores, causing the blood to circulate with greater vivacity, and restoring elasticity to their benumbed limbs. It was the majordomo who was the first to resume the conversation.

"¡Viva Dios!" he said, shaking himself joyously; "I am now quite a different man. What a fine thing a fire is when you are cold. Suppose we make use of it, comrade?"

"Do so, pray," the stranger replied, with a laugh; "but in what way?"

"Oh, that is very easy; you shall see. Are you not hungry?"

"*Caray*, it is fourteen hours since I have eaten; but unluckily I have no provisions."

"Well, I have, and we will share them."

"Very good. I see that you are a first-rate fellow."

The majordomo rose, fetched the alforjas which were fastened to his saddle, and then seated himself again by the fire.

"There!" he said, displaying his provisions with some degree of complacency.

"¡*Caramba!*" the other remarked, with a laugh; "Food was never more welcome."

The provisions which caused such delight to the two men would have made our European good wives smile with pity. They consisted of some slices of *tasajo, cicuia*, a lump of goat's cheese, and a few maize tortillas; but the majordomo produced a leather bottle, full of excellent mezcal, which had the privilege of restoring to the two adventurers all their merry carelessness.

The *tasajo* was laid on the coals, where it was soon done to a turn, and the two friends heartily attacked the supper. The frugal meal ended, they washed it down with a few sips of mezcal, fraternally passing the bottle to each other; then they lit their cigarettes, the *obligado* supplement of every Mexican repast, and began to smoke, while attentively surveying the heavy sky, which was already striped with dark bands under the influence of the early morning hours.

"Now, let us hold a council, if you are agreeable," the stranger said, as he inhaled an enormous mouthful of smoke, which he sent forth through his mouth and nostrils.

"As you are my senior on this territory," the majordomo remarked, with a laugh, "and are better acquainted with its resources than I am, you have the right to speak first."

"Very good: we are surrounded by water, and though the temporal has ceased, the streams will not return to their bed for several hours: moreover, the whole day will pass before the water is entirely absorbed by the sand."

"That is true," the majordomo said, with a significant shake of the head: "and yet we must get away from here."

"That is the question. To do so, we can only employ two means."

"Yes, we must either wait till the ground is dry, and that unfortunately will take a long time, which I cannot afford, as I am in a hurry: or at sunrise we can mount our horses, and bravely swim off, and reach the mountains, which cannot be very far distant."

"You forgot another way which is still at our service."

"I do not think so."

"We can get into a canoe, and tow our horses after us, which will tire them less than carrying us; and enable us to reach the mountains to which you refer with greater ease; and they are only two leagues at the most, from this point."

"Your opinion is certainly good, and I approve of it with all my heart; unluckily we want one very important thing to carry it out."

"What is that?"

"Why, hang it all—the canoe."

"You are mistaken, *compadre*, we have one."

"Nonsense; how can that be possible?"

"While you were in a faint," the stranger continued, with a smile, "I explored our domain. You know that, in this country, when the rainy season arrives, the inhabitants are accustomed to hide canoes in bushes, and even in trees, in order to give travellers who are surprised by the inundation the means of saving themselves."

"That is true; have you found a canoe?"

"Yes; and hidden behind the very tree against which you are leaning."

"Heaven be praised! In that case we run no risk; but is the canoe in good condition?"

"I have assured myself of that fact, and even found two pairs of new paddles."

"Heaven is very certainly on your side. In that case we will start at sunrise, if that suits you."

"Excellently; though I am not in such a hurry as you appear to be, and for certain reasons I must remain in these parts for some days longer."

"Shall we employ the few hours left us in having a sleep?"

"You can sleep if you like, but as I am not at all fatigued, I shall watch over our common safety."

"I accept your proposal as frankly as you make it. Yet, with your permission, I will not close my eyes till I have become better acquainted with you."

"How so? Are we not friends already?"

"Certainly, I am your friend, at least; but we do not know one another."

"That is to say—"

"We do not know one another—I mean who we are."

"Oh, when travelling, what value can such formalities possess?"

"A greater value than you suppose; in a few hours we shall part, it is true, perhaps never to meet again; but perhaps, at some distant period, we may require each other's assistance; now, how could I summon you, if I did not know your name?"

"You're right, comrade; as for me, I am only a poor devil of a hunter, wood ranger, or trapper—whichever you please, and my companions call me Stronghand, because, as they say, when I hold out my hand to a friend he can trust to it in perfect confidence."

"¡Viva Dios, caballero! you are well named, as I can declare; your reputation has already reached me, and I am delighted at the chance that has brought us together, as I had already desired to form your personal acquaintance."

"I thank you," the hunter replied, with a bow.

"As for me," the Mexican continued, "my name is José Paredes, and I am majordomo to the Marquis de Moguer."

"What!" Stronghand said, with a surprise he did not try to conceal; "you are majordomo at the Hacienda del Toro?"

"Yes, what do you find surprising in that?"

"The man whom his master sent two days ago to Hermosillo, to receive cash for heavy bills drawn on an English banker?"

"How do you know that?" Paredes exclaimed, in his turn overwhelmed with surprise.

"What matter, so long as I know it?" the hunter replied. "Believe me," he added, with an accent that caused the majordomo deep reflection, "our meeting is truly providential, and Heaven led us toward each other."

"That is strange," Paredes muttered; "how is it possible that a secret which my master confided to me alone should be in your possession?"

The hunter smiled. "A secret known to three persons," he said, "does not long remain a secret."

"But that third person, to whom you refer, has no right to divulge it."

"How do you know that? I will say to you in my turn, Master Paredes. Sufficient for you, for the present, to learn that I am aware of the cause of your journey. I think you said you had heard speak of me before we met?"

"That is true, Señor."

"What terms did the persons who spoke of me employ?"

"The best, I must allow. They represented you to me as a man of unspotted loyalty and dauntless courage."

"Good! Does that report satisfy you—have you confidence in me?"

"Yes; for I am convinced that you are an honest man."

"I hope that your opinion of me will not alter. I will soon prove to you that it is fortunate for you and the Marquis that we have met at the moment when you least expected it; for I was looking for you."

"Looking for me? I do not understand you."

"You do not require to understand me at the present moment; but set your mind at rest, everything will be explained ere long."

"I hope so."

"And I am certain of it. Are you devoted to your master?"

"My family have lived on the estate for two hundred years."

"That is not a reason; answer distinctly."

"I am devoted to him body and soul, and would willingly lay down my life for him."

"That is the way to answer; however, I knew it already, and only desired that your lips should confirm what I have been told."

"My master has no secrets from me."

"I know that also. Well, now, listen to me attentively, Señor Paredes, for what I have to reveal to you is of the utmost gravity."

"I am listening to you, Señor."

"Your master is at this moment in danger of being utterly ruined. He is the plaything of villains who have sworn to destroy him. The sum you are going to fetch they intend to take from you, and everything is prepared to make you fall into an infamous trap, in which you will infallibly perish."

"Are you certain of what you assert?" the majordomo exclaimed, in horror.

"I know all, I repeat to you: the men from whom I obtained your secret, who little expected that I was listening to them, at the same time revealed to me the means they intended to employ in assassinating you."

"Why, that is infamous!"

"I am completely of your opinion, and that is why, instead of setting my traps in the desert, as I ought to be doing, I am now here. I wish to foil the plots of these villains, and confound them."

"But what interest induces you to act thus?" the majordomo asked, with a shadow of distrust.

"That question I cannot answer. You must for the present lay aside all curiosity; you must place entire confidence in me, and give me, in what I propose doing, as much help as I shall offer you. Does this suit you? I fancy that the bargain I offer is entirely to your advantage, and that you will run no risk beyond what I do myself."

There was a lengthened silence. The majordomo was reflecting on what he had just heard, while the hunter, with his eyes fixed on him, was patiently waiting till he thought proper to renew the conversation. At length Paredes raised his head, and held out his hand to the hunter, who pressed it.

"Listen, Stronghand," he said to him; "all that you have told me appears extraordinary, and I confess that at once: but there is such frankness in your voice, and your reputation is so well established among your brethren, the wood rangers, who all proclaim your loyalty, that I do not hesitate to confide in you without any reservation, for I am convinced that you can have no idea of betraying me, up to the moment when you think proper to reveal to me the names of the villains into whose hands I should have infallibly fallen, had it not been for you, and who have sworn the ruin of my beloved master. I will do what you ask of me—resign my will entirely; you may regard me as a thing belonging entirely to you. Come, go, act as you think proper, and I will obey you in everything, without asking any explanation of your conduct. Now, in your turn, say if it suits you."

"Yes, my worthy friend, that pleases me. You have guessed my thought. I require this liberty to give me the means of succeeding in what I wish to do. Believe the word of an honest man. If anything can add to the confidence you have placed in me, and of which I am proud, I swear to you, by all that is most sacred in the world, that no one is more interested than I am in the Marquis de Moguer, or more sincerely desires to see him happy."

"We shall still start at sunrise, eh?"

"Yes; but not to proceed to Hermosillo. Before going to that town, we must take certain indispensable precautions. We have to deal with the most crafty bandits on the border, and must beat them by cunning. They are on our track, and we must cheat the cheaters."

"Good, good! I will call to mind my old hunter's profession."

"Remember, above all, the prairie proverb, 'The trees have eyes and the leaves ears.' Fortunately for us, the villains who are watching for you do not disturb me in any way. I reckon principally on that ignorance to foil their plots."

"But if we do not go to Hermosillo, where are we going?"

"Tomorrow, when it is daylight," the hunter answered, sententiously, "when the bright sunbeams permit me to convince myself that no one can hear us, I will tell you. For the present, sleep, rest yourself, so that you may be able to support the fatigue that awaits you."

And, as if to avoid fresh questioning, the hunter wrapped himself in his zarapé, leant his back against the larch tree, stretched out his legs to the fire, and closed his eyes. The majordomo, in spite of his lively desire to continue the conversation, imitated him; and a few minutes later, overcome by the fatigue of every description he had endured for some days, he was fast asleep.

CHAPTER XIII
THE REAL DE MINAS

For some years past—that is to say, since the day when Captain Sutter, while digging a well at his plantation in San Francisco, accidentally found a lump of virgin gold—the discovery of the rich mines of the New World has so aroused interest and excited admiration, by giving a fresh impulse to avarice and covetousness, that we consider it necessary to say a few words here about the mines. Of course we shall allude to those situated in the country where our scene is laid—that is, in Sonora.

Sonora is the richest mining country in the world. We assured ourself by official data that six hundred bars of silver and sixty bars of gold, worth together a million of piastres, were brought to the Mint of Hermosillo in 1839. To this large amount a nearly equal sum must be added, which is not brought to be assayed, in order to avoid the payment of the duty, which is five per cent, on silver and four per cent, on gold. This country also possesses most valuable copper mines, but the population generally abandons the other metals to seek virgin gold.

No country in the world possesses auriferous strata so rich and so extensive (*criaderos or placeres de oro*). The metal is found in alluvial soil in ravines after rain, and always on the surface or at a depth of a few feet. In the north of the province of Arispe, the placers of Quitoval and Sonoitac, which were found again in 1836, and to which we shall soon have to allude more specially, produced for three years two hundred ounces of gold per day,—that is to say, reducing it to our money, the large sum of two hundred and fifty thousand pounds.

The gold seekers restrict themselves to turning up the soil with a pointed stick, and only collect the nuggets that are visible; but if the streams were diverted from their course, and large washings undertaken, the profits would be far more considerable. It is not rare to find nuggets weighing several pounds; we saw at Arispe, in the hands of a miner, one that was worth nine thousand piastres, or about eighteen hundred pounds; and the Royal Cabinet at Madrid contains several magnificent specimens. We will soon describe how and why the working of these strata was interrupted.

Most of the buildings of the *pueblos*, or Missions of Sonora, serve as the gathering place of the nomadic workmen and traders who collect round any important mine so soon as its working is begun. The place where the workmen assemble takes the name of *Real de Minas* or *Mineral;* and if the mine promises to be productive for any length of time, the population definitively settles round it. Many important towns of Mexico had no other origin. The facility with which the miners earn large sums explains the enormous consumption of European goods which takes place in the provinces. Simple rancheros may frequently be seen spending in a few days seven or eight pounds of gold, which only cost them a week's toil. Unhappily, the ruinous passion for gambling—that shameful leprosy of Mexico, whose inhabitants it degrades—prevents the great mine owners from keeping a large capital on their hands, and thus checks works on a great scale.

Before resuming our narrative, we must also give the reader certain information about the Indian nations that inhabit the territory of Sonora. There are in this province five distinct tribes; the Yaquis, the Opatas, the Mayos, the Gilenos, and the Apaches. The Yaquis and Mayos occupy the country to the south of Guaymas, as far as the Rio del Huerto; they let themselves out to the creoles as farm labourers, masons, servants, miners, and divers. Their number is about forty thousand. The Opatas reside along the bank of the San Miguel de Horcasitos, the Arispe, the Los Ures, and the Oposina; they are very good workmen and excellent soldiers. They have always served the government faithfully, both Spanish and Mexican, and their number is estimated at thirty thousand.

The Gilenos spread along the banks of the Gila and Colorado rivers. The Axuas and Apaches, who belong to the Sierra Madre, are confounded under the name of Papazos. These Indians are nomadic, and only live by hunting and plunder; they were formerly encamped to the north of Chihuahua and Sonora; but being driven back by the progress of the Americans and Texans, they threw themselves upon the Mexican territory, where they cause immense damage, for they are well supplied with firearms, which they obtained in exchange for peltry and cattle at the American establishments at the Arkansas, the Missouri, and the Rio Bravo del Norte. In order to complete this brief enumeration of the Indian nations of Sonora, we will mention a mission established at the gates of Hermosillo, and in which five hundred Seris Indians lived; a thousand members of the same tribe, formerly one of the most powerful in this country, but now almost extinct, dwelt on the coast to the north of Guaymas, and in Tiburón or Sharkesland.

We will now temporarily leave Stronghand and José Paredes at the top of the hill, where they found a shelter from the inundation, and lead the reader to the Real de Minas of Quitoval, where certain important events are about to take place.

It was the evening: the streets and plazas of the pueblo were crowded with individuals of every description: Yaquis Indians, hunters, miners, gambusinos, monks, and adventurers, who composed the motley population of the Mineral, mounted and foot, incessantly jostled each other, and bowed, spoke, laughed, or quarrelled. Some were returning from the placer, where they had been at work all day; others were leaving their houses to enjoy the evening breeze; others, and they were the larger number, were entering the drinking shops, through whose doors could be heard the songs of the topers, and the shrill, inharmonious tinkling jarabes and vihuelas.

One of these *tendajos*, of a more comfortable and less dirty appearance than the rest, seemed to have the privilege of attracting a greater number of customers than all the rival establishments. After passing through a low door and descending two steps of unequal height, the visitor found himself in a species of hideous den, resembling at once a cellar and a shed, whose earthen flooring, rendered uneven by the mud constantly brought in by customers, caused persons to stumble at each step who visited the place for the first time! A hot heavy vapour, impregnated with alcoholic fumes and mephitic exhalations, escaped through the door of this den, as from the mouth of Hades, and painfully affected mouth and eyes, before the latter became accustomed to the close, obscure aspect of the place, and were enabled to pierce the thick curtain of vapour, which was constantly drawn from one side to the other by the movements of the customers. They perceived, by the dubious light of a few *candils* scattered here and there, a large and lofty room, whose once whitewashed walls had become black at the lower part by the constant friction of heads, backs, and shoulders, to which they served as a support.

Facing the door was a dais, raised about a foot above the ground; this dais occupied the entire width of the room, and was divided into two parts; that on the right contained a table forming a bar, behind which stood a tall, active fellow, with false look and ill-tempered face, the master of the tendajo. Above the head of this respectable personage, who answered to the harmonious name of Cospeto, a niche had been made in the wall, in which was a statue of the Virgin, holding the Holy Infant in her arms; in front of the statue a dozen small wax tapers, fixed on a row of iron points, were burning. The left hand portion of the dais was occupied by the musicians, or performers on jarabes and vihuelas.

On each side of the room, the centre of which remained free for the dancers, ran rickety, badly made, and dirty tables, occupied at this moment by a crowd of customers, some seated on benches, others standing, laughing, talking, shouting, quarrelling; drinking mezcal, refino, pulque, or infusion of tamarinds, or else staking at monte the gold earned during the day at the mine, and which their dirty hands fetched from the pockets of the shapeless rags that served them as garments. A few women, creatures without a name, whose features were sodden with debauchery, and eyes deep sunk with drinking, were mingled with the crowd; and all, both men and women, were smoking either cigars or husk cigarettes.

Nothing can describe the hideous aspect of this infamous Pandemonium, the refuge of all the vices of the province, overlooked by the gentle, smiling face of the statue of the Virgin, whose features, in the light of the tapers, assumed an expression of wondrous pity and sorrow.

At the moment when we invite the reader to enter this drinking shop with us the fun was at its height, the room was full of drinkers and dancers, and the whole mob laughed, yelled, and made a row which would have rendered the saint herself deaf. On the left, near the door, a man, wrapped up in a thick cloak, one end of which was raised to his face, and completely concealed his features, was sitting motionless at a separate table, looking absently and carelessly at the dancers who whirled round him. When a newcomer entered the tendajo, this man looked toward the door, and then turned his head away with an air of ill humour when he perceived that the newcomer was not the person that he had been so long expecting, for he had been sitting alone at this table for upwards of two hours. Still no one paid, or seemed to pay, any attention to him—all were too much absorbed in their own occupations to think about a man who obstinately remained gloomy and silent amid this revelry. The stranger, so often deceived in his expectations, at length gave up looking toward the door; he let his head fall on his chest and went to sleep, or pretended to do so, either for the sake of not attracting attention, or else to indulge with greater freedom in his reflections.

All at once a formidable disturbance broke out at one end of the room; a table was upset by a vigorous blow; oaths crossed each other in the air, and knives were drawn from boots; musicians and dancers stopped short, and a circle was formed round two men who, with frowning brows, eyes sparkling with intoxication and passion, a zarapé rolled as a buckler round the left arm, and a navaja in their right hand, were preparing, according to all appearance, to attack each other vigorously. The tendajero, or master of the house, then proved himself equal to the position he occupied—he leaped like a jaguar over the counter behind which he had hitherto stood coldly and indifferently, merely engaged in watching his waiters and serving customers; he closed the front door, against which he leant his powerful shoulders, in order to prevent any customer bolting without payment of his score, and prepared with evident interest to witness the fight.

The two men, with outstretched legs, left arm advanced, bodies bent forward, and knife held by the middle of the blade, were standing looking in each other's eyes, ready for attack, defence, or parry. All at once the mysterious sleeper appeared to wake with a start, as if surprised by the voice of one of the adversaries, took a hasty glance at the combatants, and then darted between them.

"What is the matter?" he asked, in a firm voice, the sound of which affected the duellists, who were astounded at an interference they had been far from expecting.

"This man," one of them answered, "has lost three ounces to me at monte, through the unexpected turn up of the ace of spades."

"Well?" the stranger interjected.

"He refuses to pay me," the gambler continued; "because he declares that the cards were packed, and that consequently I cheated him, which is not true, for—*viva Dios;* I am known to be a caballero."

At this affirmation, which was slightly erroneous, a smile of singular meaning, but which no one saw, curled the stranger's lip; he continued, in a more serious voice—"It is true that you are a caballero, and I would affirm it were it necessary; but the most honest man is subject to deceive himself, and I am convinced that this has happened to you. Hence instead of fighting with this caballero, whose honour and loyalty cannot either be doubted, prove to him that you recognise your error by paying him the three ounces, which you claimed of him through an oversight; this gentleman will apologize for having used certain ugly expressions, and all will then be settled to the general satisfaction."

"Certainly, I am convinced that this caballero is a man of honour; I am ready to proclaim it anywhere, and I regret with all my soul the misunderstanding which momentarily divided us," said the individual who had not yet spoken, though he remained on the defensive, a position that slightly contradicted the apparent good humour of his remark.

The stranger then turned to the man whose friend he had so unexpectedly made himself, and gave him a sign which the other appeared to understand.

"Well, caballero," he said, with an irony whose expression was hardly noticeable, "what do you think of this apology? For my part, I consider it complete and most honourable."

The man thus addressed hesitated for a moment; a combat was evidently going on in his mind; his furious glances seemed to challenge the company; and had he perceived on the face of one of the spectators an expression of contempt, however fugitive it might have been, he would doubtless have immediately picked another quarrel. But all the persons who surrounded him were cold and indifferent; curiosity alone was legible on their features. He unrolled his cloak, returned the knife to his boot, and held out his hand to his adversary at the same time that he gave him three ounces.

"Pardon me an involuntary error at which I am truly confused," he said, with a courteous bow, but with a sigh he could not restrain.

The other took the ounces without pressing, thrust them away in his capacious pockets with far from ordinary dexterity, returned the salute, and mingled with the crowd, who, through a lengthened acquaintance with the two men, did not at all comprehend this peaceful result.

"Now, Master Kidd," the stranger continued, as he laid his hand on the shoulder of the adventurer, who stood motionless in the middle of the room, "I suppose that all your business here is settled; so, with your permission, we will withdraw."

"As you please," Kidd answered, carelessly, for this man was no other than the bandit we came across in the opening of our story.

The groups had broken up, the crowd had dispersed, musicians and dancers had returned to their places, and the two men could consequently leave without attracting attention. The stranger, when he reached the purer atmosphere of the street, took several deep inspirations, as if trying to expel from his lungs the vitiated air he had been constrained to swallow for so long. Then he turned to his companion, who was walking silently by his side.

"¡Cuerpo de Cristo! Master Kidd," he said, in a tone of ill humour, "you are, it must be confessed, a singular fellow; you compel me, the commandant of this pueblo, to come and hunt you up at this filthy den, where, on your entreaty, I consented to meet you, and instead of watching for my arrival, you leave me among the most perfect collection of bandits I ever saw in my life."

"Excess of zeal, captain; so you must not be angry with me for that," the bandit answered, with a cunning look. "In order to be punctual at the rendezvouz I gave you, I had been for nearly four hours at worthy Señor Cospeto's. Not knowing how to spend my time, I played at cards. You know what month is; once I have the cards in my hand, and the gold on the table, I forget everything."

"Good, good," the stranger answered. "I am willing to believe you. Still, I pledge you my word, that if you dupe me in the affair you have proposed, and the information you offer to sell me is false, you will repent it. You know me, I think, Master Kidd?"

"Yes, Captain Don Marcos de Niza, and I suppose that you know me too; but of what use is this discussion? Let us settle our business first, and then you can act as you think proper."

The Captain gave him a suspicious glance. "It is well," he said, as he rapped at the door; "come in, this is my house; I prefer treating with you here to the tendajo."

"As you please," the bandit said, and followed the Captain into his house, the doors of which were closed behind them.

CHAPTER XIV
THE BARGAIN

Captain Don Marcos de Niza, whom we left commanding the post of San Miguel, and defending it against the Indians, had been a few days previously summoned to the political and military government of the Mineral of Quitoval, by an order that arrived from Mexico, and emanated from the President of the Republic himself. The fact was, that during the last few days certain events had occurred which demanded energetic action on the part of the President. All at once, at a moment when no discontent was supposed to exist among the Indians, the latter, after long councils they had held together, revolted, and had, without any declaration of war, invaded the Mexican territory at several points simultaneously. This revolt suddenly assumed serious proportions; and had become the more formidable within a short time, because the revolters were the Gilenos, that is to say, the Comanches, Apaches, and Axuas, whose dangerous country is known by the name of the Papazos.

The General commanding Sonora and Sinaloa, the two states most exposed to the depredations of the Indians, saw that he must oppose to the Indians a man who, through a lengthened residence on the borders, had acquired great experience as to their way of fighting and the tricks they employ. Only one officer fulfilled these conditions, and that officer was Captain de Niza; he, therefore, received orders to quit the post of San Miguel after dismantling it, and proceed immediately to the Mineral of Quitoval. The Captain obeyed with that promptitude which old soldiers alone can display in the execution of the orders they receive. His first care, on reaching the Mineral, was to protect the pueblo, as far as was possible, from a surprise, by digging a large trench, throwing up entrenchments, and barricading the principal streets.

Unfortunately, the general commanding the provinces had but a very limited military force at his disposal; scarce amounting to six hundred infantry and two hundred cavalry, without field artillery. Hence, in spite of his lively desire to give the Captain a respectable force, as he was obliged to scatter his troops along the whole seaboard of the two states, he found it impossible to send to Quitoval more than one hundred infantry and fifty cavalry. In spite of the numerical weakness of his troops the Captain did not despair. He was one of those men to whom the performance of duty was everything; and who carry out without a murmur the most extraordinary order.

Still, as he expected to be attacked at any moment by an army of ten or fifteen thousand veteran Indians, amply supplied with firearms, and who, through being accustomed to fight with Spaniards, could not be easily terrified, he had to augment the number of his soldiers, so as to have men enough to line the entrenchments he had thrown up round the town. He had two means by which to obtain this result, and he employed them. The first consisted in making the great mine owners understand that they must participate in the defences of the pueblo, either personally or by arming and placing under his orders a certain number of the peons they employed; for if the Indians succeeded in seizing the Mineral, the source of their wealth would be at once dried up.

The great owners understood the Captain's reasons the more easily because their interests were at stake. They therefore enthusiastically followed his advice, and raised at their common charge a corps of one hundred and fifty Opatas—brave soldiers, thoroughly devoted to the Whites. They placed this corps under the Captain's orders, pledging themselves to pay and support it so long as the danger lasted. Don Marcos thus doubled his army at one stroke. This success, which he had been far from expecting, owing to his profound knowledge of the apathy and selfishness of his countrymen, induced him to try the second plan.

This was very simple. It consisted in enlisting, for a certain bounty, as many as he could of the adventurers who always swarm on the borders, and whose neutrality is at times more formidable than declared enmity. The sum offered by the Captain was two ounces per man, one payable on enlistment, the other at the termination of the campaign. This offer, seductive though it was, did not produce all the effect the Captain expected from it. The adventurers responded but feebly to the appeal made to them. These men, in whose hearts patriotic love does not exist, and who only care for pillage, saw in the insurrection of the Indians a source of disorder, and, consequently, of rapine. They cared very little about defending a state of things which their predacious instincts led them, on the contrary, to attack.

Thirty or forty adventurers, however, responded to the call; and these immoral men, who were impatient at the yoke of discipline, were rather an embarrassment than an assistance to the Captain; still as, take them altogether, they were sturdy fellows, and thoroughly acquainted with Indian warfare, he attached them to his cavalry, which was thus raised to a strength of one hundred men. Don Marcos thus found himself at the head of two hundred and fifty infantry and one hundred horse—a force which appeared to him, if well directed, more than sufficient to withstand, behind good entrenchments, the effort of the whole Indian army.

We are aware that this number of men defending a town will produce a smile of pity among European readers, who are accustomed to see on battlefields masses of three hundred thousand men come into collision. But all is relative in this world. In America, where the population is comparatively small, great things have often been decided at the bayonet's point by armies whose relative strength did not exceed that of one of our line regiments. In the last battle fought between the Texans and Mexicans—a battle which decided the independence of Texas, the two armies together did not amount to two thousand men, and yet the collision was terrible, and victory obstinately disputed. In the actions between white men and Indians, the latter, in spite of their indomitable valour, were almost always defeated in a pitched battle, in spite of their crushing superiority of numbers. Not through the courage of their enemies, but by their discipline and military skill. The latter is certainly very limited, but sufficient for adversaries such as they have to combat.

One night, when the Captain returned home after his usual visit to the pueblo to assure himself that all was in order, a ragged lepero, more than half intoxicated with mezcal and pulque, handed him with an infinitude of bows a dirty slip of paper folded up in the shape of a letter. Don Marcos de Niza was not accustomed to neglect anything. He attached as much importance to apparently frivolous events as to those which seemed to possess a certain gravity. He stopped, took the letter, gave a real to the lepero, who went away quite satisfied, and entered his house, which was situated on the Plaza Mayor, in the centre of the pueblo.

After throwing his cap and sword on a table, the Captain opened the letter. He read it at first rather carelessly; but ere long he began frowning, and read the letter a second time, attentively weighing each word. Then at the end of a moment he folded up the letter, and said in a low voice—"I will go."

This letter came from Kidd. The Captain had been long acquainted with the bandit, and knew certain peculiar facts about him which would have been most disagreeable to the bandit, had the latter suspected that the Captain was so thoroughly initiated in the secrets of his vagabond life. Hence Don Marcos fancied he had no right to neglect the overtures the other was pleased to make; while keeping on his guard and determined to punish him severely if he deceived him. The Captain, therefore, proceeded without hesitation to the place where the adventurer appointed to meet him. He had waited for him for several hours with exemplary patience, and would probably have waited longer still, had not chance suddenly brought them face to face in the way we have described.

When the two men had entered the house, and the door closed after them, Don Marcos de Niza, still closely followed by the bandit, who, in spite of his impudence, looked around him timidly, like a wolf caught in a sheepfold, led him into a room the door of which he carefully closed. The Captain pointed to a chair, sat down at a table, laid a brace of pistols ostentatiously within his reach, and said —

"Now I am ready to hear you."

"¡Caray!" the bandit said, impudently; "that is possible; but the point is whether I am disposed to speak."

"And why not, pray, my excellent friend?"

"Hang it, Captain," he said, as he pointed to the pistols, "there are two playthings not at all adapted to set my tongue wagging."

Don Marcos looked at him in a way that made the adventurer involuntarily let his eyes fall, and then leant his elbows on the table.

"Master Kidd," he then said, in a stern voice, though a certain tone of sarcasm was perceptible in it, "I like a distinct understanding; let us therefore, before anything establish our relative positions. You have led a very agitated life, Master Kidd; your vagabond humour, your mad desire to appropriate certain things to which you have a very dubious claim have led you into a few mistakes, whose results might prove remarkably disagreeable to you."

The bandit shook his head in denial.

"I will not dwell," the Captain continued, mockingly, "on a subject which must make your modesty greatly suffer, and will come at once to the motives of your presence here, and the positions we must hold towards each other. I am commandant of this pueblo, and in that capacity compelled to watch over its external safety as well as its internal tranquillity, I think you will agree with me."

"Yes, Captain," the bandit answered, somewhat reassured at finding the conversation turned away from such delicate topics.

"Very good; you wrote me this letter, appointing a meeting and offering to sell — that is your own word — certain most important information, as you say, for the continuance of the safety and tranquillity which I am bound to maintain. Another man might have treated you in the Indian fashion. After having you arrested, he would have ordered a cord to be fastened round your temples; or your suspension by your thumbs—as you have done yourself, if report be true, on various occasions with less valid reasons; and have so thoroughly loosened your tongue that you would not have kept a single secret back. I have preferred dealing with you as an honest man."

The bandit breathed again.

"Still, as you are one of those persons with whom it is advisable to take precautions, and in whom a confidence cannot be placed, as they would not scruple to abuse it on the first opportunity, I retain not only the right, but also the means of blowing out your brains if you have the slightest intention of deceiving me."

"Oh, Captain, what an idea! Blow out my brains!" the bandit stammered.

"Do you fancy, my dear Señor," the Captain continued, still sarcastically, "that your friends will pity you greatly, if such a misfortune happened to you?"

"Hum! to tell you the truth, I do not exactly know," the adventurer answered, with at attempt to jest; "people are so unkind. But, since you accept the bargain offered to you—for you do accept it, I think, Captain?"

"I do."

"What then, will you give me in exchange for what I shall tell you?"

"You sell; I buy; it is your place to make your conditions; and, if they are not exorbitant—if, in a word, they seem to me fair, I will accept them; so, speak, what do you ask?"

"¡Caray! Captain; it is a delicate question, for I am an honest man."

"That is allowed," Don Marcos interrupted him with a laugh. "Name your price."

"Fifty ounces; would that be too much?" the bandit ventured.

"Certainly not, if the thing be worth it."

"Then," Kidd exclaimed, joyfully, "that is understood, fifty ounces."

"I repeat, if it be worth it."

"Oh, you shall judge for yourself," he remarked, rubbing his hands.

"I ask nothing better but to buy, and to prove to you that I have no intention of cheating you," he added, as he opened a drawer and took out a rather heavy purse, "here is the amount."

And the Captain made two piles each of twenty-five ounces, exactly between the pistols. At the sight of the gold the bandit's eyes sparkled like those of a wild beast.

"¡*Rayo de Dios!* Captain," he exclaimed; "There is a pleasure in treating with you. I will remember it another time."

"I ask nothing better, Master Kidd. Now speak, I am listening."

"Oh, I have not much to say; but you will judge whether it is important."

"Go on; I am all ears."

"In two words, this is the matter; the Papazos have not elected a chief, but an emperor!"

"An emperor?"

"Yes."

"What do they assert, then?"

"They mean to be free, and wish to constitute their Independence upon a solid basis."

"Do you know this emperor?"

"I have seen him, at least."

"Who is he?"

"A man who is the more formidable because he appears to belong to the white rather than the red race; and is thoroughly conversant with all the means hitherto employed by the Indians."

"Is he young?"

"He is sixty; but as active as if he were only twenty."

"Very good; proceed."

"Is that important?"

"Very important. But not worth fifty ounces, for all that."

"The Yaquis, Mayos, and Seris have allowed themselves to be seduced, and have entered the Confederation. They have taken up again their old plans of 1827—you remember, at the time of their great revolution?"

"Yes; go on."

"The first expedition the Chief of the Confederation means to undertake is the capture of the Real de Minas."

"I am aware of it."

"Yes; but do you know, Captain, that the Indians have spies even among the garrison; that all is ready for the attack, and that the Papazos intend to surprise you within the next two days?"

"Who gave you this information?"

The bandit smiled craftily.

"What use my telling you, Captain," he answered, "if the information is correct?"

"Do you know the men who have entered into negotiations with the enemy?"

"I do."

"In that case tell me their names."

"It would be imprudent, Captain."

"Why so?"

"Judge for yourself. Suppose I were to tell you their names, what would happen?"

"*¡Viva Dios!*" the Captain sharply interrupted him. "I should shoot them like the miserable dogs they are, and to serve as a warning to others."

"Well, that is the mistake, Captain."

"How a mistake?"

"Why, yes; suppose you shoot ten men?"

"Twenty, if necessary!"

"Say twenty, it is of no consequence to me; but those who remain, whom neither you nor I know, will sell you to the Indians, so that the only result will be precipitating the evil instead of preventing it."

"Ah, ah!" the Commandant said, with an expressive glance at the bandit. "And what would you do in my place?"

"Oh, a very simple thing."

"Well, what is it?"

"I would leave the scamps at liberty to prepare their treachery, while carefully watching them; and when the moment for attack arrived, I would have them quietly arrested; so that the Indians would be surprised, instead of surprising us, and we should cheat the cunning cheats."

The Captain appeared to reflect for a moment, and then said—"The plan you recommend seems to me good, and for the present I see no inconvenience in carrying it out. Give me the names of the traitors."

Kidd mentioned a dozen names, which the Captain wrote down after him.

"Now," Don Marcos continued, "there are your fifty ounces, and I shall give as many each time you bring me information as valuable as that of today. I pay you dearly, so it is your interest to serve me faithfully; but remember, that if you deceive me, nothing can save you from the punishment I will inflict on you, and that punishment, I warn you, will be terrible."

The adventurer bounded on the money like a wild beast on a prey it has long coveted, concealed it with marvellous dexterity in his wide pockets, and said to the Captain with a bow—"Señor Don Marcos, I have always thought that in this world gold was the sovereign master, and that it alone had the right to command."

After accompanying these singular words with a smiling and almost mocking expression, Kidd bowed for the last time and disappeared, leaving the Captain to his reflections.

CHAPTER XV
THE PAPAZOS

We will not return to Stronghand and José Paredes, whom we have left too long at the top of the hill. The night passed without any incident, the majordomo sleeping like a man overcome by fatigue; as for the hunter, he did not close his eyes once. The sun had risen for a long time; it was nearly nine o'clock, but the hunter, forgetting apparently what he had said to his comrade, did not dream of departure. José Paredes slept on. It was a magnificent day; the sky, swept by the night hurricane, was cloudless; the sun darted down its glowing beams; and yet the atmosphere, tempered by the storm, retained an agreeable freshness. The water was disappearing with a rapidity almost equalling that it bad displayed in rising, being drunk by the thirsty sand or by the hot sunbeams; the plain had lost its lacustrine appearance; and all led to the supposition that by midday the ground would be firm enough to be ventured on in safety.

As the canoe was unnecessary, the hunter did not try to get it down from the tree; with his back leant against the larch tree, his hands folded, and his head bowed on his chest, he was thinking, and at times taking an anxious glance at his sleeping comrade. At length the majordomo turned, stretched out his arms and legs, opened his eyes, and gave a formidable yawn.

"¡Caramba!" he said, as he measured the height of the sun; "I fancy I have forgotten myself; it must be very late."

"Ten o'clock," the hunter answered with a smile.

"Ten o'clock!" José exclaimed, as he leaped up; "And you have let me idle thus instead of waking me."

"You slept so soundly, my friend, that I had not the courage to do so."

"Hum!" Paredes replied, half laughing, half vexed; "I know not whether I ought to complain or thank you for this weakness, for we have lost precious time."

"Not at all; see, the water has disappeared; the ground is growing firm again, and when the great heat of the day is spent we will mount our horses and catch up in a few hours the time you are regretting."

"That is true, and you are right, comrade," said the majordomo, as he looked around with the practised glance of a man accustomed to a desert life. "Well, as it is so," he added, with a laugh, "suppose we breakfast, for that will enable us to kill some time."

"Very good," the hunter replied, good humouredly. They breakfasted as they had supped on the previous night. When the hour for starting at length arrived, they saddled their horses and led them down the hill; for the ascent which they had escaladed so actively by night, under the impulse of the pressing danger that threatened them, now proved extremely steep, abrupt, and difficult. When they mounted, Stronghand said—"My friend, I am going to take you to an *atepetl* of the Redskins. Do you consider that disagreeable?"

"Not personally, but I will ask what advantage my master can derive from it?"

"That question I am unable to answer at the moment. You must know, though, that we are taking this step on your master's behalf, and that his affairs, instead of suffering by it, will be greatly benefited."

"Let us go, then. One word, however, first. Are the Redskins, to whom we are proceeding, a long distance off?"

"It would be almost a journey for any persons but us."

"Hum!" said Paredes.

"But you and I," the hunter continued, "who are true guides, and who have also the advantage of being well mounted, will reach the village at three or four o'clock tomorrow afternoon at the latest."

"In that case it is not very distant."

"I told you so."

"And in what direction is the village?"

"You must have often heard it spoken of, if chance has never led your footsteps thither."

"Why so?"

"Because it is only a dozen leagues at the most from the Hacienda del Toro."

"Wait a minute," the majordomo said, frowning like a man who is collecting his thoughts; "you are right, I have never been to that village, it is true, but I have often heard it spoken of. Is not one of the chiefs a white man?"

The hunter blushed slightly.

"So people say," he answered.

"Is it not strange," the majordomo continued, "that a white man should consent to abandon entirely the society of his fellows to live with savages?"

"Why so?"

"Hang it! Because the Indians are devoid of reason, as everybody knows."

The hunter gave his companion a glance of indefinable meaning, slightly shrugged his shoulders, but made no reply; probably from the reason that he had too much to say, and considered the majordomo's rather heavy mind incapable of appreciating it. The day passed without any occurrences to interrupt the monotony of their ride, which they continued with great speed till night, only stopping from time to time to shoot a few birds for supper. Galloping, talking, and smoking, they at length reached the spot where they intended to bivouac. The road they had followed in no way resembled the one the majordomo had taken on leaving the hacienda, although they were returning in the direction of Arispe. This resulted from the fact that Paredes had kept in the regular road, while this time the two men rode Indian fashion, that is to say, straight ahead without troubling themselves about roads. They galloped on as the bird flies, crossing mountains and swimming rivers whenever they came to them, without losing time in seeking a ford.

This mode of travelling, generally adopted by the wood rangers of the savannah, where the only roads are tracks made by the wild beasts, would not be possible in civilized countries, where there are so many towns and villages; but in Mexico, especially on the Indian border, towns are excessively rare: by riding in this way distances are marvellously shortened and a considerable tract is covered between two sunrises. This is what happened to the two adventurers; for in one day they went a greater distance than Paredes had done in eight-and-forty hours, though he was well mounted. At night they camped in a wood beyond the Hacienda del Toro, which building they saw rising gloomy and tranquil like an eagle's nest on the top of its rock, and they passed close to it during the afternoon.

The country assumed a wilder and more abrupt aspect; the grass was thicker, the trees were larger, older, and closer together; it was evident that the travellers were at the extreme limit of civilization, and would soon find themselves in the Red territory, although nominally, at least on the maps, this territory figured among the possessions of the Mexican Confederation. This feature, by the way, is found everywhere throughout the New World. Even in the United States, which pretend, erroneously, we believe, to be more civilized than their neighbours, towns with high-flown names may be seen on the maps of their large possessions, which only exist in reality as a name painted on a solitary post, planted in the centre of a plain or on the bank of a river, without even a keeper to watch over the preservation of this post, which, worn by wind and sun, eventually disappears, though the town never sprung up in its place. During our travels we were too often the victim of this humorous Yankee mystification not to feel angry with this eccentric nation, which repeats to every newcomer that it marches at the head of civilization, and has a mission to regenerate the New World.

The two men, after lighting their watch fire, supped with good appetite, rolled themselves in their zarapés, and fell asleep, trusting to the instinct of their horses to warn them of the approach of any enemy, whether man or wild beast, that attempted to surprise them during their slumbers. But nothing disturbed them; the night was quiet; at sunrise they awoke, mounted, and continued their journey, which would only take a few hours longer.

"I am mistaken," the hunter said suddenly, turning to his companion.

"How so?" the latter asked.

"Because," Stronghand replied, "I told you yesterday we should not reach the *atepetl* till the afternoon."

"Well?"

"We shall be there by eleven o'clock."

"¡*Caramba!* That is famous news."

"When we have crossed that hill we shall see the village a short distance ahead of us, picturesquely grouped on the side of another hill, and running into the plain, where the last houses are built on the banks of a pretty little stream, whose white and limpid waters serve as a natural rampart."

"Tell me, comrade, what do you think of the reception that will be offered us?"

"The Papazos are hospitable."

"I do not doubt it; unluckily, I have no claims to the kindness of the Redskins. Moreover, I know that they are very suspicious, and never like to see white men enter their villages."

"That depends on the way in which white men try to enter them."

"There is another reason which, I confess, supplies me with reason for grave thought."

"What is it?"

"It is said—mark me, I do not assert it—"

"All right; go on."

"It is said that the Papazos are excited, and on the point of revolting, if they have not done so already."

"They rose in insurrection some days ago," Stronghand coolly answered.

"What?" the majordomo exclaimed, greatly startled, "and you are leading me to them?"

"Why not?"

"Because we shall be massacred, that's all."

The hunter shrugged his shoulders.

"You are mad."

"I am mad—I am mad!" Paredes repeated, shaking his head very dubiously; "it pleases you to say that, but I am not at all desirous, if I can avoid it, of thus placing myself in the power of men who must be my enemies."

"I repeat that nothing will happen to you. ¡*Viva Dios!* do you fancy me capable of leading you into a snare?"

"No; on my honour that is not my thought; but you may be mistaken, and credit these savages with feelings they do not possess."

"I am certain of what I assert. Not only have you nothing to fear, but you will have an honourable reception."

"Honourable?" the majordomo remarked, with an air of incredulity; "I am not very certain of that."

"You shall see. Woe to the man who dared to hurt a hair of your head while you are in my company."

"Who are you, to speak thus?"

"A hunter, nothing else; but I am a friend of the Papazos, and adopted son of one of their tribes; and every man, though he were the mortal enemy of the nation, must for my sake, be received as a brother by the sachems and warriors."

"Well, be it so," the majordomo muttered, in the tone of a man forced in his last entrenchments, and who resolves to make up his mind.

"Besides," the hunter added, "any hesitation would now be useless and perhaps dangerous."

"Why so?"

"Because the Indians have their scouts scattered through the woods and over the plain already; they saw and signalled our approach long ago, and if we attempted to turn back, it would justly appear suspicious; and then we should suddenly see Indians rise all round us, and be immediately made prisoners, before we even thought of defending ourselves."

"¡Demonio! that makes the matter singular, comrade; then you believe we have been seen already?"

"Would you like to have a proof on the spot?" the hunter asked, laughingly.

"Well, I should not mind, for I should then know what I have to expect."

"Well, I will give you the proof."

The travellers had reached the foot of the hill, and were at this moment concealed by the tall grass that surrounded them. Stronghand stopped his horse, and imitated the cry of the mawkawis twice. Almost immediately the grass parted, an Indian bounded from a thick clump of trees with the lightness of an antelope, and stopped two yards from the hunter, on whom he fixed his black, intelligent eyes, without saying a word. The apparition of the Redskin was so sudden, his arrival so unexpected, that, in spite of himself, the majordomo could not restrain a start of surprise.

This Indian was a man of three-and-twenty years of age at the most, whose exquisite proportions made him resemble a statue of Florentine bronze; the whole upper part of his body was naked: his unloosened hair hung in disorder over his shoulders; his clothing merely consisted of trousers sewn with horsehair, fastened round the loins by a belt of untanned leather, and tied at the ankles. A tomahawk and a scalping knife—weapons which the Indians never lay aside—hung from his belt, and he leant with careless grace upon a long rifle of American manufacture. The hunter bowed, and after stretching out his arm, with the palm turned down and the fingers straight, said in a gentle voice—"Wah! The Waconda protects me, since the first person I see, on returning to my people, is Sparrowhawk."

The young Indian bowed in his turn with the native courtesy characteristic of the Redskin, and replied in a guttural voice, which, however, was very gentle—"For a long time the sachems have been informed of the coming of the Great Bear of their Nation; they thought that only one chief was worthy saluting Stronghand on his return. Sparrowhawk is happy that he was chosen by them."

"I thank the sachems of my nation," the hunter said, with a meaning glance at the majordomo, "for having designed to do me so signal an honour. Will my son return to the village with us, or will he precede us?"

"Sparrowhawk will go ahead, in order that the guest of Stronghand, my father, may be received with the honours due to a man who comes in the company of the Great Bear."

"Good! My brother will act as becomes a chief. Stronghand will not detain him longer."

The young Indian bowed his head in assent, leapt backwards, and disappeared in the thicket whence he had emerged, with such rapidity, that if the grass had not continued to undulate after his departure, his apparition would have seemed like a dream.

"We can now start again," the hunter said to the majordomo, who was utterly confounded.

"Let us go!" the latter answered, mechanically.

"Well," answered Stronghand, "do you now believe that you have anything to fear among the Papazos?"

"Excuse me; as you said, I was a madman to fear it."

They crossed the plain, following a wild beast track which, after numberless windings, reached a ford, and in about an hour they arrived at the bank of the river. Twelve Papazo Indians, dressed in their war paint and mounted on magnificent horses, were standing motionless and in single file in front of the ford.

So soon as they perceived the two travellers, they uttered loud shouts and dashed forward to meet them, firing their guns, brandishing their weapons, and waving their white female buffalo robes, which, by-the-bye, only the most renowned sachems of the nation have the right to wear. The two white men, on their side, spurred their horses, responding to the shouts of the Indians, and firing their guns. All at once, at a signal from one of the chiefs, all the horsemen stopped, and arranged themselves round the travellers, to act as an escort. The whole party crossed the ford and entered the village, amid the deafening shouts of the women and children, with which were inharmoniously blended the bark of dogs, the hoarse notes of the shells, and the shrill sounds of the *chichikoues*.

CHAPTER XVI
THE ATEPETL

Many persons imagine that all Indians are alike, and that the men acquainted with the manners of one tribe knows them all. This is a serious error, which it is important to dissipate. Among the Indians, properly so called—that is to say, the aborigines of America—will be found as many differences in language, dialect, &c., as among the nations of the Old Continent, if not more. The number of dialects spoken by the Indians is infinite; the manners of one nation form a complete contrast with those of another living only a few leagues away; and any person who, after travelling for some time in the Far West, asserted that he was thoroughly acquainted with the character of the Indians and their mode of life, would be quite deceived; and more serious still, would deceive those whom he pretended to instruct.

The Indians are divided into two great families: the cultivating Indians—that is to say, those who are sedentary and attached to the soil they till; and hunter or nomadic Indians, who have a great resemblance to the Touaricks of Africa and the Tartars of Asia. The hunting Indians, known as *Indios Bravos*, inhabit leathern huts, easy of transport from one place to another, and only remain stationary so long as the country supplies them with the necessary forage for their horses, and the game indispensable for the men. The tame Indians, or *Indios Mansos*, on the other hand, are permanently established at a carefully selected spot; they have built actual houses, in which they shelter themselves and keep their winter provisions. These Indians, though they follow the customs of their fathers, recognise the Mexican laws, obey them ostensibly, are apparent Christians, though they secretly practise all the rites of their old faith; and their chief assumes the title of Alcalde. In a word, they are nearly as much civilized as the majority of the creoles.

The confederation of the Papazos was composed of several nations, combining both Indios Mansos and Indios Bravos. The latter, though harmless, and consequently nomadic, had, in the heart of unexplored forests or the gorges of the Sierra Madre, their winter villages—a collection of huts made of branches, and covered with mud, where, in the event of war, their squaws found refuge, and which served them, after an expedition, to hide the plunder they had made.

The Gilenos, whose powerful nation was composed of one hundred and eighteen distinct tribes, each of which had its private totem or standard, formed the principal branch of the Confederation of the Papazos. The Gilenos are essentially agricultural. At a period which it would be impossible to state with certainty, because the Indians do not write anything down, but trust to tradition, the Comanche nation, which proudly calls itself the "Queen of the Prairies," and asserts, perhaps justly, that it is descended in a straight line from the Chichimeques, the first conquerors of Mexico, was divided into two parts after a council held by the chiefs, for the sake of terminating a dispute that threatened to degenerate into a civil war. One half the nation continued to wander in the immense prairies of the Far West, and retained the name of Comanche. The other tribes settled on the banks of the Rio Gila, gave up hunting for agriculture, while retaining their independence, and only nominally obeying the Spaniards and Mexicans. Eventually they received the name of Gilenos, from the river on whose banks they originally settled. But, although separated, the two divisions of the Comanche nations continued to maintain friendly relations, recognised each other as springing from the same stem, and helping one another whenever circumstances demanded it.

The Gilenos piously preserved the faith of their fathers, maintained their customs; among others that of never drinking spirituous liquors: and never permitted the Mexican Government to establish among them that system of annoyance and rapine under which it mercilessly bows the other Indian Mansos. The Gileno villages are distinguished from all the others by their singular construction, which admirably displays the character of this people. We will attempt to convey an idea of them to the reader.

Stronghand had pointed out to the majordomo clusters of storied houses, suspended as it were from the flank of the hill. But these houses were only built temporarily, and in case of an attack on the village would be immediately destroyed. The hill, doubtless in consequence of one of those natural convulsions so common in these regions, was separated into two parts by a quebrada of enormous depth, which served as the bed of an impetuous torrent. On either side of this quebrada the Indians had built an enormous construction, of pyramidal shape, upwards of two hundred and fifty feet in height. These two towers contained the lodgings of the inhabitants, their granaries and storehouses. More than eight hundred beings, men, women, and children, resided in these singular buildings, which were connected together at the top by a bridge of lianas, boldly thrown across the abyss. These towers could only be entered by a ladder, which was drawn up each night; for as a last and essential precaution, the doors were sixty feet from the ground, in order to guard against surprise.

Nothing could be more curious or picturesque than the appearance offered at a distance by this strange village, with its two massive towers, having ladders for stairs, up and down which people were constantly moving. A few days previously, for greater safety, and to guard the village from a surprise, the chiefs had a trench dug, and a palisade erected, composed of stakes fastened together by lianas. The Indians had taken this precaution, to prevent their horses, on which they especially calculated for the success of the meditated expedition, being carried off by surprise, as so frequently happens on the border.

The travellers were conducted with great ceremony by the chiefs, who had come to receive them at the entrance of the village, to the square, on one side of which stood the "Ark of the First Man;" on the other, "The Great Medicine Lodge, or Council Hut." During the ride the majordomo fancied he saw among the crowd several individuals belonging to the white race, and mentioned it to his comrade.

"You are not mistaken," the latter replied; "several Mexicans reside in the village and trade with the Indians; but that must not surprise you, for you are aware that the Gilenos are mansos. Stay, here is a monk."

In fact, at this moment a stout, rubicund monk crossed the square, distributing blessings right and left, of which the Indians seemed to take but little notice.

"These worthy Frayles," the hunter continued, "lead here a rather monastic life, but in spite of the trouble they take, they cannot succeed in making proselytes. The Comanches are too attached to their religion to accept another; still, as they are too savage to be intolerant," he added, ironically, "they allow these poor monks entire liberty, on the express condition that they do not interfere with them. They have even permitted them to build a chapel, a very poor and simple edifice, in which a few passing adventurers offer up their prayers; for the inhabitants of the village never set foot in it."

"I will go to it," said Paredes.

"And you will act rightly. However, I will do this justice to the four monks who, through a love of proselytism, have confined themselves to this forgotten nook, of stating that they bear an excellent reputation, do all the good they can, and are generally beloved and respected by the population. This praise is the more valuable, because the Mexican clergy do not enjoy a great reputation for sanctity."

"But now that war is declared, what will become of these monks?"

"What do you think? They will remain peacefully, without fearing insult or annoyance. However savage the Indians may be, they are not so savage, be assured, as to make the innocent suffer for the crimes of the guilty."

"Forgive me, Stronghand, if I remark that I notice, with sorrow, in your mode of expressing yourself, a certain bitterness which seems to me unjust. The secret sympathies of an honest man ought not, in any case, to render him partial."

"I allow that I am wrong, my friend. When you know me better, you will be indulgent, I doubt not, to this bitterness which I frequently unconsciously display in my language. But here we are at the square, and other more urgent matters claim all our attention."

The plaza, which the travellers now reached, formed a parallelogram, and rose with a gentle ascent to the foot of the tower on the left of the village. Several streets opened into it, and the houses built on either side of it had an appearance of cleanliness and comfort which is but rarely found in Indian villages; and if this pueblo had been inhabited by white creoles, it would certainly have obtained the title of *ciudad*. In front of the council lodge stood three men, whom it was easy to recognise as the principal chiefs of the village by their hats of raccoon skin, surrounded by a gold golilla, and the silver mounted cane, like that of our beadles, which they held in their right hand. The Mexicans, among other customs they took from the Spaniards, have retained that of investing the Indian chiefs with authority. This investiture, generally performed by a delegate of the governor of the province, consists in giving them the hat and stick to which we have referred. These three chiefs, therefore, ostensibly held their power from the Mexican government, but in reality the latter had only obeyed the feudal claims of the tribes assembled at this village, by conferring the authority on these men whom their countrymen had long previously recognised as chiefs.

The procession halted before the alcaldes, or, to use the Indian term, the sachems. The latter were men of a ripe age, with a haughty and imposing mien. The eldest of them, who stood in the centre, had in his look and the expression of his features something indescribably majestic. He appeared about sixty years of age; a long white beard fell in snowy flakes on his chest; his tall form, his broad forehead, his black eyes, and his slightly aquiline nose, rendered him a very remarkable man. He did not wear the Indian costume, but that adopted by the hunters and wood rangers; a blue cotton shirt, fastened round his hips by a leather girdle, which held his arms and ammunition, wide *calzoneras* of deer hide buckled below the knee, and heavy boots, whose heels were armed with formidable spurs, the wheel of which was as large as a saucer.

In conclusion, the personage we have attempted to describe did not belong to the Indian race, as could be seen at the first glance; but in addition, the fine, elegant, nervous type of the pure Spanish race could be noticed in him. The majordomo could not check a start of surprise at the sight of this man, whose presence seemed to him incomprehensible at such a place and among such people. He leant over to Stronghand, and asked him, in a low voice, choked by involuntary emotion, — "Who is that man?"

"You can see," the hunter replied, drily, "he is the Alcalde Mayor of the pueblo. But silence! The persons surrounding us are surprised to see us conversing in whispers."

Paredes held his tongue, though his eyes were obstinately fixed on the man to whom the hunter had ironically given the title of Alcalde Mayor. A little to the rear of the chiefs, a warrior was holding a totem of the tribe, representing a condor, the sacred bird of the Incas. A crowd of Indians of both sexes, nearly all armed, filled the square, and pressed forward to witness a scene which was not without a certain grandeur. So soon as the procession halted, Sparrowhawk dismounted and walked up to the sachems.

"Fathers of my nation," he said, "the Great Bear of our tribe has returned, bringing with him a paleface, his friend."

"He is welcome," the three chiefs answered, unanimously, "as well as his friend, whoever he may be; so long as he pleases to remain among us he will be regarded as a brother."

The hunter then advanced, and bowed respectfully to the sachems.

"Thanks for myself and friend," he said; "the journey we have made was long, and we are worn with fatigue. May we be permitted to take a few hours' rest?"

The Indians were astonished to hear the hunter, a man of iron power, whose reputation for vigour was well established among them, speak of the fatigue he felt. But understanding that he had secret reasons for asking this, no one made a remark.

"Stronghand and his friend are at liberty to proceed to the calli prepared for them," one of the chiefs answered: "Sparrowhawk will guide them."

The two adventurers bowed respectfully, and, preceded by Sparrowhawk, passed through the crowd, which opened before them, and proceeded to the calli appointed for them. Let us state at once that this calli was the property of Stronghand, who inhabited it whenever business or accident brought him to the village. By the order of the chiefs, however, it had been prepared for the reception of two persons. So soon as the travellers reached the calli, Sparrowhawk retired, after whispering a few words in the ear of the hunter. The latter replied by a sign of assent, and then turned to the majordomo, who was already engaged in unsaddling his horse.

"You are at home, comrade," he said to him; "use this house as you think proper. I have to see a person to whom I will introduce you presently. I will, therefore, leave you for the present, but I shall not be absent long."

And without awaiting an answer, the hunter turned his horse, and started at a gallop.

"Hum!" the Mexican muttered, so soon as he was alone, "all this is not clear; did I do wrong in trusting to this man? I will be on my guard."

CHAPTER XVII
THE SPY

After installing the majordomo in the calli, Stronghand proceeded through the village, taking an apparently careless glance around, but in reality not letting anything unusual escape his notice. The Indians whom the hunter met addressed him as an old acquaintance; the very women and children tried to attract his attention by their hearty bursts of laughter and their greetings of welcome. For all and for each the hunter had a pleasant remark, and thus satisfied the frequently indiscreet claims of those who pressed around him. Thus occupied, he went right through the village, and, on reaching the foot of the left-hand pyramid, dismounted, threw his horse's bridle to a boy, bidding him lead the horse to his calli, and forced his way with some difficulty through the crowd, whose curiosity seemed to increase instead of diminishing. He walked up to the ladder, and after waving his hand to the Indians, hurried up it, and disappeared inside the pyramid.

This strange building, which was almost shapeless outside, was internally arranged with the utmost care and most perfect intelligence. The hunter, who was doubtless anxious to reach his destination, only took a hurried glance at the rooms he passed through; he went up an internal staircase, and soon reached the top of the pyramid. Sparrowhawk was standing motionless before a cougar's skin hung up in lieu of a door, and on seeing the hunter he bowed courteously.

"My father has not delayed," he said, with a good-tempered smile.

"Has the council begun yet?" Stronghand asked.

"For four suns the elders of the nation have remained without taking rest round the council fire; the arrival of my father was alone able to make them suspend their labours for an hour."

The hunter frowned.

"Cannot I speak to the great sachem for a moment?"

"I cannot give my father any information on that point."

"Good!" the hunter continued, apparently forming a determination. "Has Sparrowhawk no instructions for me?"

"None, but to await Stronghand, and announce his arrival."

"Wah! here I am; my brother's instructions are fulfilled."

Without replying, Sparrowhawk raised the curtain, and allowed the hunter to pass into the council hall.

In a large room, which was entirely destitute of furniture—unless that name can be given to dried buffalo skulls employed as seats—some twenty persons were gravely seated in a circle, smoking a calumet silently, whose mouthpiece constantly passed from hand to hand. In the centre of the circle was a golden brasier, in which burned the sacred fire of Motecuhzoma, a fire which must never go out. According to tradition, the last Emperor of Mexico shared it among his dearest partisans on the eve of his death; and this fire, it is also said, derives its origin from the sun itself.

The presence of this fire in the room, which was generally kept in a subterraneous vault, inaccessible to the sight of the common herd, and which is only shown to the people on grand occasions, proved the gravity of the matters the council had to discuss. Moreover, the appearance of the chiefs assembled in the room had about it something stern and imposing that inspired respect. Contrary to Indian habits, they were all unarmed. This precaution, which was owing to the advice of the principal sachem of the nation, was justified not only by the considerable number of chiefs present, but also by their belonging to various nations. Each tribe of the grand confederation of the Papazos had its representative in this assembly, where were also the sachems of nations ordinarily at war with it, but who, in the hope of a general revolt against the whites, the implacable enemies of the red race, had forgotten their hatred for a season. Here could be seen Yaquis, Mayos, Seris, and even free hunters and trappers, white and half-bred, in their grand war paint, with their heels adorned with wolves' tails, an honorary distinction to which only the great braves have a right.

Thunderbolt, the old man whose portrait we have just drawn, presided over the assembly. On the entrance of Stronghand, all the warriors rose, turned to him, and after bowing gracefully, invited him to take a seat among them. The hunter, flattered in his heart by the honour done him, bowed gravely to the members of the council, and seated himself on the right of Thunderbolt, after handing his weapons to Sparrowhawk, who carried them into an adjoining room. There was a rather long silence, during which the hunter smoked the calumet which had been eagerly offered him. At length Thunderbolt began speaking.

"My son could not arrive at a better moment," he said, addressing Stronghand; "his return was eagerly desired by his brothers. He has come from the country inhabited by our enemies; without doubt he will give us news."

The hunter rose, looked round the meeting, and replied—"I have been among the Gachupinos, I have entered their towns, I have seen their pueblos, presidios, and posts; like ourselves, they are preparing for war; they understand the extent of the danger that threatens them, and are trying to neutralize it by all means."

"The news is not very explicit; we hoped that Stronghand would give us more serious information about the movements of the enemy," Thunderbolt remarked, with a reproachful accent.

"Perhaps I could do so," the hunter remarked, calmly.

"Then why are you silent?"

The young man hesitated for a moment beneath the glances fixed on him.

"The white men have a proverb," he said, at length, "whose justice I specially recognise at this moment."

"What is it?"

"Words are silver, but silence is gold."

"Which means?" Thunderbolt continued, eagerly.

"The most formidable weapon of the white man is treachery," the hunter continued, not appearing to heed the interruption; "they have even conquered by treachery the Redskins, whom they did not dare meet face to face. Questions so interesting as those we have to settle, such serious interests as we have to discuss, must not be treated in so large an assembly ere it is quite certain that a traitor has not glided in among us. So long as merely general questions are discussed this is of slight consequence; but so soon as we discuss the means to be employed in carrying on the war, it is urgent that the enemy should not be warned of the result of our deliberations."

"We cannot act otherwise than we are doing. Yes, and that is why the whites are cleverer than we: so soon as war is declared, they appoint a commission, composed of three members, or five at the most, who have to draw up the plan of the campaign. Why do we not do the same? Nothing is more simple, it seems to me: choose, among the chiefs assembled here, a certain number of wise men accustomed to command; these men will assemble in secret, and decide on the means to be employed in conquering our enemy: in this way, if the Spaniards are informed of our movements, the traitor cannot escape us for long. The other chiefs, and the deputies of the friendly natives and other confederated tribes, will settle in the Grand

Council the common interests of the Indian natives, and the terms to be established among them, in order to stifle for ever those germs of discord which frequently spring up from a misunderstanding, and almost always degenerate into sanguinary and interminable quarrels. I have spoken: my brothers will determine whether my words deserve being taken into consideration."

After bowing to the audience, the hunter sat down again, and seemed to be plunged into deep thought. One of the instinctive qualities of the Indian race is good sense. The chiefs, in spite of the circumlocution in which the hunter had thought it necessary to envelop his remarks, had perfectly understood him: they had caught the justice of his reasoning, and the advantage of a speedy decision on a subject so interesting to the entire confederation: they guessed, under the hunter's reticence, a name which, for secret reasons of his own, he did not wish to utter, and hence his speech was greeted with a buzz of satisfaction, which is always flattering to the ears of an orator, no matter the nature of his hearers. Thunderbolt questioned the members of the council by a glance; all replied with an affirmative shake of their heads.

"Your plan is adopted," the chief said; "we recognise the necessity of carrying it out. But this time again we must apply to you to choose the members of the council whom we have to elect."

"Chance alone must decide the solution. All the sachems collected in this hall are great braves of their tribes, and the picked warriors of their nations. No matter on whom the lot falls, the members will behave honourably in the new council."

"Stronghand has spoken well, as he always does, when he is called upon to give his opinion in the council of the chiefs; now let him finish what he has so well begun, by instructing us of the way in which we are to consult chance."

"Be it so: I will obey my father."

The hunter rose and left the hall, but his absence lasted only a few minutes. During this interval the chiefs remained motionless and silent. Stronghand soon returned, followed by Sparrowhawk, who, as he had been ordered by the sachems to keep the door, had not taken part in the deliberations, though he had a right to do so. This chief carried a blanket tied up so as to form a bag.

"In this blanket," the hunter then said, "I have placed a number of bullets equal to that of the chiefs assembled in council: I have taken these bullets from the ammunition bag of every one of the chiefs. I have noticed that our guns are of different bores, and hence some of the bullets are larger, others smaller. Each of us will draw a bullet haphazard; when all have one, they will be examined; and the three chiefs, if you fix on that number, or the five, if you prefer that number, to whom chance has given the largest bullets, will compose the new council."

"That is a simple way, and will prevent any annoyance," Thunderbolt said; "I believe that we shall do well by adopting it."

The chiefs bowed their assent.

"But," the sachem continued, "before we begin drawing, let us first settle of how many members the council shall consist; shall there be three or five?"

A white trapper rose and asked leave to speak. It was a man of about forty years of age, with frank and energetic features and muscular limbs, well known all over the western prairies by the singular name of the Whistler.

"If I may be allowed," he said, "to offer my opinion on such a matter before wise men and renowned warriors—for I am only a poor rogue of a hunter—I would call your attention to the fact that, with a committee whose duties are so serious, three men are not sufficient to discuss a question advantageously, because it is so easy to obtain a majority. On the other hand, five men mutually enlighten each other, by exchanging their ideas and starting objections: hence, I am of opinion that the council ought to be composed of five members. I will add one word: Will the white and half-breed hunters and trappers here present take part in the election?"

"Do they not fight with us?" Thunderbolt asked.

"This is true," the Whistler continued; "still it would be, perhaps, better for you to settle the matter among yourselves; we are, in reality, only your allies."

"You are our brothers and friends; in the name of the chiefs of the confederation. I thank you, Whistler, for the delicate proposal you have made; but we do not accept your offer, for all must be in common between you and us."

"You will do as you please. I spoke for your good; and it does not suit you, say no more about it."

While these remarks were exchanged between the trapper and Thunderbolt, the chiefs had decided that the military commission should be composed of five members. The drawing at once began; each warrior went, in his turn, to draw a bullet from the bag held by Sparrowhawk; then the verification was begun with that good faith and impartiality which the Indians display in all their actions when dealing with one another. On this occasion chance was intelligent, as happens more frequently than is supposed, when it is left free to act: the chiefs chosen to form the committee were exactly those who, if another mode of election had been employed, would have gained all the votes through their talent, experience, and wisdom. Hence, the sachems frankly applauded the decision of fate, and in their superstition, derived from this caprice of accident a favourable augury for the result of the war. The committee was composed as follows Thunderbolt, Sparrowhawk, Stronghand, the Whistler, and a renowned Apache chief, whose name was the Peccary.

When the election was over, just as the chiefs were returning to their seats, Stronghand approached a trapper, who, ever since his entrance, had seemed to shun his eye, and conceal himself, as far as possible, behind the other chiefs. Tapping him on the shoulder, he said in a low but imperative voice—"Master Kidd, two words, if you please."

The adventurer, for it was really he, started at the touch, but immediately recovering himself, he turned his smiling face to the hunter's, and said, with a respectful bow—"I am quite at your service, caballero; can I be so happy as to be able to help you in anything?"

"Yes," the hunter answered, drily.

"Speak, caballero, speak; and as far as lies in my power—"

"A truce to these hypocritical protestations," Stronghand rudely interrupted him, "and let us come to facts."

"I am listening to you," the other said, trying to hide his anxiety.

"This is the point—rightly or wrongly, your presence here offends me."

"What can I do to prevent that, my dear Señor?"

"A very simple thing."

"What is it, if you please?"

"Leave the tower at once, mount your horse, and be off."

"Oh!" the bandit said, with a forced laugh, "Allow me to remark, my dear señor, that the idea seems to me a singular one."

"Do you think so?" the hunter remarked, coldly; "Well, opinions differ. For my part, I consider it quite natural."

"Of course you are jesting."

"Do you fancy me capable of jesting—before all, with a man like you? I think not. Well, I repeat, be off; be off as quickly as possible. I advise you for your own good."

"I must have an excuse for such a flight. What will the Indian chiefs who did me the honour of summoning me to their grand council, and my friends the hunters suppose, on seeing me thus abandon them without any apparent motive, at the very moment when the war is about to begin?"

"That does not concern me; I want you to be off at once; if not—"

"Well?"

"I shall blow out your brains in the presence of all as a traitor and a spy. You understand me now, my master, I think?"

The bandit started violently; his face became livid, and for some minutes he fixed his viper eye on the hunter, who examined him ironically; then bending down to his ear, he said, in a voice choked with rage and shame, "Stronghand, you are the stronger, and any resistance on my part would be mad; I shall go, therefore; but remember this, I shall be avenged."

Stronghand shrugged his shoulders contemptuously. "Do so," he said, "if you can; but, in the meanwhile, be off if you do not wish me to carry out my threat!" and he turned his back on the bandit. Kidd gave him a parting look of fury, and without adding a word, left the hall. Ten minutes later he was galloping on the road to the Real de Minas, revolving the most sinister schemes.

CHAPTER XVIII
THE COUNCIL OF THE SACHEMS

Although the chiefs had guessed from Stronghand's gestures what was going on between him and the American bandit, not one of them made the slightest allusion to Kidd's departure, or even seemed to notice it. The Canadian trapper, named Whistler, alone went up to the hunter, and pressing his hand, said, with a coarse laugh—

"By heavens! Comrade, you did not miss your game, but brought it down at the first shot. Receive my sincere congratulations for having freed us of that skunk, who is neither fish nor flesh, and whose roguish face did not at all please me."

"It would please you much less, my good fellow, if you knew him," the hunter replied, with a smile.

"I beg you to believe that I have no desire to form a closer acquaintance with that pícaro; only too many like him may be met on the prairies."

The chiefs had resumed their seats, and the council which had been momentarily interrupted, was re-opened by Thunderbolt. The Indians, though people think proper to regard them as savages, could give lessons in urbanity and good breeding to the members of parliamentary assemblies in old Europe. Among them a speaker is never interrupted by those coarse and inopportune noises for which some M.P.'s seem to possess a privilege. Each speaks in his turn. The speakers, who are listened to with a religious silence, have the liberty of expressing their ideas without fearing personalities, which are frequently offensive. When the debate is closed, the speaker—that is to say, the oldest chief, or the one of the highest position either through bravery or wisdom—sums up the discussion in a few words, takes the opinion of the other chiefs, who vote by nodding their heads, and the minority always accepts, without complaint or recrimination of any sort, the resolution of the majority.

Before going further, we will explain, in a few words, the cause of the dissatisfaction which had induced the Indians to revolt once again against the whites. At the period of the Spanish conquests, the Indians, in spite of the obstinate assertions to the contrary, were happy, or at any rate were, through the intelligent care of the Government, placed in a situation which insured their existence under very satisfactory conditions. It is indubitable that if Spain had retained her colonies for fifty or sixty years longer, she would have gradually succeeded in converting the aborigines of her vast territories, attaching them to the cultivation of the soil, and making them give up a nomadic existence, and adopt the far preferable life in villages.

All Spanish America, both North and South, was covered with missions; that is to say, agricultural colonies, established on a large scale; where monks, in every way respectable, through their complete abnegation of the enjoyments of the world, and their inexhaustible charity, taught the Indians not only the paternal precepts of the Gospel, and their duty to their neighbour, but preaching by example, they became weavers, labourers, cobblers, and blacksmiths, in order to make their docile apprentices more easily understand the way to set to work. These missions contained, at the time of the War of Independence, several hundred thousand Indians, who had given up their nomadic life of hunting, and patiently assumed the yoke of civilization. This magnificent result, obtained by courage and perseverance, and which would have speedily resulted in the solution of a problem declared to be insoluble—the emancipation of the red race, and its aptitude to assume the sedentary condition of a town life, was unhappily not carried further.

When the Mexicans had proclaimed their independence, their first care was to destroy all that the Spaniards had raised, and utterly overthrow the internal governmental system established by them. Naturally, the missions were not exempted from this general overthrow; they were perhaps more kindly treated than the institutions created by the old oppressors. The philosophic spirit of the eighteenth century, when it forced its way into Mexico, was naturally misunderstood and ill appreciated by men who were plunged into the grossest ignorance, and who believed that they displayed the independence and nobility of their character by deadly hatred of the clergy, and abolishing their prerogatives at one stroke. It is true that, by an inevitable reaction, the Mexicans, whose revolution was almost entirely effected by priests, and who, at the outset, displayed themselves as such daring skeptics, ere long fell again, through their superstition, beneath the power of the same clergy, and became more devoted slaves to them than ever.

Unfortunately, the death blow had been dealt to the missions or agricultural colonies, although the Government recognized its mistake, and sought by all means to palliate it. They never recovered, only languished, and eventually the majority of them fell into ruin, and were utterly abandoned by the Indians, who returned to that desert life from which they had been drawn with such difficulty. Nothing is so heart-rending as the sight now offered by these missions, which were once so rich, so full of life, and so flourishing; only a few Indians can be seen, wandering about like ghosts in the deserted cloisters, led by an old, white-haired monk, whom they would not leave, and who had vowed to die among his children.

The Mexican Government did not stop here. Returning to the old errors of the conquistadors, it grew accustomed to regard the Indians as slaves; imposing on them exorbitant tariffs for articles of primary necessity, which it sold to them through special agents, bowing them to any Draconian law, and carrying their injustice so far as to deny them intellect, and brand them with the name of *Gente sin razón,* or people without reason. The consequences of such a system can be easily comprehended. The Indians, who, at the outset, contented themselves with passively withdrawing, and seeking in the desert the liberty that was refused them, on finding themselves so unjustly treated, and urged to desperation by such insults, thought about avenging themselves, and requiting evil for evil.

Then recommenced those periodical invasions of the Indian borders which the Spaniards had repressed with such difficulty and such bloodshed. Murder and pillage were organized on a grand scale, and with such success, that the Comanches and Apaches, to vex the whites, gave the ironical name of the "Mexican moon" to the month they selected to commit their periodical depredations. The subjected Indians—that is to say, those who, in spite of the constant vexations to which they were victims, remained attached to their villages—revolted several times, and on each occasion the Mexican government succeeded in making them return to their duty by promises and concessions, which were violated and forgotten so soon as the Redskins had laid down their arms. The war, consequently, became generalized and permanent in the Border states of the confederation.

But with the exception of a few invasions more serious than others, the Indians had almost entirely confined themselves to keeping the whites on the alert, when the great insurrection of 1827 broke out, which all but succeeded in depriving Mexico of her richest provinces. This insurrection was the more terrible, because on this occasion the Indians, guided by experienced chiefs, possessing firearms, and carrying out tactics entirely different from those they had hitherto employed, waged a serious war, and insisted on retaining the provinces they had seized. The Redskins elected an emperor and established a government; they displayed a settled intention of definitively regaining their independence and reconstituting their nationality.

The Mexicans, justly terrified by these manifestations, made the greatest sacrifices in order to quell this formidable revolt, and succeeded, though rather owing to the treachery and disunion they managed to sow among the chiefs than by the power of their arms. But this uprising had caused them to reflect, and they saw that it was high time to come to an arrangement with these men, whom they had hitherto been accustomed to regard as irrational beings. Peace was concluded on conditions very advantageous to the Indians and their forces; and the Mexicans, owing to the fright they had endured, were compelled to keep their promises, or, to speak more correctly, pretended to do so.

For several years the Indians, satisfied with this apparent amelioration in the relations between them and the whites, remained peacefully in their villages, and the Mexicans had only to defend their borders against the attacks of the wild or unsubjected Indians. This was a task, we are bound to confess, in which they were not very successful; for the Indians eventually passed the limits the Spaniards had imposed on them, permanently established themselves on the ruins of the old Creole villages, and by degrees, and gaining ground each year, they reduced the territory of the Mexican Government in an extraordinary way.

Still, when the remembrance of the great Indian insurrection seemed to have died out, and the Indios Mansos had apparently accepted the sovereignty of Mexico, the annoyances recommenced. Though at first slight, they gradually became more and more frequent, owing to the apathetic resignation of the Indians, and the patience with which they uncomplainingly endured the unjust aggressions of which they were made the systematic victims. The concessions granted under the pressure of fear were brutally withdrawn, and matters returned to the same state as before the insurrection. The Indians continued to suffer, apparently resigned to endure all the insults it might please their oppressors to make them undergo: but this calm concealed a terrific storm, and the Mexicans would shortly be aroused by a thunderclap.

The Redskins behaved, under the circumstances, with rare prudence and circumspection, in order not to alarm the persons they wished to surprise. They would certainly have succeeded in deceiving the Mexicans as to their plans, had it not been for the treachery of the agents of the Mexican Government, continually kept in their villages to watch them, among whom was Kidd, whom Stronghand had so suddenly unmasked and contemptuously turned out. Still these agents, in spite of their lively desire to make themselves of importance by magnifying facts, had only been able to give very vague details about the conspiracy the Indians were secretly forming. They knew that an emperor had been elected, and that he was a white man, but they did not know who he was or his name. They also knew that the Confederation of the Papazos had placed itself at the head of the movement, and intended to deal the first blow, but no one was aware when or how hostilities would commence.

This information, however, incomplete though it was, appeared to the Mexicans, on whose minds at once rushed the sanguinary memories of the last revolution, sufficiently serious for them to place themselves in a position to resist the first attack of the Redskins, which is always so terrible, and to place their frontiers in such a state as would prevent a surprise—a thing they had never yet succeeded in effecting. The Mexican Government, warned of what was going on by the commandants of the States of Sonora and Sinaloa, the two most menaced of the Confederation, and recognising the gravity of the case, resolved to send troops from the capital to reinforce the border garrisons. This plan, unfortunately, could not be carried out, and was the cause of fresh and very dangerous complications.

It is only in the old Spanish colonies, which are in the deepest state of neglect and disorganization, that such acts are possible. The troops told off to proceed to Sonora, so soon as they learned that they were intended to oppose the Indians, peremptorily refused to march, alleging as the reason, that they were not at all desirous of fighting savages who did not respect the law of nations, and had no scruples about scalping their prisoners. The President of the republic, strong in his right and the danger the country ran, tried to insist and force them to set out. Then a thing that might be easily foreseen occurred: not only did the troops obstinately remain in revolt, but set the seal on it by making a pronunciamiento in favour of the general chosen to command the expedition, and who, we may do him the justice of saying, had been the first to declare against the departure of the troops from the capital.

This pronunciamiento was the spark that fired the powder train. In a few days the whole of Mexico was a prey to the horrors of civil war; so that the governors of the two States, being reduced to their own forces, and not knowing whether they would retain their posts under the new president, were more embarrassed than ever, did not dare take any initiative, and contented themselves with throwing up such intrenchments as they could, though they had quite enough to do in keeping their troops to their duty, and keeping them from deserting. Such was the state of things at the moment we have now reached. This information, upon which we have purposely laid a stress, in order to make the reader understand certain facts which, without this precaution, would seem to belong rather to the regions of fancy than to that of history, as they are so strange and incredible, was reported by Stronghand to the council of the sachems, and listened to in a religious silence.

"Now," he added, in conclusion, "I believe that the moment has arrived to strike the grand blow for which we have so long been preparing. Our enemies hesitate; they are demoralized; their soldiers tremble; and I am convinced they will not withstand the attack of our and the great Beaver's warriors. This is what I wished to say to the council. Still it was not advisable that such important news should reach the ears of our enemies. The sachems will judge whether I have acted well, or if my zeal carried me too far in dismissing from the council a paleface who, I am convinced, is a traitor sold to the Mexicans. I have spoken."

A flattering murmur greeted the concluding remarks of the young man, who sat down, blushing.

"It appears to me," Whistler then said, "that the debate need not be a long one. As war is decided on, the council of the Confederation has only to seek allies among the other Indian nations, in order to augment the number of our warriors, if that be possible. As regards the operations, and the period when the Mexican territory is to be invaded, that will devolve on the military committee, who pledge themselves to the profoundest secrecy about their discussions, until the hour for action arrives. I have spoken."

Thunderbolt rose.

"Chiefs and sachems of the Confederation of the Papazos," he said in his sympathetic and sonorous voice, "and you, warriors, our allies, the moment for dissolving your council has at length arrived. Henceforth the committee of the five chiefs will alone sit. Each of you will return to his tribe, arm his warriors, and order the scalp dance to be performed round the war post; but the eighth sun must see you here again at the head of your warriors, in order that all may be ready to act when the invasion is decided on. I have spoken. Have I said well, powerful men?"

The chiefs rose in silence, resumed their weapons, and immediately left the village, starting in different directions at a gallop. Thunderbolt and Stronghand were left alone.

"My son," the old man then said, "have you nothing to tell me?"

"Yes, father," the young man respectfully answered; "I have very serious news for you."

CHAPTER XIX
THE RANCHO

Before describing the conversation between Thunderbolt and Stronghand, we are obliged to go back, and tell the reader certain facts which had occurred at the Hacienda del Toro, a few days before the majordomo set out for Hermosillo. Mexican girls, born and bred on the Indian border, enjoy a liberty which the want of society renders indispensable. Always on horseback upon these immense estates, which extend for twenty or five-and-twenty leagues, their life is spent in riding over hill and dale, visiting the wretched huts of the vaqueros and peons, relieving their wants, and rendering themselves beloved by their simple graces and affecting goodness of heart.

Doña Mariana, who had been exiled for several years at a convent, so soon as she returned home, eagerly renewed her long rides through forests and prairies, to see again the persons in her father's employ, with whom she had sported as a child, and of whom she had such a pleasant recollection. At times followed by a servant, specially attached to her, but more usually alone, the maiden had therefore recommenced her rides, going to visit one and the other, enjoying her gallop, careless as a bird, pleased with everything—the flowers she culled as she passed, the reviving breeze she inhaled, and smiling gaily at the sun which bronzed her complexion; in a word, she revealed the voluptuous and egotistic apathy of a child in whom the woman is not yet revealed, and who is ignorant that she possesses a heart.

Most usually Doña Marianna guided her horse to a rancho situated about three leagues from the hacienda, in the midst of a majestic forest of evergreen oaks and larches. This rancho, which was built of adobes, and whitewashed, stood on the bank of a stream, in the centre of a field sufficiently cleared to grow the grain required for the support of the poor inhabitants of the hovel. In the rear of the rancho was an enclosure, serving as a corral, and containing two cows and four or five horses, the sole fortune of the master of this rancho, which, however, internally was not so poverty stricken as the exterior seemed to forebode. It was divided into three parts, two of which served as bedrooms, and the third as sitting room, saloon, kitchen, &c. In the latter, the fowls impudently came to pick up grain and pieces of tortillas which bad been allowed to fall.

On the right was a sort of low fireplace, evidently for culinary purposes; the middle of the room was occupied by a large oak table with twisted legs; at the end, two doors opened into the bedrooms, and the walls were covered with those hideous coloured plates which Parisian trade inundates the New World with, and under which intelligent hawkers print the names of saints, to render the sale more easy. Among these engravings was one representing Napoleon crossing the St. Bernard, accompanied by a guide, holding his horse. It bore the rather too fanciful title, "The great St. Martin dividing his cloak with a beggar." A fact which imparts incomparable meaning to this humorous motto is, that the general, far from wishing to give his cloak to the guide, who does not want it, seems to be shivering with cold, and wrapping himself up with extreme care. Lastly, a few *butacas* and *equipales* completed the furniture, which, for many reasons, might be considered elegant in a country where the science of comfort is completely ignored, and the wants of material life are reduced to their simplest expression.

This rancho had been for many years inhabited by the same family, who were the last relics of the Indians dwelling here when the country was discovered by the Spaniards. These Indians, who were mansos, and long converted to Christianity, had been old and faithful servants of the Marquises de Moguer, who were always attached to them, and made it a point of honour to heighten their comforts, and give them their protection under all circumstances. Hence the devotion of these worthy people to the Moguer family was affecting, through its simple self-denial. They had forgotten their Indian name, and were only known by that of Sanchez.

At the moment when we introduce this family to the reader, it consisted of three persons: the father, a blind old man, but upright and hale, who, in spite of his infirmity, still traversed all the forest tracks without hesitation or risk of losing himself, merely accompanied by his dog Bouchaley; the mother, a woman about forty years of age, tall, robust, and possessing marked features, which, when she was younger, must have been very handsome; and the son, a young man of about twenty, well built, and a daring hunter, who held the post of tigrero at the hacienda.

Luisa Sanchez had been nurse to Doña Marianna, and the young lady, deprived at an early age of her mistress, had retained for her not merely that friendship which children generally have for their nurse, and which at times renders the mother jealous, but that craving for affection, so natural in young hearts, and which Doña Marianna, restrained by her father's apparent sternness, could not indulge. The maiden's return to the hacienda caused great joy at the rancho; father, mother, and son at once mounted and proceeded to the Toro to embrace their child, as they simply called her. Halfway they met Doña Marianna, who, in her impatience to see them again, was galloping like a mad girl, followed by her brother, who was teasing her about this love for her nurse.

Since then, not a day passed on which the young lady did not carry the sunshine of her presence to the rancho, and shared the breakfast of the family—a frugal meal, composed of light cakes, roasted on an iron plate, boiled beef seasoned with chile Colorado, milk, and *quesadillas*, or cheesecakes, hard and green and leathery, which the young lady, however, declared to be excellent, and heartily enjoyed. Bouchaley, like everybody else at the rancho, entertained a feeling of adoration for Doña Marianna. He was a long-haired black and white mastiff, about ten years old, and spiteful and noisy as all his congeners. In reality, the dog possessed but one good quality—its well-tried fidelity to its master, whom it never took its eyes off, and constantly crouched at his feet. Since the young lady's return, the heart of the worthy quadruped had opened to a new affection; each morning it took its post on the road by which Doña Marianna came, and as soon as it saw her, saluted her by leaps and deafening barks.

Mariano Sanchez, the tigrero, had for his foster sister an affection heightened by the similarity of name—a similarity which in Spanish America gives a right to a sort of spiritual relationship. This touching custom, whose origin is entirely Indian, is intended to draw closer the relations between *tocayo* and *tocaya*, and they are almost brother and sister. Hence the tigrero, in order to be present each morning at his tocaya's breakfast, often rode eight or ten leagues in the morning, and found his reward in a smile from the young lady. As for Father Sanchez, since the return of his child, as he called her, he only felt one regret. It was that he could not see her and admire her beauty; but he consoled himself by embracing her.

It was about eleven o'clock in the morning; the sun illumined the hut; the birds were singing merrily in the forest. Father Sanchez had taken up the hand mill, and was grinding the wheat, while his wife, after sifting the wheat, pounded it, and formed it into light cakes, called tortillas, which, after being griddled, would form the solid portion of the breakfast.

Bouchaley was at his post on the road, watching for the arrival of the young lady.

"How is it," the old man asked, "that Mariano is not here yet? I generally hear the sound of his horse earlier than this."

"Poor lad! Who knows where he is at this moment?" the mother answered. "He has for some days been watching a band of jaguars that have bitten several horses at the hacienda. He is certainly ambushed in some thicket. I only trust he will not be devoured some day by the terrible animals."

"Nonsense, wife," the old man continued, with a shrug of the shoulders. "Maternal love renders you foolish. Mariano devoured by the tigers!"

"Well, I see nothing impossible in that."

"You might just as well say that Bouchaley is capable of chasing a peccary; one thing is as possible as the other. Besides, you forget that our son never goes out without his dog Bigote, a cross between a wolf and a Newfoundland dog, as big as a six months' old colt, and who is capable of breaking the loins of a coyote at one snap."

"I do not say no, father; I do not say no," she continued, with a shake of her head; "that does not prevent his being a dangerous trade, which may one day or another, cost him his life."

"Stuff! Mariano is too clever a hunter for that; besides, the trade is lucrative; each jaguar skin brings him in fourteen piastres—a sum we cannot afford to despise, since my infirmity has prevented me from working. It would be better for my old carcass to return to the earth, as I am no longer good for anything."

"Do not speak so, father; especially before our daughter, for she would not forgive you: for what you are saying is unjust; you have worked enough in your time to rest now, and your son take your place."

"Well, tell me, wife," the old man said, laughingly, "was I devoured by the jaguar? And yet I was a tigrero for more than forty years, and the jaguars were not nearly so polite in my time as they are now."

"That is all very well; it is true that you have not been devoured, but your father and your grandfather were. What answer have you to that?"

"Hem!" the old man went on, in some embarrassment; "I will answer—I will answer—"

"Nothing, and that will be the best," she continued; "for you could not say anything satisfactory."

"Nonsense! What do you take me for, mother? If my father and grandfather were devoured, and that is true, it was—"

"Well, what? I am anxious to hear."

"Because they were treacherously attacked by the jaguars," he at length said, with a triumphant air; "the wretches knew whom they had to deal with, and so played cunning. Otherwise they would never have got the best of two such clever hunters as my father and grandfather."

The ranchera shrugged her shoulders with a smile, but she considered it unnecessary to answer, as she was well aware she would not succeed in making her husband change his opinion as to her son's dangerous trade. The old man, satisfied with having reduced his wife to silence, as he fancied, did not abuse his victory; with a crafty smile he rolled and lit a cigarette, while Na Luisa laid the table, arranged and dusted everything in the rancho, and listened anxiously to assure herself that the footfall of her son's horse was not mingled with the sounds that incessantly rose from the forest.

All at once Bouchaley was heard barking furiously. The old man drew himself up in his butaca, while Na Sanchez rushed to the doorway, in which Doña Marianna appeared, fresh and smiling.

"Good morning, father! Good morning, mother!" she exclaimed in her silvery voice, and kissed the forehead of the old man, who tenderly pressed her to his heart. "Come, Bouchaley, come, be quiet!" she added, patting the dog, which still gamboled round her. "Mother, ask my tocayo to put Negro in the corral, for the good animal has earned its alfalfa."

"I will go, Querida," the old man said; "for today I take Mariano's place." And he left the rancho without awaiting an answer.

"Mother," the young lady continued, with a shade of anxiety, "where is my foster brother? I do not see him."

"Has not arrived yet, niña."

"What! Not arrived?"

"Oh, I trust he will soon be here," she said, while stifling a sigh.

The maiden looked at her for a moment sympathetically.

"What is the matter, mother?" she at length said, as she seized the poor woman's hand; "Can any accident have happened?"

"The Lord guard us from it, Querida," Luisa said, clasping her hands.

"Still, you are anxious, mother. You are hiding something from me. Tell me at once what it is."

"Nothing, my child; forgive me. Nothing extraordinary has occurred, and I am hiding nothing from you; but—"

"But what?" Doña Marianna interrupted her.

"Well, since you insist, Querida, I confess to you that I am alarmed. You know that Mariano is tigrero to the hacienda?"

"Yes; what then?"

"I am always frightened lest he should meet with an accident, for that happens so easily."

"Come, come, mother; do not have such thoughts as these. Mariano is an intrepid hunter, and possesses far from common skill and tact."

"Ah, hija, you are of the same opinion as my old man. Alas! If I lost my son, what would become of you?"

"Oh, mother, why talk in that way? Mariano, I hope, runs no danger. The delay that alarms you means nothing; you will soon see him again."

"May you be saying the truth, dear child!"

"I am so convinced of it, mamita, that I will not sit down to table till he arrives."

"Well, you will not have to wait long, hijita," the old man said, as he re-entered the rancho.

"Is he coming?" the mother joyously exclaimed, as she furtively wiped away a tear.

"I knew it," the maiden remarked.

"There, do you hear his horse?" the old man said. In fact, the furious gallop of a horse echoed in the forest, and approached with the rapidity of a hurricane. The two females darted to the door. At this moment a horseman appeared on the skirt of the clearing, riding at full speed, with his hair floating in the breeze, and his face animated by the speed at which he rode. This horseman, who was powerfully and yet gracefully built, and had a manly, energetic face, was Mariano, the tigrero. His dog, a black and white Newfoundland, with powerful chest and enormous head, was running by the side of the horse, and looking up intelligently every moment.

"¡Viva Dios! ¡Querida tocaya!" the young man exclaimed, as he leaped from his horse. "I am glad to see you, for I was afraid that I should arrive too late. Bigote," he added, addressing his dog and throwing the bridle to it, which the animal seized with its mouth, "lead Moreno to the corral."

The dog immediately proceeded thither, followed by the horse, while Mariano and the two females returned to the rancho. The young man kissed his father's forehead, and took his hand, saying, "Good morning, papa!" and then returned to his mother, whom he embraced several times.

"Cruel child," she said to him, "why did you delay so long?"

"Pay no attention to what your mother says, muchacho," the old man remarked; "she is foolish."

"Fie! You must not say that!" the young lady exclaimed; "You would do better in scolding Mariano, for I, too, felt alarmed."

"Do not be angry with me," the young man replied; "I have been for some days on the track of a family of jaguars, which is prowling about the neighbourhood, and I could not possibly come sooner."

"Are they about here?"

"No; they are prowlers brought here by the drought; and are the more dangerous because, as they do not belong to these parts, they rest where they please—sometimes at one place, sometimes at another, and it becomes very difficult to follow their trail."

"I only hope they will not think of coming here," the mother said, anxiously.

"I do not believe they will, for wild beasts shun the vicinity of man. Still, Doña Marianna had better, for some days to come, restrict her rides, and not venture too far into the forest."

"What can I have to fear?"

"Nothing, I hope; still it is better to act prudently. Wild beasts are animals whose habits it is very difficult to discover, especially when they are in unknown parts, as these are."

"Nonsense!" the young lady said, with a laugh; "You are trying to frighten me, tocayo."

"Do not believe that; I will accompany you with Bigote to the hacienda."

The dog, which had returned to its master's side after performing its duties, wagged its tail, and looked up in her face.

"I will not allow that, tocayo," the young lady replied, as she passed her hand through the dog's silky coat, and pulled its ears; "let Bigote have a rest. I came alone, and will return alone; and mounted on Negro, I defy the tigers to catch me up, unless they are ambuscaded on my road."

"Still, niña—" Mariano objected.

"Not a word more on the subject, tocayo, I beg; let us breakfast, for I am literally dying of hunger; and were the tigers here," she added, with a laugh, "they might frighten me, but not deprive me of my appetite."

CHAPTER XX
LOST!

They sat down to table; but the meal, in spite of Doña Marianna's efforts to enliven it, suffered from the anxiety which two of the party felt, and tried in vain to conceal. The tigrero was vexed with his foster sister for not letting him accompany her, for he had not liked to express his fears, lest the young lady on her return to the hacienda might meet the ferocious animals he had been pursuing for some days past, without being able to shoot them.

The jaguar, which, is very little known in Europe, is one of the scourges of Mexico, and would figure advantageously in zoological gardens. There is only one in the Parisian Jardin des Plantes, and that is a very small specimen. Let us describe this animal, which is more feared by the Indians and white men of North America, than is the lion by the Arabs. The jaguar (*Felis onca, or onza*) is, next to the tiger and lion, the largest of the animals of its genus; it is the great wild cat of Cuvier, and is called indiscriminately "the American tiger," and the "panther of the furriers." It is a quadruped of the feline race; its total length is about nine feet, and its height about twenty-seven inches. Its skin is handsome, and in great request; while of a bright tawny hue on the back, it is marked on the head, neck, and along the flanks with black spots: the lower part of the body is white, with irregular black spots.

But few animals escape the pursuit of the jaguar: it obstinately hunts horses, bulls, and buffaloes; it does not hesitate to leap into rivers to catch certain fish it is fond of, fights the alligator, devours otters and picas, and wages a cruel warfare with the monkeys, owing to its agility, which enables it to mount to the top of trees, even when they are devoid of branches, and upwards of eighty feet high. Although, like all the carnivora of the New World, it shuns the proximity of man, it does not hesitate to attack him when urged by hunger or tracked by hunters; in such cases it fights with the utmost bravery, and does not dream of flight.

Such were the animals the tigrero had been pursuing for the last few days, and had not been able to catch up. According to the sign he had found, the jaguars were four in number—the male, female, and two cubs. We can now understand what the young man's terror must be on thinking of the terrible dangers to which his foster sister ran a risk of being exposed on her return to the hacienda: but he knew Doña Marianna too well to hope he could make her recall her decision. Hence, he did not try to bring the conversation back to the subject, but resolved to follow her at a distance, in order to come to her aid if circumstances required it.

As always happens under such circumstances, Doña Marianna, seeing that no one referred again to the jaguars, was the first to talk about them, asking her foster brother the details of their appearance in the country, and the mischief they had done, in what way he meant to surprise them, and a multitude of other questions; to which the young man replied most politely, but limiting himself to brief answers, and without launching into details, which are generally so agreeable to a hunter. The tigrero displayed such laconism in the information he gave the young lady, that the latter, vexed in spite of herself at seeing him so cold upon a subject to which he had seemed to attach such importance a few moments before, began jeering him, and ended by saying, with a mocking look, that she was convinced he had only said what he did to frighten her, and that the jaguars had only existed in his imagination. Mariano gaily endured the raillery, confessed that he had perhaps displayed more anxiety than the affair deserved, and taking down a jarabe that hung on the wall, he began strumming a fandango with the back of his hand, in order to turn the conversation.

Several hours passed in laughing, talking, and singing. When the moment for departure at length arrived, Mariano went to the corral to fetch the young lady's horse, saddled it with the utmost care, and led it to the door of the rancho, after saddling his own horse, so that he might start so soon as Doña Marianna was out of sight of the rancho.

"You remained a long time in the corral, tocayo," she said with a laugh; "pray, have you discovered any suspicious sign?"

"No, Niña; but as I am also going to leave the rancho, after saddling your horse, I saddled mine."

"Of course you are going to hunt your strange jaguars again?"

"Oh, of course," he answered.

"Well," she said, with feigned terror, "if you do meet them, pray do not miss them."

"I will do all in my power to avoid that, because I desire to make you a present of their skins, in order to prove to you that they really existed."

"I thank you for your gallantry, Tocayo," she replied with a laugh; "but you know the proverb—'A hunter must not sell the skin of a—jaguar, before—'"

"Well, well, we shall soon know who is right, and who wrong," he interrupted her.

The maiden, still laughing, embraced the ranchero and his wife, lightly bounded into the saddle, and bending down gracefully offered her hand to Mariano.

"We part friends, tocayo," she said to him. "Are you coming my way?"

"I ought to do so."

"Then why not accompany me?"

"Because you would suppose, Niña, that I wished to escort you."

"Ha! Ha! Ha!" the young lady said, merrily; "I had forgotten your proposal of this morning. Well, I hope you will be successful in your bunt; and so, good-bye till tomorrow. Come, Negro."

After uttering these words, she gave a parting wave of the hand to her nurse, and started at a gallop. The young man, after watching her for a while, to be certain of the road she followed, then re-entered the rancho, took his gun, and loaded it with all the care which hunters display in this operation, when they believe that life depends on the accuracy of their aim.

"Are you really about to start at once?" his mother asked him, anxiously.

"At once, mother."

"Where are you going?"

"To follow my foster sister to the hacienda, without her seeing me."

"That is a good idea. Do you fear any danger for her?"

"Not the slightest. But it is a long distance from here to the hacienda; the Indians are moving, it is said. We are no great distance from the border, and, as no one can foresee the future, I do not wish my sister to be exposed to any chance encounter."

"Excellently reasoned, muchacho. The niña is wrong in thus crossing the forest alone."

"Poor child!" the ranchero said; "An accident happens so easily; lose no time, muchacho, but be off. On reflection, I think you ought to have insisted on accompanying her."

"You know, father, she would not have consented."

"That is true; it is better that it should be as it is, for she will be protected without knowing it. The first time I see Don Ruiz, I will recommend him not to let his sister go out thus alone, for times are not good."

But the young man was no longer listening to his father: so soon as his gun was loaded, he left the rancho, followed by his dog. Two minutes later he was in the saddle, and riding at full speed in the direction taken by Doña Marianna.

So soon as the young lady found herself at a sufficient distance from the rancho, she had checked her horse's pace, which was now proceeding at an amble. It was about five in the afternoon; the evening breeze was rising, and gently waving the tufted crests of the trees; the sun, now almost level with the ground, only appeared on the horizon in the shape of a reddish globe; the atmosphere, refreshed by the breeze, was perfumed by the gentle emanations from the flowers and herbs; the birds, aroused from the heavy lethargy produced by the heat, were singing beneath all the branches, and filling the air with their joyous songs.

Doña Marianna, whose mind was impressionable, and open to all sensations, gently yielded to the impressions of this scene, which was so full of ineffable harmony, and gradually forgetting where she was and surrounding objects, had fallen into a voluptuous reverie. What was she meditating? She certainly could not have said; she was yielding unconsciously to the influence of this lovely evening, and travelling into that glorious country of fancy of which life is but too often the nightmare. Doña Marianna was too young, too simple, and too pure yet to possess any memory either sad or sweet; her life had hitherto been an uninterrupted succession of sunshiny days; but she was a woman, and listened for the beatings of her heart, which she was surprised at not hearing. With that curiosity which is innate in her sex, the maiden tried with a timid hand to raise a corner of the veil that covered the future, and to divine mysteries which are incomprehensible, so long as love has not revealed them by sufferings, joy, or grief.

Doña Marianna had rather a long ride through the forest before reaching the plain; but she had so often ridden the road at all hours of the day, she was so thoroughly persuaded that no danger menaced her, that she let the bridle hang on her horse's neck, while she plunged deeper and deeper into the delicious reverie which had seized on her. In the meanwhile, the shades grew deeper; the birds had concealed themselves in the foliage, and ceased their songs; the sun had disappeared, and the hot red beams it had left on the horizon were beginning to die out; the wind blew with greater force through the branches, which uttered long murmurs; the sky was assuming deeper tints, and night was rapidly approaching. Already the shrill cries of the coyotes rose in the quebradas and in the unexplored depths of the forest; hoarse yells disturbed the silence, and announced the awakening of the savage denizens of the forest.

All at once a long, startling, strident howl, bearing some resemblance to the miauling of a cat, burst through the air, and fell on the maiden's ear with an ill-omened echo. Suddenly startled from her reverie, Doña Marianna looked up, and took an anxious glance around her. A slight shudder of fear passed over her body, for her horse, so long left to its own devices, had left the beaten track, and the maiden found herself in a part of the forest unknown to her—she had lost her way. A person lost in an American forest is dead!

These forests are generally entirely composed of trees of the same family, which render it impossible to guide oneself, unless gifted with that miraculous intuition which the Indians and hunters possess, and which enables them to march with certainty in the most inextricable labyrinths. Wherever the eye may turn, it only perceives immense arcades of verdure, infinitely prolonged, wearying the eye by their desperate monotony, and only crossed at intervals by the tracks of wild beasts, which are mixed strangely together, and eventually lead to unknown watering places, nameless streams, that run silently and gloomily beneath the covert, and whose windings cannot possibly be followed.

The spot where the maiden was, was one of the most deserted in the forest; the trees, of prodigious height and size, grew closely together, and were connected by a network of lianas, which, growing in every direction, formed an impassable wall; from the end of the branches hung, in long festoons to the ground, that greyish moss known as Spanish beard, while the tall straight grass that everywhere covered the ground, showed that human foot had not trodden the soil here for a lengthened period. The maiden felt an invincible terror seize upon her. Night had almost completely set in; then the stories her foster brother had told her in the morning about the jaguars returned to her mind in a flood, and were rendered more terrible by the darkness that surrounded her, and the mournful howling that burst forth on all sides. She shuddered, and turned pale as death at the thought of the fearful danger to which she had so imprudently exposed herself.

Then, collecting all her strength for a last appeal, she uttered a cry; but her voice died out without raising an echo. She was alone—lost in the desert by night. What could she do? What would become of her?

The maiden tried to find the route by which she had come, but the road followed haphazard through the herbage no longer existed; the grass trodden by her horse's hoof had sprung up again behind it. Moreover, the night was so dark that Doña Marianna could not see four paces ahead of her; and she soon found that her efforts to find the road would only result in leading her further astray. Under such circumstances, a man would have been in a comparatively far less dangerous position. He could have lit a fire to combat the night chill, and keep the wild beasts at bay; in the event of an attack, his weapons would have allowed him to defend himself: but Doña Marianna had not the means to light a fire; she had no weapons, and had she possessed them, she would not have known how to use them. She was forced to remain motionless at the spot where she was for the whole night, at the hazard of dying of cold or terror.

This position was frightful. How she now regretted her imprudent confidence, which was the cause of what was now occurring! But it was too late; neither complaints nor recrimination aught availed. She must yield to her fate. With energetic natures, however little accustomed they may be to peril, when that peril proves inevitable, and they recognise that nothing can protect them from it, a reaction takes place; their thoughts become clearer, their courage grows with their will, and they accept, with a proud and resolute resignation, all the consequences of the danger they are compelled to confront, however terrible they may be. This was what happened to the maiden when she perceived that she was really lost. A profound despair seized upon her—for a moment the weakness natural to her sex gained the upper hand, and she fell sobbing on the ground; but gradually the reaction set in, and, pious as all Spanish women are, she clasped her bands, and addressed a fervent and touching prayer to God, who was her last hope.

It has been justly said that prayer not only consoles, but strengthens and restores hope. Prayer, with those who sincerely believe, is the expression of the real feelings of the soul; only those who have looked death in the face, either on the battlefield or during a storm at sea, will understand the sublimity of prayer—the last appeal of the weak victim to the omnipotent Intelligence which can alone save him. Doña Marianna prayed, and then rose calmer, and, above all, stronger. She had placed herself in the hands of Deity, and, in her simple faith, was convinced that He would not abandon her.

Her horse, whose bridle she had not let loose, was standing motionless by her side. The maiden gently patted the noble animal, the only friend left to her; then, by a sudden inspiration, she began unfastening the girths, tearing her little hands without knowing it, and lacerating her fingers with the iron tongues of the buckles.

"Poor Negro," she said, in a soft voice, as she removed the trappings, "you must not be the victim of my imprudence; resume your liberty; for the noble instinct with which your Creator has endowed you will perhaps enable you to find your road. Go, my poor Negro; you are now free."

The animal gave a whinnying of delight, made a prodigious leap, and disappeared in the darkness. Doña Marianna was alone—really alone, now.

CHAPTER XXI
STRONGHAND

It is impossible to imagine what terrors night brings with it under its thick mantle of mist, when the earth is no longer warmed by the sparkling sunbeams, and darkness reigns as supreme lord. At that time everything changes its aspects, and assumes in the flickering rays of the moon a fantastic appearance; the mountains seem loftier, the rivers wider and deeper; the trees resemble spectres—gloomy denizens of the tomb, watching for you to pass, and ready to clutch you in their fleshless arms. The imagination becomes heated, ideas grow confused, you tremble at the fall of a leaf, at the moaning of the night breeze, at the breakage of a branch; and, suffering from a horrible nightmare, you fancy at every moment that your last hour is at hand.

In the American forests, night has mysteries still more terrible. Beneath these immense domes of verdure, which the sun is powerless to pierce even at midday, and which remain constantly buried in an undecided clear obscure, the darkness may, so to speak, be felt; nothing could produce a flash in this chaos, excepting, perhaps, the luminous eyeballs of the wild beasts, that dart electric sparks from the thickets. Here Night is truly the mistress; the darkness is peopled by the sinister denizens of the forest, whom the obscurity drives from their unknown hiding places, and who begin their mournful prowling in search of prey. From each clump, from each ravine, issue confused sounds that have no name in human language; some clear and sharp, others hoarse and low, and others, again resembling miauling, or sardonic laughter, are blended in horrible concert. Then come the heavy footfalls on the ground, and the sullen flapping of birds' wings, as well as that incessant indistinct murmur, which is nought else but the continual buzz of the infinitely little, mingled with the hollow moan always heard in the desert, and which is only the breath of Nature travailing with her incomprehensible secrets. A night passed in the forest, without fire or weapons, is a terrible thing for a man; but the situation becomes far more frightful for a woman—a girl—a frail and delicate creature, accustomed to all the comforts of life, and unable to find within herself those thousand resources which a strong man, habituated to struggle, manages to procure, even in the most desperate situations.

Without dwelling further on the subject, the reader can imagine without difficulty the painful situation in which Doña Marianna found herself. So long as she could hear the sound of her horse's hoofs, as it fled at full speed, she stood with her body bent forward and outstretched ears, attaching herself to life, and, perchance, to hope, through the sound which was so familiar to her; but when it had died out in the distance, when a leaden silence once again weighed on her, the maiden shuddered, and, folding her hands on her chest, sank in a half-fainting condition at the foot of a tree—no longer thinking or hoping, but awaiting death. For what succour could she expect in the tomb of verdure, which, though so spacious, was not the less secure?

How long did she remain plunged in this state of prostration, which was only an anticipated death—one hour or five minutes? She could not have said. For wretched people, whom everything, even hope, abandons, time seems to stand still—minutes become ages, and an hour seems as if it would never end. All at once a feeble, almost indistinguishable sound smote her ear, and she instinctively listened. This sound grew louder with every second, and ere long she could not be mistaken; it was a rapid mad gallop through the forest. This sound Doña Marianna recognised with terror; for it was produced by the return of her horse. For the noble animal to come back with such velocity, it must be pursued, and that closely, by ferocious animals, such was Doña Marianna's idea, and, unfortunately, she only too soon recognised its correctness. The horse gave a snort of terror, which was immediately answered by two loud, sharp growls. Then, as if dreaming, Doña Marianna heard prodigious leaps; she saw ill-omened shadows pass before her with the rapidity of a lightning flash, and then a fearful struggle, in which groans of agony were mingled with yells of delight.

However terrible the maiden's position might be she felt tears slowly course down her cheeks—her horse, her last comrade, had succumbed—the liberty she had granted it had only precipitated its destruction. Strange to say, though, at this supreme moment Doña Marianna did not think for an instant that the death of her horse probably only preceded her own by a brief space, and that it was a sinister warning to her to prepare for being devoured.

When terror has attained a certain degree, a strange effect is produced upon the individual; animal life still exists in the sense that the arteries pulsate, the heart palpitates; but intellectual life is completely suspended; the brain, struck by a temporary paralysis, no longer receives the thought; the eyes look without seeing; the voice itself cannot force its way through the contracted throat; in a word, terror produces a partial catalepsy, by destroying for a period, longer or shorter, all the noblest faculties of man.

Doña Marianna had reached such a point that, even had she possessed the means of flight, she would have been incapable of employing them, so thoroughly was every feeling extinct in her—even the instinct of self-preservation, which usually remains when all the others are destroyed.

Fortunately for the girl, the jaguars—for there were several of them—were to leeward; moreover, they had tasted blood, and this was a double reason which temporarily saved her, by depriving their scent of nearly all its delicacy. No other sound was audible, save that produced by the crushing of the horse's bones, which the wild beasts were devouring, mingled with growls of anger, when one of the banqueters tried to encroach on its neighbour's share of the booty. There could be no doubt about the fact; the animals enjoying this horrible repast were the jaguars, so long hunted by the tigrero, and which her evil star had brought across the maiden's track.

By degrees, Doña Marianna became—not familiarized with the danger hanging over her head, for that would have been impossible; but as, according to the law of nature, anything that reaches its culminating point must begin to descend, her first terror, though it did not abandon her, produced a strange phenomenon. She felt involuntarily attracted towards these horrible animals, whose black outlines she could distinguish moving in the darkness; suffering from a species of vertigo with her body bent forward, and her eyes immoderately dilated, without, even accounting for the strange feeling that urged her to act thus, she kept her eyes eagerly fixed upon them, following with a febrile interest their slightest movements, and experiencing at the sight a feeling of inexplicable pleasure, which produced a mingled shudder of joy and pain. Let who will try to explain this singular anomaly of human nature; but the fact is certain, and among our readers many will, doubtless, bear witness to its truth.

All at once the jaguars, which had hitherto been greedily engaged with the corpse of the horse, without thinking of anything beyond making a hearty meal, raised their heads and began sniffing savagely. Doña Marianna saw their eyes, sparkling like live coals, fixed upon her; she understood that she was lost; instinctively she closed her eyes to escape the fascination of those metallic eyeballs, which seemed in the darkness to emit electric sparks, and prepared to die. Still the jaguars did not stir; they were crouching on the remains of the horse, and, while continuing to gaze at the maiden, gracefully passed their paws over their ears with a purr of pleasure—in a word, they were coquettishly performing their toilet, appearing not only most pleased with the meal they had just ended, but with that which was awaiting them.

Still, in spite of the calmness affected by the two animals—for the cubs were sleeping, rolled up like kittens—it was evident that for some unknown motive they were restless; they lashed the ground with their weighty tails, or laid back their ears with a roar of anger, and, turning their heads in all directions, sniffed the air. They scented a danger; but of what nature was it? As for Doña Marianna, they appeared so sure of seizing her whenever they thought proper, and saw how harmless she was, that they contented themselves with crouching before her, and did not deign to advance a step. All at once the male, without stirring, uttered a sharp, quick yell. The female rose, bounded forward, seized one of her cubs in her mouth, and with one backward leap disappeared in a thicket; almost immediately she reappeared, and removed the second in the same way; then she returned calmly and boldly to place herself by the side of the male, whose anxiety had now attained formidable proportions.

At the same instant a flash traversed the air—a shot echoed far and wide—and the male jaguar writhed on the ground with a roar of agony. Almost immediately a man dashed from the tree at the foot of which Doña Mariana was crouching, stood in front of her, and received the shock of the female, which, at the shot, had instinctively bounded forward. The man tottered, but for all that kept his feet: there was a frightful struggle for a few minutes, and then the jaguar fell back with a last and fearful yell.

"Come," the hunter said, as he wiped on the grass the long machete with which he had stabbed the beast, "my arrangements were well made, but I fancy that I arrived only just in time. Now for the cubs; for I must not show mercy to any member of this horrible family."

Then this man, who seemed to possess the faculty of seeing in the darkness, walked without hesitation towards the spot where the female had hidden her cubs. He resolutely entered the thicket, and came out again almost immediately, holding a cub in either hand. He smashed their heads against the trunk of a tree, and threw the bodies on those of their father and mother.

"That is a very tidy butchery," he said; "but what on earth is Don Hernando's tigrero about, that I am obliged to do his work?"

While saying this, the hunter had collected all the dry wood within reach, struck a light, and within a few minutes a bright flame rose skywards. This duly accomplished, the stranger hurried to the assistance of Doña Marianna, who had fainted.

"Poor girl!" he muttered, with an accent of gentle pity, as he lifted her in his arms, and carried her to the fire; "How is it that the fright has not killed her?"

He gently laid her on some firs he had arranged for her bed, and gazed at her for a moment with a look of delight impossible to describe. But then he felt considerably embarrassed. Accustomed to the hardships of a desert life, and a skilful hunter as he had proved himself, this man was naturally a very poor sick nurse. He knew how, at a pinch, to dress a wound or extract a bullet, but he was quite ignorant how to bring a fainting woman round.

"Still, I cannot leave her in this state, poor girl," gazing on her sorrowfully; "but what am I to do?—how can I relieve her?"

At length he knelt down by the young lady's side, gently raised her lovely head, which he laid on his knee, and, opening with his dagger point her closed lips, poured in a few drops of Catalonian refino contained in a gourd. The effect of this remedy was instantaneous. A nervous tremour passed over the maiden's body; she heaved a sigh, and opened her lips. At the first moment she looked around her wildly, but ideas seemed gradually to return to her brain; her contracted features grew brighter, and fixing her eyes on the hunter, who was still bending over her, she muttered, with an expression of gratitude which made the young man's heart beat, "Stronghand!"

"Have you recognised me, señorita?" he exclaimed, with joyous surprise.

"Are you not my Providence?" she answered. "Do you not always arrive when I have to be saved from some fearful danger?"

"Oh, señorita!" he murmured, in great embarrassment.

"Thanks! Thanks, my saviour!" she continued, seizing his hand, and pressing it to her heart; "Thanks for having come to my help, Stronghand, for this time again. I should have been lost without you."

"I really believe," he said, with a smile, "that I arrived just in time."

"But how is it that you came so opportunely?" she asked, curiously, as she sat up and wrapped herself in the furs, for the feminine instinct had regained its power over her.

At this question, simple though it was, the hunter turned red.

"Oh," he said, "it is very simple. I have been hunting in these parts for some days past. I had tracked this family of jaguars, which I obstinately determined to kill, I know not why; but now I understand that it was a presentiment. After pursuing them all day, I had lost them out of sight, and was seeking their trail, when your horse enabled me to recover it."

"What!—my horse?" she exclaimed, in amazement.

"Do you not remember that it was I who gave you this poor Negro on our first meeting?"

"That is true," she murmured, as she let her eyes fall beneath the hunter's ardent glance.

"I saw you for a moment this morning when you were going to Sanchez' rancho."

"Ah!" she remarked.

"Sanchez is a friend, of mine," he continued, as if to explain his remark.

"Go on."

"On seeing the horse, which I at once recognised, I feared that some accident had happened to you, and set out after it. But the jaguars had scented it at the same time, and in spite of my thorough acquaintance with this forest, it was impossible for me to run as fast as they did. Luckily, they were hungry, and amused themselves by devouring poor Negro; otherwise I should not have arrived in time."

"But how was it that you came by this strange road?"

"In the first place, I was bound to save your life, as I knew that if I killed one jaguar, the other would leap upon you, in order to avenge it."

"But you ran the risk of being torn in pieces by the horrible animals," she said, with a shudder of retrospective terror, as she thought of the frightful dangers from which she had been so miraculously preserved.

"That is possible," he said, with an unmistakable expression of joy; "but I should have died to save you, and I desired nothing else."

The maiden made no reply. Pensive and blushing, she bowed her head on her chest. The hunter thought that he had offended her, and also remained silent and constrained. This silence lasted several minutes. At length Doña Marianna raised her head and offered her hand to the young man.

"Thank you again!" she said, with a gentle smile.

"Your heart is good. You did not hesitate to sacrifice your life for me, whom you scarce know, and I shall feel eternally grateful to you."

"I am too amply repaid for my services by these words, señorita," he replied, with marked hesitation; "still I have a favour to ask you, and I should be pleased if you would deign to grant it."

"Oh, speak, speak! Tell me what I can do!"

"I know not how to explain it; my request will appear to you so strange, so singular—perhaps so indiscreet."

"Speak; for I feel convinced that the favour you pretend to ask of me is merely another service you wish to render me."

Stronghand bent a searching glance on the maiden, and then seemed to make up his mind.

"Well, señorita," he said, "it is this:—should you ever, for any reason neither you nor I can foresee, need advice, or the help of a friend, either for yourself or any member of your family, do nothing till you have seen me, and explained to me unreservedly the motives that impelled you to come to me."

Doña Marianna reflected, while the hunter gazed at her attentively.

"Be it so," she at length said; "I promise to act as you wish. But how am I to find you?"

"Your foster brother is my friend, señorita; you will request him to lead you to me, and he will do so; or, if you prefer it, you can warn me through him to proceed to any place you may point out."

"Agreed."

"I can count on your promise?"

"Have I not passed my word?"

All at once a loud noise, resembling the passage of a wild beast, was heard in the forest glade; the maiden started, and instinctively clung to the hunter.

"Fear nothing, señorita," the latter said; "do you not recognise a friend?"

At the same moment the tigrero's dog leaped up to fondle her, followed almost instantaneously by Mariano.

"Heaven be blessed!" he said, joyfully, "She is saved!" and pressing the hunter's hand cordially, he added, "Thanks; it is a service I owe you, brother."

CHAPTER XXII
THE RETURN

How was it that the tigrero, whom we saw leave the rancho almost as soon as Doña Marianna, and follow in her track, arrived so late? We will explain this in a few sentences. The young man, feeling certain that his foster sister thoroughly knew the road she had to follow, which was, moreover, properly traced, had not dreamed of the chance of her missing her way, and not troubling himself to follow the horse's footmarks, he pushed straight on, fancying Doña Marianna ahead of him, crossed the forest, and then entered the plain, without perceiving the person he fancied he was following.

Still, on reaching the cultivated land, he looked carefully ahead of him, for he was surprised at the advance the young lady had gained on him in so short a time. But, though he examined the horizon all around, he saw nothing of her. Mariano was beginning to grow anxious; still, as there was a chaparral some distance ahead, whose tufted trees might conceal her whom he sought, he became reassured, and pushed onward, increasing the already rapid pace of his steed. It took him some time to pass through the chaparral; when he reached its skirt, and again entered the plain, the sun had set about half an hour previously, and darkness was invading the earth; the darkness was, indeed, so thick, that in spite of all his exertions, he could distinguish nothing a few paces ahead of him.

The tigrero halted, dismounted, placed his ear on the ground, and listened. A moment later he heard, or fancied he heard, a distant sound resembling a horse's gallop; his alarm was at once dissipated. Convinced that the young lady was in front of him, he mounted again and pushed on. As he was only two leagues from the Hacienda del Toro, he soon reached the foot of the rock. Here he stopped, and asked himself whether he had better go up, or regard his mission as fulfilled, and turn back. While unable to form any decision, he saw a black outline gliding along the path, and soon distinguished a horseman coming toward him.

"*Buena noche, Caballero,*" he said, when the latter crossed him.

"*Dios le de a usted buena,*" the other politely replied, and he passed on, but suddenly turned round again. The tigrero rode to meet him.

"Ah!" the horseman said, when they met, "I felt sure that I was not mistaken. How is No Mariano?"

"Very well, and at your service," the tigrero answered, recognising the majordomo; "and you, No Paredes?"

"The same, thank you; are you going up to the toro, or returning to the rancho?"

"Why that question?"

"Because in the former case I would bid you good night, while in the latter we would ride together."

"Are you going to the rancho?"

"Yes; the Señor Marquis has sent me."

"Tell me, No Paredes, would there be any indiscretion on my part in asking you what you are going to do at the rancho at so late an hour?"

"Not the slightest, compadre. I am simply going to fetch Doña Marianna, who has remained today later than usual with her nurse. Her father is anxious about her long absence, and asked me to go and meet her if she were on her road home, or if not, push on to the rancho."

This revelation was a thunderclap for the young man, who fancied that he had misunderstood.

"What!" he exclaimed, anxiously, "Is not Doña Marianna at the hacienda?"

"It seems not," the majordomo answered, "since I am going to fetch her."

"Why, that is impossible!" the other continued, in extreme agitation.

"Why so?" said Paredes, beginning to grow anxious in his turn. "What do you mean?"

"I mean that Doña Marianna left the rancho full three hours ago; that I followed her without her knowledge to watch over her safety, and that she must have been at the hacienda for more than half an hour."

"Are you quite sure of what you assert?"

"¡Caray! I have asserted it."

"In that case, Heaven have pity on the poor girl! For I apprehend a frightful misfortune."

"But she may have entered the hacienda without your seeing her."

"Nonsense, compadre; that is impossible. But come, we'll convince ourselves."

Without losing time in longer argument the two men dashed up the rock at a gallop, and in a few minutes reached the first gate of the hacienda. No one had seen Doña Marianna. The alarm was instantly given; Don Hernando wished to ride off at the head of his people, and beat up the country in search of his daughter; and it was with great difficulty that he was induced to abandon the project. Don Ruiz and the majordomo, followed by some twenty peons, provided with ocote wood torches, started in two different directions.

Mariano had an idea of his own. When he was quite certain that his foster sister had not returned, he presumed the truth—that she was lost in the forest. He did not consider for a moment that she had been carried off by Indian marauders, for he had not noticed any trace of a party of horsemen; and Bigote, whose nose was infallible, had evinced no anxiety during the ride. Hence Doña Marianna must be lost in the forest. The tigrero let Don Ruiz, the majordomo, and the peons pass him, and then bent his steps towards the rancho, closely followed by his dog, in spite of the exhortations of his young master and No Paredes, who wanted him to accompany them. When he was in the forest he stopped for a moment, as if to look round him; then, after most carefully examining the spot where he was, he dismounted, fastened his horse's bridle to the pommel, tied the stirrups together to keep them from clanking, and gave his horse a friendly smack on the crupper.

"Go along, Moreno," he said to it; "return to the rancho. I shall not want you again tonight."

The horse turned its fine intelligent head to its master, gave a neigh of pleasure, and started at a gallop in the direction of the rancho. The tigrero carefully examined his gun, the priming of which he renewed, and began inspecting the ground by the light of a torch. Bigote, gravely seated on its hind legs, followed its master's every movement, and was evidently much perplexed. After a very lengthened search, the tigrero probably found what he was looking for, for he rose with an air of satisfaction, and whistled his dog, which at once ran up.

"Bigote," he said, "smell these marks; they were made by the horse of your mistress, Marianna; do you recognise them?"

The noble animal did as its master ordered, then fixed its sparkling eyes upon him with an almost human expression, and wagged its tail with delight.

"Good, Bigote! Good, my famous dog!" the tigrero continued, as he patted it; "And now let us follow the trail; forward, Bigote, pick it up clean."

The dog hesitated for a moment, then it set out with its nose to the ground, closely followed by its master, who had extinguished his torch, which would henceforth be useless. But all we have narrated occupied considerable time; and the tigrero would have arrived too late to save the maiden, had not Heaven sent the hunter across her path. The dog did not once check its speed through the numberless windings of the course Negro had followed; and master and dog together reached the spot where the horrible drama we recently described occurred.

"When I heard Stronghand's shot," the tigrero added, as he concluded his narrative, "I experienced a sound of deadly agony, for I understood that a frightful struggle was going on at the moment, and that the beast might conquer the man. Well, tocaya, will you now believe in the jaguars?"

"Oh, silence, Mariano!" the young lady said, with a shudder; "I almost went mad with terror when I saw the eyes of the horrible animals fixed upon me. Oh! Had it not been for this brave and honest hunter, I should have been lost."

"Brave and honest, indeed!" the tigrero, said, with frank affection; "You are right, señorita, for Stronghand might just as fairly be called Goodheart, for he is ever so ready to assist strangers, and relieve the unfortunate."

Doña Marianna listened with lively pleasure to this praise of the man who had saved her life; but Stronghand felt terribly embarrassed, and suffered in his heart at a deed which he thought so simple, and which he was so delighted to have done, being rated so highly.

"Come, come, Mariano," he said, in order to cut short the young man's compliments, "we cannot remain here any longer; remember that while we are quietly resting by the fireside and talking nonsense, this young lady's father and brother are suffering from deadly anxiety, and scouring the plain without any hope of finding her. We must arrange how to get away from here as soon as possible, and return to the hacienda."

"Caray, master, you are right, as usual; but what is to be done? Both you and I are on foot, and we cannot dream for a moment that the señorita could walk such a distance."

"Oh, I am strong," she said with a smile; "under your escort, my friends, I fear nothing, and can walk."

"No, señorita," the hunter said, with an accent of gentle authority, "your strength would betray your courage; on so dark a night, and in a forest like this, a man accustomed to desert life could hardly expect to walk without falling at every step. Put yourself in our hands, for we know better than you do what is best to be done under the circumstances."

"Very good," she answered; "act as you think proper. I have suffered enough already today, by refusing to listen to the advice of my tocayo, to prevent me being obstinate now."

"That is the way to talk," the tigrero said gaily. "What are we going to do, Stronghand?"

"While you skin the jaguars—for I suppose you do not wish to leave them as they are—"

"What!" the tigrero interrupted him, "Those skins belong to you, and I have no claim to them, as you killed the beasts."

"Pooh!" the hunter said with a laugh, "I am not a tigrero, except by accident; the skins are yours, and fairly so; so you had better take them."

"Since that is the case I will not decline; but as for my part, I promised to give my foster sister the skins to make a rug, I will beg her to accept them."

"Very good," she answered, giving the hunter a look which filled him with joy; "they will remind me of the fearful danger I incurred, and the way in which I escaped it."

"That is settled, then," the hunter said; "and I will; cut down with my machete some branches to form a litter."

"Caray, that is an idea which would not have occurred to me," Mariano remarked, with a laugh; "but it is very simple. To work."

Hunters and trappers are skilful and most expeditious men; in a few minutes Mariano had skinned the jaguars, and Stronghand formed the litter; the skins, after being carefully folded, were securely fastened on the back of Bigote, who did not at all like the burden imposed on him; but after a while he made up his mind to put up with it. Stronghand covered the litter with leaves and grass, over which he laid the saddlecloth of the horse the jaguars had devoured; then he requested the young lady to seat herself on this soft divan, which was so suddenly improvised, and the two men, taking it on their strong shoulders, started in the direction of the hacienda, joined by Bigote, who trotted in front with glad barks.

Although the hunters had, from excess of precaution, formed torches of ocote wood to help them, the darkness was so complete—the trees were so close together—that it was with extreme difficulty that they succeeded in advancing in this inextricable labyrinth. Forced to take continual *detours*— obliged at times to walk in water up to their waists—deafened by the discordant cries of the birds, which the flash of the torches aroused—they saw all around them the wild beasts flying, with hoarse roars and eyes glaring through the darkness. It was then that Doña Marianna fully comprehended what frightful peril she had escaped, and how certain her death would have been, had not the hunter come to her assistance with such noble self-devotion; and at the remembrance of all that had occurred, and which was now but a dream, a convulsive tremor passed over her limbs, and she felt as if she were about to faint. Stronghand, who seemed to guess what was going on in the maiden's mind, frequently spoke to her, in order to change the current of her ideas by compelling her to answer him. They had been marching for a long distance, and the forest seemed as savage as when they started.

"Do you believe," Doña Marianna asked, "that we are on the right road?"

"Even admitting, señora, what might be possible," the hunter answered, "that Mariano and myself were capable of falling into an error, we have with us an infallible guide in Bigote, who, you may be quite certain, will not lead us astray."

"Within ten minutes, señorita," the tigrero said, "we shall enter the road that runs from the rancho to the hacienda."

All at once the two men stopped. At the same moment Doña Marianna heard shouts that seemed to answer each other in various directions.

"Forward! Forward!" said Stronghand; "Let us not leave your relatives and friends in anxiety longer than we can help."

"Thanks," she answered.

They continued their march; and, as the tigrero had announced, in scarce ten minutes they reached the road to the hacienda.

"What shall we do now?" Marianna asked.

"I think," Stronghand answered, "that we ought to announce our presence by a cry for help, and then proceed in the direction of those who answer us. What is your opinion, señora?"

"Yes," she said, "I think we ought to do so; for otherwise we run a risk of reaching the hacienda without meeting any of the persons sent to seek me, and who might continue their search till morning, which would be ingratitude on my part."

"You are right, niña; for all these worthy people are attached to you, and besides, your brother and Don Paredes are also seeking you."

"That is a further reason why we should hasten to announce our return," the young lady answered.

The two hunters, after consulting for a moment, uttered together that long shrill yell, which, in the desert as in the mountains, serves as the rallying cry, and may be heard for an enormous distance. Almost immediately the whole forest seemed to be aroused; similar cries broke out in all directions, and the hunters noticed red dots running with extreme rapidity between the trees, and all converging on the spot where they stood, as if they radiated from a common centre. Certain of having been heard, the hunters once again uttered their shout for help. The reply was not delayed; the galloping of horses soon became distinct, and then riders, holding torches, appeared from all parts of the forest coming at full speed, waving their hands, and resembling the fantastic huntsmen of the old German legends. In a few minutes all the persons were assembled round the litter on which the young lady reclined; and Don Ruiz and the majordomo were not long ere they arrived. We will not describe the joy of brother and sister on seeing each other again.

"Brother," Doña Marianna said to Don Ruiz, "if you find me still alive, you owe it to the man who before saved us both from the pirates of the prairies; had it not been for him, I should have been lost."

"You may safely say that, and no mistake," Marianna said, in confirmation.

"Where is he?" Don Ruiz asked—"Where is he? that I may express all my gratitude to him."

But he was sought for in vain. During the first moment of confusion, Stronghand had summoned a peon to take his place—had glided unnoticed into the forest and disappeared—no one being able to say in what direction he had gone.

"Why this flight?" Doña Marianna murmured, with a stifled sigh; "Does this strange man fear lest our gratitude should prove too warm?"

And she thoughtfully bowed her head on her bosom.

CHAPTER XXIII
CHANCE WORK

Although he allowed nothing to be visible, Don Ruiz was vexed at heart with the affectation the hunter seemed to display in avoiding him, and escaping from his thanks. This savageness in a man to whom he owed such serious obligations appeared to him to conceal either a disguised enmity, or dark schemes whose accomplishment he feared, though he could not assign any plausible motive for them, especially after the manner in which the hunter had not hesitated on two occasions to imperil his life in assisting himself and his sister. These thoughts, which incessantly thronged to the mind of Don Ruiz, plunged him into deep trouble for some moments; still, when the peons he had sent off to seek the hunter all returned one after the other, declaring that they could not possibly find his trail, the young man shook his head several times, frowned, and then gave orders for the start.

Doña Marianna's return to the hacienda was a real triumphal procession. The peons, delighted at having found their mistress again safe and sound, gaily bore her on their shoulders, laughing, singing, and dancing along the road, not knowing how otherwise to express their joy, and yet desirous to make her comprehend the pleasure they felt. In spite of the fatigue that crushed her, and the state of exhaustion into which she had fallen through the terrific emotions she had undergone, Doña Marianna, sensible of these manifestations of gratitude, made energetic efforts in order to appear to share their joy, and prove to them how greatly she was affected by it. But, although she gave them her sweetest smiles and gentlest words, she could not have endured much longer the constraint, and she was really exhausted when the little party at length reached the hacienda.

The Marquis, who was suffering the most frightful agitation, had gone to the last gate to meet them, and would possibly have gone further still, had not Don Ruiz taken the precaution, so soon as his sister was found, to send off a peon to tranquillize his mind and announce the successful result. At the first moment the Marquis completely forgot his aristocratic pride, only to think of the happiness of pressing to his heart the child he feared he had lost for ever. Don Rufino Contreras, carried away by the example, shared in the general joy, and pretended to pump up a tear of sympathy while fixing on the young lady his huge grey eyes, to which he tried in vain to give a tender expression.

The maiden threw herself with an outburst of tears into her father's arms, and at length, yielding to her feelings, fainted—an accident which, by arousing the anxiety of the spectators, cut short all the demonstrations. Doña Marianna was conveyed to her apartments, and the peons were dismissed after the majordomo had, by the order of the Marquis, distributed among them *pesetas* and tragos of refino, which set the crown of the delight of these worthy fellows.

In spite of the offer of No Paredes, who invited him to spend the night at the hacienda, the tigrero would not consent; and after freeing Bigote from the jaguars' skins, which seemed to cause the dog considerable pleasure, they both started gaily for the rancho. It was about two o'clock, a.m., and a splendid night, and the tigrero, with his gun under his arm and his dog at his heels, was walking at a steady pace while whistling a merry jarana, when, just as he was entering the shadow of the forest, Stronghand suddenly emerged from a thicket two paces ahead of him.

"Hilloh!" the tigrero said, on recognising him; "Where the deuce did you get to just now, that it was impossible to find you? What bee was buzzing in your bonnet?"

The hunter shrugged his shoulders.

"Do you fancy," he replied, "that it is so very pleasant to be stared at by those semi-idiotic peons for performing so simple a deed as mine was?"

"Well, opinions are free, compadre, and I will not argue with you on that score; still, I should not have run off in that way."

"¿Quién sabe? You are more modest than you like to show, brother; and I feel certain that, under similar circumstances, you would have acted as I did."

"That is possible, though I do not believe it; still, I thank you," he added, with a laugh, "for having discovered in me a quality which I was not aware I possessed. But where on earth are you going at such an hour?"

"I was looking for you."

"In that case all is for the best, since you have found me; what do you want of me?"

"To ask hospitality of you for a few days."

"Our house is not large, but sufficiently so to contain a guest, especially when you are he; you can remain with us so long as you please."

"I thank you, gossip, but I shall not abuse your complaisance; I am obliged to remain for a few days in these parts, and, as the nights are fresh, I will confess that I prefer passing them under a roof instead of the star spangled arch of heaven."

"As you please, Stronghand; the door of my humble rancho is ever open to let you in or out. I do not want to know the reason for your stay here; but the longer you remain with us, the greater honour and pleasure you will afford us."

"Thanks, comrade."

All was settled in a few words. The two men continued their walk, and soon reached the rancho. The tigrero led the hunter to his bedroom, where they lay down side by side, and soon fell asleep. A few days elapsed, during which the hunter saw Doña Marianna several times, while careful not to let her notice him, although it was evident to Stronghand that the young lady would have liked nothing better than meeting him; perhaps she really desired it, without daring to confess it to herself.

One day, about a week after the scene with the jaguars, the hunter was lying half asleep in a copse whose leafy branches completely hid him from sight, and quietly enjoying his siesta during the great midday heat, when he fancied he heard the sound of footsteps not far from the spot where he was. He instinctively opened his eyes, raised himself on his elbow, and looked carefully around him; he checked a cry of surprise on recognising the man, who had stopped close to the thicket and dismounted, like a man who has reached the spot he desired. This man was Kidd, the bandit, with whom the reader has already formed acquaintance.

"What does that scoundrel want here?" the hunter asked himself. "He is doubtless plotting some infamy, and I bless the chance that brings him within earshot, for this demon is one of the men who cannot be watched too closely."

In the meanwhile Kidd had removed his horse's bit, in order to let it graze freely; he himself sat down on a rock, lit a husk cigarette, and began smoking with all the *nonchalance* of a man whose conscience is perfectly at its ease. Stronghand racked his brains in vain to try and discover the motive for the presence of the bandit in these parts, so remote from the ordinary scene of his villainy, when chance, which had already favoured him, gave him the clue to the enigma, which he had almost despaired of obtaining. A sound made him turn his head, and he saw a stout horseman, with rubicund face and handsomely dressed, coming up at an amble. When he reached the adventurer, the latter rose, bowed respectfully, and assisted him to dismount.

"Ouf!" the stout man said, with a sigh of relief, "What a confounded ride!"

"Well," the bandit replied with a grin, "you must blame yourself, Don Rufino, for you arranged it. May the fiend twist my neck if I would damage myself, no matter for what purpose, and ride across the plain at this hour of the day."

"Everybody is the best judge of his own business, Master Kidd," Don Rufino remarked, drily, as he wiped his steaming face, with a fine cambric handkerchief.

"That is possible; but if I had the honour to be Don Rufino Contreras, enormously rich, and senator to boot, hang me if I would put myself out of my way to run after an adventurer like Master Kidd, whatever pleasure I might take at other times in the conversation of that worthy caballero."

The senator began laughing.

"Ha! Ha! Scoundrel; you have scented something."

"Hang it!" the bandit replied, impudently, "I do not deceive myself, and am well aware that whatever attractions my conversation may offer, you would not have come this distance expressly to hear it."

"That is possible, scamp. However, listen to me."

"I can see from your familiarity that the job will be an expensive one; well, I do not dislike that way of entering upon the subject, for it forebodes a good business."

The senator shrugged his shoulders with ill-disguised contempt. "Enough of this," he said, "let us come to facts."

"I ask nothing better."

"Are you fond of money?"

"I certainly have a weakness for gold."

"Good. Would you hesitate about killing a man to earn it?"

"What do you mean?"

"I ask you, scoundrel, whether in a case of necessity you would kill a man for money?"

"I perfectly understood you."

"Then why make me repeat it?"

"Because your doubt is offensive to my feelings."

"How so?"

"Hang it, I fancy I speak clearly. Killing a man is nothing when you are well paid for it."

"I will pay well."

"Beforehand?"

"Yes, if you like."

"How much?"

"I warn you that the man I refer to is but a poor fellow."

"Yes, a poor fellow who is troublesome to you. Well, go on."

"One thousand piastres. Is that enough?"

"It is not too much."

"Confound it, you are expensive."

"That is possible; but I do my work conscientiously. Well, tell me who the man is that is in your way."

"José Paredes."

"The majordomo at the Toro?"

"Yes."

"Do you know that he is not an easy man to kill? You must owe him a sore grudge, I suppose?"

"I do not know him."

The bandit looked in amazement at the speaker.

"You do not know him, and yet offer one thousand piastres for his death? Nonsense!"

"It is so."

"But you must have a reason. Caray, a man is not killed as one twists a fowl's neck. I know that, bandit though I am."

"You said it just now. He is in my way."

"That is different," the adventurer replied, convinced by this peremptory reason.

"Listen to me attentively, and engrave my words on your mind."

"Go on, señor. I will not lose a word."

"In two or three days the majordomo will leave for Hermosillo, carrying bills to a considerable amount."

"Good," the bandit said, rubbing his hands gleefully; "I will kill him as he passes, and take possession of the bills."

"No, you will let him go on in peace, and you will kill him on his return, when he has cashed the bills."

"That is true. Where the deuce was my head? That will be much better."

Don Rufino looked at him ironically.

"You will deliver to me the sum this man is the bearer of," he said.

The bandit gave a start of alarm,

"I suppose the sum is large?"

"Fifty thousand piastres."

"¡Viva Dios! Surrender such a fortune? I would sooner be burned alive."

"You must, though,"

"Never, señor."

"Nonsense," the senator remarked, contemptuously. "You know you are in my hands. All the worse for you if you hesitate, for you will then lose two thousand piastres."

"You said one thousand."

"I made a mistake."

"And when will you give them to me?"

"At once."

"Have you the amount about you?"

"Yes."

Suddenly the bandit's eye gleamed with a sinister flash; he drew himself up, and leaped, knife in hand, upon the senator. But the adventurer had a powerful adversary. Don Rufino had long known the man he was treating with, and, while conversing, had not once taken his eye off, and attentively watched all his movements. Hence, though Kidd's action was so rapid, Don Rufino was before him; he seized his arm with his left hand, while with the right he placed a pistol to his chest.

"Hilloh, my master," he said, coldly, and with the most perfect tranquillity, "are you mad, or has a wasp stung you?"

Abashed by his failure, the bandit gave him a savage look.

"Let me loose!"

"Not before you have thrown your knife away, scoundrel!"

Kidd opened his hand, the knife fell on the ground, and Don Rufino put his foot upon it.

"You are not half clever enough," he said, sarcastically; "you deserve to have your brains blown out, in order to teach you to take your measures better another time."

"I do not always miss my mark," he replied, with a menacing accent.

There was a moment of silence between the two men. Stronghand still watched them, not losing one of their words or gestures, which interested him to the highest degree. At length Don Rufino spoke.

"Have you reflected?" he asked the bandit.

"Of what?" the latter remarked, roughly; "Of this proposal?"

"Yes."

"Well, I accept."

"But you understand," the senator continued, laying a stress upon every word, "you must deal frankly this time. No trickery, eh?"

"No, no," Kidd answered, with a shake of the head; "you may be sure of that."

"I reckon on your honesty. Moreover, profit by what has occurred today. I am not always so good tempered; and if a misunderstanding, like that just now, again arose between us, the consequences might be very serious to you."

These few words were uttered with an intonation of voice, and accompanied by a look, that produced a profound impression on the bandit.

"All right," he said, shrugging his shoulders savagely; "there is no need to threaten, as all is settled."

"Very good."

"Where shall I come to you after the business?"

"Do not trouble yourself about that. I shall manage to find you."

"Ah!" he said, with a side-glance; "then that is your affair?"

"Yes."

"Very good. Give me the money."

"Here it is. But remember, if you deceive me—"

"Nonsense," the bandit interrupted him. "Did I not tell you that it was all settled?"

The senator drew from his pocket a long purse, through whose meshes gold coins could be seen. He weighed it for an instant in his hand, and then threw it twenty paces from him.

"Go and fetch it," he said.

The bandit dashed at the gold, which as it fell produced a ringing sound. Don Rufino took advantage of this movement to get into his saddle.

"Good-bye," he said to the bandit. "Remember!" and he started at a gallop. Kidd made no reply, for he was too busy counting the ounces contained in the purse.

"All right," he at last said, with a smile upon his features, as he hid the purse in his bosom. "No matter," he added, as he looked savagely after the senator, "I allow that I am in your power, demon; but if I ever had you in my hands as you had me today, and I manage to discover one of your secrets, I should not be so mad as to show you any mercy."

After this soliloquy the bandit went up to his horse, tightened the girths, and set out in his turn, but in a direction opposite to that which the senator had taken. So soon as he was alone, the hunter rose.

"Oh, oh!" he muttered, "That is a dark plot. That man cannot want to kill Paredes merely to rob him; it is plain that the blow is meant for the Marquis. I will be on my guard."

We have already seen that the hunter religiously kept his promise.

CHAPTER XXIV
FATHER AND SON

Now that we have given the reader all necessary information about the events accomplished at the Hacienda del Toro, we will resume our narrative at the point where we were compelled to leave it—that is to say, we will return to the village of the Papazos, and be present at the conversation between Thunderbolt and Stronghand in the Pyramid. The two men, walking side by side, went up to the top of the Pyramid. They traversed the bridge of lianas thrown over the Quebrada at a great height, and entered the Pyramid on the right. They descended to the first floor—the Indians they met bowing respectfully to them—and stopped before a securely fastened door. On reaching it, Thunderbolt gave it two slight taps; an inner bolt was drawn, the door opened, and they went in. They had scarce crossed the threshold ere the young Indian who had opened the door closed it again after them. A strange change had taken place in the two men; the Indian stoicism they had hitherto affected made way for manners that revealed men used to frequent the highest society of cities.

"Maria," Thunderbolt said to the girl, "inform your mistress that her son has returned to the village." In giving this order the old gentleman employed Spanish, and not the Comanche idiom which he had used up to the present.

"The señora was already aware of her son's return, *mi amo*," Maria answered, with a smile.

"Ah!" said the old man, "then she has seen somebody."

"The venerable Padre Fray Serapio came an hour ago to pay the señora a visit, and he is still with her."

"Very good; announce us, my child."

The girl bowed and disappeared, returning a moment after to tell the two gentlemen that they could enter. They were then introduced into a rather spacious room, lighted by four glazed windows—an extraordinary luxury in such a place—in front of which hung heavy red damask curtains. This room, entirely lined with stamped Cordovan leather, was furnished in the Spanish style, with that good taste which only the Castilians of the old race have kept, and was, through its arrangement, half drawing room, half oratory. In one corner an ebony *prie-dieu*, surmounted by an ivory crucifix, which time had turned yellow, and several pictures of saints, signed by Murillo and Zurbaran, would have caused the apartment to be taken for an oratory, had not comfortable sofas, tables loaded with books, and butacas, proved it to be a drawing room. Near a silver brasero two persons were sitting in butacas.

Of these, one was a lady, the other a Franciscan monk; both had passed midlife, or, to speak more correctly, were close on fifty years of age.

The lady wore the Spanish garb fashionable in her youth—that is to say, some thirty years before. Although her hair was beginning to grow white, and a few deep wrinkles altered the purity of her features, still it was easy to see that she must have been very lovely once on a time. Her skin, of a slightly olive hue, was extremely fine, and in the firm marked lines of her face, the distinctive character of the purest Aztec race could be recognised. Her black eyes, shaded by long lashes, and whose corners rose slightly, like those of the Mongolians, had an expression of strange gentleness, and her whole face revealed mildness and intelligence. Although she was below the ordinary height of women, she still retained the elegance of youth; and her exquisitely modelled hands and feet were almost of a microscopic smallness. Fray Serapio was the true type of the Spanish monk—handsome, majestic, and dreamy—and seemed as if he had stepped out of a picture by Zurbaran. When the two gentlemen entered, the lady and the Padre rose.

"You are welcome, my darling child," the old lady said, opening her arms to her son.

The latter rushed into them, and for some minutes there was an uninterrupted series of caresses between mother and son.

"Forgive me, Padre Serapio," Stronghand at length said, as he freed himself from the gentle bondage; "but it is so long since I had the pleasure of embracing my mother, that I cannot leave off."

"Embrace your mother, my child," the monk answered, with a smile; "a mother's caresses are the only ones that do not entail regret."

"What are you about, Padre?" Thunderbolt asked; "Are you going to leave us already?"

"Yes; and pray excuse me for going away so soon; but after a lengthened separation, you must have much to say to one another, and a third person, however friendly he may be, is always in the way at such a time. Moreover, my brothers and I have a good deal to do at present, owing to so many white hunters and trappers being in the village."

"Are you satisfied with your neophytes?"

The monk shook his head mournfully.

"No," he at length answered; "the Indians love and respect us, owing to the protection you have deigned to afford us, Señor Don—"

"Silence!" the chief interrupted him, with a smile; "no other name but that of Thunderbolt."

"That is true; I always forget that you have surrendered the one received at your baptism; still it is one of the most noble in the martyrology. Well," he continued with a sigh, "the will of Heaven be done! The glorious days of conversion have passed since we have become Mexicans; the Indians no longer believe in the Spanish good faith, and sooner than accept our God, persist in their old errors. This makes me remember that I have a favour to ask of you."

"Of me? Oh, it is granted beforehand, if it be in my power to satisfy you."

"Doña Esperanza, with whom I have spoken about it, leads me to hope that you will not refuse it."

"Did you not say to me one day that the señora's name brought you good luck? It will probably be the same today."

The monk took a furtive glance at the old lady.

"This is the matter, my dear," she said, mingling in the conversation; "the good father wishes your authority to follow, with another monk, the warriors during the coming expedition."

"That is a singular idea, father; and what may your object be? For I presume you do not intend to fight in our ranks."

"No," the monk answered with a smile, "my tastes are not warlike enough for that; but if I may judge from the preparations I see you making, this will be a serious expedition."

"It will," the old man answered, pensively.

"I have noticed that generally, during these expeditions, the wounded are left without assistance. I should like to accompany the Indians, in order to attend to their wounds, and console those whose hurts are so serious that they cannot recover; still, if the request appear to you exorbitant, I will recall it, though I shall do so reluctantly."

The old gentleman gazed at the monk for a moment with an expression of admiration and tenderness impossible to describe.

"I grant your request, Padre," he at length said, affectionately pressing his hand. "Still, I am bound to make one remark."

"What is it?"

"You run a risk of falling into the hands of the Mexicans."

"Well, what matter? Can they regard it as a crime if I perform on the battlefield the duties which my religion imposes on me?"

"Who knows? Perhaps they will regard you as a rebel."

"And in that case—"

"Treat you as such."

"That is to say—"

"You will run a risk, father, of being shot; and that is worth thinking about, I suppose."

"You are mistaken, my friend; between duty and cowardice no hesitation is possible. I will die, if it be necessary—but with the conviction that I have fulfilled to the close the sacred mission I have undertaken. Then you grant my request?"

"I do so, father, and thank you for having made it."

"Blessings on your kindness, my son; and now the Lord be with you. I shall retire."

In spite of much pressing, the worthy father insisted on going away, and was conducted to the door of the apartment by the two gentlemen, in spite of his efforts to escape a mark of honour of which he considered himself unworthy. When the door closed after him, and the three persons were really alone, Doña Esperanza, after a long look at her son, gently drew him towards her, and obliging him to sit down on an equipal, she lovingly parted off his forehead his clustering locks, and said in a sweet, harmonious voice, in which all the jealous tenderness of a mother was revealed—

"I find you sad, Diego; your face is pale, your features are worn, and your eyes sparkle with a gloomy fire. What has happened to you during your absence?"

"Nothing extraordinary, mother," he answered, with an embarrassment he tried in vain to conceal. "As usual, I have hunted a great deal, travelled a long distance, and consequently, endured great fatigue; hence, doubtless, comes the pallor you notice upon my face."

The old lady shook her head with an incredulous air.

"A mother cannot be deceived, my boy," she said, gently. "Since you have been a man I have seen you return only too often, alas, from long and perilous expeditions. You were fatigued—at times ill, but that was all; while today you are gloomy, restless—"

"Mother!"

"Do not argue, for my mind is made up, and nothing will alter it. If you refuse me your confidence, Heaven grant that you may select a confidant who understands you so thoroughly."

"Oh, mother! This is the first time a reproach has passed your lips."

"Because, Diego, this is the first time you have refused to let me read your heart."

The young man sighed and hung his head, without replying. Thunderbolt, who had hitherto been a silent spectator of the scene, gave Doña Esperanza a meaning glance, and walked up to her son.

"Diego," he said to him, as he laid his hand on his shoulder, "you forget that you have to give me a report of the mission I entrusted to you."

Stronghand started, and eagerly sprang up.

"That is true, father," he replied; "forgive me. I am ready to furnish you with all the details you desire of what I have been doing during my absence from the village."

"Sit down, my son; your mother and I give you permission."

The young man took a chair, and after reflecting for a few seconds, at a further remark from his father, he commenced the recital of all he had been doing while away. The narrative was long, and lasted nearly two hours; but we will not relate it, because the reader is acquainted with most of the facts the young man stated. Thunderbolt and Doña Esperanza listened without interruption, and gave unequivocal signs of the liveliest interest. When he had concluded his story, his mother fondly embraced him, while congratulating him on his noble and generous conduct. But Thunderbolt regarded the matter from another point of view.

"Then," he asked his son, "the man who arrived with you is the majordomo of this Don Hernando de Moguer?"

"Yes, father."

"Though I am an Indian by adoption, I will not forget that Spanish blood flows in my veins. You will pay this Paredes, as you call him, the amount of the bills, and I will send them to Hermosillo to be cashed hereafter. You did well in bringing him with you, for an honest man must not fall a victim to a villain. Although this affair does not in any way concern us, I am not sorry to do a service to an old fellow countryman. Let the majordomo leave the village this very night; in order to prevent any accident on the road, you will have him escorted to the hacienda by Whistler and Peccary, and three or four warriors. They will be more than sufficient to frighten any scoundrels that may attempt to stop him; and as, moreover, we are in a direction entirely opposed to that in which the Hermosillo road runs, no one will think of stopping him."

"I can accompany him myself, with your permission, father."

The old gentleman gave him a piercing glance, which compelled him to look down.

"No," he replied; "I want you here."

"As you please, father," he said, with feigned indifference.

And he rose.

"Where are you going?"

"To carry out your orders, father."

"There is no hurry; the day is not very advanced yet, and I want to talk with you; so return to your chair."

The young man obeyed. Thunderbolt reflected for a moment, and then said—

"How do you call this hacienda?"

"El Toro."

"Let me see," the old man continued, as if striving to remember; "it is not built on the exact site of the ancient Cosala?"

"So people say, father."

Doña Esperanza listened to this conversation with considerable anxiety. In vain did she try to discover her husband's meaning, and ask herself why he thus obstinately brought the conversation back to so hazardous a subject.

"Is it not a strong place?" the sachem continued.

"Yes, father; substantially built, and crowned with almenas."

"In truth, I now remember having seen it formerly! It is an excellent strategical position."

Doña Esperanza looked at her husband with amazement blended with alarm; she could neither account for his coldness nor his persistence. He continued—

"Have you ever entered this hacienda."

"Never, father."

"That is vexatious; still, I presume you are acquainted with some of its inhabitants. A man cannot save," he added, ironically, "the life of such a man as this Don Hernando de Moguer must be, without his trying to testify his gratitude to the man who did him the service."

"I know not whether that is Don Hernando's idea, for I never had the honour of seeing him."

"That is strange, Don Diego; and I cannot understand why you did not try to form his acquaintance; however, that is of little consequence, as far as my plans are concerned."

"Your plans, father?" the young man asked, in amazement.

"I will explain to you that we intend to commence the expedition with a thunder stroke; our first attempt will be to seize the Real de Minas of Quitovar, where the main body of the Mexican forces is now collected. The Hacienda del Toro, situated scarce ten leagues from Arispe, commanding the three roads to Hermosillo, Ures, and Sonora, and built at a very strong position, is of immense importance to us for the success of the war. I had thought of appointing you to carry it by surprise, but as you have no friends in the place, and seem not to care greatly about it, let us say no more on the subject. I will give the command of the expedition to Whistler and Peccary; they are two experienced chiefs, endowed with far from common tact, and will carry the hacienda by a surprise, because the Spaniards, not anticipating such an attack, will not be on their guard. As for you, my son, you will follow me to the Real de Minas. And now, my dear Diego, I have nothing more to say to you, and you can withdraw."

The young man had listened in secret horror to this revelation of his father's plans. He was so full of terror that he did not notice that Thunderbolt, though he pretended at the beginning not to know the hacienda even by name, had described its position with a precision that showed that, on the contrary, he must be perfectly acquainted with it. He stood for a moment crushed by the thought of the terrible danger Doña Marianna would incur if the Apaches took the hacienda. His father took a side-glance at him, and attentively watched the various feelings reflected in his face.

"Forgive me, father," the young man at length said, with an effort; "but I should like to offer an objection."

"What is it, my son? Speak, I am listening."

"I do not think it would be prudent to try and surprise, with a band of savages, a house so far advanced in the interior of the country."

"That is why I selected you. You would have taken a band of white and half-breed trappers and hunters, and would have passed unnoticed, owing to the colour of your skins. Your refusal greatly annoys me, I confess; but, as I do not wish to force your inclinations—"

"But I did not refuse, father," the young man exclaimed.

"What! You did not refuse?"

"No, father; on the contrary, I ardently wish to be entrusted with this confidential mission."

"In that case, I misinterpreted your silence and ambiguous remarks. Then you accept?"

"Gladly, father."

"Very good; that is settled. Now go and send off that Paredes, for it is time for him to return to his master. As for you, my son, breathe not a syllable of what we have discussed; you understand the importance of discretion under such circumstances. Embrace your mother, and leave us."

The young man threw himself into his mother's arms, who tenderly embraced him, and whispered in his ear, "Hope!"

Then he withdrew, after bowing respectfully to his father.

"Well, Esperanza," the old gentleman said, rubbing his hands, so soon as his son had left the room, "do you now begin to guess my plans?"

"No," she answered with a gentle smile; "but I believe that I understand them."

CHAPTER XXV
THE HATCHET

Stronghand quitted the Pyramid in a state of indescribable agitation. The word his mother had whispered in his ear at parting incessantly recurred to his mind, and led him to suppose that Doña Esperanza, with that miraculous intuition Heaven has given to mothers, that they may discover the most hidden feelings of their children, had divined the secret he fancied he had buried in the remotest corner of his heart, and which he did not dare avow to himself. On the other hand, the strange conversation he had held with his father, and the proposal which concluded it, plunged him into extraordinary perplexity. His father's conduct appeared to him extraordinary, in the sense that he did not understand how the old gentleman, who justly enjoyed among the Indians a reputation for stainless honour, could be preparing treacherously to attack the man to whose succour he came at the same moment with such noble disinterestedness. All this seemed to him illogical, incomprehensible, and in direct opposition with the word "hope," which he fancied he could still hear buzzing in his ear. Still, as he was obliged to cross the torrent, and go some distance before reaching his calli, he had time to restore some degree of order in his ideas, and resume his coolness and self-mastery before he reached his own door. Two men were standing there—Whistler and Peccary.

"Come along, Stronghand," the trapper shouted, so soon as he saw him; "we have been waiting for you a long while."

"Waiting for me?" he asked, in surprise.

"Yes. Sparrowhawk warned us, on the part of Thunderbolt, that the chief and myself were to hold ourselves in readiness to escort the man who entered the village with you wherever he thinks proper to go."

"Ah! Whistler has spoken well," Peccary remarked, laconically.

"What else has happened?"

"Nothing, except that Thunderbolt has made this man a present of a mule, laden with rich wares, as Sparrowhawk says. But go on, and he will tell you about it himself."

Stronghand entered, and found the majordomo busily engaged in making his preparations for a start. So soon as he saw the hunter, Paredes eagerly walked up to him, and shook his hand several times.

"You are welcome, comrade," he said. "¡Caray! you are a man of your word, so forgive me."

"Forgive you for what?" the young man asked, with a smile.

"For having doubted you, caramba."

"Doubted me?"

"Yes, on my word. When I saw you leave me this morning in this hole, like a useless or noxious animal, I doubted your sincerity. In a word, as you know, anger is an evil counsellor; still, all sorts of stupid thoughts occurred to me, and I was on the point of running away."

"You would have done wrong."

"Caray! I see it now; hence I feel quite confused at my folly, and beg you once again to forgive me."

"Nonsense," the hunter said, with a laugh, "it is not worth while to torment yourself about such a trifle. An escort of resolute men will accompany you to the hacienda, and as in all probability your master, on seeing that you have brought the money he sent you to fetch, will not ask about what may have happened to you on your journey, I think it unnecessary for you to give him details which would interest him but very slightly, and give rise to unpleasant comments."

"That's enough," the majordomo said, with a knowing smile; "I will not breathe a syllable."

"That will be the best."

"Be easy. Ah! that reminds me that, as I have received the money from you, you must have the bills. Here they are, and once again I thank you."

The hunter took the bills and concealed them in his bosom. There was a moment of silence. The majordomo walked about the calli with an air of embarrassment, though his purpose was now finished, and the hunter comprehended that he had something to say, but did not know how to begin it.

"Come," he asked him, "what else is there that troubles you, my friend? Let me hear."

"On my faith," the Mexican replied, at length forming a resolution. "I confess that I should be delighted to prove my gratitude to you for the service you have done me, and I should not like to leave without doing so; but, unluckily, it embarrasses me more than I can express."

"What, is that all?" the hunter said, gaily. "Why that is a very easy matter."

"Is it?" he remarked, with surprise. "Well, you will not believe that I have been racking my brains over it for more than half an hour, and brought nothing out."

"Because you seek badly, my friend; that is all."

"Then you have found it?"

"You shall see."

"¡Caray! You cannot imagine what pleasure you will cause me."

"You know that I frequently hunt in your parts?"

"Yes; I am aware of that."

"Well, the first time I find myself near the hacienda, I will come and ask hospitality of you."

"Ah! That is what I call a good idea; and even if you brought ten comrades with you, you would see how I should receive you. I only say this much,—I am in a position to treat you well."

"I take you at your word; so that is settled."

"You pledge me your word?"

"I do."

"Very good. Now I shall start happy. Come by day or night, as you may think proper, and you will always be welcome."

"I fancy it would be rather difficult to get into the hacienda by night."

"Not at all. You will only have to mention my name."

"Well, that is settled; and now be off. Only four hours of daylight remain, so do not delay any longer."

"You are right; so good-bye. Do not be long ere you remind me of my promise."

"I will bear you in mind."

They left the calli. Seven or eight hunters and Indians were mounted, and awaiting at the door their guest's good pleasure to start. The majordomo shook the hunter's hand for the last time, mounted his horse, gave the signal for departure, and the little band started at a gallop through a crowd of women and children that had collected through curiosity. Stronghand looked after them as long as he could see them, and then thoughtfully returned to the calli. For a very long time he remained plunged in earnest thought, then he stamped his foot passionately, and exclaimed, in Spanish—"No; a thousand times no. I will not take advantage of the man's kindness to abuse his confidence like a coward. It would be a disgraceful deed."

These words doubtless contained the result of the hunter's reflections, and were the expression of the resolutions he had just formed.

Several days elapsed, and nothing of an interesting nature occurred in the village. The military committee sat several hours during the interval. The plan of the coming campaign was definitively arranged and the collection of the Indian forces was the only thing that delayed the outbreak of hostilities. Whistler returned to the village four days after his departure, and reported to the hunter that Paredes reached the hacienda without any accident, and nothing had disturbed the tranquillity of the journey.

In the meanwhile, the different Indian tribes forming the great confederation of the Papazos began flocking into the village. Ere long there were no quarters left for them, and they were compelled to camp on the plain, which, however, was no hardship to men accustomed to brave all weather. On the twelfth day after Paredes' departure, the hachesto convened all the chiefs to a general meeting at sunset, in order to perform the mystic rites of the great medicine before opening the campaign. At the moment when the sun disappeared below the horizon in clouds of purple vapour, the amantzin, or first sorcerer of the nation, mounted the roof of the medicine hut, and by a sign commanded silence.

"The sun has withdrawn its vivifying heat from us," he said in a powerful voice, "the earth is covered with darkness, and this is the mystic hour when man must prepare for the struggle with the genius of evil—begin the great medicine."

At the same instant, animals of every description appeared from all the lodges, from the corners of the streets, gliding down the ladders of the pyramids, or coming from the plain; quadrupeds, birds, and reptiles collected in the village square, with horrible cries, overflowed the streets on all sides, and spread out over the country for a league round. These animals were Indian chiefs, clothed in the skins of the beasts they wished to represent. Not only do the Indians imitate with rare perfection the different cries of animals, but they have also made a special study of their manners, habits, mode of progression, and even of the way in which they eat and sleep. Nothing can furnish an idea of the horrible concert composed of these cries—hisses, snapping, and roars, mingled with the furious barking of the dogs. There was something savage and primitive that powerfully affected the imagination. At intervals silence was suddenly re-established, and the sorcerer's voice rose alone in the night.

"Is the evil principle conquered?" he asked; "Have my brothers trampled it under foot?"

The animals responded by horrible yells, and the noise began again worse than before. This lasted the whole night through. A few minutes before sunrise the sorcerer repeated the question for the last time, which had received no other answer but furious yells. This time the pure and melodious voice of a young girl rose in the silence, and pronounced these words:—"The Master of Life has pity on his red children; he sends the sun to their help. The evil principle is conquered."

At the same instant the sun appeared in its radiance. The Indians saluted it with a cry of joy, and throwing off their disguises, they fell on their knees, with faces turned up to heaven. The sorcerer, holding in his right hand a calabash full of water, in which was a sprig of wormwood, sprinkled a few drops to each of the cardinal points, crying with an inspired air—"Hail, O sun! Visible minister of the invisible Master of Life! Listen to the prayers of thy red sons. Their cause is just; give them the scalps of their enemies, that they may attach them to their waist belts. Hail, O sun! All hail!"

All the Indians repeated in chorus—

"Hail, O Sun! All hail!"

Then they rose to their feet. The first part of the mysteries of the great medicine was accomplished, and the sorcerer retired. The hachesto, or public crier took his place, and invited the principal chiefs of the confederation to dig up the war hatchet. This characteristic ceremony consists in going in procession into the medicine lodge, where the oldest chief digs up the ground with his scalping knife at a spot the sorcerer indicates, and draws out the great war hatchet, the emblem of the strife about to commence. When the hatchet is unburied, the chiefs quit the hut in the same way as they entered it. At their head marches, with the chief entrusted with the sacred token of the nation, and the brave of the great calumet, the chief who has dug up the hatchet, which he holds with both hands to his breast, with the edge turned outwards. On leaving the lodge, chiefs silently draw up in front of the ark of the first man, opposite the war post, and chance decides which chief shall have the honour of dealing the first blow on the emblematic post with the sacred hatchet.

The Indians, like all primitive peoples, are extremely superstitious; hence they attach an immense importance to this ceremony, because they fancy they can draw a good omen from the way in which the blow has been dealt, and the depth of the notch made by the edge of the blade. Lots were drawn, and chance selected Stronghand. A flattering murmur greeted this name, which was loved by the Indians, and belonged to a man whom they regarded as one of their greatest heroes. Stronghand quitted the ranks, walked into the open space in front of the ark of the first man, and seizing the hatchet which the chief presented to him, he raised it above his head, whirled it round with extreme dexterity, and then dealt a terrible stroke at the war post. The blow was dealt with such violence, the hatchet penetrated the wood so deeply, that when the sorcerer attempted to withdraw it, according to the usual custom, in spite of all his efforts he could not succeed, and was obliged to give up the attempt.

The warriors uttered a shout of joy, which, spreading along the crowd assembled to witness the ceremony, was soon converted into a hideous clamour. The war would be lucky. The omens were excellent. Never, even by the confession of the oldest sachems, had such a blow been dealt the post. Stronghand was congratulated by the chiefs and warriors, who were delighted at the result he had obtained. When the hatchet was at length removed from the post, the warriors retired to make way for the squaws, and the scalp dance began.

This dance is exclusively performed by women, and in this affair alone the men make way for them. This dance, which is regarded as sacred by the untamed Indian nations, only takes place under grand circumstances—at the beginning of an expedition, or at its close, when it has been successful— that is to say, when the warriors bring back many scalps and horses, and have suffered no loss themselves. The women display an excitement in this dance which speedily degenerates into a frenzy, which fills the minds of the warriors with martial ardour. When this dance was ended, and the squaws had ceased their insensate cries and gestures, the final ceremony was proceeded with. This ceremony, of which we only find vestiges among a few tribes of the Upper Missouri, and the Aucas, or Pampas Indians, seems peculiar to the Papazos. It consists in sacrificing a brood mare, which has not yet foaled, and reading the future in its entrails.

We can easily understand that the sorcerer who undertakes the explanation says what He pleases, and must be believed through the impossibility of contradicting his statements. On this occasion, either because he wished to share in the general joy, or that, through deceiving others, he had succeeded in deceiving himself, and putting faith in his own falsehoods, he announced to the attentive warriors the most splendid and successful results for the coming expedition. These prophecies were greeted as they deserved to be—that is to say, with the greatest favour—

and, according to custom, the body of the mare was given to the sorcerer; and this was, doubtless, the greatest profit he derived from the whole affair.

Then, when all the rites were performed, the order was given for each warrior to prepare his horses, his weapons, and his provisions, for the expedition might set out at any moment. The Papazos chiefs had succeeded in collecting beneath their totems 30,000 warriors, all mounted on excellent horses, and about 4000 armed with guns. It is true that the Indians, though so skilful in the use of the axe, the lance, and the bow, are deplorable marksmen, and have an instinctive dread of firearms, which prevents their taking a proper aim. Still, some of them succeed in attaining a relative skill, and are dangerous in a fight. But the greatest strength of the Indian army consisted of the sixty or eighty white and half-breed hunters, whom the hope of plunder had induced to join them.

Thunderbolt, while retaining the supreme command of the army, appointed three chiefs as generals of division; they were Sparrowhawk, Whistler, and Peccary. Stronghand took the command of twenty-five white hunters, whom he selected among the bravest and most honourable, and was entrusted with a special mission by his father. All being then in readiness to begin the war, the Indians, according to their invariable custom, only awaited a moonless night to invade the territory of their enemies under cover of the darkness.

CHAPTER XXVI
THE WHITE-SKINS

The return of José Paredes to the hacienda caused Don Hernando a lively pleasure. Still, the sum he brought, though considerable, was far from sufficing for the constant outlay in working the mine, and would hardly coyer the demands of the moment. Don Rufino did not in any way show the amazement the sight of the majordomo occasioned him, after the measures he had taken to get rid of him. Still this surprise was converted into anxiety, and ere long into terror, when he reflected on the time that had elapsed since his departure.

In fact, it would take three weeks to proceed from the hacienda to Hermosillo and back, even at a good pace, and yet the majordomo had only been absent for nine days. It was evident to the senator that Paredes had not been to Hermosillo, and yet he brought back the money for the bills! What did all this mean? There was something obscure in the whole affair, which Don Rufino burned to clear up; but, unhappily, that was very difficult, if not impossible.

He was supposed to be ignorant of the motive of the majordomo's journey, and consequently could not interrogate him; and then, again, even had he ventured to do so, Paredes would probably not have answered him, or, if he had done so, it would only have been in mockery; for the worthy majordomo, with the infallible scent which upright and faithful men possess, had detected the wolf in sheep's clothing, and although he had no apparent motive, as he was unaware that the senator was the concoctor of the plot to which he had all but fallen a victim, he felt an instinctive aversion for that person, and displayed a marked affectation in trying to avoid any meeting with him.

In Sonora, as in other countries, it is not easy to meet at a moment's notice persons who will discount large bills to render you a service. The man who had given the money for these must be very rich, and most desirous to assist the Marquis. However much the senator thought of the subject, he could not call to mind any landowner for fifty leagues round capable of acting in such a way. Moreover, the discounter must have been aware of the plot formed against the majordomo, for otherwise he would not have proposed to take the bills. Could Kidd be the traitor? In a moment the senator recognised the absurdity of such a suspicion. It was not probable that the bandit had declined to kill the majordomo; but that he should have allowed him to escape without robbing him was an utterly unlikely circumstance. Moreover, Kidd had everything to fear from the senator, and would not have risked playing him such a malicious trick.

As always happens when a man indulges in probabilities without any settled starting point, and proceeds from one deduction to another, Don Rufino attained such a monstrous conclusion, that he was really terrified by it. Still, throughout all his wanderings, a very logical remark escaped him, which proved that, if he had not discovered the truth, he was not very far from it.

"The Redskins are right," he muttered, "and their proverb is true. In the desert, trees have ears, and leaves have eyes. I remember that my conversation with that pícaro of a Kidd took place near a very close growing thicket; perhaps it contained a traitor. Henceforward I will only discuss business at the top of an entirely unwooded hill; and yet," he added with a sigh, "who knows whether a spy may not be concealed in a prairie-dog hole?"

All these reflections the senator made while walking in extreme agitation up and down the room, when the door opened, and Don Ruiz made his appearance.

"Señor Don Rufino," he said to him, after a mutual exchange of compliments, "will you kindly come to the drawing room? Our majordomo, who, as you may have noticed, has been absent for some days, has brought most important news, which my father would like you to hear."

The senator started imperceptibly, and gave the young man a suspicious glance; but nothing in Don Ruiz's open face caused him to suppose any hidden meaning in his words.

"Is anything extraordinary happening, my dear Don Ruiz?" he asked, in a mellifluous voice.

"I have as yet received but very imperfect information about the grave events that threaten us; but if you will kindly follow me, you will soon learn all."

"Be it so, my dear sir—I am at your service;" and he followed Don Ruiz to the saloon, where Doña Marianna, the Marquis, and José Paredes were already assembled.

"Why, what can be the matter, my dear señor?" the senator asked, as he entered; "I confess that Don Ruiz has startled me."

"You will be more startled when you know the events. But sit down, pray," the Marquis answered, and then said to the majordomo, "you have your information from a good source?"

"I can assert that all I have told you is true, *mi amo*. The Papazos have allied themselves with I know not how many other tribes of ferocious pagans, and we may expect to see them burst upon us at any moment."

"¡Caspita! that is serious," the senator said.

"Much more than you suppose; for the Indians are this time resolved to expel the white men for ever from Sonora, and establish themselves in their place," answered Paredes.

"Oh, oh," Don Rufino said, "they are undertaking a rude task."

"Laugh if you like, but it is so."

"I do not laugh, my worthy friend; still, I do not believe the Indians capable of attempting so mad an enterprise."

"In the first place, I am not your friend, señor," the majordomo said, roughly; "and next, it is probable that when you have seen the Indians at work, your opinions about them will be considerably modified."

The senator pretended not to notice the bitterness contained in this remark, and replied, lightly—"I never saw any wild Redskins, and Heaven preserve me from doing so. Still, I strongly suspect the inhabitants of this country of making them more formidable than they really are."

"You are wrong to have such an opinion, my friend; and if you remain any time with us, will soon have proof of it," the Marquis said.

"Are you going to remain here, exposed to the attacks of the pagans, papa?" Doña Marianna asked with terror.

"We have nothing to fear from the Indians," the Marquis replied. "The rock on which my hacienda is built is too hard for them. They will break their nails before they can pull out a single stone."

"Still, father, we cannot be too prudent," Don Ruiz observed.

"You are right, my son; and as I do not wish your sister to retain even a shadow of anxiety, we will immediately place ourselves in a position of defence, though it is unnecessary. During the grand insurrection of 1827, the Indians did not once attempt to approach El Toro, and I greatly doubt whether they will attack it this time."

"*Mi amo,*" Paredes replied, "believe me, do not neglect any precaution; this insurrection will be terrible."

"Come, come," Don Rufino asked, "tell me, Señor Majordomo, who the person is that informed you so well?"

Paredes gave him a side-glance, and replied, with a shrug of his shoulders—"It is enough that I know it; no matter the name of the man to whom I owe the information. If you fancy that it is a friend who warned me, you will be near the truth."

"Permit me, señor," the senator answered, with a frown, "this is more important than you fancy. You must not thus create an alarm in a family, and then refuse to give proofs in support of your assertions."

"My master knows me, señor; he knows that I am devoted to him, and also that I am incapable of uttering a falsehood."

"I do not doubt, señor, either your honesty or your truthfulness; still, a thing so serious as you announce requires, before being taken into consideration, to be based on evidence with proofs, or a respectable name, in default of anything else."

"Stuff! Stuff! The main point is to be on your guard."

"Yes, when we know whether we really ought to do so. Consequently, in my quality as a magistrate—and I ask the Señor Marquis a million pardons for acting thus in his presence—I command you to reveal to me at once the name of the man who gave you these alarming news."

"Nonsense!" The majordomo said, with a shrug of his shoulders; "What good would it do if I were to tell you the name of an individual you do not know, and whom you never heard mentioned?"

"That is not the question. Be good enough to answer me, if you please."

"It is possible that you may be a magistrate, señor, and I do not care if you are. I recognise no other masters but the Señor Marquis and his children here present; they alone have the right to question me, and them alone I will answer."

The senator bit his lips, and turned to the Marquis.

"Come, Paredes, answer," the latter said. "I really do not at all understand your obstinacy."

"Since you order me to speak, *mi amo,*" the majordomo continued, "you must know that the person who told me of the insurrection of the pagans is a white hunter, called Stronghand."

"Stronghand?" brother and sister exclaimed simultaneously.

"Is not that," the Marquis asked, "the hunter to whom we already are so greatly indebted?"

"Yes, *mi amo*," the majordomo replied, musingly; "and it is probable that he has not yet finished."

Although it was the first time the senator heard the hunter's name mentioned, by a kind of intuition he felt a species of emotion for which he could not account.

"Oh," Doña Marianna cried, eagerly, "we must place entire confidence in Stronghand's statements."

"Certainly we must," Don Ruiz added. "It is plain that he wished to warn us, and put us on our guard."

"But who is this man who inspires you with such profound sympathy?" the senator asked.

"A friend," Doña Marianna replied, warmly, "for whom I shall feel an eternal gratitude."

"And whom we all love," the Marquis added, with emotion.

"Then you accept his bail for Paredes?"

"Yes; and believe me, my friend, that I shall not neglect the advice he gives me."

"Very good, señor; you will therefore permit me to remark that Señor Paredes' obstinacy in not revealing his name must fairly appear to me extraordinary."

"Señor Rufino, Paredes is an old servant who enjoys a very pardonable freedom, and believes that he has acquired the right of being believed on his word. Now," he added, "let us discuss the means to prevent a surprise. Paredes, you will at once mount your horse, and order all the peons and vaqueros to bring the ganado and horses into the hacienda. You, Don Ruiz, will prepare the necessary corrals and cuartos to lodge the men and animals; collect as much forage and provisions as you can, for, in the event of a siege, we must not run the risk of being reduced by famine. How many peons have you under your orders, Paredes?"

"Excellency, we have about eighty able to bear arms, and do active duty, without counting the women, children, and old men, whom we can always turn to some account."

"Oh, oh," the Marquis said, "there are many more than we require; I see that it will be unnecessary to summon our miners from Quitovar."

"The more so," Paredes objected, "because Captain de Niza, whose position is far more exposed than ours will already have enlisted them in his service."

"That is probable," the Marquis answered, as he rose. "Go and carry out my orders without delay."

The majordomo bowed to his master, and went out.

"Will it please you, señor, to grant me a moment's interview?" the senator then said.

"I am at your orders, señor."

"Oh, do not disturb yourselves," the senator said, addressing Don Ruiz and his sister, who had risen to leave the room: "I have nothing secret to say to the Marquis."

The young people sat down again.

"I confess to you that what this man has just said," Don Rufino continued, "has greatly startled me. I never saw any Indian bravos, and have a horrible fear of them. I should therefore wish, Don Hernando, however strange so sudden a request may appear to you, to obtain your permission to leave you so soon as possible."

"Leave me!" the Marquis replied, with amazement, "At this moment?"

"Yes; it seems as if coming events will be very serious. I am not a man of war, nor anything like it, for I am frightened at anything that bears a likeness to a quarrel; but Congress claims my immediate presence at Mexico, were it only to inform the Government of the situation in which this state is, and urge it to assume energetic measures."

"Señor Don Rufino, you are at liberty to act as you please. Still, I fear that the roads are not quite safe, and that you will expose yourself to serious dangers by obstinately insisting on departing."

"I have thought of that; but I fancy that when I have once reached Arispe, which is no great distance from here, I shall have nothing more to fear. Will you allow Don Señor Ruiz to escort me to that town?"

"I can refuse you nothing, señor. My son will accompany you, since you do him the honour of desiring his escort."

"Yes," the senator continued, taking a side-glance at Doña Marianna, who had let her head drop on her chest; "I wish to entrust Don Ruiz with an important letter for you."

"Why write? It would be far more simple to tell me what you wish in a couple of words."

"No! No! That is impossible," Don Rufino answered, with a smile that resembled a grimace; "that would demand too much time: moreover, dear sir, you know better than I do that there are certain things which can only be settled by ambassadors."

"As you please, señor. When do you propose to start?"

"I frankly confess that, in spite of the regret I feel at leaving you, I fancy that the sooner I set out the better."

"It is only ten o'clock," said Don Ruiz, as he rose; "by hurrying a little, we can reach Arispe tonight."

"Famous! That is better. Allow me, Don Hernando, to take leave of you, as well as of your charming daughter, and pray accept my thanks for the noble hospitality I have received in your mansion."

"What! Are you not afraid of travelling in the great heat of the day?"

"I only fear the sight of the Indians, and that fear is enough to make me forget all others. Excuse me, therefore, for leaving you so suddenly, but I feel convinced that I should die of terror if I heard the war cry of those frightful savages echo in my ears."

Don Ruiz had left the room to give the requisite orders, and his sister followed him, after making a silent curtsey to the senator, whose intention she was far from suspecting. The apprehension expressed by Don Rufino was greatly exaggerated, if it was not entirely fictitious; but he instinctively felt that the ground was beginning to burn beneath his feet at the hacienda, and he wanted to get away, not only to guard himself against the perils he foresaw from the ill success of his plot, but also to try and refasten the broken threads of his intrigue, and carry out his plans with the shortest possible delay.

The revolt of the Indians, by interrupting the work, paralyzing commercial transactions, and consequently creating enormous difficulties for the Marquis, admirably assisted the senator in the realization of the plans he had long been forming in the dark. Moreover he desired, during the short ride he was going to take with Don Ruiz, to obtain in the young man a precious ally, who would serve him the better because he would do so without any afterthought, and without seeing Don Rufino's object. He also thought it better to write and detail his intentions to the Marquis in a letter, rather than discuss them with him, for the grand diplomatic reason that the man who writes is the only speaker, must be heard, and consequently does not fear a refutation till he has completely explained his ideas.

After a few moments, Don Ruiz returned to state that the escort had mounted, and that all was ready for a start. Don Rufino repeated his farewells to the Marquis, but the latter would not let him depart before he had drunk, according to the hospitable fashion of the country, the stirrup cup—that is to say, a glass of iced orangeade. Then all three left the room, for in spite of the entreaties and objections of the senator, his host insisted on accompanying him to the patio, and witnessing his departure. Two minutes later, Don Rufino Contreras, accompanied by Don Ruiz, and followed by six confidential peons, well armed and mounted, left the hacienda, and took the direction of Arispe, which they reached at nightfall; after a rather fatiguing journey, it is true, but which, however, was not troubled by any accident of an alarming nature. The only thing the travellers noticed, and which proved to them how thoroughly the news of an approaching invasion of the Indians had spread along the border, was the complete solitude of the country, which resembled a desert.

All the ranchos they passed were deserted; the doors, windows, and furniture had been removed by the inhabitants, and carried off by them in their flight; they had burned or destroyed all they were compelled to leave behind them; their horses and cattle had also disappeared, which gave a look of indescribable melancholy to the numerous plains the little party crossed. The crops had been cut in the green, or burned, in order that the Indians might not profit by them; and thus, ere the wretched country was ravaged by the Redskins, it had already been completely ruined by its inhabitants.

Don Rufino contemplated with stupor the desolate aspect of the country, for he could not at all understand the strange tactics of the inhabitants. When they reached the gates of Arispe, they found them closed, and guarded by powerful detachments of soldiers and cívicos—a species of national militia, paid by the rich inhabitants to repress the devastation of the marauders who swarm on the Indian border. It was only after interminable debates and infinite precautions that the barrier guards at length consented to let the travellers pass. All the streets in Arispe were defended by strong barricades. The town resembled one large camp. The soldiers were bivouacked on all the squares, and sleeping round the bivouac fires, which were lighted as much to keep off the sharp night cold, as to cook their scanty rations.

Don Rufino possessed, on the Plaza Mayor of Arispe, a large and handsome mansion, at which he resided when business summoned him to Arispe. It took him more than an hour to reach it, owing to the numberless turnings he was compelled to take, and the barricades he was forced to scale. The door of the house was open, and a dozen soldiers were quietly bivouacked in the zaguán and patio; but Don Rufino did not at all protest against this arbitrary violation of his domicile; on the contrary, he boasted of his senatorial title, and seemed very pleased with the liberty the soldiers had taken. Don Rufino would not allow Don Ruiz and his peons to seek a shelter anywhere but in his own house; he forced them to accept his hospitality, and they did so without any excessive pressure, for both men and horses were beginning to feel the want of a few hours' rest, after an entire day's journey, made in the stifling heat of the sun.

CHAPTER XXVII
SERIOUS EVENTS

Nothing equals the rapidity with which a new fortune is established, except, perhaps, that with which an old family falls, through the eternal balancing of accident, which elevates some and lowers others, thus producing incessant contrasts, which are one of the claims of existing society, and of the equilibrium that presides over the things of this world. With a few exceptions, the first and last of a race are always two powerful men, created by the struggle, endowed with great and noble qualities, and who are always equal to circumstances. Unfortunately, of these two men, one, sustained by capricious chance and the benign influence of his star, sees all obstacles fall before him, and his rashest combinations succeed. In a word, success frequently crowns his efforts, contrary to his expectations. The other, on the contrary, unconsciously yielding through the law of contrast to the malign influence attaching to his race—having fallen by the fault of his predecessors from an elevated position—compelled to struggle on unequal terms with enemies prejudiced against him, and who render him responsible for the long series of errors of which his ancestors have been solely culpable—sees himself, so to speak, placed without the pale of the common law; his most skilful combinations only succeed, in delaying for a few years an inevitable fall, and frequently render that fall the more startling and certain.

What we say here is applicable to all the degrees of the social stage; not only to royal families, but to the miserable beggar's brood. Each revolution that changes the face of an empire, by bringing up to the surface unknown geniuses, at the same time plunges into an abyss of wretchedness and opprobrium those who for centuries have oppressed entire generations, and have in their time placed themselves on a level with the Deity, by believing everything allowed them.

Time, that impassive leveller, bringing progress in its train, incessantly passes its inexorable square over all that raises its head too high—thus pleasing itself by raising some and humiliating others. It has constituted itself the sole arbiter of human ambitions, and the real representative of that moral equality which would be an Utopia, if the great organic law of the harmony of the universe had not thus proclaimed its astonishing principles.

On the very day when Don Ruiz, after escorting Don Rufino Contreras to Arispe, returned to the hacienda, a courier arrived simultaneously with him. This man, who was mounted on an utterly exhausted steed, had apparently ridden a great distance, and was in an excessive hurry. No sooner had he reached the Toro than he was introduced into the Marquis's study with whom he remained shut up for a long time. Then the courier, on leaving the study, remounted his horse, and set off again without speaking to a soul. The almost fantastic apparition of this man caused the occupiers of the hacienda that instinctive fear which people generally experience from things they cannot account for.

The Marquis, whose face was usually imprinted with an expression of sad and resigned melancholy, had, after this interview, become of a cadaverous pallor; deep wrinkles furrowed his forehead, and his eyes stared wildly. He walked up and down the huerta for a long time in extreme agitation, with his arms crossed on his back, and his head bowed over his chest. At times he stopped, beat his forehead furiously, uttered incoherent words, and then resumed his walk mechanically—obeying an imperious want of locomotion rather than any other motive.—

Doña Marianna, seated at a window of her boudoir, behind a muslin curtain, followed her father's movements, for she felt frightened at his state, and had a foreboding that she would have to share some of the sorrow which had fallen on him. The Marquis at length stopped, looked round him like a man who is waking up, and, after a moment of reflection, returned to his apartments. A few minutes after, a servant came to inform Doña Marianna that her father was awaiting her in the red chamber. In spite of herself, the maiden felt her apprehensions redoubled, but hastened to obey.

This red chamber, into which we have already had opportunity to introduce the reader, and which Don Hernando had not entered since the day when his brother was so inexorably disinherited by their father, was as cold and gloomy as when we saw it. The sole difference was, that time, by tarnishing the lustre of the hangings and tapestry, and blackening the furniture, had imparted to it a tinge of sadness, which made the visitor shudder as soon as he entered. When Doña Marianna reached the red chamber, she found her father already there; he gave her a silent sign to take a seat, and she sank into an armchair in a state of undisguised alarm. A few minutes after Don Ruiz entered, followed by José Paredes. The Marquis then seated himself in the spacious armchair that occupied the centre of the dais; he ordered the majordomo to close the door, and began in a feeble, trembling voice—

"My children, I have summoned you hither because we have to discuss matters of the deepest gravity. I have called to our council Paredes, as an old servant of the family, whose devotions we have known so long, and I trust you will not think that I have exceeded my rights in doing so."

The young people bowed their assent, Paredes placed himself by their side, and the Marquis continued—"My children, our family has for many years been tried by adversity. Hitherto, respecting the happy carelessness of childhood, I have sought to keep within my own breast the annoyances and grief with which I was incessantly crushed; for, after all, of what good would it have proved to lay a portion of the burden on your shoulders? Misfortune advances with gigantic strides; it catches us up one after the other, and it was better to let you enjoy the too short days of your happy youth. I have therefore struggled for all of us, concealing the grief which at times overwhelmed me, restraining my tears, and always offering to you the calm brow and the tranquil appearance of a man, who, if he were not entirely happy, was satisfied with his share of good and evil Heaven had allotted to him. Believe me, my children I should have continued this conduct, and kept to myself all the cares and annoyances of such a life as I lead, had not a sudden, terrible, and irremediably misfortune, which has fallen on me today, forced me, against my will, to impart to you the melancholy, frightful condition we are now in, and acquaint you with the posture of my affairs, which are yours, for I am only entrusted with the fortune which will be yours some day if we succeed in saving it."

The Marquis stopped for a moment, overcome by the emotion which contracted his throat.

"Father," Don Ruiz replied, "you have ever been the best of parents to my sister and myself. Be assured that we have anxiously awaited this confidence, which has been so long delayed in the fear of causing us a temporary sorrow; for we hoped we might be able to assume a portion of the burden, and thus restore you the courage necessary to support the gigantic struggle in which you have engaged with adverse fortune."

"My son," the Marquis said, "I know your heart and your sister's. I am aware of the respectful affection you feel for me; and in the misfortune that is now bursting on me, it is a great satisfaction to have the intimate conviction that my children will heartily combine in supporting and consoling me."

"Be kind enough then, father, to tell us what the matter is, without further delay. The courier with whom you were shut up so long this morning cannot be a stranger to the determination you have formed. Doubtless he was the bearer of evil tidings?"

"Alas! My son," the Marquis answered, "for some years past fortune has been treating our house with incomprehensible severity; everything is leagued against us, and our fortune, which was immense under the Spanish rule, has constantly diminished since the proclamation of Mexican independence. In vain have I tried to contend against the torrent which carried us away; in vain have I forgotten all I owe to my name and rank, and attempted to regain what I had lost by honourable enterprise. All has been of no avail, and my efforts have only served to prove the inutility of my attempts. Still, I had hoped a few days back that I should be able to render fortune more favourable to me. I foresaw a chance of saving some fragments of our old fortunes; but today I have attained the melancholy conviction that I am entirely ruined unless a miracle intervene."

"Oh, things cannot be so bad as that, father!" Doña Marianna exclaimed.

"Yes, my children, we are ruined—reduced to utter misery," the Marquis continued sadly. "We have lost everything; even this hacienda, built by one of our ancestors, which will be speedily sold—perhaps tomorrow—for the benefit of our creditors."

"But how has such a great misfortune occurred?"

"Alas! in the same way as misfortunes always happen when fate has resolved on ruining a man. For a long time past business has been in a state of collapse, owing to the disastrous negligence of the Government; and the news of the fresh revolt of the Indian mansos and bravos has raised the alarm of the merchants to the highest pitch. The panic is general among the bankers and persons whose capital is engaged in mines; several houses at Hermosillo, Ures, Arispe, Sonora, and even Mexico, have already suspended payment, and thus everything has been paralyzed at a single blow. Then, to complicate matters even more, a pronunciamiento has taken place in Mexico, and at this moment we have not only an Indian border war, but the interior of the country is suffering from all the horrors of a civil war."

"Do you know this officially, father?"

"Unfortunately, I cannot entertain the slightest doubt on the subject. For this reason; under such circumstances as the present, one thing inevitably happens. Creditors insist on the immediate repayment of their advances, while persons indebted to you, if they do not fail, defer payment so long that it is practically of no service. Now, the letters I received this morning, and they are numerous, may be divided into two classes; my debtors refuse to pay me, while my creditors, fearing a loss, have taken out writs against me, so that if I have not paid them within eight days the round sum of 380,000 piastres, I shall be declared bankrupt, imprisoned, expelled from my estate, and this hacienda, the last thing left us, will be put up to auction, and probably purchased for a trifle by one of the ex-vassals of our family, who has grown rich at our expense, and does not blush to take our place."

"Three hundred and eighty thousand piastres!" Don Ruiz muttered with stupor.

"That is the amount."

"How can we possibly get it together?"

"It is useless to dream of it for the present, my son. This hacienda alone is worth double. At other times I could have offered a mortgage, and as I have nearly 300,000 piastres owing to me, you see that I could have easily confronted this fresh stroke of fortune. But now it cannot be thought of; it will be better to give way, and allow our creditors to divide the spoil. I hope you do hot suppose, Ruiz, that I have the intention of defrauding my creditors of the little that is left me?"

"Oh no, father; but what do you propose doing?"

"¡Caray!" Paredes then said, "that is easily settled. I possess, through the liberality of the Moguer family a rancho, which owes nothing to anybody. It is yours, *mi amo*. My mother and I can easily find another shelter. Well, if this wretched lodging is not so fine or handsome as this, it will, at any rate, afford you a shelter, and save you from applying for it to strangers. Is it so, Excellency? Will you honour the old house of your servant by your presence?"

The Marquis seemed to reflect for a moment, and then held out his hand to Paredes, who kissed it.

"Be it so, my friend. I accept your offer," he said. "Not that I intend to inconvenience you for any length of time, but merely during the few days I shall require to save, if possible, some fragments of my children's fortune from the general shipwreck."

"Do not think of us, father," Doña Marianna said, with emotion. "We are young, and will work."

Paredes was delighted at the acceptance of his offer.

"Oh, do not be frightened, *mi amo*," he said; "the old rancho is not so dilapidated and miserable as might be supposed. I trust, with the help of Heaven, that you will not be very uncomfortable there, and, at any rate, you will have no cause to fear the visits of certain parties."

"You are unjust, Paredes," the Marquis replied. "Don Rufino Contreras, to whom you allude, is one of my best friends, and I must speak of his behaviour in the highest terms of praise."

"That is possible, *mi amo*, that is possible," the majordomo said, shaking his head with an air of conviction; "but if I may be permitted to express an opinion about that gentleman, I fancy we had better wait a while before fully making up our minds about him."

"What do you mean?"

"Nothing, *mi amo*, really nothing. I have an idea, that is all."

"That reminds me, father, that on leaving me, Don Rufino gave me a letter, which he begged me to deliver to you so soon as I reached the hacienda."

"Yes; he informed me of his intention of writing."

"Hum!" the majordomo said, between his teeth, but loudly enough for the Marquis to hear him; "I always had a bad idea of men who prefer blackening paper to explain themselves frankly in words."

During this aside, the Marquis had opened and read the letter.

"This time, at any rate," he said, "Don Rufino cannot be accused of want of frankness, or of not explaining himself clearly. He warns me of the measures taken against me, and after showing me, in a most gentlemanly manner, the precarious nature of my position, he ends by offering me the means of escaping from it in the most honourable way; in one word, he asks for my daughter's hand, and offers her a dowry of one and a half million piastres, besides liquidating my debts."

Doña Marianna was crushed by the blow so suddenly dealt her. The Marquis continued, with the bitter accent he had hitherto employed—"Such is the state we have reached, my children; we, the descendants of a race of worthies noble as the king, and whose escutcheon is unstained, have so fallen from our lofty social position, that we are too greatly honoured by the offer of a man whose grandfather was our vassal. But such is the way of the world, and why blame it when we live in an age in which everything is possible?"

"What answer will you give to this strange letter, father?" Don Ruiz asked, anxiously.

Don Hernando drew himself up proudly.

"My son," he replied, "however poor I may be, I do not the less remain the Marquis de Moguer, the only thing, perhaps, which cannot be taken from me. I know the obligations I owe to the honour of my name. Your sister is free to accept or reject the offer made her. I do not wish, under any pretext, to influence her determination in so serious a matter. She is young, and has still many years to live; I have no right to enchain her existence with that of a man she does not love. She will reflect, and follow the impulse of her own heart. Whatever her resolution may be, I approve of it beforehand."

"Thanks, father," the maiden answered, gently. "And now grant me a last favour."

"What is it, my child?"

"I wish for a week before answering this request, for I am so surprised and confused, that it would be impossible for me to form any resolution at present."

"Very good, my child; in eight days you will give me your answer. And now withdraw: but do you remain, Paredes; before leaving the hacienda for ever, I wish to make some arrangements in which your help will be necessary."

Brother and sister, after bowing respectfully to their father, slowly quitted this fatal chamber, which persons never entered save through a misfortune.

CHAPTER XXVIII
THE TIGRERO

Don Ruiz and his sister left the red chamber together, gloomy, sad, and despairing, and not daring to communicate their impressions, because they knew that they had nothing to hope from an exchange of conventional consolation. When they reached the hall whence ran the stairs leading to their different suites of rooms, Don Ruiz let loose his sister's arm, and kissed her on the forehead.

"Courage, Marianna," he said, gently.

"Are you leaving me, brother?" she remarked, with a slight tinge of reproach in her voice.

"Are you not going to your own rooms?" he asked her.

"And what do you intend doing?"

"To tell you the honest truth, sister," he replied, "after what has occurred in the red chamber, I feel in such a state of excitement, that I want to breathe the fresh air; did I not, I fancy I should be ill."

"Do you propose going out, then?"

"In leaving you, my dear sister, it is my firm intention to saddle Santiago, and ride about the country for two or three hours."

"If that be the case, Ruiz, I will ask you to do me a service."

"What is it?"

"Saddle Madrina at the same time."

"Your mare?"

"Yes."

"Are you going out too?"

"I want to pay a visit to my nurse, whom I have not seen for a long time. I am anxious to speak a few words with her."

"Will you go alone to the rancho?"

"Unless you give me the pleasure of your company."

"Do you doubt it, sister?"

"Yes and no, Ruiz."

"Why this reticence?"

"I will explain it to you, brother. To be frank with you, I want to see my nurse, and I may spend the night at the rancho; in the event of that happening, I do not wish you to make an attempt to dissuade me by entreaty or otherwise."

"Reflect, sister, that the country is not tranquil, and that you may incur danger in a wretched rancho, where any resistance would be impossible."

"I have thought of that, and calculated all the chances. But I repeat to you, I must go to the rancho, and may be obliged to pass there not only a night, but a day or two."

Don Ruiz reflected for a moment.

"Sister," he then said, "you are no ordinary woman, and everything you do is carefully calculated. Although you do not tell me the motives for this visit, I guess that they are serious, and hence will make no attempt to thwart your wishes. Act as you please, and I will do all you wish."

"Thank you, Ruiz," she answered, warmly; "I anticipated you would say that, for you understand me: my visit has a serious motive, as you have divined."

"Then I will go and saddle the horses," he remarked, with a smile.

"Do so, brother," she replied, as she gently pressed his hand. "I will wait for you here."

"I only require five minutes."

The young man went out. Doña Marianna leant on the balustrade, and fell into deep thought. Don Ruiz returned, leading the horses by the bridle: brother and sister mounted, and at once left the hacienda. It was about four in the afternoon; the great heat of the day was spent, the birds were singing gaily beneath the foliage; the sun, now level with the lowest branches, had lost much of its heat; and the coming breeze, which was beginning to rise, refreshed the atmosphere, and bore far away the clouds of mosquitoes which had for several hours darkened the air. The young people galloped silently side by side, absorbed in their thoughts, and only taking absent glances at the splendid scenery unfolded around them as they advanced further into the country. They thus reached the rancho without exchanging a word.

Bouchaley, faithful to his friendship for Doña Marianna, had long before announced her arrival to the inhabitants of the rancho, who had hurried out to welcome her. With a hurried glance, Marianna assured herself of the presence of her foster brother, which seemed to cause her great satisfaction.

"Goodness! You here so late, niña?" the ranchero said, in his delight; "What blessed wind has blown you?"

"The desire of seeing you, madresita," the young lady answered, with a smile; "it is so long since I embraced you, that I could not wait any longer."

"It is a good idea, niña," the ranchero said; "unfortunately it is late, and we shall only be able to converse with you for a few moments."

"How do you know, old father?" she replied, as she leaped off her horse, and threw her arms round his neck; "Who told you I should not spend the night at the rancho?"

"Oh, oh, you would not do us that honour, niña," the old man answered.

"You are mistaken, father, and the proof is that I ask my brother to leave me here, and return alone to the hacienda."

"Then I am discharged," Don Ruiz said, laughingly.

"Yes, brother; but you have no cause of complaint, for I warned you."

"That is true; hence I do not complain, little sister; still, before we part, tell me at what hour I am to come and fetch you tomorrow?"

"Do not trouble yourself about that, Ruiz; Mariano will bring me home."

"And this time I shall not behave as the last, niña: may the Lord confound me if I lose sight of you even for a moment," the tigrero said, as he took the horse's bridle to lead it to the corral.

"Will you be so cruel, Marianna," Ruiz observed, "as to force me thus to return at once?"

"No; I grant you an hour to rest and refresh yourself, but when that time has elapsed you will start."

"Agreed, little sister."

They entered the rancho: No Sanchez, with that hospitable speed all Mexican rancheros display, had already covered the table with pulque, mezcal, Catalonian refino, orangeade, and infusion of tamarinds. The young people, thirsty from their long ride, and not wishing to grieve the worthy persons who received them so kindly, did honour to the refreshments thus profusely offered them. Don Ruiz, while teasing his sister about her strange fancy for spending the night at the rancho, though he felt convinced that she must have a very serious reason for it, conversed gaily according to his fashion, and displayed a dazzling wit which is easier in Mexico than elsewhere; for, owing to the natural intelligence of the people, no matter their rank, they are certain to understand. When day began to fall, the young gentleman took leave of the rancheros, mounted his horse, and started for the hacienda.

In Mexico, as in all intertropical countries, evening is the pleasantest part of the day: at that time the inhabitants are all in the open air. At night they sit in front of the rancho doors, conversing, singing, or dancing; two or three in the morning arrives before they dream of going to bed. But on this day, contrary to her habit when she paid her nurse a visit, Doña Marianna seemed fatigued: at times she had difficulty in checking a yawn, and her desire for rest was so evident that the nurse was the first to invite her to retire. The young lady required no pressing, and after bidding the old folks good night, entered the rancho, and the room prepared for her. So soon as Marianna had left them, the old couple also retired to rest. As for Mariano, after making his usual tour of inspection round the rancho, he hung up a hammock under the portico, as he preferred sleeping in the open air to being shut up within walls which the sun's heat had rendered stifling. An hour later all the inhabitants of the rancho were plunged into the deepest sleep.

Suddenly the tigrero felt a hand gently laid on his shoulder; he opened his eyes, and by the light of the stars, which was as brilliant as day, recognised Doña Marianna. The young man who had thrown himself fully dressed upon the hammock, started up, and looked at his foster sister anxiously.

"What is the matter with you, niña?" he asked, in evident alarm.

"Silence, Mariano!" she answered in a low voice, and laying her finger on her lips; "All is quiet, at least I suppose so, but I wish to speak with you."

"Go on, tocaya," he replied, as he leaped from the hammock and folded it up.

"Yes, but I am sorry at having woken you; you were sleeping so soundly, that I looked at you for nearly a quarter of an hour ere I dared to disturb your rest; for sleep is such a blessed thing."

"Nonsense," he answered with a laugh; "you were wrong, niña; we wood rangers sleep so quickly that an hour is sufficient to rest us, and if I am not mistaken, I have been lying down for more than two. Hence speak, niña; I am attentive, and shall not miss a word of what you say to me."

The young lady reflected for a moment.

"You love me, I think, Mariano?" she at length said, with a certain hesitation in her voice.

"Like a sister, niña," he said, warmly; "in truth, are we not tocayo and tocaya? Why ask such a question?"

"Because I want you to do me an important service."

"Me, niña? ¡Caray! Do not be alarmed; I am devoted to you body and soul, and whatever you may ask—"

"Do not pledge yourself too hastily, tocayo," she interrupted him, with a meaning laugh.

"A man cannot do that when he firmly intends to keep his promise."

"That is true; still there are things from which a man at times recoils."

"There may be such, niña, but I do not know them; however, explain your wishes to me, frankly."

"I think, Mariano, that you are on friendly terms with the hunter, called Stronghand?"

"Very intimate, niña; but why do you ask the question?"

"Is he an honest man?"

The tigrero looked at her.

"What do you mean by that?" he asked her.

"Why," she said, with considerable embarrassment, "I mean a man of heart—a man, in short, whose word may be taken."

Mariano became serious.

"Señorita," he said, "Stronghand saved my life under circumstances when my only hope was in Heaven. I have seen this man perform deeds of incredible courage and audacity, for the sole object of serving people who frequently did not feel the slightest gratitude to him. To me he is more than a friend—more than a brother; whatever he bade me I would do, even if I had to lay down the life he saved, and which belongs to him. Such, niña, is my opinion about the hunter called Stronghand."

The young lady gave a glance of pleasure.

"You are deeply attached to him?" she murmured.

"As I told you, he is more to me than a brother."

"And you often see him?"

"When I want him, or he wants me."

"Does he live in the neighbourhood, then?"

"A short time back he stayed several days at the rancho."

"And will he return?"

"Who knows?"

"What did he during his stay here?"

"I am not aware; I believe that he hunted, though I did not see a single head of game he had killed whilst he was here."

"Ah!" she said, pensively.

There was a silence. Mariano looked at her, somewhat surprised that she should have woke him for the sake of asking him such unimportant questions.

"Well," she continued, presently; "if you wanted to see Stronghand, do you know where to find him?"

"I think so."

"You are not certain?"

"Forgive me, niña, I am certain; we have a spot where we are safe to meet."

"But he might not be there."

"That might happen."

"What would you do in that case?"

"Go and seek him at another place, where I should be sure of finding him."

"Ah! And where is that?"

"At the village he inhabits."

"What village is that? I know of none in the vicinity."

"Pardon me, niña; there is one."

"A long way from here, I presume?"

"Only a few leagues."

"And what is this pueblo?"

"A village of the Papazos."

"What?"

"Yes, I have forgotten to tell you that. Although he is a white man, Stronghand has, for reasons I am ignorant of, joined the Indians, and been adopted by one of their most powerful tribes."

"That is singular," the young lady murmured.

"Is it not?" the tigrero replied; understanding less than ever the object of the conversation.

The maiden shook her head coquettishly, and seemed to form a sudden resolution.

"Mariano," she said, "I asked you to do me a service."

"Yes, niña, and I answered that I was ready to do it."

"That is true; are you still of the same mind?"

"Why should I have altered it?"

"This is what I want of you."

"Speak."

"I wish to see Stronghand."

"Very good; when?"

"At once."

"What?" he asked, in amazement.

"Do you refuse?"

"I do not say that, but—"

"There is a but, then?"

"There always is one."

"Let me hear yours."

"It is long past midnight."

"What matter is that?"

"Not much, I allow."

"Well, what next?"

"It is a long journey."

"Our horses are good."

"We risk not finding the hunter at our usual meeting place."

"We will push on to his village."

The tigrero looked at her attentively.

"You have a great need to see Stronghand in that case?" he asked.

"Most extreme."

"It is more serious than you suppose, señorita."

"Why so?"

"Hang it! It is not so easy to enter an Indian village."

"But you do so."

"That is true; but I am alone and well known."

"Well, I will go on after you; that is all."

"Are you aware that the Indians have revolted?"

"That does not concern you, as you are a friend of theirs."

Mariano shook his head.

"You ask a very difficult thing again, tocaya," he said, "in which you run a great risk."

"Yes, if I fail; but I shall succeed."

"It would be better to give up this excursion."

"Confess at once," she said, impatiently, "that you do not wish to keep the promise you made me."

"You are unjust to me; I am only trying to dissuade you from an enterprise which you will repent when it is too late."

"That is my business, I repeat, Mariano," she continued, with a marked stress in her words; "it is not to gratify a caprice that I wish to see the hunter. I have reasons of the utmost importance for wishing to speak with him; and, to tell you all, he urged me to summon him under certain circumstances, and told me I need only apply to you in order to find him. Are you satisfied now? will you adhere to your doubts, and still refuse to accompany me?"

The young man had listened to Doña Marianna with earnest attention. When she had ended, he replied—"I no longer hesitate, niña; as things are so, I am bound to obey you. Still, I beg you not to make me responsible for any events that may happen."

"Whatever may occur, my kind Mariano, be assured that I shall be grateful to you for the immense service you have rendered me."

"And you wish to start at once?"

"How far have we to ride?"

"Some ten or twelve leagues."

"Oh, that is nothing."

"Not on a regular road; but I warn you that we shall be compelled to follow hardly visible wild beast tracks."

"The night is clear; we shall have sufficient light to guide us, so let us start."

"If you wish it," the young man answered.

A few minutes later they left the rancho at a gallop. It was about two in the morning; and the moon, which was at its full, lit up the landscape as in bright day.

CHAPTER XXIX
THE EXCURSION

As we have already said, Doña Marianna, although still so young, was gifted with an ardent soul and an energetic character, which the unusual dangers of a border life had, so to speak, unconsciously ripened. In life these select organizations do not know themselves; events alone, by exciting their living strength, reveal to them what they are capable of at a given moment, by urging them bravely to endure the attack of malignant fortune, and to contend resolutely with their adversary. When the Marquis, forced by the necessities of his unhappy condition, had a frank explanation with his children, and confessed to them into what difficulties he was suddenly thrown, Doña Marianna had listened to him with the most sustained attention. Then, by degrees, a species of revolution took place in her. Stronghand's words reverted to her mind, and she had a vague idea that he could avert the danger that was suspended over her father's head.

On recapitulating all that had occurred to her since her departure from Rosario—the help the hunter had rendered her on various occasions with unexampled devotion—the conversation she had held with him a few days previously, and the promise she had made him—it appeared evident to her that Stronghand, better informed than perhaps the Marquis himself was about the machinations of his enemies, held in his hands the means of saving the Moguer family, and parrying the blows which were about to be dealt them in the dark.

Then, full of hope, and confiding in the promises of this man, who had never made his appearance except to prove his devotion to her, her resolution was spontaneously formed, and without informing anyone of the project she had conceived, for fear lest an effort might be made to dissuade her, she went to her nurse's rancho, in order to obtain an interview with the hunter by the agency of her foster mother. Under existing circumstances, the step taken by Doña Marianna was not at all easy, or without dangers. The daughter of the Marquis de Moguer galloping at night along the Indian border, only accompanied by one man—devoted, it is true, but who, in spite of all his courage, would be powerless to defend her against an attack—displayed more than temerity in this action; and however great her bravery was, and the confidence she had in the honesty of the enterprise she was thus blindly undertaking, still she could not refrain from an internal shudder on thinking of her isolated position, and the ease with which she might be surprised, carried off, or even massacred by the revolted Indians. Too proud, however, to allow any of the secret fears that agitated her to be seen, Doña Marianna affected a tranquillity and freedom of mind she was far from feeling. She conversed in a low voice with her foster brother, teasing and scolding him about the difficulty he had made in granting her request, and describing her delight at a ride through such exquisite scenery on so magnificent a night.

Mariano did not think, and consequently did not understand what he supposed was a girl's fancy. Accustomed since childhood to yield to all the wishes of his foster sister, and obey her as a slave, he had on this occasion done what she desired without trying to account for such an unusual excursion, so happy did he feel at obliging her. At the same time, he felt a lively pleasure at accompanying her, and thus passing a few hours in her company. We must not mistake the feelings that animated the tigrero for Doña Marianna. He loved his foster sister with his whole soul, and would have gladly died for her; but this feeling, lively as it was, had nothing personal or interested about it; it was merely friendship, but a friendship elevated to the most complete self-denial and the most entire devotion—in a word, to the most sublime degree which this feeling can attain in the human heart. Hence the tigrero, comprehending the responsibility weighing on him, rode on, as is commonly said, with his beard on his shoulder, carefully examining the bushes, listening to the desert sounds, and ready, on the slightest alarm, bravely to defend the girl who had placed herself under his guard. The country they were traversing, though rather varied, was not, however, completely wooded: owing to the transparent brightness of the night, the view extended for a great distance, which removed all fears of a surprise, and gave a certain security to the travellers; still, they at times, fancied they saw great shadows moving on the riverbank, and flying at their approach. The young lady looked round her curiously, and then asked the tigrero whether they would soon reach the spot where Stronghand was. Mariano pointed out to her a gentle eminence forming a bend of the river, on the top of which the fugitive gleams of an expiring fire could be seen at intervals.

"That is where we are going," he said.

"Then we have only a few minutes' ride, and it is useless to hurry our horses."

"You are mistaken, niña. Not only is the track we are following very winding, and will detain us, but, through an optical illusion easy to be understood, this hill which you fancy so near to us is at least two leagues distant as the crow flies; so that, taking into account the windings, the distance is nearly doubled."

"Can we not cut across country, and thus shorten the distance?"

"Heaven forbid, niña! We should get into trembling prairies, in which we should be swallowed up in a few minutes."

"I trust to you in that case, Mariano; besides, now that, thanks to that fire, I am certain of meeting the hunter, my anxiety is less lively, and I will await patiently."

"Permit me to remark, my dear tocaya, that I did not say certainly that we should find Stronghand at this bivouac."

"What did you tell me, then?"

"Simply that we might hope to meet him here, because it is the spot where he generally encamps when hunting in these parts."

"Still, as we can perceive the flame of that watch fire—for that is really a flame, is it not?"

"Certainly; still, we have yet to learn whether this fire has been kindled by Stronghand or some other hunter. This mound is one of the most suitable places of encampment, owing to the height of the hill, which allows the country to be surveyed, and thus avoid a surprise."

"Then probably we shall not find the hunter at the encampment?"

"I do not say that either, niña," Mariano answered, with a laugh.

"But what do you mean?" the young lady said, impatiently patting the pommel of her saddle with her little hand; "you are really unendurable."

"Do not be angry, tocaya; I may be mistaken. If Stronghand is not here, perhaps we may find a hunter who will tell us where he is."

"Why not an Indian?"

"Because there are no Indians at that campfire."

"Tocayo, I must really ask this time how you can possibly know that?"

"Very easily, niña; I do not require to be a sorcerer to guess so simple a thing."

"Do you consider it so simple?"

"Certainly; nothing can be more so."

"In that case I will ask you to explain, for it is always worth while learning."

"You fancy you are joking, niña; and yet there is always something to be learned in the desert."

"Good, good, tocayo; I know that; but I am waiting for your explanation."

"Listen then. This fire, as I told you, is not an Indian fire."

"That is not exactly what you said to me. Go on, however."

"The Indians, when they camp on the white man's border, never light a fire, for fear of revealing their presence; or if compelled to light one in order to cook their food, they are most careful to diminish the flame, in the first place by digging a deep hole in the ground, and next by only using extremely dry wood, which burns without crackling, flaming, or producing smoke, and which they carry with them for long distances, in case they might not find it on their road."

"But, my friend, that fire is scarce visible."

"That is true; but still it is sufficiently so for us to have perceived it a long distance off, and thus discovered the existence of a bivouac at this spot which, under present circumstances, would entail the surprise and consequent death of the imprudent men who lit it, if they were Indians instead of hunters."

"Excellently reasoned, compañero, and like a man accustomed to a desert life!" A rough, though good-humoured voice suddenly said, a few yards from them.

The travellers started and pulled up sharply, while anxiously investigating the surrounding thickets. Mariano, however, did not lose his head under these critical circumstances; but with a movement swift as thought raised his rifle, and covered a man who was standing by the side of a thicket, with his hands crossed on the muzzle of a long gun.

"Hold, compadre!" the stranger continued, not at all disturbed by the tigrero's hostile demonstration; "Pay attention to what you are about. A thousand fiends! Do you know that you run a risk of killing a friend?"

Mariano hesitated for a moment; and then, without raising his rifle, remarked—

"I fancy I recognise that voice."

"By Jove!" the other said, "It would be a fine joke if you did not."

"Wait a minute; are you not Whistler?"

"All right, you remember now," the Canadian said with a laugh; for the person was really the hunter whom the reader saw for a moment at the village of the Papazos.

The tigrero uncocked his rifle, which he threw over his shoulder, and said to Marianna—"It is a friend."

"Are you quite sure of this man?" she asked in a low, quick voice.

"As of myself."

"Who is he?"

"A Canadian hunter or trapper. He has all the defects of the race, but at the same time all its qualities."

"I will believe you, for his countrymen are generally regarded as honest men. Ask him what he was doing on the skirt of the track."

Mariano obeyed.

"I was attending to my business," Whistler replied with a grin; "and pray what may you be doing, so poorly accompanied at this hour of the night, when the Indians have taken the field?"

"I am travelling, as you see."

"Yes, but every journey has an object, I suppose."

"It has."

"Well, I do not see what end yours can achieve by continuing in that direction."

"Still, we are going to do so till we have found the man we are in search of."

"I will not ask you any questions, although I may perhaps have a right to do so; still, I fancy you would act more wisely in turning back than in obstinately going on."

"I am not able to do so."

"Why not?"

"Because I have not the command of the expedition, and I cannot undertake such a responsibility."

"Ah, who is the chief, then? I only see two persons."

"You seem to forget, señor," Doña Marianna said, joining in the conversation for the first time, "that one of these two persons is a female."

"Of course she must command," the trapper answered with a courteous bow; "pray excuse me, madam."

"I the more willingly do so, because I hope to obtain from you important information about the object of the journey we have undertaken, perhaps somewhat too carelessly, in these desolate regions."

"I shall be too happy to be agreeable to you, my lady, if it be in my power."

"Permit me, in that case, to ask you a few questions."

"Pray do so."

"I wish to know what the camp is whose watch fires I perceive a short distance off."

"A hunter's bivouac."

"Only hunters?"

"Yes, they are all white hunters or trappers."

"I thank you, señor. Do you know these men?"

"Very well, considering I am a member of the band." Doña Marianna hesitated for a moment.

"Forgive me, sir," she continued, "I am in search of a hunter with whom grave reasons force me to desire an immediate interview; perhaps he is among your comrades."

"Do you know him personally, madam?"

"Yes, and am under great obligations to him. He is called Stronghand."

The trapper eagerly walked up to the young lady, and attentively examined her.

"You wish to have an immediate interview with Stronghand?"

"Yes, I repeat, señor, for reasons of the highest importance."

"In case you are Doña Marianna de Moguer."

"What!" she exclaimed, in surprise, "You know my name?"

"That needs not astonish you, madam," he said, with the most exquisite politeness; "I am the intimate friend of Stronghand. Without entering into any details that might justly offend you, my friend told me that you might perchance come and ask for him at our campfire."

"He knew it, then," she murmured, in a trembling voice; "but how did he learn it?"

Though these words were uttered in a whisper, Whistler heard them.

"He doubtless hoped it would be so, without daring to credit it, madam," he answered.

"Good heavens!" she continued, "What does this mean?"

"That my friend, in his eager desire to be agreeable to you, and foreseeing the chance of your coming during his absence, warned me, in order to spare you a very difficult search, and thus induce you to grant me a little of that confidence you deign to honour him with."

"I thank you, sir. Now that you know me, would it be taxing your courtesy too greatly to ask you to guide my companion and myself to your bivouac?"

"I am at your orders, madam, and believe me that you will receive a proper reception, even though my friend does not happen to be there at the moment."

"What!" she said, suddenly checking her horse, "Can he be absent?"

"Yes, but do not let that cause you any anxiety; he will soon return.

"Good heavens!" she murmured, clasping her hands in grief.

"Madam," Whistler again continued, "I understand that the reasons which urged you to undertake such a journey must be of the utmost importance; let me, therefore, go on ahead to the camp, and make all the preparations for your reception."

"But Stronghand, señor?"

"Warned through me, madam, he will be back by daybreak."

"You promise me that, señor."

"On my honour."

"Go, then, and may Heaven requite you for the goodwill and courtesy you show me."

Whistler bowed respectfully to the young lady, took his rifle under his arm, and soon disappeared in the forest.

"We can now go on without fear," said Mariano; "I know Whistler to be an honest, worthy fellow, and he will do what he has promised."

"Heaven grant I may see the man whom I have come so far to meet."

"You will see him, be assured; moreover, all precautions were taken in the event of your visit."

"Yes," she murmured, pausing; "and it is this which renders me alarmed. Well, I put my trust in the Virgin."

And flogging her horse, she went on her way, followed by the tigrero, who, according to his habit, could not at all comprehend this remark, after the desire the young lady had evinced to see the hunter.

CHAPTER XXX
THE HUNTER'S CAMP

It was no great distance to the bivouac, and the travellers reached it about half an hour after Whistler. Still, though this period was so short, the worthy Canadian had profited by it to erect for the young lady, who thanked him by a smile, a jacal of branches, under which she found a shelter as comfortable as desert life permits. The hunters' camp had a military look, which greatly perplexed Doña Marianna. Strong wooden palisades defended all the approaches; the horses, which were ready saddled, were fastened to pickets; several watch fires, lighted at regular distances, sufficiently illumined the plain to prevent the approach of an enemy, whether man or beast; and four sentinels, standing rifle in hand on the entrenchments, followed with a vigilant eye the slightest undulations of the lofty pass. Some thirty men, with harsh and irregular features, clothed after the fashion of wood rangers, in fur caps, cotton shirts, and leather calzoneras, were lying in front of the fires, rifle in hand, in order to be ready for the first alarm.

Orders had probably been given beforehand by Whistler, for the sentinels allowed the two travellers to pass unquestioned through a breach in the entrenchments, which was immediately closed after them again. The Canadian was awaiting them in front of the jacal; he helped Doña Marianna to dismount, and the horses were led to join the others, and supplied with a copious meal of alfalfa.

"You are welcome among us, señora," he said with a respectful bow; "in this jacal, which no one will enter save yourself, there is a bed of skins, on which you can take a few hours' rest while awaiting Stronghand's arrival."

"I thank you, señor, for this graceful attention, by which I cannot profit, however, till you have reiterated your promise."

"Señorita, two horsemen have already set out to fetch Stronghand, but I repeat, that he cannot be here for some hours; now, if you will accept the humble refreshment prepared for you—"

"I only require rest, señor; still I am not the less obliged to you for your offer. With your permission, I will retire."

"You are the mistress here, madam."

The young lady smiled, pressed her foster brother's hand, and entered the jacal. So soon as Doña Marianna had let fall after her the blanket which formed the doorway, the tigrero quietly removed his zarapé from his shoulders, and laid it on the ground.

"What is that for, comrade?" Whistler asked, astonished at the performance.

"You see, compadre, I am making my bed."

"Do you mean to sleep there?"

"Why not?"

"As you please; still, you will be cold, that is all."

"Nonsense! A night is soon spent, especially when so far advanced as this one is."

"I trust that you do not doubt us."

"No, Whistler, no; but Doña Marianna is my foster sister, and I am bound to watch over her."

"That care concerns me at the moment; so do not be at all alarmed."

"Two sentries are better than one; besides, you know me, do you not? Although I place the utmost confidence in you, I will not surrender the guardianship of my tocaya to another man; that is my idea, whether right or wrong, and I shall not give it up."

"As you please," the trapper said, with a laugh.

And he left him at liberty to make his arrangements as he pleased. The tigrero, though he knew most of the hunters, or, perhaps, because he knew them, did not wish to leave his foster sister unprotected among these reckless men, who, accustomed to the utter license of a desert life, might, under the influence of strong liquors, forget the sacred duties of hospitality, and insult Doña Marianna. In this the young man, in spite of his desert experience, was completely mistaken.

We have no intention to attempt the rehabilitation of these men, who, generally endowed with evil instincts, and who do not wish to yield to the demands of civilization, retire into the desert in order to live as they like, and seek liberty in license; still, we will mention in their honour, that a nomadic life, after a certain lapse of time, completely modifies their character, curbs their passions, and so subjects them that they gradually become purified by constant danger and privations, by getting rid of all that was bad in them, and retaining beneath their rough bark and coarse manners principles of honesty and devotion of which they would have been considered incapable at an earlier period. What we say here is scrupulously true of about two-thirds at least of the bold pioneers who traverse in all directions the vast savannahs of the New World; the others are incorrigible, and within a given time end by becoming real bandits, and carry their contingent of crime to those formidable bands of pirates of the prairies, who ambush like hideous birds of prey to await the passage of caravans, and plunder and massacre the travellers.

But, whether good or bad, the dwellers on the prairie—no matter if whites, half-breeds, or Redskins, trappers, pirates, or Indians—have one virtue in common, and whose duties they carry out with remarkable punctuality and generosity, and that is hospitality. A traveller surprised by night, and wearied by a long journey, may, if he see a campfire in the huts of an Indian village, present himself without fear, and claim hospitality. From that moment he is sacred to the men he applies to, no matter if they be Indians, bravos, hunters, or even pirates. These individuals, who would not have scrupled to assassinate him by the side of a ditch, treat him like a brother, show him the most delicate attentions, and will never make any insulting allusions to the length of his stay among them; on the contrary, he is at liberty to remain as long as he pleases, and when he takes leave his hosts say good-bye regretfully. At the same time it is true that, if they meet him a week after in the forest, they will kill him without mercy to raise his hair and take his weapons; but this need only be apprehended with the pirates and some Indian tribes of the far west. As for the hunters, when a stranger has once slept by their side and shared their food, he is for ever sacred to them.

The tigrero, therefore, was completely mistaken when he feared lest Doña Marianna might be insulted by these men, who, although coarse, were honest and loyal in the main; and who, flattered by the confidence this lovely, innocent girl placed in them, would, on the contrary, have gladly defended her had it been necessary.

Whistler went off with a laugh, and lay down by the side of his comrades. As we have already said, the night was far advanced when Doña Marianna and her travelling companion reached the camp of the hunters; a few hours at the most separated them from sunrise: and the young lady, who at first resolved to spend these hours awake, overcome by fatigue, had yielded to sleep, and enjoyed a calm and refreshing rest. So soon as day began to appear, Doña Marianna repaired as well as she could the disorder produced in her dress by her lengthened journey, rose and went to the door of the jacal. The camp was still plunged in the deepest silence: with the exceptions of the sentries still on the watch, the hunters were fast asleep.

The dawn was just breaking, and striping the horizon with wide vermillion bands; the sharp and rather cold morning breeze rustled softly through the branches; the flowers that enamelled the prairie raised themselves, and expanded the corollas to receive the first sunbeams; the numberless streams, whose silvery waters made their way through the tall grass, murmured over the white and grey pebbles as they bore their tribute to the Rio Bravo del Norte, whose capricious windings could be guessed in the distance, owing to the thick cloud of vapour that constantly rose from it and brooded over its bed. The birds, still hidden beneath the foliage, were timidly preluding their harmonious concert; the glad earth, the bright sky, the serene atmosphere, the pure light—all, in a word, revealed that the day which had now entirely appeared was about to be tranquil and lovely.

The maiden, refreshed by the rest she had enjoyed, felt herself newborn as she breathed the first exhalations of the flowers and the sharp odour which is found in the desert alone. Without venturing to quit the jacal, in front of which the tigrero was lying, she surveyed the surrounding landscape, which, thanks to the elevation she stood at, lay expanded at her feet for a long distance. The profound calmness of reawakening nature, the powerful harmonies of the desert, filled the maiden's heart with a gentle melancholy; she pensively indulged in those thoughts which the great spectacles of nature ever arouse in minds unaffected by human passions. In the meanwhile the sun ascended the horizon, and the last shadows melted away in the dazzling beams propelled by the daystar. Suddenly the girl uttered an exclamation of delight, for she noticed a band of horsemen fording the stream, and apparently coming in the direction of the hill. At the cry his foster sister uttered, the tigrero bounded to his feet and stood by her side, rifle in hand, ready to defend her if necessary.

"Good morning, tocayo," she said to him.

"Heaven keep you, niña!" he replied, with a shade of anxiety. "Have you slept well?"

"I could not have done so better, Mariano."

"All right then; but why did you utter that cry?"

"I cried out, my friend, and scarce know why."

"Ah, yes—stay; look at those horsemen coming up at full speed."

"Caray! How they gallop! They will be here within half an hour."

"Do you think that Stronghand is among them?"

"I suppose so, niña."

"And I am sure of it," said Whistler, with a respectful bow to the young lady; "I have recognised him, señorita; so will you allow that I have kept my promise?"

"Most fully, señor; and I know not how to express my thanks for the hearty hospitality you have given me."

"I have no claim to any thanks from you, señorita, as I have only carried out my friend's intention; niña, it is to him alone you should offer thanks, if you consider that you ought to make them."

In the meanwhile the camp was aroused; the hunters were yawning, and turned to their daily avocations; some led their horses to the watering place, others kindled the fires; some cut the wood requisite to keep them up, while two or three of the older men acted as cooks, and got breakfast ready for the party. The camp changed its appearance in a minute; it lived the nervous, agitated life of the desert, in which each man performs his task with the feverish speed of persons who are aware of the value of time, and do not wish to lose it. The young lady, at first surprised by the cries, laughter, and unaccustomed movement that prevailed around her, began to grow used to it, and eagerly watched the occupations of the men she had beneath her eyes. A sharp challenge of "Who goes there?" suddenly made her raise her head.

"A friend!" a voice she at once recognised answered from without.

Suddenly a band of horsemen entered the camp, at their head being Stronghand. The young man dismounted, and after exchanging a few words with Whistler, he went straight up to the maiden, who was standing motionless in the doorway of the jacal, and watching his approach with amazement. In fact, as we have said, Stronghand was not alone; several persons accompanied him, among them being Thunderbolt and Doña Esperanza; the rest were confidential Indian servants. When Stronghand came in front of the young lady, he bowed to her respectfully, and then turned to the persons who accompanied him.

"Permit me, señorita," he said to her, "to present to you my mother, Doña Esperanza, and my father; both love you, though they do not know you, and insisted on accompanying me."

The maiden, blushing with joy at this delicate attention on the part of the hunter, who thus placed their interview beneath the safeguard of his father and mother, replied with emotion—"I am delighted, señor, with this kind inspiration of your heart; it augments, were it possible, the confidence I have placed in you, and the gratitude I felt for the eminent services you have rendered me."

Doña Esperanza and the sachem embraced the girl, who, at once ashamed and joyous at the friendship of these persons, whose exterior was at once so imposing and so venerable, knew not how to respond to their caresses and the kindness they evinced to her. In the meanwhile the hunters had raised, with great skill and speed, a tent, under which the four persons were at once protected from the curious glances of the persons who surrounded them. Through that innate feeling of women, which makes them love or detest each other at the first glance, Doña Esperanza and the young lady at once felt attracted to each other by a natural movement of sympathy, and leaving the gentlemen to their occupations, they withdrew on one side, and began an animated and friendly conversation. Doña Marianna, subjugated by Doña Esperanza's seductive manner, and drawn toward her by a feeling of attraction for which she did not attempt to account, as she felt so happy with her, spoke to her open-heartedly; but then she was greatly surprised to see that this lady, whom she was bound to suppose an entire stranger, was perfectly acquainted with all that related to her family, and knew her father's affairs better than she did herself; her amazement increased when Doña Esperanza explained in the fullest details the reasons that occasioned her presence in the hunter's camp, and the precarious position to which the Marquis de Moguer was reduced.

"I could add many more surprising things, my dear girl," Doña Esperanza continued with a smile, "but I do not wish to fatigue you at present; sufficient for you to know that we really take an interest in your family, and that it will not be our fault if your father is not soon freed from all his cares."

"Oh, how good you are, madam!" the young lady exclaimed, warmly; "How can I have merited such lively interest on your part?"

"That must not trouble you at all, my dear girl; the step you have taken today to come to your father's assistance, and the confidence you have placed in my son, are for us proofs of the loftiness of your feelings and the purity of your heart. Although we are almost Indians," she added with a smile, "we have white blood enough in our veins to remember what we owe to persons of that race."

The conversation went on thus between the two ladies on a footing of frank friendliness, until the moment when Stronghand came to interrupt it, by stating that breakfast was ready, and that they were only waiting for them to sit down. The tigrero and the Canadian had both been invited to share the meal, but they declined the invitation under the pretext that they did not like to eat with persons so high above them in rank, but in reality, because the worthy wood rangers preferred breakfasting without ceremony. Stronghand did not press them, and allowed them to do as they pleased. Doña Marianna bit her lips in order to suppress a smile when the hunter informed her that they were about to sit down to table; for, owing to her recent journey and her life on the Indian border, the young lady was well aware that such meals were extremely simple, and eaten on the grass. Hence her surprise was at its height when, after passing into a separate compartment of the tent, she perceived a table laid with a luxury which would have been justly admired even in Mexico: nothing was wanting, even to massive plate and valuable crystal. The dishes, it is true, were simple, and merely consisted of venison and fruit; but all had a stamp of true grandeur, which it was impossible not to appreciate at the first glance. The contrast offered by this table, so elegantly and comfortably laid, was the greater, because, behind the canvas of the tent, desert life could be seen in all its simplicity.

The young lady seated herself between Thunderbolt and Doña Esperanza, Stronghand sat down opposite to her, and two menservants waited. In spite of the agreeable surprise which the impromptu comfort of this repast, prepared for her alone, caused her, the young lady did not at all display her surprise, but she ate heartily and gaily, thus thanking her hosts for the delicate attentions they showed her. When the dainties were placed on the table, and the meal was drawing to a close, Stronghand bowed to Doña Marianna.

"Señorita," he said, with a smile, "before we begin a serious conversation, which might, at this moment, appear to you untimely, be kind enough to permit my mother to tell us one of the charming Indian legends with which she generally enlivens the close of our meals."

Doña Marianna was at first surprised by this proposition, made, without any apparent motive, at the close of a lively conversation; but imagining that the hunter's remarks concealed a serious purpose, and that the legend, under its frivolous aspect, would entail valuable results for her, she answered with her sweetest smile—"I shall listen with the greatest pleasure to the narrative the señora is about to tell us, because my nurse, who is of Indian origin, was wont to lull me to sleep with these legends, which have left a deep and most agreeable impression on my mind."

CHAPTER XXXI
THE LEGEND

Doña Esperanza exchanged a look with the sachem, and after reflecting a moment, as if recalling her ideas, she said to Doña Marianna, in her gentle, sympathising voice—"My dear girl, before beginning my narrative, I must inform you that I belong to the Aztec race, and am descended in a direct line from the kings of that people. Hence, the story you are about to hear, though simple in its form, is completely exact, and has dwelt among us intact for generations. I trust," she added, with a stress, "that it will interest you."

Then turning to one of the criados who stood motionless behind the guests, she said—"The quipos."

The criado went out, and almost immediately returned with a bag of perfumed tapir skin, which he handed his mistress with a bow. The latter opened it, and drew out several cords plaited of different coloured threads, divided at regular distances by knots mingled with shells and beads. These cords are called quipos, and are employed by the Indians to keep up the memory of events that have occurred during a long course of years, and thus represent books. Still, it requires a special study to understand these quipos, and few people are capable of deciphering them, the more so as the Indians, who are very jealous about keeping their historical secrets, only permit a small number of adepts to learn the explanation, which renders any knowledge of Indian history almost impossible for white men. Doña Esperanza, after attentively examining the quipos, selected one, replaced the others in the bag, and letting the knots of the rope glide through her fingers, much as a monk does with his beads when telling his rosary, she began her narrative.

For fear of injuring this story, whose truth cannot be doubted, and which we ourselves heard told in an atepetl of the Papazos, we will leave it in all its native rudeness, without attempting to adorn it with flowers of European metaphors, which, in our opinion, would deprive it of its peculiar character. Doña Esperanza spoke as follows:—"At a certain period of the year," she said, while beginning to feel the quipos, which served her, as it were, as a book, "long before the appearance of white men on the red territory, a numerous band of Chichimeques and Toltequez, who originally dwelt at the lakes, becoming dissatisfied, resolved to emigrate to the south-west in pursuit of the buffaloes, and carried out their resolve."

"At Salt Lake they divided, and those who remained continued to bear their primitive name; while the others, for an unknown motive, assumed that of Comanches. These Comanches, more enterprising than their brothers, continued their journey till they reached the banks of the Rio Gila, where they encamped and divided again. One band, which resolved not to go farther, was christened by the others, who determined to press on, the 'Great Ears;' but the whites who first discovered them called them 'Opatas.' The remainder of the band continued to march in the same direction, and found the Rio Bravo del Norte at the mouth of the Rio Puerco. They had only two principal chiefs left, and gave themselves the name of Neu-ta-che, which means, 'those who reach the river's mouth.' One of the chiefs had an only son, and the other a lovely daughter, and the young people loved each other. But this raised the anger of the father of the unhappy girl to such a height, that he made his band arm and prepare to fight. But the father and the young man crossed the Rio Gila, and buried themselves with their band in the territory afterwards called by the white man Señora or Sonora, where they settled, and continued to reside peacefully until the period when the whites, ever in search of new lands, arrived there in their turn, and after many cruel wars, succeeded in gaining possession of the country."

"The Comanches had founded several towns in Sonora, and, in accordance with their constant habit, in the neighbourhood of the gold and silver mines they discovered, and begun to work. One of their towns, perhaps the richest and most populous, had for its chief a warrior justly renowned for his wisdom in council, and valour in the combat. This chief was called Quetzalmalin—that is to say, the 'Twisted Feather.' His nobility was great, and very ancient; he justly declared that he was descended in a direct line from Acamapichtzin, first king of Mexico, whose hieroglyphic he retained on the totem of his tribe, through that veneration which our fathers displayed for their ancestors. This hieroglyphic, which his descendants have preciously retained, is composed of a hand grasping a number of reeds, which is the literal translation of the name of the noble chief of the race. Twisted Feather had a daughter, eighteen summers old, lovely and graceful: her name was Ova, and she ran over the prairie grass without bending it; gentle, pensive, and timid as the virgin of the first loves, her black eyes had not yet been fixed on one of the warriors of the tribe, who all sought to please her."

"Ova wore a tunic of water-green colour, fastened round her waist by a wampum belt, with a large golden buckle. When she danced before her father, the old man's forehead became unwrinkled, and a sunbeam passed into his eyes. Her father had often told her that it was time for her to marry, but Ova shook her head with a smile; she was happy, and the little bird that speaks to the heart of maidens had not yet sung to her the gentle strains of love."

"Still a moment arrived when Ova lost all her careless gaiety. The young girl, so laughing and so wild, became suddenly pensive and dreamy—she loved."

"Ova went to find her father. The chief at this moment was presiding over the great council of the nation in the great medicine calli. The maiden advanced, and knelt respectfully before her father."

"'What is it, my daughter?' the chief said, as he passed his hand gently through her long hair, which was fine as aloe threads."

"'My father,' she replied, looking down modestly, 'I love, and am beloved.'"

"'My daughter, what is the name of the chief who is so happy that your choice should have fallen on him?'"

"'He is not a chief, my father; he is, perchance, one of the most obscure warriors of the tribe, although he is one of the bravest. He works in the gold mine that belongs to you.'"

"The chief frowned, and a flash of anger sparkled in his glance."

"'My father,' the maiden continued, as she embraced his legs, 'if I did not marry him, I should die.'"

"The chief gazed at his daughter for a moment, and saw her so sad and resigned, that pity entered his heart. He, too, loved his daughter—his only child; for the Master of Life had called away the others to the happy hunting grounds. The aged man did not wish his daughter to die."

"'You shall marry the man you love,' he said to her."

"'Do you promise it to me on the sacred totem of the nation, father?'"

"'On the sacred totem of the nation I promise it; speak, therefore, without fear. What is the name of the man you love?'"

"'He is called the Clouded Snake, father.'"

"The old man sighed."

"'He is very poor,' he muttered."

"'I am rich enough for both.'"

"'Be it so. You shall marry him, my daughter.'"

"Ova rose, sparkling with joy and happiness, bowed to the assembly, and left the medicine lodge."

"Clouded Snake was poor, it is true—even very poor, since he was constrained to work in the gold mine; but he was young, he was brave, and was considered the handsomest of all the warriors of his age."

"Tall, robust, and muscular, Clouded Snake formed as complete a contrast with Ova, who was pale and frail, as a noble buffalo does with a graceful antelope. Perhaps their love emanated from this contrast."

"The young man, though he was so poor, found means to give his betrothed perfumes of grizzly bears' grease, necklaces of alligators' teeth, and wampum girdles."

"The young people Were happy. On the eve of the marriage, Clouded Snake laid at Ova's feet buckles of gold and two bracelets of shells, mingled with beads of pure gold."

"Ova accepted these presents with a smile, and said to her betrothed, as she left him, —"

"'Farewell; we part today to see each other tomorrow, and tomorrow we shall be united for ever.'"

"On the next day Clouded Snake did not come. Ova waited for several months; Clouded Snake did not reappear."

"In vain, by the chief's orders, was the young man sought for throughout the country; no one had seen him, no one had heard speak of him."

"Clouded Snake no longer existed, except in the heart of Ova."

"She wept for him, and people tried to make her believe that he had gone to fight the white men; but Ova shook her head, and wiped away her tears."

"Forty times did the snow cover the summit of the mountains, and yet it had been impossible to clear up the mystery of Clouded Snake's disappearance."

"One day some labourers at work in the gold mine, which had belonged to Ova's father, and was now her property, while going far down an old gallery which had been abandoned for a long time, exhumed a corpse as miraculously preserved as the mummies of the *teocallis* are in their bandages."

"The warriors flocked up to see this strange corpse, clothed in a dress belonging to another age, and no one recognised it."

"Ova, who was then old, and who, to please her father had married the great chief of his nation when her last hope expired, went with her husband to the spot where the corpse was exposed to the sight of visitors."

"Suddenly she started, and tears darted from her eyes; she had recognised Clouded Snake, as handsome as on the day when she left him with the hope of a speedy reunion. She, on the other hand, aged and bowed down more by grief than years, was weak and tottering."

"Ova wished that the corpse of the man whom she had been on the point of marrying, and whom the evil spirit had torn from her, should be restored to the mine from which it had been removed after forty years. The mine, by the orders of the chief's wife, although extremely rich, was abandoned and shut up."

"Ova ordered a hieroglyphic to be carved on the stone that covers the body of her betrothed, which may be thus translated:—'This sepulchre is without a body; this body is without a sepulchre; but by itself it is a sepulchre and a body.'"

"Such," Doña Esperanza added, as she finished the legend, and laid down the quipos, "is the story of the lovely Ova, daughter of the great chief Twisted Feather, and of Clouded Snake the miner, just as it occurred, and just as Ova herself ordered it to be preserved by a special quipos for future ages."

Doña Esperanza stopped, and there was a moment's silence.

"Well, señorita," the sachem asked, "has the legend interested you?"

"Through its simplicity it is most touching, señor," the young lady answered; "still, there is something vague and unsettled about the whole story, which impairs its effect."

Thunderbolt smiled gently.

"You find, do you not, that we are not told the precise spot where the events of the narrative occurred, that Sonora is very large, and that the town in which Twisted Feather commanded is not sufficiently indicated?"

"Pardon me, señor," the young lady remarked, with a blush, "such geographical notions, though doubtless very useful in settling the spot where events have occurred, interest me personally very slightly. What I find incomplete is the story itself; the rest does not concern me."

"More so than you suppose, perhaps, señorita," the sachem remarked; "but pray be good enough to state your objections more fully."

"Excuse me, señor, but I have not yet recovered from the surprise which the events that have occurred during the last few hours have occasioned me, and I explain myself badly, in spite of my efforts."

"What do you mean, señorita, and to what events are you referring?"

"To those which are taking place at this very moment. Having started from home to ask an interview of a wood ranger, whom I naturally supposed encamped in the open air, and shared the life of privations of his fellows, I meet, on the contrary, persons who overwhelm me with attentions, and, under an Indian appearance, conceal all the refinements of the most advanced civilization. You can understand how this strange contrast with what surrounds me must surprise, almost frighten me, who am a young girl, ignorant of the world, and have undertaken a step which many persons would disapprove if they knew it."

"You are going too far, my dear child," Doña Esperanza replied, as she tenderly embraced her; "what you have seen here ought not to surprise you. My husband is one of the principal chiefs of the great Confederation of the Papazos; but he and I, in other times, lived the life of white men. When we withdrew to the desert, we took with us our civilized habits, and that is the entire mystery. As for the step you have taken, it has nothing that is not most honourable to you."

"I thank you for these kind remarks, and the interpretation you are pleased to give to a step conceived, perhaps, a little too giddily, and executed more giddily still."

"Do not regret it, señorita," said Thunderbolt; "perhaps it has helped your father's affairs more than you suppose."

"As for the story of Ova," Doña Esperanza continued, with a gentle smile, "this is how it ended:—the poor woman died of despair a few days after the discovery of the man she ought to have married, and whom she had held in such tender memory for so long a time. At her last hour she expressed a desire to be united in death to the man from whom she had been separated in life. This last wish was carried out. The two betrothed repose side by side in the mine, which was at once closed again, and no one has dreamed of opening it up to the present day."

"I thank you, señora, for completing your narrative. Still," Marianna said, with a sigh, "this gold mine must, in my opinion, be very poor, since the Spaniards, when they seized the country, did not attempt to work it."

"Not at all, my dear child; on the contrary, it is excessively rich. But Ova's secret has been so well kept that the Spaniards remained in ignorance of its existence."

The two ladies were by this time alone, as the sachem and his son had left the tent.

"It is strange," the maiden murmured, answering her own thoughts rather than Doña Esperanza's remark.

The earnestness with which the lady insisted on referring to the legend astounded and interested her. A secret foreboding warned her that the story had a hidden object, whose importance still escaped her, though she was burning to discover it. Doña Esperanza attentively followed in her face the various feelings that agitated her, and were reflected in her expressive face as in a mirror. She continued—"This is why the mine was not discovered when the Spaniards seized the town where it was situated. It had been stopped up for a very long time. The old inhabitants were killed or expelled by the conquerors; and those who escaped were careful not to reveal this secret to their oppressors. The latter destroyed the town, and built an immense hacienda over its mines."

"But—pardon me for questioning you thus, señora—how have all these facts come to your knowledge?"

"For a very simple reason, my dear child. Ova was my ancestress, and the knowledge of this mine is consequently a family secret for us. I am, perhaps, the only person in the world who at the present day knows its exact position."

"Yes, I understand you," the young lady said, becoming very pensive.

"Still you are trying to discover, are you not, my dear child?" the old lady continued, kindly interrogating her, "Why, instead of letting you speak of the important matters that brought you here, my son urged you to ask this story of me; and why, without pity for your filial sorrow, I consented to do so; and why, now that it is ended, I am anxious for you to learn the minutest details."

The girl hid her face in the old lady's bosom, and burst into tears.

"Yes," she said, "you have understood me, madam, and pray pardon me."

"Pardon you for what, my dear child? For loving your father? On the contrary, you are quite right. But yours is no common nature, my child; though we have only been acquainted for a few hours, you have sufficiently appreciated my character, I think, to recognise the interest I take in you."

"Yes, yes, I believe you, madam; I must believe you."

"Well, console yourself, my dear girl; do not weep thus, or I shall be forced to follow your example; and I have still some details to add to this interminable story."

The maiden smiled through her tears. "Oh, you are so kind, madam," she answered.

"No, I love you, that is all, and," she added, with a sigh, "I have done so for a long time."

Doña Marianna gazed at her with amazement.

"Yes, that surprises you," she continued, "and I can well understand it. But enough of this subject for the present, my darling, and let us return to what I wanted to say to you."

"Oh, I am listening to you, madam."

"I will now tell you where Ova's town stood, and its name. It was called Cibola."

"Cibola!" the girl exclaimed.

"Yes, dear child, the very spot where the Hacienda del Toro was afterwards built by your ancestor, the Marquis de Moguer. Now do you understand me?"

Without replying, Doña Marianna threw herself into the old lady's arms, who pressed her tenderly to her bosom.

CHAPTER XXXII
KIDD REAPPEARS

Kidd had left the atepetl of the Papazos with rage in his heart, and revolved in his mind the most terrible schemes of vengeance. Not that the bandit had in his gangrened heart any sensitive chord which noble sentiment could cause to vibrate; to him it was a matter of the slightest importance that he had been publicly branded and expelled like the lowest scoundrel; humiliation glided over him without affecting him, and what most enraged him was to see the fortune dried up which Don Marcos de Niza had momentarily flashed before his greedy eyes, and which he hoped, by dissimulation and treachery, to invest in his capacious pocket in the shape of gold ounces. Now he could no longer dream of it; the slightest information he could henceforth accidentally pick up would not be sufficiently important to be paid for at the price given for the first.

There was something desperate in such an alternative for a man like the bandit; but what should he do? With all his other qualities, the adventurer combined the rather strange one, for him, of only being brave like the Coyotes, which only attack in pairs, and when they are certain of conquering; that is to say, he was an utter coward when compelled to meet an enemy face to face, although he would not hesitate to kill him from behind a bush. The adventurer did not deceive himself about this peculiarity of his character, and the mere idea of picking a quarrel with Stronghand caused him an instinctive terror, externally revealed by a general trembling.

He therefore very sadly and despairingly proceeded, along the road to the Real de Minas, not knowing yet whether he should enter the pueblo, or push further on and seek fortune elsewhere, when his attention was attracted to the left hand of the road he was following by an unusual and continuous undulation of the tall grass. The bandit's first impulse was to stop, dismount, and conceal himself and his horse behind an aloe tree, which afforded a temporary shelter. It is extraordinary to see how villains, who care nothing for the life of others, display remarkable instinct of self-preservation, and what tricks they employ to escape an often imaginary danger. When the bandit believed himself in safety, at least for the moment, he began watching most carefully the undulation of the grass, which incessantly drew nearer to him.

A quarter of an hour passed thus; then the grass parted, and the bandit perceived three horsemen coming towards him, entirely dressed in black. With that peculiar scent scoundrels have for detecting policemen, Kidd did not deceive himself; he at once recognised the three persons as belonging to the noble corporation of Alguaciles. A fourth, also dressed in black, in whose ugly features an expression of bestial craft and wickedness seemed to be reflected, was evidently the leader of the party,—an Alguacil mayor, a race of rapacious vultures, without heart or entrails; a manso Indian, dressed in torn trousers, and with bare head, arms, and legs, was running in front of the others, and evidently acting as guide.

"Hold, José!" the most important of the men shouted to the Indian, employing the general nickname of these poor fellows. "Hold, José! Mind you do not lead us astray, scoundrel, if you do not want to have your ribs broken; we must arrive this night at the Real de Minas of Quitovar, whither important business summons us."

"You would arrive there before two o'clock, Excellency," the Indian answered, with a crafty laugh, "if instead of riding at a foot pace you would consent to give your mule the spurs; if not we shall not get there till after sunset."

"¡Válgame dios!" the first speaker said, angrily; "What will my honourable client, El Señor Senator Don Rufino Contreras say, who must have been awaiting my arrival for several days with the utmost impatience?"

"Nonsense, Excellency! You will arrive soon enough to torture honest people."

"What do you dare to say, scoundrel?" the bailiff exclaimed, raising the chicote he held in his hand.

The Indian parried with a stick the blow which would have otherwise fallen on his loins, and answered drily, as he seized the mule by the bridle, and made it rear, to the great alarm of the rider,—

"Take care, señor; though you call me José, and treat me no better nor worse than a brute, we are no longer in one of your civilized towns, but on the prairie; here I have my foot on my native heath, and will not put up with the slightest insult from you. Treat me as an idiot, if you like, and I shall not care for it, as it comes from one whom I utterly despise; but bear this in mind,—on the slightest threatening gesture you make, I will immediately thrust my knife into your heart."

And while saying this, the man flashed in the bailiffs terrified face a long knife, whose blue blade had a sinister lustre.

"You are mad, José—quite mad," the other answered, affecting a tranquillity he was far from feeling at the announcement; "I never intended to insult you, and I shall never do so; so let go my mule's bridle, pray, and we will continue our journey in peace."

"That will do," the Indian said, with his eternal grin; "that is the way you must speak for us to remain good friends during the period we shall have to pass together."

And after letting go the mule, he began trotting in front with that swinging pace of which Indians alone possess the secret, and which enables them to follow a trotting horse for several days, without becoming tired.

The conversation had taken place sufficiently near to Kidd's lurking place for him to overhear every syllable. Suddenly he started. An idea doubtless crossed his mind, for after allowing the horsemen to go on, but not too far for him to catch them up, he left his thicket, and went after them, growling between his teeth,—"What the deuce relations can these birds of night have with Don Rufino Contreras? Well, we shall soon see."

On turning into the track he saw the party a short distance ahead of him. The latter, whom the sound of his horse's hoofs stamping on the dry ground, had already warned, looked back rather anxiously, the more so because the bandit, in spite of the ease he tried to effect, had nothing very prepossessing about his appearance or face. Policemen could form no mistake about him. Hence they did not do so, and at the first glance recognised him as what he really was—that is to say, a bandit. But in Mexico, as in many other countries which pretend, rightly or wrongly, to be civilized, policemen and ruffians have the best possible reasons for living on friendly terms; and had it not been for the solitary spot where he was, Don Parfindo Purro (such was the Alguacil's name) saw nothing very disagreeable in meeting the adventurer. The latter continued to advance, talking to his horse, tickling its flanks with his spur, galloping, with his fist proudly placed on his hip, and his hat pulled impudently over his right ear.

"*Santas tardes, caballeros,*" he said, as he joined the party of men in black, and slightly checked his horse, so that it should keep pace with the others, "by what fortunate accident do I meet you so late on this desolate road?"

"Fortune is with us, caballero," Don Parfindo answered, politely; "this accursed Indian has led us a roundabout road; I really believe, whatever he may say, that we have lost our way, or shall soon do so."

"That is possible," Kidd observed; "and without being too curious, will you allow me to ask whither you are going? Moreover, to set you at your ease by displaying confidence, I will inform you that I am going to Quitovar."

"Ah!" said the bailiff, "That is very lucky."

"Why so?"

"Because I am going there too, in the first instance. Are we still a great distance from the pueblo?"

"Only a few leagues; we shall arrive before two o'clock, and if you will allow me to take your guide's place, I shall be delighted to show you the way, which, I confess, is not very easy to find."

"Your proposal delights me, caballero, and I most heartily accept it."

"That is agreed; if you do not know the pueblo, I will take you to a capital house, where you will be excellently treated."

"I thank you, caballero; it is the first time I have been to Real de Minas. I am a bailiff at Hermosillo."

"A bailiff!" the bandit said; "¡Caray! That is a famous profession."

"At your service, were I competent for it," Don Parfindo said, puffing himself out.

"I do not say no," Kidd continued, giving himself an air of importance. "When a man carries on a large business, as I do, the acquaintance of a caballero so distinguished as you appear to be can only be most advantageous."

"You confound me, señor."

"Oh, do not thank me, for what I say I really think; I was speaking about it only a few days back to Don Rufino Contreras, who is also very rich, and consequently has numerous trials."

"Do you know Don Rufino?" the bailiff asked, with rising respect.

"Which one? — The illustrious senator?"

"Himself."

"He is one of my most intimate friends. Are you acquainted with him too?"

"He has instructed me to proceed in his name against certain debtors of his."

"¡Viva Dios! This is a strange meeting," the adventurer exclaimed, with a radiant face.

"What a worthy señor!" the bailiff remarked, "And so honourable!"

The two scoundrels understood each other. The acquaintance was formed, and confidence sprang up quite naturally. The conversation was continued on the best possible terms; Kidd adroitly led the other to make a general confession, and the latter, believing that he had to do with an intimate of Don Rufino, told him the secret of the negotiations he was intrusted with, without any visible pressure. Altogether this is what the adventurer learned:—Don Rufino Contreras, impelled by some motive unknown, had secretly bought up the claims of all the persons to whom the Marquis de Moguer was indebted. So soon as he held them, he had taken out writs, through a third party, against the Marquis, so as to dispossess him of the small property left him—among other things, the Hacienda del Toro, which he evinced a great desire to possess. His proposal to marry Doña Marianna was only a bait offered to the good faith of Don Hernando, in order to lull his prudence and remove his suspicions. What he wanted was to become, at any price, proprietor of the hacienda. But still, wishing to retain the mask of friendship, by the aid of which he had hitherto deceived the Marquis, he had put the matter in the hands of a man of his own, who had orders to push matters to extremities, and accept no arrangement. Don Parfindo Purro was the bailiff selected: he was the bearer of the most perverse instructions and strictest orders, and was resolved to accomplish to the letter what he emphatically called his duty.

In Mexico, we are compelled to allow that justice is the most derisive buffoon and horrible thing imaginable. The judges, most of whom are utterly ignorant, and who act *gratis*, as their salaries are never paid, requite themselves for this annoyance on the contending parties, whom they plunder without pity or shame; and this is carried to such an extent, that, so soon as the trial is begun, it is known who will win and who lose. It is little consequence whether the trial be criminal or civil. Money decides everything. To give only one instance: A man commits a murder, the fact is confirmed—known by all; the assassination has been performed in bright day, in the open street, and in the presence of a hundred persons. The relations of the victim go before the *juez de lettras*—that is to say, the criminal judge; he lets them explain the affair in its fullest details, and gives no signs of approval or disapproval; but when they have finished, he asks them the simple question—

"Have you any witnesses?"

"Yes," the relatives answer.

"Very good; and these witnesses are doubtless men of good position and of a certain value?"

"Certainly. Each of them is worth a thousand piastres."

"Well," says the judge, "and how many may there be?"

"Ten."

"What a pity!" he then continues, in his mildest accents; "Your adversary, who between ourselves, appears to me a highly distinguished caballero, has exactly the same number of witnesses as you; but his are far more important people, for each is worth two thousand piastres."

The matter is settled. If the relatives of the murdered man are not rich enough to make a higher bid, the assassin is not only acquitted, but discharged without a stain on his character, and is at perfect liberty, if he think proper, to kill another of his enemies on the same day and the same terms. Such is the way in which the Mexicans understand justice. We can therefore understand how an enormously rich man like Don Rufino Contreras could defeat the Marquis, the state of whose fortune did not allow him to buy the judges.

The adventurer listened with the most earnest attention to the revelations the bailiff made with a certain degree of complacency. Kidd, who was accustomed to fish in troubled waters, had found an opportunity for a famous haul in these revelations. His plan was at once formed, and so soon as he came in sight of the pueblos his arrangements were made. It was late when the travellers reached the barriers of the Real de Minas; the sun had set long before, and the sentries, although they recognised the adventurer as one of their side, made some difficulty about letting him and his companions into the town. They were engaged for nearly an hour in parleying outside, and it was only by the express orders of the commandant that they obtained permission at last to enter the pueblo, which had been converted into a regular fortress.

Kidd, still continuing to act as guide to his comrades, led them straight to a mesón, where he left them at liberty to rest themselves, after warmly recommending them to the landlord. Then the bandit, after placing his horse in the corral, and carefully wrapping himself up in his zarapé, and pulling the brim of his hat over his eyes to escape recognition, glided through the darkness to the house of Don Marcos de Niza, which he entered. The captain, as we said, was accessible at all hours of the day or night, to any person who had news to communicate. At this moment he was in the same study where he had already held a conversation with Master Kidd. On noticing the adventurer, the captain raised his eyes, and without leaving his chair, he said—"Ah, is that you, Master Kidd? Your absence has been long; but for all that, you are welcome, if you bring good news."

The bandit gave a meaning smile.

"My news is excellent, captain," he said, laying a marked stress on the words, "especially for you."

"*¡Cuerpo de Cristo!* I hope so, for am I not commandant of the town?"

"Yes; but I am not going to talk with you about politics at present, Excellency."

"In that case, go to the deuce, scoundrel," the captain said, shrugging his shoulders angrily; "do you think I have nothing more important to do than listen to the rubbish you may please to invent and tire my ears with?"

"I invent nothing, Excellency. Fortune has this very day granted me the opportunity of catching a secret it is most important for you to know—that is all."

"Well, tell me what this mighty secret is."

"It relates to your private affairs, Excellency."

"My affairs!" the captain repeated, bursting into a laugh; "Hang it all! Have I any?"

"If the secret does not relate directly to you, it interests in a most eminent degree one of your nearest relatives?"

"Ah! who is he?"

"The Marquis de Moguer."

The captain became serious; he frowned with a menacing expression, which made Kidd tremble in spite of his well-bred effrontery.

"Speak, and be brief," he said to him.

"Nothing will suit me better."

The captain took several ounces from the table drawer, which he threw to the bandit, who caught them in their flight, and stowed them away with a grin of satisfaction in his huge pockets.

"You will not regret your money, Excellency," he said.

"I hope not; and now go on, scoundrel, as you are paid."

Kidd, without further pressing, related in its fullest details all that had occurred between himself and the bailiff on the road. The captain listened with the most earnest attention.

"Is that all?" he asked, when the other stopped.

"Yes, Excellency."

"Good; now be off. You will continue to watch this man, and report to me all he does."

And he dismissed him with a wave of the hand. The adventurer bowed, and went away. When alone, the captain reflected for a few minutes, and then wrote a letter, sealed it, and summoned his orderly, who at once made his appearance.

"Isidro," the captain said to him, "at all risks this letter must be in the hands of the Marquis de Moguer within six hours at the most. You understand me? —at all risks?"

"It shall be done, captain."

"Take this for yourself," —and he handed him some gold coins, —"and this pass, which will enable you to go in and out. You must be off at once."

Without replying, the soldier withdrew, after concealing the letter in the breast of his uniform.

"And now," the captain muttered to himself; "let them come on."

CHAPTER XXXIII
COMPLICATIONS

After leaving the captain's study, Kidd halted in the anteroom, not because he had any plan formed, but through that instinct which urges villains of his species not to leave a good place till compelled. He had heard the captain summon his asistente. The latter, after a few moments' absence, returned to the anteroom with a look of importance which at once caused the adventurer to reflect, and suggested to him the idea of knowing what the conversation was the soldier had held with his chief. Isidro, the captain's asistente, was an Opatas Indian, of tried bravery and fidelity. Unluckily, though he did his duty in the battlefield, his intellect was rather restricted, and, like all Indians, he had a propensity for strong liquors, which had several times brought him to great grief. Kidd was familiar with the soldier, and knew his weakness; hence his plan was formed in a moment.

"Since you remain here," he said to him, "I shall be off: when I came to speak to the captain, I left a nearly full bottle of mezcal at the tocanda of Master Cospeto, and on my word I feel inclined to go and finish it. I will not invite you to accompany me, for your duty keeps you here; otherwise you may be assured that I should be delighted to empty it with you."

"My duty does not keep me here," the Indian answered; "on the contrary, I have a long ride to make this very night."

"A long ride!" the adventurer exclaimed; "¡Caray! It is the same case with me, and as I know no better preservative against the night cold than mezcal, that is why I meant to empty the bottle before mounting. If your inclinations lie the same way, it is at your service."

We will allow that the asistente hesitated.

"Have you also a ride to take?" he asked.

"Yes, and I suspect that yours is as long as mine: well, I am going a long distance; what direction do you follow?"

"The captain sends me to Arispe," the bandit answered, boldly.

"Why, how singular that is! We shall follow the same road."

"That is indeed strange. Well, is it settled?—Will you drink the stirrup-cup with me?"

"Upon due reflection, I see no harm in it."

"Let us make haste, then," the brigand continued, for he feared lest the captain might catch him with his asistente; "we have no time to lose."

For reasons best known to himself, the adventurer left the Indian at the house door, bidding him bring his horse to Cospeto's rancho, where he would join him in a few minutes, and they would set out on their journey together. Kidd merely wanted to warn the mesonero, with whom he had lodged the bailiff, not to let him go away on any excuse—"Watch him closely, and at the slightest suspicious movement go and inform Captain Don Marcos Niza"—who, for reasons connected with the public safety, did not wish to let these strangers out of sight. The mesonero promised to carry out his instructions faithfully; and, re-assured on this point, the adventurer fetched his horse from the corral, and went to join the Opatas at Señor Cospeto's rancho, as had been agreed on. On reaching the inn by one street, to his great satisfaction he saw the orderly arriving by another, mounted, and ready to start. The two friends entered the rookery to which we have already conducted the reader.

The adventurer honourably kept his word: not only did he order a bottle of mezcal, but at the same time one of excellent Catalonian refino. The Indian's prudence was entirely routed by such generosity; the more so because he had no reason to distrust the bandit, with whom he had already made several excursions, and regarded him as an excellent comrade. Kidd, in order to avoid any doubts on the part of his comrade, was careful not to ask him any questions; he merely poured him out glass after glass, and when the bottles were empty, the Indian had drunk the greater part of their contents, as Kidd desired to retain his coolness. When they had finished, the bandit rose, paid the score, and called for another bottle of refino.

"This is for the road," he said.

"An excellent idea," remarked the asistente, whose eyes flashed like carbuncles, and who was beginning to have a very vague notion of the state of affairs. They left the rancho, and mounted their horses. Kidd was rather anxious as to how he should get out of the rancho, as he had no pass of any sort; for if it were difficult to get into the Real de Minas, it was quite as much to get out of it. Luckily, for the adventurer, Isidro's pass was in perfect order, and when he showed it at the gate, where he was perfectly well known to all the soldiers on duty, he said, pointing to Kidd, "This caballero goes with me." The soldiers, aware that Isidro was the confidential man of the captain, did not offer the slightest difficulty, but allowed them to pass, and wished them a lucky journey. When the adventurer found himself in the open country he drew a deep breath of relief, as he gave his too confiding comrade a sarcastic glance.

"Now," he said, "we must take the shortest road, in order to arrive sooner."

"What, are there two roads?" Isidro asked.

"There are ten," Kidd replied coolly; "but the shortest runs almost in a right line, and passes close to the Hacienda del Toro."

"Let us take that, then."

"Why that more than another?"

"Because I am going to the hacienda."

"Ah," the adventurer said, pleasantly, "let us take a drink, and start." Uncorking the bottle, he took a pull, and then handed it to his companion, who imitated him, with an evident expression of pleasure.

"You say, then," Kidd resumed, as he smacked his lips, "That you are going to the Hacienda del Toro?"

"Yes, I am."

"It is a good house, and most hospitable."

"Do you know it?"

"¡Caray! I should think so. The majordomo is my intimate friend. What happy days I have spent with that excellent Señor Paredes!"

"Since it is your road, why not call there with me as you are certain of a kind reception?"

"I do not say I will not; I suppose you are going to ask the Marquis for some men, as soldiers are scarce at the pueblo?"

"I do not think that is the case. Don Hernando has already authorized the captain to enlist his miners, and the peons left him he will need to defend the hacienda in the event of an attack."

"That is true; besides, it is no business of mine. Let every man have his own secrets."

"Oh, I do not think there is any great secret in the matter: the captain is a near relation of the Marquis; they often write to each other, and the letter I am ordered to deliver will only refer, I expect, to family matters and private interests."

"That is probable; the more so, because it is said that the Marquis's affairs are in a very bad state at present."

"So it is said; but I have heard that they are about to be settled."

"¡Caray! I wish it with all my heart, for it is a pity to see one of the oldest families of the province reduced. Suppose we drink the health of the Marquis?"

"With pleasure."

The bottle was hugged for the second time by the two companions. A man may be an Opatas Indian, that is to say, of herculean stature, with a breast arched like a tortoiseshell; but he cannot swallow with impunity such a prodigious quantity of alcohol as Isidro had absorbed without beginning to feel intoxicated. The asistente, strong though he was, tottered on his horse: his eyes began to close, and his tongue to grow thick. But, excited as he was by liquor, the more difficulty he experienced in speaking the more he wanted to do so. The adventurer eagerly followed the progress of his comrade's intoxication, while careful not to let him see that he was aware of his condition.

"Yes, yes," the Indian continued, "the affairs of the Marquis might easily be arranged sooner than is supposed, comrade."

"With his name it cannot be difficult for him to procure money."

"Nonsense! That is not the point, and I know what I know."

"Exactly, Señor Isidro; and as what you know may be a secret, I will not urge you to tell it me."

"Did I say that it was a secret?" the Indian objected.

"No, but I suppose so."

"You are wrong to suppose so; and, besides, you are my friend, are you not?"

"I believe so," the adventurer answered, modestly.

"Well, if you are my friend, I have nothing to conceal from you."

"That is true; still, if you consider it your duty to hold your tongue—"

"Hold my tongue! Why so? Have you any pretence to silence me?"

"I? Heaven forbid, and the proof is, here's your health."

The Indian began laughing.

"That is what is called an unanswerable argument," he said, as he placed the bottle to his lips and threw back his head, as if contemplating the stars.

He remained in this position till all the remaining liquor had passed down his throat.

"Ah!" he said, with an accent of regret, "It was good."

"What do you mean?" Kidd exclaimed, with pretended surprise; "Is there none left?"

"I do not think so," the Indian remarked, with a drunkard's gravity; "it is a pity that these bottles are so small."

And with that he threw it into the road.

"I agree with you that the rancheros are robbers."

"Yes," said the asistente, with a hiccough, "robbers; but soon—we shall drink as much as we like."

"Eh, eh, that will not be unpleasant; but where will it be?"

"Where? Why, at the Hacienda del Toro."

"Yes, they never refuse a draught of mezcal to an honest man in that house."

"Nonsense, a draught! You are jesting, comrade; whole bottles would be nearer the truth. Besides, do you fancy the Marquis will look into matters so closely at his daughter's marriage."

"What?"

"Where on earth do you come from, that you are ignorant of that? Nothing else is spoken of in the country."

"It is the first I have heard of it."

"Well, all the better; I will tell you. Doña Marianna, a pretty girl, caray, is going to marry a senator, no one less."

The adventurer suddenly pricked up his ears.

"A senator?" he repeated.

"This seems to surprise you. Why should not a pretty girl marry a senator? I consider you a curious comrade to doubt my word."

"I do not doubt it."

"Yes, you do; ugly brute that you are."

The intoxication of the Opatas was at its height. Excited even more by the horse's gallop and the adventurer's artfully managed contradiction, Isidro felt passion mount to his head. The intoxication of Indians is horrible: they become raving madmen; their heated brain gives birth to the strangest hallucinations, and under the influence of spirits they are capable of the greatest crimes. The bandit was aware of all these peculiarities, by which he hoped to profit; he had drawn from the Indian all that he wanted to learn from him; he had squeezed him like a lemon, and now only wanted to throw away the peel. We need hardly say that at this hour of the night the road the two travellers were following was completely deserted, and that Kidd did not fear any overlookers of what he intended doing. They were riding at this moment along the course of a small stream, a confluent of the Rio Bravo del Norte, whose wooded banks afforded sufficient concealment. The adventurer made his horse bound on one side, and drawing his machete, exclaimed—

"Brute yourself, you drunken Opatas!" At the same moment he dealt the poor follow such a sudden blow that he fell off his horse like a log. But he rose to his feet tottering, and though stunned by the attack, and seriously wounded, he drew his sabre, and rushed on the bandit with a yell of fury. But the latter was on his guard; he attentively watched his enemy's movements, and urged his horse forwards. The Indian, thrown down by the animal's chest, rolled on the ground where he lay without stirring. Was he dead? Kidd supposed so; but the bandit was a very prudent man, Indians are crafty, and this death might be a feint. Kidd therefore watched quietly a few paces from his victim, for he was in no hurry.

A quarter of an hour elapsed, and the Indian had not made a movement. Reassured by this complete immobility, the bandit resolved to dismount and go up to him. All at once the Opatas rose; with a tiger leap he bounded on the adventurer, twined his arms round him, and the two men rolled on the ground, uttering savage yells, and trying to take each other's life. It was a short but horrible struggle. The Opatas, in spite of his wounds, derived a factitious strength from the fury that animated him and the excitement produced by intoxication, which was heightened by his ardent desire to take revenge for the cowardly treachery of which he was the victim.

Unhappily, the efforts he was compelled to make opened his wounds, and his blood flowed in streams; and with his blood he felt his life departing. He made a supreme effort to strangle the miserable adventurer in his clenched fingers; but the latter, by a sudden and cleverly calculated movement, succeeded in liberating himself from the Indian's iron grasp. He rose quickly, and at the moment when the asistente recovered from his surprise, and prepared to renew the fight, Kidd; raised his machete, and cleft the poor fellow's head.

"Dog! Accursed dog!" he yelled.

The Indian remained on his feet for a moment, tottering from right to left; he took a step forward with outstretched arms, and then fell with his face to the ground and the death rattle in his throat. This time he was really dead.

"Well," Kidd muttered, as he thrust his machete several times into the ground, in order to remove the blood, "that was tough work; these demons of Indians must be killed twice to make sure they do not recover. What is to be done now?"

He reflected for a few moments; then walked up to the corpse, turned it over, and opened the breast of the uniform to obtain the letter. He had no difficulty in finding it; he placed it in his own pocket, and then stripped his victim, on the chance that he might want to use his uniform. But two things troubled him: the first was the soldier's horse; the second, his bag. The horse he made no attempt to seize; so soon as its master was wounded, the animal started off at a gallop into the wood; and as it would have been madness to try and find it on so dark a night, the adventurer did not attempt it. Still the flight of the horse alarmed him. Any person who found it would take it back to the pueblo, and then suspicions would be aroused which might soon be fixed on him, although he felt almost certain that the soldiers who saw him leave the town with the asistente had not recognized him; but his absence from the pueblo would appear suspicious to the captain, who was acute, and as he knew Kidd so well, would not hesitate to accuse him.

The affair was embarrassing; but luckily for him, the adventurer was a man of resources. Any other person would have fastened a stone to the body, and thrown it into the stream, but the bandit carefully avoided that. Such an expeditious method, while getting rid of the victim, would only have increased the suspicions; besides water is not a good keeper of secrets; one day or another the body would rise perhaps to the surface, and then the nature of the wounds would reveal the hand that dealt them. Kidd hit upon a more simple or sure plan, or at least he thought so. With horrible coolness he scalped the corpse, and threw the scalp into the stream, after rolling it round a large stone; this first profanation accomplished, he made a cross cut on the victim's chest, plucked out his heart, which he also threw into the river, and then plaiting together a few flexible lianas, he formed a cord, which he fastened to the feet of the corpse, and hung it from the main branch of a tree.

"There!" he said, with satisfaction, when the horrible task was completed, "That is all right, caray! I am ready to wager my share of paradise with the first comer that the cleverest people will be taken in. The Indians are in the field at this very moment, and hang me if everyone will not be convinced that this drunken scoundrel was scalped by the Apaches."

In fact, all the hideous mutilating which this villain has made his victim undergo is employed by the Indian bravos upon their enemies. Frightful though the deed was, Kidd consequently, in the impossibility he found of disposing of the body, had employed the best mode in which to divert suspicion.

Before leaving the scene of the murder, the bandit carefully washed the soldier's clothes, and removed any blood stains from his own; then, after assuring himself by a searching glance that there was nothing to denounce the crime of which he had been guilty, he whistled up his horse, and mounted, after carefully fastening the soldier's uniform behind him. He rolled a cigarette, lit it, and set out again, with the satisfaction of a man who had just succeeded in a most important affair, which had caused him great anxiety.

It was somewhat by chance that Kidd originally told the asistente that he was proceeding to Arispe; but the discovery of the letter, and the soldier's confidential remarks, had converted this chance into certainty. The bandit had discovered, amid all poor Isidro's drunken maundering, one leading idea, and scented a profitable stroke of business. He comprehended of what importance it would be to Don Rufino to be informed of all that was going on at the pueblo at the Hacienda del Toro, that he might be able to arrange his plans with certainty. Consequently, the adventurer resolved to ride at full speed to Arispe, determined to make the senator pay dearly for the news he brought, while making a mental reservation, with that adventurous logic he was so skilful in, to betray Don Rufino on the first opportunity, if his own interests demanded that painful sacrifice of him. All this being thoroughly settled in his mind, the bandit started at full speed in the direction of Arispe, which city he reached by sunrise.

CHAPTER XXXIV
TWO VILLAINS

As Kidd was well known, he easily obtained admission to the town; but when he had passed the gates, he reflected that it was too early for him to call on the senator, who would still be asleep. Hence he proceeded straight to a rancho he knew, a suspicious den, the usual gathering place of fellows of his sort, where he was certain of a hearty welcome by payment. In fact, the ranchero, who on first seeing him assumed an ill-omened grimace, greeted him with the most agreeable smile when he flashed before his eyes some piastres and gold coins.

The adventurer entered the rancho, left his horse in the corral, and immediately began to arrange his toilette, which was as a general rule neglected, but which his struggle with the asistente and his hurried ride had rendered more disorderly than usual; and then waited, smoking and drinking, for the hour to arrive when he should pay his respects to Don Rufino.

The ranchero, who was thoroughly acquainted with his man and his habits, prowled round him in vain to try and sound him and learn the causes of his appearance in Arispe, where, for certain reasons the police did not care to see him. This rendered his journeys to that town rather few and far between; for the police there, as elsewhere, are very troublesome to a certain class of citizens. But vainly did the ranchero try all his cleverest ruses, his most delicate insinuations; Kidd only answered his questions by insignificant phrases, crafty smiles and winks; but in the end he remained perfectly impenetrable, a want of confidence by which the ranchero was greatly insulted, and he swore to himself to be avenged on the bandit for it some day.

When the Cabildo clock struck nine, Kidd thought it was time to be off; he rose, majestically threw a piastre on the table in payment of his score, wrapped his zarapé round him, and left the house.

"Whom can he have assassinated to be so rich?" the ranchero asked himself, as he cunningly watched him depart.

A reflection which proved that the worthy ranchero was well acquainted with his man.

Kidd felt he was watched, and hence carefully avoided going straight to the senator's house; on the contrary, affecting the careless demeanour of a lounger, he set out in the diametrically opposite direction. The adventurer then walked about the town for half an hour, while carefully avoiding the more frequented streets, for fear of attracting attention on himself; thus he gradually approached the senator's mansion, and hurriedly slipped under the zaguán, after assuring himself by a glance all around that no one had seen him enter.

"Halloa, you fellow!" a voice suddenly shouted to him, making him start and stop; "Where the deuce are you going like that? And what do you want here?" The adventurer raised his eyes, and saw an individual of a certain age, easily to be recognized as a domestic by his clothing, who was standing in the hall door, and resolutely barring his way.

"What do I want?" the bandit repeated, to give himself time to seek an answer.

"Yes, what do you want? That is clear enough, I suppose?"

"¡Caray! It is clear; what can I want except to see his Excellency, Senator Don Rufino Contreras?"

"Excellent," the other said, derisively; "and do you suppose his Excellency will receive you without knowing who you are?"

"And why not, if you please, señor?"

"Because you do not look like drawing room company."

"Do you think so?" the bandit said, haughtily.

"Why, that is plain enough; you much more resemble a lepero than a caballero."

"You are not polite, my good fellow; what you say may be correct, but the remark is uncalled for; patched clothes often conceal very honourable caballeros, and if I have been ill treated by fortune, that is no reason why you should throw it in my teeth so sharply."

"Enough of this, and be off."

"I shall not stir till I have seen the senator."

The manservant gave him a side look, which the other endured with imperturbable coolness.

"Do you mean that?" he asked him.

"I really do."

"For the last time, I order you to be gone," the valet went on, menacingly.

"Take care of what you are doing, comrade; I have to talk with the señor, and he is expecting me."

"Expecting you?"

"Yes, me!" the scoundrel answered, majestically. The servant shrugged his shoulders contemptuously: still he reflected, and asked with a more conciliatory tone than he had yet employed—"Your name?"

"You do not want to know it; merely tell your master that I have just come from the Hacienda del Toro."

"If that is the case, why did you not tell me so before?"

"Probably because you did not ask me. Go and announce me to your master; you have kept me waiting too long already."

The domestic went off without replying, and Kidd took advantage of his departure to instal himself in the vestibule. For a hundred reasons he did not like the vicinity of the street, and he was glad to be no longer exposed to the curious glances of passers-by. The absence of the servant was not long, and when he returned, his manner was entirely changed.

"Caballero," he said, with a bow, "if you will do me the honour of following me, his Excellency is waiting for you."

"Fellow! Too insolent before, too humble now," the adventurer said, crushing him with a contemptuous glance; "show the way."

And, laughing in his beard, he followed the footman, who was red with anger and shame at this haughty reprimand.

Mexican houses, except in the great cities, are ordinarily built but one story high; they are generally very slightly constructed, owing to the earthquakes, which are extremely frequent in intertropical countries, and destroy in a few seconds towns, and entirely ruin them. The result of this mode of building is that nearly all the apartments are on the ground floor; and then there are no staircases to ascend or descend, which, in our opinion, is very agreeable. The adventurer remarked with some degree of pleasure that the valet led him through several rooms before reaching the one in which the senator was sitting; at length he turned the handle of the door, threw it open, and stepped aside to let the bandit pass. The latter walked in boldly, like a man certain of a hearty reception.

"Ah!" said the senator, starting slightly at seeing him, "It is you."

"Yes," he replied, with a graceful bow.

"Retire," Don Rufino said to the valet; "I am not at home to anyone, and do not come in till I call you." The valet bowed, went out, and closed the door behind him. As if by common accord, the two stood silently listening till the valet's footsteps died away in the distance; then, without saying a word, Kidd threw open the folding doors.

"Why do you do that?" Don Rufino asked him.

"Because we have to talk about serious matters; the *tapetes* spread over the floors of your rooms deaden footsteps, and your servant has an excellent spy's face."

The senator made no remark; he doubtless recognised the correctness of his singular visitor's argument.

"It is you then, bandit," he said at last.

"I fancy I can notice that you did not expect me?"

"I confess it; I will even add that I did not in the slightest desire your visit."

"You are very forgetful of your friends, Don Rufino, and it makes me feel sorry for you," the bandit answered, with a contrite air.

"What do you mean, scoundrel, by daring to use such language to me?"

Kidd shrugged his shoulders, drew up a butaca, and fell into it with a sigh of relief.

"I must observe," he said, with the most imperturbable coolness, "that you forgot to offer me a chair."

Then, crossing one leg over the other, he began rolling a cigarette, a task to which he gave the most serious attention. The senator frowningly examined the adventurer; for this bandit to dare assume such a tone with him, he must have very powerful weapons in his hands, or be the bearer of news of the highest importance. In either case he must be humoured. Don Rufino immediately softened the expression of his face, and handed the adventurer a beautifully chased gold mechero.

"Pray, light your cigarette, my dear Kidd," he said, with a pleasant smile.

The bandit took the mechero, and examined it with admiration.

"Ah!" he exclaimed, with a splendidly feigned regret, "I have dreamed for years that I possessed such a toy, but, unluckily, fortune has ever thwarted me."

"If it please you so much," Don Rufino answered, with a mighty effort, "I shall be delighted to make you a present of it."

"You are really most generous. Believe me, señor, that any present coming from you will always be most precious in my eyes."

And, after lighting his cigarette, he unceremoniously placed the mechero in his pocket.

"Of course your visit Has an object?" the senator said, after a moment's interval.

"They always have, señor," the other answered, as he enveloped himself in a cloud of blue smoke, which issued from his nose and mouth; "the first was to see you."

"I thank you for the politeness; but I do not think that is sufficient reason for forcing your way in here."

"Forcing is rather a harsh word, señor," the bandit said, sorrowfully; but he suddenly changed his tone, and assumed his usual sharp, quick way. "Come, Don Rufino, let us deal fairly, and not waste our time in compliments which neither of us believes."

"I wish nothing better; speak, then, and the plague take you."

"Thank you. I prefer that mode of speech, for at least I recognise you. I am about to give you an example of frankness; I have come, not to propose a bargain, but to sell you certain information, and a letter of the utmost importance to you, which I obtained—no matter how—solely on your account."

"Good; let us see whether I can accept the bargain."

"In the first place, allow me to say two words, so as to thoroughly establish our reciprocal position. Our situation has greatly changed during the last few days; I no longer fear you, but you, on the contrary, are afraid of me."

"I afraid of you?"

"Yes, señor, because I hold your secret, and you can no longer threaten to kill me, as you did at our last interview."

"Oh! Oh! And why not, if you please?" the senator asked.

"Because we are alone, you are unarmed, I am stronger than you, and at your slightest movement would blow out your brains like those of a wild beast. Do you now comprehend me, my dear sir?" he added, as he drew a brace of pistols from under his zarapé; "what do you think of these playthings?"

"They are tolerably good, I should fancy," the senator replied, coldly; "and what do you say to these?" he added, as he uncovered a brace of magnificent pistols hidden under the papers scattered over the table at which he was seated.

"They are detestable."

"Why so?"

"Because you would not dare use them."

The senator smiled ironically.

"Laugh, if you like, my master; I like best to see you treat the matter in that way; but I repeat that you are in my power this time, instead of my being in yours. I have delivered to Captain Don Marcos Niza certain papers, which, were they opened by him, might, I fear, gravely compromise you: there is one among them, the tenor of which is as follows:—'I, the undersigned, declare that my valet, Lupino Contrarias, has treacherously assassinated and deserted me in a frightful desert, and there plundered me of everything I possessed, consisting of two mules laden with gold dust, and two thousand three hundred gold ounces in current money. On the point of appearing before my God, and not hoping to survive my wounds, I denounce this wretch, etc. etc. Signed—.' Shall I tell the name of the signer? But what is the matter with you, my dear sir? Do you feel ill? You are as pale as a corpse."

In truth, on hearing the narrative, which the bandit told with a species of complacency, the senator was seized with such a violent fit of terror, that for a moment he was on the point of fainting.

"It is extraordinary," the bandit continued, "how nothing can be trusted to in this world. Just take the case of this excellent Lupino, who had arranged a most delicious trap in the adroitest manner: for more surety, he waited till they were on the other side of the Indian border, at a spot where not a soul passes once in two years; he fires his pistols point blank into his master's back, and goes off, of course taking with him the fortune so honourably acquired. Well, fatality decrees that the master whom he had every reason for believing dead is not quite so; he has time to take out his tablets, and write in pencil a perfectly regular denunciation, and then this demon of a fatality, which never does things by halves, brings to these parts a hunter, who picks up the tablets. It is enough to make a man turn honest, deuce take me if it is not, had he not quite made up his mind to the contrary."

During this long harangue the senator had time to recover from the shock, and regain his coolness. By a supreme effort of the will he had restored calmness to his face, and forced his lips to smile.

"¡Caray!" he said, with a laugh that resembled gnashing of teeth, "that is a wonderful story, and admirably arranged. Permit me, dear señor, to congratulate you on your inventive faculty; it is charming, on my word. But who on earth do you expect to believe such a story?"

"You, first of all, señor, for you know the truth of the story better than anybody."

"Nonsense! You are mad, upon my honour."

"Not quite so mad as you fancy, for the proofs are in my hands."

"I do not say they are not; but admitting the reality of the facts you allege, they took place a long time ago; this Lupino Contrarias has disappeared; he is dead, perhaps: as for his master, the pistols were too well loaded to give him a chance of escape. Who takes any interest in a dead man—especially in our country?"

"How do you know that the weapons were so carefully loaded?"

"I suppose so."

"Suppositions are always the plague in business matters. Between ourselves, do you think it would be so difficult to find this Lupino Contrarias in Rufino Contreras? I think not."

The senator felt his face flush involuntarily.

"Señor," he said, "such an insinuation—"

"Has nothing that needs offend you," Kidd interrupted him, calmly; "it is a supposition, nothing more; now, continuing our suppositions, let us admit for a moment that this master, whom his valet is persuaded he killed, should be, on the contrary, alive and—"

"Oh, that is quite impossible."

"Do not interrupt me so, señor. And, I say, were to lay his hand on his valet's shoulder, as I lay mine on yours, and assert, 'This is my assassin!' what answer would you give to that?"

"I—I!" the senator exclaimed, wildly; "What answer should I give?"

"You would give none," the bandit continued, as he took and thrust into his belt the pistols which the senator, in his trouble, had let fall; "overcome by the evidence, and crushed by the very presence of your victim, you would be irretrievably lost."

There was a second of horrible silence between these two men, who looked at each other as if about to have a frightful contest. At length the senator's emotion was calmed by its very violence; he passed his hand over his damp forehead, and, drawing himself up to his full height, said, sharply—

"After this, what would you of me?"

"I am waiting to hear your resolution before I offer any conditions."

Don Rufino Contreras remained for some minutes plunged in deep thought. Kidd watched him attentively, ready to make use of his weapons if he saw the senator attempt any suspicious movement; but the latter did not even dream of it. Annihilated by the adventurer's staggering revelation, he looked round him wildly, racking his mind in vain to discover some way of escape from the terrible dilemma in which he was placed. At length he raised his head, and looked the bandit fiercely in the face.

"Well, yes," he said to him resolutely, "all that you have narrated is true. I cowardly assassinated, to rob him of his fortune, the man who offered me a helping hand in my misery, and treated me as a friend rather than a servant. But this fortune, however badly it may have been acquired, I possess; by its means I have acquired a position in the world; by roguery and falsehood I have succeeded in imposing on everybody; I have rank and a name; and death alone could make me resign this position, so hardly attained. Now that I have spoken frankly with you, it is your turn to do the same. Tell me the conditions you intend to impose on me, and if they are fair, I will accept them; if not, whatever the consequences may be, I shall refuse them. Take care, for I am not the man to remain at the mercy of a villain like you; sooner than accept so horrible a situation I would denounce myself, and drag you down in my fall. Reflect carefully, then, before answering me, comrade, for my proposition is in earnest. Once the bargain is concluded between us, we will say no more about it. I give you ten minutes to answer me."

This clear and categorical proposal affected the bandit more than he liked to show. He understood that he had to do with one of those indomitable men who, once they have made their mind up, never alter it. The adventurer had nothing to gain by ruining Don Rufino, on the contrary; moreover, that never entered into his plan: he hoped to terrify him, and had succeeded; and now the only thing to be done by these two men, so well suited to understand each other, since they had frankly settled facts, was to attack the pecuniary question, and treat it as skilfully as they could; Kidd, therefore prepared to begin the assault.

CHAPTER XXXV
A FRIENDLY BARGAIN

Don Rufino, with his head resting on his right hand, was carelessly playing with a paper knife, and patiently waiting till his visitor thought proper to speak. This affected indifference perplexed the adventurer: men of Kidd's species instinctively distrust all that does not appear to them natural, and he felt embarrassed by this coolness, for which he could not account, and which he feared might contain a snare. At length he suddenly broke the silence.

"Before all, Don Rufino," he said, "I must tell you the motives of my visit."

"I do not at all care about them," the senator answered, negligently; "still, if you think my knowledge of them may be useful, pray let me hear them."

"I think that when you have heard me, you will change your opinion, señor, and recognise the importance of the service I propose to do you."

"That is possible, and I do not deny it," the senator said, ironically; "but you will allow, my dear Señor Kidd, that you interfere so thoroughly in my affairs, that it is difficult for me to decide, among all the combinations your mind takes pleasure in forming, whether your intentions are good or bad."

"You shall judge."

"Pray speak, then."

"I will tell you, in the first place, that a certain Alguacil, Don Parfindo Purro by name, arrived yesterday at the pueblo of Quitovar."

"Very good," the senator answered, looking fixedly at the bandit.

"Now, I do not know how it is, but the bailiff had scarce reached the pueblo ere by some strange fatality, Captain de Niza was informed of his arrival."

"Only think of that," the senator remarked, ironically; "ever that fatality of which you now spoke to me; it is really being the plaything of misfortune."

In spite of the strong dose of effrontery with which nature had endowed him, the adventurer felt involuntarily troubled.

Don Rufino continued, with a light laugh—

"And still, through this implacable fatality, the captain was not only informed of the arrival of this worthy Don Parfindo, but also of the reasons that brought him."

"How do you know that?" Kidd exclaimed, with pretended surprise.

"Oh, I guess it, that is all," the senator replied, with a slight shrug of his shoulders; "but go on, pray; what you tell me is beginning to become most interesting."

The bandit went on with imperturbable coolness.

"As you are aware, the captain is a relation of the Marquis de Moguer."

"Yes, and a very near relation."

"Hence he did not hesitate, but at once sent off a messenger to the Hacienda del Toro, carrying a letter in which he probably gave the most circumstantial details about the bailiff, and the mission he is charged with."

At this revelation, Don Rufino suddenly doffed the mask of indifference he had assumed, and smote the table fiercely with his fist.

"Ah, that letter!" he exclaimed, "That letter! I would give its weight in gold for it."

"Very well, señor," the bandit remarked, with a smile; "as I am anxious to prove to you the honesty of my intentions, I give it you for nothing."

He took the letter from his pocket, and handed it to the senator; the latter bounded on it like a tiger on its prey, and tore it from Kidd's hands.

"Gently, gently; be good enough to remark that the seal is not broken, and that, as the letter has not yet been opened, I am naturally ignorant of its contents."

"That is true," the senator muttered, as he turned it over and over; "I thank you for your discretion, señor."

"You are most kind," Kidd replied, with a bow.

"But," the senator continued, "how did this letter, addressed to Don Hernando de Moguer, fall into your hands?"

"Oh, very simply," the other replied, lightly; "just fancy that the man the captain selected to carry his missive was a friend of mine. As I intended to pay you a visit at Arispe, and as I felt grieved at seeing this man traverse such a dangerous road alone by night, I offered to accompany him, and he consented. I do not know how it occurred, but on the road we began quarrelling. In short, without any evil intentions on my part, I declare to you, in the heat of the argument I gave him a blow on the head with my machete, so well dealt that he was compelled to die. It grieved me deeply, but there was no remedy; and as I was afraid lest the letter might get into bad hands, I carried it off. That is the whole story."

"It is really most simple," Don Rufino remarked, with a smile, and broke the seal.

Kidd discreetly sat down again in his butaca, in order to leave the senator at liberty to peruse this despatch, which seemed to interest him greatly. He read it through with the utmost attention, and then let his head hang on his chest, and fell into deep thought.

"Well," the adventurer at length asked, "is the news that letter conveys so very bad, that it must entirely absorb you?"

"The news is of the utmost importance to me, señor; still, I ask myself for what purpose you seized it?"

"Why, to do you a service, it strikes me."

"That is all very well; but, between ourselves, you had another object."

The bandit burst into a laugh.

"Did I not tell you that I wish to make a bargain?"

"That is true; but I am awaiting a full explanation from you."

"That is very difficult, señor."

"I admit that it is; well, I will put you at your ease."

"I wish for nothing better."

"I will offer you the bargain you do not like to propose."

"I see that you are beginning to understand me, and that, between the pair of us, we shall come to something."

"You are not rich," the senator remarked, frankly approaching the point.

"I am forced to confess that I am not actually rolling in wealth," he answered, with an ironical glance at his more than ragged attire.

"Well, if you like I will make you a rich man at one stroke."

"What do you mean by rich, señor?" the bandit asked, distrustfully.

"I mean to put you in possession of a sum which will not only protect you from want, but also allow you to indulge your fancy, while living honestly."

"Honesty is a virtue only within reach of those who can spend money without wanting it," the adventurer remarked sententiously.

"Be it so; I will render you rich, to use your language."

"It will cost a good deal," Kidd answered, impudently, "for I have very peculiar tastes."

"I dare say; but no matter. I have in Upper California a hacienda, of which I will hand you the title deeds this very day."

"Hum!" said Kidd, thrusting out his upper lip contemptuously; "Is the hacienda a fine one?"

"Immense; covered with ganado and manadas of wild horses; it is situated near the sea."

"That is something, I allow; but that is not wealth."

"Wait a minute."

"I am waiting."

"I will add to this hacienda a round sum of one hundred thousand piastres in gold."

The bandit's eyes were dazzled.

"What," he said, rising as if moved by a spring, and turning pale with joy, "did you say—one hundred thousand?"

"Yes, I repeat," the senator continued, internally satisfied with the effect he had produced; "do you think that with such a sum as that it is possible to be honest?"

"*¡Viva Cristo!* I should think so!" he exclaimed, gleefully.

"It only depends on yourself to possess it within a week."

"Oh, yes, I understand; there is a condition. ¡Caray! It must be very hard for me to refuse it."

"This is the condition; listen to me, and, above all, understand me thoroughly."

"¡Caray! I should think I would listen; a hacienda and one hundred thousand piastres—I should be a fool to refuse them."

"You must not impede my prospects in any way; allow me to espouse Doña Marianna, and on the day of the marriage hand me the tablets which you took from the gentleman so unhappily assassinated by his valet."

"Very well. Is that all?"

"Not yet."

"Very good; go on."

"I insist that when you deliver me the tablets, you will supply proof that the writer is really dead."

"¡Caray! That will be difficult."

"That does not concern me; it is your business."

"That is true; and how long will you give me for that?"

"Eight days."

"¡Cuerpo de Cristo! It is not enough; the man is not so easily to be taken unawares."

"Yes; but once that he is dead, you will be rich."

"I know that, and it is a consideration. No matter; caray! It will be a tough job, and I shall risk my hide."

"You can take it or leave it."

"I take it, viva Cristo! I take it. Never shall I find again such a chance to become an honest man."

"Then that matter is quite settled between us?"

"Most thoroughly; you can set your mind at rest."

"Very good; but as you may change your mind someday, and feel an inclination to betray me—"

"Oh, señor, what an idea!"

"No one knows what may happen. You will at once sign a paper on which these conditions will be fully detailed."

"¡Caray! What you ask is most compromising."

"For both of us, as my proposals will be equally recorded."

"But, in that case, what is the good of writing such a paper, as it will compromise you as much as me?"

"For the simple reason that if some day you feel inclined to betray me, you cannot ruin me without ruining yourself, which will render you prudent, and oblige you to reflect whenever a bad thought crosses your brain."

"Do you distrust me, señor?"

"Have you any excessive confidence in me?"

"That is different; I am only a poor scamp."

"In one word, you will either accept the conditions I offer, or any bargain between us will be impossible."

"Still, supposing, señor, I were to use the paper I hold, as you employ such language to me?"

"You would not dare."

"Not dare!" he exclaimed; "And pray why not?"

"I do not know the motive; but I feel sure that if you could have used that document, you would have done so long ago. I know you too well to doubt it, Señor Kidd; it would be an insult to your intellect, whose acuteness, on the contrary, it affords me pleasure to bear witness to. Hence, believe me, señor, do not try to terrify me further with this paper, or hold it to my chest like a loaded pistol, for you will do no good. Your simplest plan will be to accept the magnificent offer I make you."

"Well, be it so, since you are so pressing," he replied; "I will do what you ask, but you will agree with me that it is very hard."

"Not at all; that is just where you make the mistake; I simply take a guarantee against yourself, that is all."

The adventurer was not convinced; still, the bait conquered him, and, with a sigh of regret, he offered no further resistance. Don Rufino immediately wrote down the conditions agreed on between the two men —a sword of Damocles, which the senator wished to hold constantly in suspense over the head of his accomplice, and which, if produced in a court of justice, would irretrievably destroy them both. While the senator was writing, the bandit sought for the means to escape this formidable compromise, and destroy the man who forced it on him when he had received the money. We should not like to assert that Don Rufino had not the same idea. When the senator had concluded this strange deed of partnership, which rendered them mutually responsible, and riveted them more closely together than a chain would have done, he read in a loud voice what he had written.

"Now," he said, after reading, "have you any remark to offer?"

"Deuce take the remarks!" the bandit exclaimed, roughly; "Whatever I might say, you would make no alteration, so it is better to leave it as it is."

"That is my opinion, too—so sign; and to soften any painful effect it may produce on you, I will give you one hundred ounces."

"Very good," he replied, with a smile; and taking the pen from Don Rufino's hand, he boldly placed his signature at the foot of this document, which might cost him his life. But the promise of the hundred ounces made him forget everything; and besides, Kidd was a bit of a fatalist, and reckoned on chance to liberate him from his accomplice ere long.

When Kidd had signed with the greatest assurance, the senator sprinkled gold dust over the paper, folded it, and placed it in his bosom.

"And here," he said, as he thrust his hand into a coffer, "is the promised sum."

He piled the ounces on the table, and Kidd pocketed them with a smile of pleasure.

"You know that I am at your orders, and ready to obey you," he said; "and, as a beginning, I restore you the pistols, which I no longer require."

"Thanks. Have you anything to detain you at Arispe?"

"Not the slightest."

"Then you would offer no objection to leaving the town?"

"On the contrary, I intend to do so as soon as possible."

"That is most fortunate; I will give you a letter for Señor Parfindo, to whom I will ask you to deliver it immediately on your arrival."

"Then you want to send me to the pueblo?"

"Have you any repugnance to return there?"

"Not the slightest; still, I shall not remain there on account of that night's business."

"Ah, yes, that is true, the soldier's death—take care."

"Oh, I shall only remain at the pueblo just long enough to perform the duty you entrust to me, and then leave it immediately."

"That will be most prudent. But no, stay; upon reflection, I think it will be better for you not to return to the Real de Minas. I will send my letter by another person."

"I prefer that. Have you any other order to give me?"

"None; so you can do what you think proper: but remember that I expect you in a week, and so act accordingly."

"I shall not forget it, caray!"

"In that case, I will not detain you. Good-bye."

"Till we meet again, señor."

The senator struck a gong, and the manservant appeared almost immediately. Don Rufino and Kidd exchanged a side-glance. It was evident that the criado, curious, like all servants, had listened at the door, and tried to learn for what reason his master remained so long shut up with a man of the adventurer's appearance; but, thanks to the precautions Kidd had taken, even the sound of the voices, which were purposely suppressed, did not reach him.

"Show this caballero out," the senator said.

The two men bowed for the last time, as if they were the best friends in the world, and then separated.

"Villain!" Don Rufino exclaimed, so soon as he was alone; "if ever I can make you pay me for all the suffering you have forced on me today, I will not spare you."

And he passionately dashed down a splendid vase, which was unluckily within his reach.

For his part, the adventurer, while following the servant through the apartment, indulged in reflections which were anything but rosy coloured.

"Hang it all!" he said to himself; "The affair has been hot. I believe that I shall act wisely in distrusting my friend: the dear señor is far from being tender-hearted, and if he has a chance of playing me an ill turn he will not let it slip. I did act wrong to sign that accursed paper; but, after all, what have I to fear? He is too much in danger to try and set a trap for me; but for all, I will be prudent, for that can do me no harm."

When he had ended this soliloquy he found himself under the zaguán, where the manservant took leave of him with a respectful bow. The adventurer pulled his wide hat brim over his eyes, and departed. In returning to the rancho he employed the same precautions he had used in going to the senator's house, for he was not at all anxious to be recognised and arrested by the Alguaciles; for, as we know, the streets of the town, for certain reasons, were not at all healthy for him. Kidd found the ranchero standing in his doorway, with straddled legs, attentively surveying the approaches to his house.

"Eh!" the host said, with a bow, "Back already?"

"As you see, compadre; but let me have my breakfast at once, for I have a deal to do."

"Are you going to leave us already?"

"I do not know; come, pray make haste."

The ranchero served him without further questioning. The adventurer made a hearty meal, paid liberally to appease his host's ill temper, saddled his horse, and set out, without saying whether he should return or not. A quarter of an hour later he was in the open country, and inhaling with infinite pleasure the fresh, fragrant breeze that reached him from the desert.

CHAPTER XXXVI
THE HACIENDA DEL TORO

We will now leap over an interval of a fortnight, and return to the Hacienda del Toro; but before resuming our story we will cursorily describe the events that occurred during this fortnight, in order to make the reader thoroughly understand by what a strange concourse of events accident brought all our characters face to face, and produced a collision among them, from which an unforeseen *dénouement* issued.

Doña Marianna, persuaded by Doña Esperanza, or, perhaps, unconsciously attracted by the secret longings of her heart, had consented to remain a couple of days with her. These days were occupied with pleasant conversation, in which the maiden at length disclosed the secret which she imagined to be buried in the remotest nook of her heart. Doña Esperanza smiled with delight at this simple revelation of a love which she already suspected, and which everything led her to encourage.

Stronghand, for his part, had yielded to the magical fascination the maiden exercised over him. Feeling himself beloved, his restraint and coldness melted away to make room for an honest admiration. Carried away by the feelings that agitated him, he displayed all the true prudence and goodness contained in his character, which was, perhaps, rather savage, but it was that loyal and powerful savageness which pleases women, by creating in them a secret desire to conquer these rebellious natures, and dominate them by their delicious seductions. Women, as a general rule, owing to their very weakness, have always liked to subdue energetic men, and those who are reputed indomitable; for a woman is proud to be protected, and blushes when she is compelled to defend the man whose name she bears. Contempt kills love. A woman will never love a man except when she has the right to be proud of him, and can say to him, "Spare foes too weak for you, and unworthy of your anger."

During the two days the young couple did not once utter the word love, and yet they clearly explained it and no longer entertained a doubt as to their mutual attachment.

Still it was time to think about returning to the hacienda. It was settled that Doña Marianna should inform her father about what she had learned from Doña Esperanza, that she should not positively refuse Don Rufino's hand, and quietly await events.

"Take care," the maiden said, as she held out her hand to the hunter; "my only hope is in you: if you fail in your plans I shall be left alone defenceless, and death alone will remain to me, for I shall not survive the loss of all my hopes."

"Trust to me, Doña Marianna; I have staked my happiness and my life on the terrible game I am preparing to play, and I feel convinced that I shall win it."

"I will pray to Heaven for both you and myself with such fervour, that I feel confident my prayers will be granted."

These words, with which the young people parted, were equivalent to a mutual engagement. Doña Esperanza tenderly embraced the maiden.

"Remember the legend," she said to her, and Doña Marianna replied with a smile.

The tigrero held the horses by the bridle. Stronghand and ten hunters prepared to follow the travellers at a distance, in order to help them, should it be necessary. The journey was performed in silence. Doña Marianna was too much engaged in restoring some degree of order to her thoughts, which were upset by what had happened during the two days she spent among the hunters, to dream of saying a word to her companion; while he, for his part, confounded by the way in which he had been treated in camp, tried to explain the luxury and comfort which he had never before witnessed in the desert, and which plunged him into a state of amazement from which he could not recover.

As Doña Marianna had expressed a wish to reach their journey's end as quickly as possible, Mariano took a different road from that which he had previously followed, and which ran to El Toro without passing by the rancho.

At about 3 p.m. they came in sight of the rock, and began scaling the path, and then noticed the hunters, commanded by Stronghand, drawn up in good order on the skirt of the forest. When the young lady reached the first gate of the hacienda, the sound of a shot reached her ear, and a white puff of smoke floating over the horsemen made her guess who it was that had fired it. Doña Marianna waved her handkerchief in the air. A second shot was fired, as if to show her that the signal was seen, and then the hunters turned round and disappeared in the forest. Doña Marianna entered the hacienda, and the first person she met was Paredes.

"*¡Válgame dios!* niña," the worthy majordomo exclaimed; "Where have you come from? The Marquis has been excessively anxious about you."

"Does not my father know that I have been to pay a visit to my nurse?"

"Your brother told him so, niña; but as your absence was so prolonged, the Marquis was afraid that some accident had happened to you."

"You see that it was not so, my good Paredes; so set your mind at rest, and go and re-assure my father, to whom I shall be delighted to pay my respects."

"Don Hernando will be pleased at your return, niña; he is at this moment engaged with Don Ruiz in inspecting the walls on the side of the huerta, in order to make certain that they are in a sound condition for we fear more and more an attack from the Indians."

"In that case do not disturb my father, and I will go and rest in the drawing room, for I am exhausted with fatigue; and when my father has completed his inspection, you will inform him of my return. It is unnecessary to importune him now."

"Importune him!" exclaimed the honest majordomo, "Excuse me, señorita, if I am not of your opinion on that head. *¡Viva dios!* the Marquis would not forgive me if I did not immediately inform him of your return."

"In that case, act as you think proper, my worthy Paredes."

The majordomo, who had probably only been waiting for this permission, ran off.

"My dear Mariano," the young lady then said, addressing her foster brother, "it is not necessary to tell what we have been doing during our absence. Everybody must suppose that I have not quitted my nurse's rancho; you understand, and I count on your discretion. When the time arrives, I intend myself to inform my father of all that has occurred."

"Enough, niña; you know that your wishes are orders for me. I will not say a word—besides, it is no business of mine."

"Very well, Mariano; now receive my sincere thanks for the services you have rendered me."

"You know that I am devoted to you, niña; I have merely done my duty, and you have no occasion to thank me for that."

The young lady offered him her hand with a smile, and entered her apartments. The tigrero, when left alone, took the bridles of the two horses, and led them to the corral, through the crowd of rancheros, who, by the Marquis's orders, had sought refuge in the hacienda, and had erected their jacales in all the courtyards. Doña Marianna was not sorry to be alone for a few minutes, in order to have time to prepare the conversation she intended to have with her father and brother, whose difficulties she did not at all conceal from herself.

The hacienda was very large, and hence, in spite of all his diligence, it was not till he had spent half an hour in sterile search, that the majordomo succeeded in finding his master. Don Hernando heard, with a lively feeling of joy, of his daughter's return, and immediately gave up his inspection in order to hurry to her. The more heavily misfortune pressed upon the Marquis, the greater became the affection he entertained for his children; he felt a necessity for resting on them, and drawing more closely the family ties. When he entered, with Don Ruiz, the room in which Doña Marianna was awaiting him, he opened his arms and embraced her tenderly.

"Naughty girl!" he exclaimed; "What mortal anxiety you have caused me! Why did you remain so long absent in these troublous times?"

"Forgive me, my dear father," the girl answered, as she returned his caresses; "I incurred no danger."

"Heaven be praised! But why did you stay away from us for three days."

The young lady blushed.

"Father," she answered, as she lavished on her parent those tender blandishments of which girls so thoroughly possess the secret, "during my entire absence I was only thinking of you."

"Alas!" the Marquis murmured, with a choking sigh, "I know your heart, my poor child; unhappily my position is so desperate that nothing can save me."

"Perhaps you may be saved, father," she said, with a toss of her head.

"Do not attempt to lead me astray by false hopes, which, in the end, would render our frightful situation even more cruel than it is."

"I do not wish to do so, father," she said, earnestly, "but I bring you a certainty."

"A certainty, child! That is a very serious word in the mouth of a girl. Where do you suppose it possible to find the means to conjure ill fortune?"

"Not very far off, father; at this very place, if you like."

Don Hernando made no reply, but let his head drop on his chest mournfully.

"Listen to Marianna, father," Don Ruiz then said; "she is the angel of our home. I believe in her, for I am certain that she would not make a jest of our misfortunes."

"Thanks, Ruiz. Oh, you are right; I would sooner die than dream of increasing my father's grief."

"I know it, child," the Marquis answered, with sad impatience; "but you are young, inexperienced, and doubtless accept the wishes of your heart as certainties."

"Why not listen to what my sister has to say, father?" Don Ruiz said. "If she is deceiving herself—if what she wishes to tell us does not produce on you the effect she expects from it, at any rate she will have given an undeniable proof of the lively interest she takes in your affairs; and were it only for that reason, both you and I owe her thanks."

"Of what good is it, children?"

"Good heavens, father! In our fearful situation we should neglect nothing. Who knows? Very frequently the weakest persons bring the greatest help. Listen to my sister first, and then you will judge whether her remarks deserve to be taken into consideration."

"As you press it, Ruiz, I will hear her."

"I do not press, father—I entreat. Come, speak, little sister; speak without fear, for we shall listen—at least I shall—with the liveliest interest."

Doña Marianna smiled sweetly, threw her arms round her father's neck, and laid her head on his shoulder with a charming gesture.

"How I love you, my dear father!" she said; "How I should like to see you happy! I have nothing to tell you, for you will not believe me; and what I might have to say is so strange and improbable, that you would not put faith in it."

"You see, child, that I was right."

"Wait a moment, father," she continued; "if I have nothing to tell you, I have a favour to ask."

"A favour!—yes, my dear."

"Yes, father, a favour; but what I desire is so singular—coming from a girl—that I really do not know how to make my request, although the thought is perfectly clear in my mind."

"Oh, oh, little maid," the Marquis said, with a smile, though he was much affected, "what is this thing which requires such mighty preparations? It must be very terrible for you to hesitate so in revealing it to me."

"No, father, it is not terrible; but, I repeat, it will appear to you wild."

"Oh, my child," he continued, as he shrugged his shoulders with an air of resignation, "I have seen so many wild things for some time past, that I shall not attach any importance to one now; hence you can explain yourself fully, without fearing any blame from me."

"Listen to me, father; the favour I have to ask of you is this—and, in the first place, you must promise to grant it to me."

"¡Caramba!" he said, good-humouredly, "you are taking your precautions, señorita. And suppose that I refuse?"

"In that case, father, all would be at an end," she replied, sorrowfully.

"Come, my child, re-assure yourself: I pledge you my word, which you ask for so peremptorily. Are you satisfied now?"

"Oh, father, how kind you are! You really mean it now. You pledge your word to grant me what I ask of you?"

"Yes, yes, little obstinate, I do pledge my word."

The girl danced with delight, as she clapped her pretty little hands, and warmly embraced her father.

"On my word, this little girl is mad!" the Marquis said, with a smile.

"Yes, father, mad with delight; for I hope soon to prove to you that your fortune has never been more flourishing than it now is."

"Why, her mind is wandering now."

"No, father," said Don Ruiz, who, with his eyes fixed on his sister, was listening with sustained interest, and was attentively following the play of her flexible face, on which the varied emotions that agitated her were reflected; "I believe, on the contrary, that Marianna is at this moment revolving in her mind some strange scheme, for carrying out which she requires full and entire liberty."

"You have read the truth, Ruiz. Yes, I have a great project in my head; but in order that it may be thoroughly successful, I must be mistress of my actions, without control or remarks, from eight o'clock this evening till midnight. Do you grant me this power, father?"

"I have promised it," Don Hernando replied, with a smile. "A gentleman has only his word; as you desire, from eight o'clock till midnight you will be sole mistress of the hacienda: no one, not even myself, will have the right to make a remark about your conduct. Must I announce this officially to our people?" he added, sportively.

"It is unnecessary, father: only two persons need be told."

"And who are these two privileged persons, if you please?"

"My foster brother Mariano, the tigrero, and José Paredes."

"Come, I see you know where to place your confidence. Those two men are entirely devoted to us, and this gives me trust in the future. Go on, my child; what must be done further?"

"These men must be provided with picks, spades, crowbars, and lanterns."

"I see you are thinking about digging."

"Possibly," she said, with a smile.

"Stories about buried treasure are thoroughly worn out in this country, my child," he said, with a dubious shake of his head; "all those that have been buried were dug up long ago."

"I can offer you no explanation, father. You are ignorant of my plan, and hence cannot argue upon a matter you do not know: moreover, you must make no remarks, and be the first to obey me," she said, with an exquisite smile. "You ought not to give an example of rebellion to my new subjects."

"That is perfectly true, my dear child; I am in the wrong, and offer you an ample apology. Be good enough to go on with your instructions."

"I have only a word to add, father. You and Ruiz must also provide yourselves with tools, for I expect you all four to work."

"Oh, oh, that is rather hard—not on me who am young," Don Ruiz exclaimed, laughingly, "but on our father. Come, little sister, do not expect such toil from him."

"I may have to lend a hand myself," Doña Marianna replied. "Believe me, Don Ruiz, you should not treat this affair lightly; it is far more serious than you suppose, and the consequence will be of incalculable importance for my father and the honour of our name. In my turn I will take an oath, since you refuse to believe my word."

"Not I, sister."

"Yes, Ruiz, you doubt it, although you do not like to allow it. Well, I swear to you and my father, by all I hold dearest in the world—that is to say, you two—that I am perfectly well aware of what I am doing, and am certain of success."

Such enthusiasm sparkled in the girl's brilliant eyes, there was such an expression of sincerity in her accent, that the two gentlemen at length confessed themselves vanquished; her conviction had entered their minds, and they were persuaded.

"What you desire shall be done, daughter," Don Hernando said; "and, whatever the result may be, I shall feel grateful to you for the efforts you are making."

Don Ruiz, by his father's orders, warned the majordomo and the tigrero, who was already preparing to return to the rancho. But so soon as the young man knew that his presence was necessary at the hacienda, he remained without the slightest remark, and delighted at having an opportunity to prove to his masters how greatly he was devoted to them. Then what always happens under similar circumstances occurred: while Doña Marianna was calmly awaiting the hour she had herself fixed for action, the Marquis and his son, on the other hand, suffered from a feverish curiosity, which did not allow them a moment's rest, and made them regard the delay as interminable. At length eight o'clock struck.

"It is time!" said Doña Marianna.

CHAPTER XXXVII
THE HUERTA

All southern nations are fond of shade, flowers, and birds; and as the heat of the climate compels them, so to speak, to live in the open air, they have arranged their gardens with a degree of comfort unknown among us. The Italians and Spaniards, whose houses, during the greater part of the year, are only inhabitable for a few hours a day, have striven to make their gardens veritable oases, where they can breathe the fresh evening air without being annoyed by those myriads of mosquitoes and gnats unknown in temperate climates, but which in tropical latitudes are a real plague. At midday they may be seen wheeling in countless myriads in every sunbeam. The Hispano-Americans especially have raised the gardening art to a science, being always engaged in trying to solve the problem of procuring fresh air during the hottest hours of the day—that is to say, between midday and three p.m., during which time the earth, which has been heated since dawn by the burning heat of a torrid sun, exhales deadly effluvia, and so decomposes the air that it is impossible to breathe it.

The Spanish language, which is so rich in expressions of every description, has two words to signify a garden. There is the word *jardín*, by which is meant the parterre properly so called—the garden in which flowers are cultivated that in those countries grow in the open air, but with us only in hothouses, where they are stunted and decrepit; and, secondly, the *huerta*, which means the kitchen-garden, the vineyard, and their clumps of trees, wide avenues, cascades, streams, and lakes—in a word, all that we, very improperly in my opinion, have agreed to call a park. The Hacienda del Toro possessed a huerta, which the Marquises de Moguer had in turn sought to embellish. This huerta, which in Europe would have seemed very large—for life among us has been reduced to the conditions of a mean and shabby comfort—was considered small in that country. It contained in all only thirty acres—that is to say, a surface of about twelve square miles; but this relative smallness was made up for by an admirable disposition of the ground, and an extent of shade, which had made a great reputation for the Huerta del Toro throughout Sonora.

At eight o'clock precisely the curfew was rung, as was the custom at the hacienda. At the sound of the chapel bell all the peons and vaqueros retired to their jacales in order to sleep. Paredes had placed sentinels at night on the walls ever since an attack from the Indians had been apprehended, and the precaution was the more necessary at this time, as there was no moon, and it is that period of the month which the Redskins always select to begin their invasions. When the majordomo had assured himself that the sentries were at their posts, he made a general inspection of the whole hacienda to have the lights extinguished, and then proceeded, accompanied by the tigrero, to the Blue Room, where Don Hernando and his son and daughter were assembled.

"All is in order, *mi amo*," he said; "everybody has retired to his jacal, the hacienda gates are closed, and the sentries placed on the walls."

"You are quite certain, Paredes, that no one is walking about the corals or huerta?"

"No one; I made my rounds with the greatest strictness."

"Very good; now, daughter, you can give your orders, and we are ready to obey you."

Doña Marianna bowed to her father with a smile.

"Paredes," she said, "have you procured the tools my brother ordered you to provide?"

"Niña," he answered, "I have placed six picks, six crowbars, and six spades in a clump of carob trees at the entrance of the large flower garden."

"Why such a number of tools?" she asked, laughingly.

"Because, señorita, some may break; the work we have to do must be performed quickly, and had I not taken this precaution, we might have met with delay."

"You are right. Follow me, señora."

"And the lanterns?" Don Ruiz observed.

"We will take them with us, but not light them till we reach the spot whither I am taking you. Although the night is dark, with your knowledge of localities we shall be able to guide ourselves without difficulty through the darkness. Our lights might be seen and arouse suspicions, and that is what we must avoid most of all."

"Excellently reasoned, daughter."

Doña Marianna rose, and the four men followed her in silence. They crossed the apartments instead of passing through the *patios*, which were thronged with sleepers, and entered the huerta by large double doors, from which the garden was reached by a flight of steps. On leaving the

Blue Room Doña Marianna took the precaution to blow out the candles, so that the hacienda was plunged into complete darkness, and all appeared asleep. The night was very dark; the sky, in which not a single star twinkled, seemed an immense pall; the breeze whistled hoarsely through the trees, whose branches rustled with an ill-omened murmur. In the distance could be heard the snapping bark of the coyotes, and at times the melancholy hoot of the owl arose in the dark, and broke the mournful silence which brooded over nature. This night was excellently chosen for a mysterious expedition of such a nature as Doña Marianna was about to attempt.

After an instant—not of hesitation, for the maiden, although her heart was beating loudly, was firm and resolute—but of reflection, Doña Marianna rapidly descended the steps and entered the garden, closely followed by the four men, who also experienced an internal emotion for which they could not account. They had gone but a few yards when they halted; they had reached the thicket in which the tools were concealed. The majordomo and the tigrero took them on their shoulders, while the Marquis and his son carried the lanterns. In spite of the darkness, which was rendered even more intense by the dense shadow cast by the old trees in the huerta, the young lady rapidly advanced, scarce making the sand creak beneath her little feet, and following the winding walks with as much ease as if she were traversing them in the bright sunshine.

The Marquis and his son felt their curiosity increase from moment to moment. They saw the girl so gay, and so sure of herself, that they involuntarily began to hope, although they found it impossible to explain the nature of their hopes to themselves. Paredes and Mariano were also greatly puzzled about the purpose of the expedition in which they were taking part; but their thoughts did not travel beyond this: they supposed that there was some work for them to do, and that was all.

The young lady still walked on, stopping at times and muttering a few words in a low voice, as if trying to remember the instructions she had previously received, but never hesitating, or taking one walk for another; in a word, she did not once retrace her steps when she had selected her course. Night, especially when it is dark, imparts to scenery a peculiar hue, which completely changes the appearance of the most familiar spots; it gives the smallest object a formidable aspect; all is confounded in one mass, without graduated tints, from which nothing stands out: a spot which is very cheerful in the sunshine becomes gloomy and mournful when enveloped in darkness. The huerta, which was so pretty and bright by day, assumed on this night the gloomy and majestic proportions of a forest; the fall of a leaf, the accidental breaking of a branch, the dull murmur of invisible waters— things so unimportant in themselves—made these men start involuntarily, although they were endowed with great energy, and any real danger would not have made them blench.

But darkness possesses the fatal influence over the human organization of lessening its faculties, and rendering it small and paltry. A man who, in the midst of a battle, electrified by the sound of the cannon, intoxicated by the smell of powder, and excited by the example of his comrades, performs prodigies of valour, will tremble like a child on finding himself alone in the shadow of night, and in the presence of an unknown object, which causes him to apprehend a danger which frequently only exists in his sickly imagination. Hence our friends involuntarily underwent the formidable influence of darkness, and felt a certain uneasiness, which they tried in vain to combat, and which they could not succeed in entirely dispelling, in spite of all their efforts. They walked on silent and gloomy, pressing against each other, looking around them timidly, and in their hearts wishing to reach as speedily as possible the end of this long walk. At length Doña Marianna halted.

"Light the lanterns," she said.

This was the first remark made since they left the Blue Room. The lanterns were instantly lighted. Doña Marianna took one, and handed another to her brother.

"Show me a light, Ruiz," she said to him.

The spot where they found themselves was situated at nearly the centre of the huerta; it was a species of grass plot, on which only stubbly, stunted grass grew. In the centre rose a sort of tumulus, formed of several rocks piled on one another without any apparent symmetry, and which the owners of the hacienda had always respected in consequence of its barbarous singularity. An old tradition asserted that one of the old kings of Cibola, on the ruins of which town the hacienda was built, had been buried at the spot, which was called "The Tomb of the Cacique" after the tradition, whether it were true or false. The first Marquis de Moguer, who was a very pious man, like all the Spanish conquistadors, had to some extent authorized this belief, by having the mound blessed by a priest, under the pretext—a very plausible one at that time—that the tomb of a pagan attracted demons, who would at once retire when it was consecrated.

With the exception of the name it bore, this mound had never been held in bad repute, and no suspicious legend was attached to it. It was remote from the buildings of the hacienda, and surrounded on all sides by dense and almost impenetrable clumps of trees. Persons very rarely visited it, because, as it stood in the centre of an open patch of grass, it offered no shelter against the sun; hence the place was only known to the family and their oldest servants.

"Ah! Ah!" said the Marquis, "So you have brought us to the cacique's tomb, my girl?"

"Yes, father; we can now begin operations without fear of being seen."

"I greatly fear that your hopes have led you astray."

"You promised, father, to make no remarks."

"That is true, and so I will hold my tongue."

"Very good, father," she said, with a smile; "be assured that this exemplary docility will soon be duly rewarded."

And the young lady continued her investigations. She looked attentively at every stone, seeming to study its position carefully, while comparing it with a point of the compass.

"In which direction does the clump of old aloes lie?" she at length asked.

"That I cannot tell you," said Don Ruiz.

"With your permission, I will do so," Paredes observed.

"Yes, yes," she said, eagerly.

The majordomo looked about for a moment, and then, placing himself in a certain direction, said,—"The aloes of Cibola, as we call them, are just facing me."

"Are you certain of it, Paredes?"

"Yes, niña, I am."

The young lady immediately placed herself by the majordomo's side, and bending down over the stones, examined them with extreme care and attention. At length she drew herself up with a start of joy.

"My father," she said, with emotion, "the honour of dealing the first stroke belongs to you."

"Very good, my child; where am I to strike?"

"There!" she said, pointing to a rather large gap between two stones.

Don Hernando drove in the pick, and, pressing on it forcibly, detached a stone, which rolled on the grass.

"Very good," said the girl. "Now stop, father, and let these young men work; you can join them presently, should it prove necessary. Come, Ruiz—

come tocayo—come, Paredes—to work, my friends! Enlarge this hole, and make it large enough for us to pass through."

The three men set to work ardently, excited by Doña Marianna's words, and soon the stones, leaping from their bed of earth, began to strew the ground around in large numbers. Not one of the three men suspected the nature of the task he was performing, and yet such is the attraction of a secret, that they drove in their picks with extraordinary ardour. Ruiz alone possibly foresaw an important discovery behind the task, but could not have explained what its nature was. The work, in the meanwhile, progressed; the hole became with every moment larger. The stones, which had been apparently thrown upon each other, were not bound by any mortal, and hence, so soon as the first was removed, the others came out with extreme facility. Now and then the labourers stopped to draw breath; but this interruption lasted only a short time, so anxious were they to obtain the solution of the problem. All at once they stopped in discouragement, for an enormous mass of rock resisted their efforts. This rock, which was about six feet square, was exactly under the stones they had previously removed, and as no solution of continuity could be perceived, everything led to the supposition that this rock was really very much larger, and that only a portion of it was laid bare.

"Why are you stopping, brother?" Doña Marianna asked.

"Because we have reached the rock, and should break our picks, without getting any further."

"What! Reached the rock? Impossible!"

The Marquis leant over the excavation.

"It would be madness to try and get any further," he said; "it is plain that we have reached the rock." Doña Marianna gave an angry start.

"I tell you again that it is impossible," she continued.

"Look for yourself, sister."

The young lady took a lantern and looked; then, without answering her brother, she turned to Paredes and the tigrero.

"You," she said, "are old servants of the family, and I can order you without any fear of being contradicted; so obey me. Remove, as rapidly as possible, all the stones round that supposed rock, and when that is done, I fancy I shall convince the most incredulous."

The two men resumed work; and Don Ruiz, piqued by his sister's remark, imitated them. The Marquis with folded arms and head bowed on his chest, was overcome by such persistency, and began to hope again. Ere long the stones were removed, and the mass of rock stood solitary.

The young lady turned to the Marquis.

"Father," she said to him, "you dealt the first blow, and must deal the last; help these three men in removing this block."

Without replying, the Marquis seized a pick, and placed himself by the side of the workers. The four men dug their tools into the friable earth which adhered to the rock; then, with a common and gradual effort, they began raising the stone until it suddenly lost its balance, toppled over, and fell on the ground, revealing a deep excavation. At the sight of this, all uttered a cry of surprise.

"Burn some wood to purify the air," the young lady said.

They obeyed with that feverish activity which, in great circumstances, seizes on apparently the slowest natures.

"Now come, father," Doña Marianna said, as she seized a lantern and boldly entered the excavation.

The Marquis went in, and the rest followed him. After proceeding for about one hundred yards along a species of gallery, they perceived the body of a man, lying on a sort of clumsy dais, in a perfect state of preservation, and rather resembling a sleeping person than a corpse. Near the body the fleshless bones of another person were scattered on the ground.

"Look!" said the maiden.

"Yes," the Marquis answered, "it is the body interred under the tumulus."

"You are mistaken, father; it is the body of a miner, and the fancied tumulus is nothing but a very rich gold mine, which has remained for ages under the guard of this insensate body, and which it has pleased Heaven to make known to you, in order that you may recover the fortune which you were on the point of losing. Look around you," she said, raising the lantern.

The Marquis uttered a cry of delight and admiration, doubt was no longer possible. All around he saw enormous veins of gold, easy of extraction almost without labour. The Marquis was dazzled; weaker in joy than in suffering, he fell unconscious on the floor of this mine, whose produce was about to restore him all that he had lost.

CHAPTER XXXVIII
THE ASSAULT ON QUITOVAR

While these events were taking place at the Hacienda del Toro, others of an even more important nature were being carried out at the Real de Minas. Kidd the adventurer, had scarce left Don Rufino Contreras, after the interesting conversations we have recorded, ere the senator made his preparations for departure, and at once set out for the Real de Minas, though careful to be accompanied by a respectable escort, which protected him from the insults of marauders. At eight a.m. of the following day the senator entered the pueblo, and his first business was to present himself to the town commandant, Don Marcos de Niza. The captain not only received him coldly, but with a certain amount of constraint. This did not escape the senator's quick eye, but he was not at all affected by it.

"My dear captain," he said, after the usual compliments, "I am pleased at having been selected by the Presidential Government as its delegate to the military authorities of the State of Sonora for two reasons, apart from the honour I shall acquire by accomplishing this confidential duty."

The captain bowed, but said nothing.

"The first of these reasons," the senator continued with his eternal smile, "is that I make the acquaintance of an excellent caballero in yourself; the second, that before being joined in the command with you, and desiring to make myself as agreeable to you as I could, I asked for the rank of lieutenant-colonel for you, a step which, between ourselves, you have long deserved, and I was so fortunate as to obtain it for you. Permit me to hand you the commission with my own hands."

And drawing from his pocketbook a large folded paper, he laid it in the hand which the captain mechanically held out. The senator had justly counted on the skilfully managed surprise. The captain, confounded by the tardy justice done him, could not find a word to answer, but from this moment Don Rufino's cause was gained in his mind; and unless some unforeseen event occurred, the senator was convinced that he had nothing now to fear from this man, whom he had cleverly managed to lay under an obligation, without it costing him anything. The truth was, that a few days previously the captain's nomination had reached the Governor of Arispe from Mexico; the senator accidentally heard of it, and offered to deliver it to the captain. As the governor had no reason to refuse, he entrusted the nomination to the senator, and he turned it to the good purpose we have seen.

"And now," he continued, cutting short the thanks which the new colonel thought himself bound to offer him, "permit me to change the conversation, my dear colonel, and speak to you about things which interest me privately."

"I am listening to you caballero," Don Marcos answered; "and if I can be of any service to you—"

"Oh, merely to give me some information," the senator interrupted him; "I will explain the matter in two words. I am, as you are probably aware, very intimate with a relative of yours, the Marquis de Moguer, and an alliance between us is being arranged at this moment."

Don Marcos gave a deep bow.

"Now," the senator continued, "the Marquis, as you of course know, has been seriously tried of late; in a word, between ourselves, he is almost ruined. Several times already I have been so fortunate as to render him important services; but, as you know, where misfortune is pressing a family, the best intentions often can only succeed in retarding an inevitable downfall. Being most desirous to save a man with whom I shall be probably closely connected within a few days, not merely by the ties of friendship, but also by the closer links of relationship, I have bought up all his debts; in a word, I have become his sole creditor, and that is as much as telling you that the Marquis does not owe a farthing now. The man whom I entrusted with this difficult negotiation will arrive immediately in this town, where I gave him the meeting."

"He arrived some days ago," the colonel remarked.

"Indeed!" Don Rufino exclaimed, affecting surprise, "It seems in that case that he has worked quicker than I expected. But that is a thousand times better, as I will claim a service at your hands."

"A service!" Don Marcos exclaimed, with instinctive distrust.

"Yes," the senator continued, tranquilly; "I hardly know how to explain it to you, for it is so difficult, however friendly you may be with a man whose daughter you are about to marry, to say to him 'You owed enormous sums; I have bought up your debts, here are the receipts; burn them, for you owe nothing now;' it would be looking so much like trying to impose conditions to act thus—in a word, to make a bargain—that I feel a repugnance from it;

and if a common friend does not consent to come to my assistance in the matter, I confess to you that I am completely ignorant how I shall get out of the difficulty."

"What!" the colonel exclaimed, in admiration, "Would you do that?"

"I never had any other thought," the senator replied simply.

"Oh, it is a great and generous action, caballero."

"Not at all; on the contrary, it is quite natural. Don Hernando is my intimate friend; I am going to marry his daughter, and my line of duty is plain. I only did what anyone else in my place would have done."

"No, no," Don Marcos said, shaking his head with an air of conviction; "no, señor, no one would have acted as you have done, I feel certain. Alas! Hearts like yours are rare."

"All the worse, all the worse, and I feel sorry for humanity," Don Rufino said, as he raised his eyes piously to the ceiling.

"What is the service you expect from me, señor?"

"A very simple thing. I will give you in a few moments those unlucky receipts, which I will ask you to be kind enough to hand to the Marquis. You can make him understand better than I can the purity of my intentions in this affair; and, above all, pray assure him that I have not done it for the purpose of forcing him to give me his daughter's hand."

The senator went away, leaving the colonel completely under the charm. He proceeded hastily to the mesón where Don Parfindo was lodged; he took the receipts from him, rewarded him handsomely, and did not leave him till he saw him and his bailiff out of the pueblo; then he walked slowly back to the colonel's house, rubbing his hands, and muttering, with an ironical smile—

"I fancy that I shall soon have no cause to fear that worthy Señor Kidd's denunciations. By the bye, where can he be? His absence from Quitovar is not natural, and I must free myself from him at our next interview."

The senator's conversation with his agent had occupied some time, and when Don Rufino returned to the colonel's house, he found the latter busy in making known his new rank to his officers. The colonel eagerly took advantage of the opportunity to introduce the senator to them, and to tell them that Don Rufino was delegated by the Government to watch the operations of the army, and that hence they must obey him like himself. The officers bowed respectfully to the senator, made their bows, and retired. When the two gentlemen were alone again, the ice was completely broken between them, and they were the best friends in the world.

"Well," the colonel asked.

"All is settled," the senator replied, as he produced the vouchers.

"¡Caramba! You have lost no time."

"The best things are those done quickly. Take all these documents, and make what use of them you think proper. I am delighted at having got rid of them." While saying this, Don Rufino threw the papers on the table with an excellent affectation of delight.

"With your leave, caballero," the colonel said, with a laugh, "I will take these papers, since you insist on it, but I will give you a receipt."

"Oh, no," the senator exclaimed, "that would spoil the whole business."

"Still—"

"Not a word," he interrupted him, quickly; "I do not wish to have in my possession the shadow of a claim upon Don Hernando."

The colonel would have probably pressed the point, had not a great noise been heard in the anteroom, and a man rushed into the colonel's sanctum, shouting at the top of his lungs, "The Indians! The Indians!"

The colonel and the senator rose. The man was Kidd; his clothes were torn and disordered; his face and hands were covered with blood and dust, and all apparently proved that he had just escaped from a sharp pursuit. A strange uproar outside the house, which soon assumed formidable proportions, corroborated his statement.

"Is that you, Kidd?" the colonel exclaimed.

"Yes," he replied; "but lose no time, captain; here are the pagans! They are at my heels, and I am scarce half an hour ahead of them."

Without waiting to hear anything more, the colonel dashed out of the room.

"Where have you come from?" Don Rufino asked the bandit, so soon as he was alone with him.

The latter gave a start of disappointment on recognising the senator, whom he had not noticed at the first moment. This start did not escape Don Rufino.

"How does that concern you?" the adventurer answered, roughly.

"I want to know."

Kidd made a meaning grimace.

"Every man has his own business," he said.

"Some treachery you have been preparing, of course."

"That is possible," he replied, with a knowing grin.

"Against me, perhaps."

"Who knows?"

"Will you speak?"

"What is the use of speaking, since you have guessed it?"

"Then you are still trying to deceive me?"

"I mean to take my precautions, that is all."

"Scoundrel!" the senator exclaimed, with a menacing gesture.

"Nonsense!" the other said, with a shrug of his shoulders; "I am not afraid of you, for you would not dare kill me."

"Why not?"

"In the first place, because it would cause a row, and because I do not think you such a friend of the captain that you would venture to take such a liberty in his house."

"You are mistaken, villain, and you shall have a proof of it."

"Holloa!" the adventurer exclaimed, as he retired precipitately to the door.

But, with a gesture rapid as thought, Don Rufino seized one of Don Marcos's pistols, cocked it, and ere Kidd could effect the retreat he was meditating, he fired, and the adventurer lay on the ground with a bullet in his chest.

"Die, brigand!" the senator shouted, as he threw down the weapon he had used.

"Yes," the bandit muttered, "but not unavenged. It was well played, master; but your turn will soon arrive—"

And stiffening with a final convulsion, the ruffian expired, retaining on his features even after death an expression of mocking defiance, which caused the senator an involuntary tremor.

"What is the matter here?" the colonel asked, suddenly entering.

"Nothing very important," Don Rufino said, carelessly. "I was carried away by my passion, and settled this scoundrel."

"¡Viva Dios! You were right, señor; I only regret that you have anticipated me, for I have proofs of his treachery.—Ho, there! Remove this carrion, and throw it out," he shouted to some soldiers who accompanied him, and had remained in the anteroom.

The soldiers obeyed, and the adventurer's body was thrown unceremoniously into the street.

"Are the Indians really coming up?"

"The dust raised by their horses' hoofs can already be perceived. We have not a moment to lose in preparing for defence. I suppose I can reckon on you?"

"¡Rayo de Dios!! I should hope so."

"Come, then, for time presses."

Kidd had in reality prepared, with his usual Machiavelism, a new treachery, of which, unluckily for him, he was destined to be the first victim. The whole pueblo was in an uproar: the streets were crowded with soldiers proceeding to their posts; with women, children, and aged persons flying in terror; with rancheros, who arrived at a gallop to find shelter in the town, and heightened the general alarm by the terror depicted on their faces; cattle were dashing madly about the streets, deserted by their herds, who were compelled to proceed to the intrenchments; and on the distant plain the body of Indians could be seen through the dust clouds, coming up at headlong speed.

"They are numerous," the senator whispered to the colonel.

"Too many," the latter answered; "but silence! Let us look cheerful."

There were twenty minutes of indescribable anxiety, during which the defenders of the pueblo were enabled to examine their enemies, and form an idea of the terrible danger that menaced them.

Unhappily, the sun was on the point of setting, and it was evident that the Redskins had calculated their march so as to arrive exactly at that moment, and continue the attack through the night. The colonel, foreseeing that he might possibly be compelled to have recourse to flight, collected a band of fifty resolute horsemen, whom he gave orders not to leave the Plaza Major, and be ready for any eventuality. After their first charge the Indians retired out of musket range, and did not renew their attack. A few horsemen, better mounted than the rest, were scattered over the plain, picking up the dead and wounded, and capturing the straggling horses; but the colonel gave orders that they should not be fired at—not through humanity, but in order to spare his ammunition, of which he possessed a very small stock.

Night set in, and a deep gloom covered the earth; but the redskins lit no fires. This circumstance alarmed the colonel; but several hours passed, and nothing led to the possibility of an attack being suspected. Profound silence brooded over the pueblo and the surrounding plains, and the Indians seemed to have disappeared as if by enchantment. The Mexicans tried in vain to distinguish any suspicious forms in the darkness; they saw and heard nothing. This expectation of a danger, which all felt to be imminent and terrible, had something frightful for the besieged.

Suddenly an immense light lit up the plain; the black outlines of the Indians rose like diabolical apparitions, galloping in all directions; a horrible, discordant, and shrill yell echoed in the ears of the Mexicans, and clouds of blazing arrows fell upon them from all sides at once, while the hideous heads of the Redskins appeared on the crest of the entrenchments. Then, in the light of a forest, kindled by the Indians to serve them as a beacon, an obstinate hand-to-hand fight began between the white men and redskins.

The pueblo was captured; any further resistance became not only impossible, but insensate. Several houses were already ablaze, and in a few minutes the Real de Minas would only be one immense furnace. The senator and the colonel had fought bravely so long as a gleam of hope was left them and the struggle appeared possible. At this moment they thought of saving the few wretches who still existed, and had escaped the frightful massacre by a miracle. Collecting around them all the men they possessed, they dashed to the Plaza Major, where, in spite of the fight raging round them, the squadron picked by Don Marcos had remained motionless, and leaping on their horses, they gave the order to start. Then the little band rushed forward like a hurricane, overthrowing and crushing all the obstacles that stood in their way; and after losing one-third their number, the rest succeeded in leaving the pueblo, traversing the enemy's lines, and taking the road to the Hacienda del Toro, without any close pursuit.

CHAPTER XXXIX
THE VENGEANCE OF HEAVEN

The Marquis's faint lasted but a short time, thanks to the attentions his son and daughter paid him. He had scarce regained his senses ere he drew Doña Marianna gently to him.

"My dear child," he muttered, as he pressed her to his heart, "you are our saviour."

The girl, delighted with this praise, freed herself, with a blush, from her father's embrace.

"Then," she said, with a pretty toss of her head, "you now allow, I think, father, that I have really kept my word."

"Oh, my child," he said, with much emotion, as he looked around him in delight, "there are here fifty fortunes equal to the one I have lost."

The girl clapped her hands in delight.

"Ah, how happy I am! I felt certain that she would not deceive me."

This remark, which escaped from the fullness of Doña Marianna's heart, struck Don Hernando.

"To whom are you alluding, daughter? And who is this person who inspires you with such confidence?"

"The one who revealed the existence of this treasure to me, father," she answered.

The Marquis did not press her.

"Mariano," he said to the tigrero, "you will pass the night here; allow no one to approach this excavation, for it would be imprudent to let strangers know of the existence of such a treasure before we have time to take certain precautions indispensable for its safety."

"You can go without fear, *mi amo*," the brave lad answered; "no one shall approach the mine while I am alive."

"Besides," Don Hernando continued, "your watch will cease at sunrise."

"As long as you please, *mi amo*."

And the tigrero, collecting the tools and lanterns, installed himself in the excavation itself, a few yards from the body still lying on the dais.

The other four slowly returned to the hacienda, conversing about this marvellous discovery, which, at the moment when all seemed desperate, saved the family. In fact, the gold veins were so rich, that it would be possible to detach in a single day enough nearly to cover all the debts contracted by the Marquis. They re-entered the blue room; and though it was very late, not one of them felt the slightest inclination to sleep; on the contrary, they wanted still to converse about the mine.

"Well," the Marquis said, "you did not dream that so rich a mine existed on the estate; you allowed as much just now."

"In truth, father, someone was kind enough to give me the information by which I found it."

"But who can this person be, who is better acquainted than myself with a property which has been in the hands of the family more than three hundred years, and yet nobody suspected that it contained this treasure?"

"The probability is that the secret was well kept, father."

"Of course; but by whom?"

"By the old owners of the soil, of course."

"Nonsense! You are jesting, daughter. Those poor Indians disappeared long ago from the face of the earth."

"I am not of that opinion, father," Don Ruiz observed.

"The more so," Paredes struck in, "because I know for a fact that the tribe to which you allude still exists; it is one of the most powerful in the great confederation of the Papazos."

"And you know, father, with what religious exactitude the Indians preserve secrets confided to their conscience."

"That is true; but in that case some man must have spoken."

"Or some woman," Doña Marianna said, smilingly.

"Well, be it so—a woman," the Marquis continued; "that is already a valuable piece of news. I know that you have obtained your information about the mine from a woman, my child."

"Unhappily, father, I am prohibited from saying any more."

"Humph! Prohibited!"

"Yes, father. However, re-assure yourself: this mine is really yours— your lawful property. Its owner has freely surrendered it in your favour."

Don Hernando frowned with an air of dissatisfaction.

"Charity!" he muttered.

"Oh, no, but a gift you can accept, father, I swear to you. Besides, the person to whom you are indebted for it promised me to make herself known to you ere long."

On the next morning, by the orders of the Marquis, the majordomo selected ten confidential rancheros and peons from those who had sought shelter at the hacienda, and the work commenced at once. The mine had been abandoned exactly in the state in which it was when the body of the miner was found by the Indians; hence the mere sweepings formed a considerable amount, and at the expiration of four or five days the sum collected was sufficient, not only to pay off all the debts, but also to leave at the disposal of the Marquis a sum thrice as large as he owed. With the exception of the legitimate anxiety caused by the apprehension of an Indian attack, joy had returned to the hacienda; the Marquis had begun to smile again, and seemed younger—so great is the privilege of wealth to alter men. The first thought that occurred to the Marquis was to settle with his creditors, and determine his position.

"My dear child," he said one evening to Doña Marianna, at the moment when she was about to retire for the night, "you have not yet given me an answer on the subject of Don Rufino Contrera's request for your hand; but the week has long since passed. Tomorrow, Paredes is going to start to place in his hands certain letters of importance for the settlement of my affairs, and I wish to take advantage of the opportunity. What answer shall I give Don Rufino?"

The young lady blushed; but at length subduing the trouble that agitated her, she said, with a slight tremour in her voice, —

"Father, I am doubtless highly honoured by this Caballero's demand; but do you not think as I do, that the moment is badly chosen for such a thing, menaced as we incessantly are by terrible dangers?"

"Very good, daughter; I do not at all wish to force your inclinations. I will answer the senator in that sense; but if he come himself to seek his answer, what shall we do?"

"It will be time enough to think of it then," she replied, with a laugh.

"Well, well, that is true, and I was wrong to dwell on the matter so. Good night, my child, and sleep soundly. As for me, I shall probably spend the whole night in my study with your brother, engaged with my accounts."

The young lady withdrew.

"Señor Marquis," said Paredes, suddenly opening the door, "excuse my disturbing you so late; but Mariano, the tigrero, has just arrived at the hacienda with his whole family; he is the bearer of such strange and terrible news, that you will perhaps sooner hear it from his lips than from mine."

"What does he say?" Don Ruiz asked, who entered the room at this moment.

"He says that the Indians have risen, that they have surprised the Mineral of Quitovar, fired the pueblo, and massacred all the inhabitants."

"Oh, that is frightful!" the Marquis exclaimed.

"Our poor cousin!" the young man added.

"That is true; our unhappy cousin commanded at the pueblo. What a horrible disaster! Send the tigrero in to me, Paredes; go and fetch him at once."

Mariano was shown in, and related in their fullest details, though with some exaggeration, the events recorded in our last chapter, which threw his hearers into a profound stupor. Among all the incomprehensible things which daily occur, there is one which will never be explained; it is the rapidity with which all news spreads even for considerable distances. Thus, the capture of Quitovar was unhappily only too true, and the details furnished by Mariano were substantially correct; but how could the tigrero have become acquainted with a fact that had happened scarce three hours previously, and at more than ten leagues from the hacienda? He could not have explained this himself; he had heard it from somebody, but could not remember whom.

This terrible news caused the Marquis to reflect deeply. Now that the roads were probably infested with marauders, and communication intercepted by the Indians, he could not think of sending Paredes to Hermosillo, and the journey had become literally impossible. He must busy himself without delay in organizing the defence of the hacienda, in order vigorously to repulse the attack which would, in all probability, not be long delayed. In spite of the advanced hour, all were at work in an instant at the Toro; the walls were lined with defenders, and reserves established in all parts of the hacienda.

The whole night was spent in preparations. About two hours after sunrise, at the moment when the Marquis, wearied by a long watch, was preparing to take a little repose, the sentries signalled the approach of a body of horsemen, coming at full gallop towards the hacienda. The Marquis went up on the walls, took a telescope, and had a look at them. After a short examination, he perceived that these horsemen were Mexicans, although, owing to the distance, he could not distinguish whether they were soldiers or rancheros. Still, he had all preparations made to give them a hearty reception, if they evinced a desire to halt at the hacienda, as the direction they were following seemed to indicate.

Some time elapsed ere these horsemen, who were climbing the hill, reached the hacienda gates. Then all doubts were removed: they were soldiers, and a few paces ahead of the troop rode Don Rufino Contreras and Colonel Don Marcos de Niza. But both leaders and soldiers were in such disorder, so blackened with gunpowder, so covered with dust and blood, that it was plain they had come from a recent fight, from which they had escaped as fugitives. Men and horses were utterly exhausted, not alone by the extraordinary fatigue they had undergone, but also by the gigantic struggle they had sustained ere they dreamed of flight. It was unnecessary to ask them any questions. The Marquis ordered refreshments to be served them, and beds got ready.

Don Marcos de Niza and the senator had hardly the strength to say a few words explanatory of the wretched condition in which they presented themselves, and yielding to fatigue and want of sleep, they fell down in a state of complete insensibility, from which no attempt was made to rouse them, but they were both carried to bed. The Marquis then withdrew to his room, leaving his son to watch over the safety of the hacienda in his stead, for in all probability it would be speedily invested by the Redskins.

At three in the afternoon a fresh band of horsemen was signalled in the plain. This considerable party was composed entirely of hunters and wood rangers. Don Ruiz gave orders to let them advance, for the arrival of these hunters, nearly one hundred in number, was a piece of good fortune for the hacienda, as the number of its defenders was augmented by so many. Still, when Don Ruiz saw them enter the track, he noticed such a regularity in their movements, that a doubt crossed his mind like a flash of lightning, and a thought of treachery rose to his brain. Hence he rushed to the outer gate of the hacienda to give Paredes orders not to open; but the majordomo checked him at the first word.

"You cannot have looked, niño," he said, "when you order such a thing."

"On the contrary, I do so because I have looked," he replied.

"Then you must have seen badly," the majordomo said; "otherwise you would have perceived that the horseman at their head is one of your most devoted friends."

"Whom do you mean?"

"Who else than Stronghand?"

"Is Stronghand coming with those horsemen?"

"He is at the head of the column, niño."

"Oh, in that case let them enter."

"Ah, I felt certain of it."

The hunters had no necessity even of parleying; they found the hacienda gates wide open, and rode straight in without drawing rein. Don Ruiz recognised Stronghand, who, on his side, rode up to him and held out his hand.

"Grant me one favour, Don Ruiz," he said.

"Speak," the young man answered.

"Two words of conversation in your sister's presence; but wait a moment, another person must accompany me, for reasons you will soon appreciate; this person desires temporarily to maintain the most inviolable incognito. Do you consent?"

Don Ruiz hesitated.

"What do you fear?" the hunter continued; "Do you not put faith in me? Do you believe me capable of abusing your confidence?"

"No; I do not wish even to suppose it, I pledge you my word."

"And I mine, Don Ruiz."

"Act as you think proper."

The hunter gave a signal, and a horseman dismounted and came up to them. A long cloak entirely covered him, and the broad brim of his hat was pulled down over his eyes. He bowed silently to the young man, who, though greatly perplexed by this mystery, made no remark; and after requesting the majordomo to take care of the newcomers, he led his guests to the room in which Doña Marianna was seated, engaged with her tambour-work. The young lady, on hearing the door open, mechanically raised her eyes.

"Oh!" she exclaimed, joyfully, "Stronghand!"

"Myself, señorita," the young man replied, with a respectful bow; "I have come to ask the fulfilment of your promise."

"I shall keep it, no matter what may happen."

"Thanks, señorita."

"Ruiz," she said to her brother, eagerly; "until further orders, my father must not know of the presence of these caballeros here."

"What you ask of me is very difficult, sister; think of the immense responsibility I assume in acting thus."

"I know it, Ruiz; but it must be, my dear brother, for my happiness is at stake," she continued, clasping her hands imploringly; "and besides, what have you to fear? Do you not know this hunter?"

"Yes, I know him; I am even under great obligations to him; but his companion?"

"I answer for him, Ruiz."

"You know, then, who he is?"

"No matter what I know, brother; I only beg you to grant what I ask."

"Well, for your sake I will be silent."

"Oh! Thanks, thanks, brother!"

At this moment a sound of footsteps was heard in the adjoining room.

"What is to be done?" the maiden murmured.

Stronghand laid his finger on his lips, and, leading away his companion—who, through the thick cloak he wore, resembled a phantom rather than a man—disappeared behind a curtain. At the same instant a door opened, and two persons entered. They were Don Marcos and the senator. They had scarce exchanged the first compliments with Don Ruiz and Doña Marianna, when the Marquis entered the room.

"You are up at last, I am happy to see," he said, cheerfully. "¡Viva Dios! You were in a most deplorable state on your arrival; I am glad to see you so fully recovered."

"A thousand thanks, cousin, for your hospitality, of which we stood in great need."

"No more about that; I am the more pleased at the chance which has brought us together, Don Rufino, because I intended to write to you immediately."

"My dear sir," the senator said, with a bow.

"Are you not expecting an answer from me?"

"It is so, but I did not dare to hope."

The Marquis cut him short.

"Let us come to the most important point first," he continued, with a smile. "Don Rufino, you have behaved to me like a real friend. By a miracle—for I can only attribute to a miracle the good fortune that has befallen me—I am in a position to arrange my affairs, and discharge my debt to you, although, be assured, I shall never forget the services you have rendered me, and the obligations I have contracted toward you."

The senator was so surprised, that he turned pale, and took a side-glance at the colonel.

"Obligations far greater than you suppose," the latter said, warmly.

"What do you mean, cousin?" the Marquis asked, in surprise.

"I mean that Don Rufino, unaware of the happy change in your fortunes, and wishing to save you from the frightful position in which you were, had bought up all your liabilities, and so soon as he had all the vouchers in his possession, he hurried with them to me, and implored me to destroy them. Here they are, cousin," he added, as he drew a bundle of papers from his pocket.

The various actors in this singular scene were affected by strange feelings. Don Ruiz and his sister exchanged a look of despair, for they understood that the Marquis would now be unable to refuse his consent to his daughter's marriage.

"Oh!" the Marquis exclaimed, "I cannot accept such an act of generosity."

"From a stranger, certainly not," Don Rufino remarked, in an insinuating voice; "but I flattered myself that I was not such to you, my dear sir."

There was a silence.

"What is going on at this moment is so strange; I feel taken so unawares," the Marquis presently continued; "my thoughts are so confused, that I must beg you, Don Rufino, to defer till tomorrow the remainder of this conversation. By that time I shall have been able to regain my coolness, and then, believe me, I will answer you in the way that I ought to do."

"My dear sir, I understand the delicacy of your remarks, and will wait as long as you think proper," the senator replied, with a bow, and an impassioned glance at Doña Marianna, who was pale and trembling.

"Yes," said the colonel, "let us put off serious matters till tomorrow; the shock we have suffered has been too rough for us to be fit for any discussion just at present."

"What has happened to you? The pagans have not seized the Mineral de Quitovar? Or at least I hope not."

"Yes, they have, cousin; the pueblo has been captured by the Redskins, sacked, and burnt. We had great difficulty in making our escape, and passed through extraordinary dangers ere we were so lucky as to reach your hacienda."

"That is disastrous news, cousin; I had been told of it, but was unwilling to believe it."

"It is unhappily but too true."

"Well, thank Heaven, cousin, you are in safety here. As for you, Don Rufino, I am happy that you escaped from the horrible massacre; you are not a soldier, you are—"

"An assassin!" a sepulchral voice suddenly exclaimed, and a hand was laid heavily on the senator's shoulder.

The company turned with horror. Stronghand's companion had let fall the hat and cloak that disguised him, and was standing, stern and menacing, behind the senator.

"Oh!" the latter exclaimed, as he recoiled with terror, "Rodolfo! Don Rodolfo!"

"Brother, do I see you again after so many years?" the Marquis said, joyfully, as he advanced towards the stranger.

"The great sachem," Doña Marianna murmured.

The sachem thrust back with a gesture of sovereign contempt the startled senator, and walked into the centre of the group.

"Yes, it is I, brother; I, the proscript, the disinherited, who enter the house of my father after an absence of twenty years, in order to save the last representative of my family."

"Oh, brother! Brother!" the Marquis exclaimed, sorrowfully.

"Recover yourself, Hernando! I entertain no feelings of hatred or rancour for you; on the contrary, I have always loved you, and though I was far away from you I have never lost you out of sight. Come to my arms, brother; let us forget the past, only to think of the joy of being reunited."

The Marquis threw himself into his brother's arms; Don Ruiz and Doña Marianna imitated him, and for some minutes there was an uninterrupted interchange of embraces among the members of this family, who had so long been separated.

"It was through me that you received the sum which Paredes was to receive at Hermosillo", Don Rodolfo continued; "to me you also owe the discovery of the gold mine which has saved you. But I have not come here solely to embrace you and yours, brother; I have come to punish a villain! This man," he said, pointing to the senator, who was trembling with rage and terror—"this man was my valet; in order to rob me, he attempted to assassinate me cowardly, treacherously, and behind my back. Such is the man whose dark machinations had succeeded in deceiving you, and to whom you were on the point of giving your daughter: let him contradict me if he dare!"

"Oh!" the senator muttered, with a furious gesture.

"Villain!" the Marquis exclaimed; "Help! Help! seize the monster!"

Several servants rushed into the room, but before they could reach Don Rufino the latter had bounded with a tiger leap upon Don Rodolfo, and buried a dagger in his chest. The sachem fell back with a cry of pain into the arms of his brother and his son. After the crime was committed, the assassin threw down his weapon, and said to the startled spectators, with an air of defiance and satisfied hatred,—

"Now you can do whatever you like to me, for I am avenged."

CHAPTER XL
FUNERAL OF A SACHEM

Two days had elapsed since the atrocious attack made by Don Rufino on Don Rodolfo de Moguer. The Papazos had captured the hacienda without a blow, as the gates were opened to them; for the stupor and terror of the Mexicans at this horrible crime were so great, that they forgot all precautions. But we must do the Redskins the justice of stating that, contrary to their habits, they committed no excesses in the hacienda, either by virtue of superior orders, or in consequence of the sorrow which the wound of their great sachem caused them. Doña Esperanza had arrived with Padre Serapio at the same time as the Indian warriors, and she and Doña Marianna did not leave the wounded man's bed.

Don Hernando was inconsolable, and the colonel could not forgive himself for having supposed for a moment that the senator was an honest man. The whole hacienda was plunged into sorrow, and Don Rodolfo alone watched death approach with a calm brow. Fray Serapio dressed his wound: his night was tolerably quiet, and in the morning the monk entered the wounded man's room. At a sign from Don Rodolfo his wife and niece, who had watched the whole night through by his bedside, withdrew.

"Now, padre," he said, when they left the room, "it is our turn."

And he helped him to remove the bandages. The monk frowned.

"I am condemned, am I not?" said Don Rodolfo, who attentively followed in the monk's face the feelings that agitated him.

"God can perform a miracle," the Franciscan stammered, in a faint voice.

The sachem smiled softly.

"I understand you," he replied; "answer me, therefore, frankly and sincerely. How many hours have I still to live?"

"What good is that, my dear, good master?" the monk murmured.

"Padre Serapio," the chief interrupted him, in a firm voice, "I want to know, in order that I may settle my affairs on earth, before I appear in the presence of God."

"Do you insist on my telling you the truth?"

"Pray do so—the entire truth."

The poor man stifled a sigh, and answered, in a voice broken by emotion—"Unless a miracle occur, you will give back your soul to your Creator at sunset."

"I thank you, my friend," the sachem said, his austere face not displaying the slightest trace of emotion. "Ask my brother to come here, for I have to talk with him. Keep back my wife and niece until I ask for them. Go, father; I will see you again before I die."

The worthy monk withdrew, choked with sobs. The interview of the two brothers was long, for Don Hernando had many faults to ask pardon for at the hands of him whose place he had taken. But Don Rodolfo, far from reproaching him, tried on the contrary to console him, by talking to him in a cheerful voice, and reminding him of the happy days of their childhood. He also thanked his brother warmly for having freed him from the heavy burden of supporting the family honour, and allowing him to live in accordance with his tastes and humour. Many other things were talked of, after which the Marquis retired, with pale brow and eyes swollen with tears, which he tried in vain to repress, that he might not sadden the last moments of the man whose great soul was revealed to him at this supreme moment—of the brother whom he had so cruelly misunderstood, and who had even sacrificed his life to insure his brother's happiness.

Doña Marianna and Doña Esperanza then returned to the dying man's room, followed by Padre Serapio, and a few moments after the Marquis came back, accompanied by Stronghand. The young man, in spite of his Indian education and affected stoicism, knelt down sobbing by his father's side. For some moments father and son talked together in a low voice; no one save God knew what words were uttered by these two men during the solemn interview.

"Come here, niece," Don Rodolfo at length said, addressing Doña Marianna.

The maiden knelt down sobbing by the hunter's side. The aged man looked for a moment tenderly at their two young faces, pale with sorrow, which were piously leaning over him; then making an effort to sit up, and supported on one side by his brother, on the other by Doña Esperanza, he said, in a voice that trembled with emotion—"Niece, answer me as you would answer God; for the dying, you know, no longer belong to this world. Do you love my son?"

"Yes, uncle," the maiden answered through her tears—"yes, I love him."

"And you, Diego, my son, do you love your cousin?"

"Father, I love her," the young man answered, in a voice crushed by emotion.

Don Rodolfo turned to his brother, who understood his glance.

"Bless our children, brother," he said, "according to the wish you expressed to me; Padre Serapio will unite them in your presence."

The wounded man stretched out his trembling hands over the two young people.

"Children," he said, in a powerful voice, though with an accent of ineffable tenderness, "I bless you; be happy."

And, crushed by the efforts he had been forced to make, he fell back in a half-fainting state on his bed. When he regained consciousness, through the attention of Don Esperanza and his niece, he perceived an altar by the side of his bed. On his expressing a desire that the ceremony should take place at once, Padre Serapio, assisted by José Paredes, who was weeping bitterly, read the marriage mass. After the nuptial benediction, Don Rodolfo received the last sacraments, amid the tears and sobs of all present.

"And, now, my friends," he said, "that I have accomplished my duties as a Christian and Spanish gentleman, it is time for me to perform my duties as an Indian chief; so allow the Papazo warriors to enter."

The doors opened, and the warriors entered: they were sad, gloomy, and thoughtful. The sachem had sat up to receive them, supported by his son Stronghand. The warriors silently surrounded the bed on which their venerated chief lay, among them being Sparrowhawk and Peccary. The sachem looked calmly round the circle, and then spoke in a calm and deeply accentuated voice:—

"The Master of Life has suddenly recalled me to Him. I did not fall in action, but beneath the dagger of a cowardly assassin. I regret leaving my nation before I had completed the task which I undertook for their happiness. What I had not time to do, another will doubtless terminate. My brothers must continue the war they have so happily and gloriously commenced; and though I am leaving them, my mind will remain among them. The warriors of my nation must never forget that the Master of Life created them free, and that they must live and die free. The Papazos are brave men, invincible warriors, and slavery is not made for them. On the point of appearing before the Master of Life, I implore the chiefs not to forget that the white persons who surround me form part of my family. If my brothers retain after my death any recollection of the good which I have continually sought to do them, they will be kind to the palefaces whom I love. I have only one more word to add: I desire to give back my soul to the Master of Life beneath the buffalo hide cabin of the warriors of my nation, and in the midst of my nation. I desire also that all the rites customary at the death of the chiefs should be performed for me."

A tremor of joy ran along the ranks of the redskin warriors on hearing the last words; for they had feared in their hearts that the sachem would wish to be interred after the fashion of the white men. The Peccary then replied, in the name of all—

"My father's wishes are orders for his children; never, so long as the powerful confederation of the Papazos exists, shall an insult be offered to the palefaces whom he loves. Our father can die in peace; all his wishes will be religiously carried out by his children."

A flash of joy sparkled in the sachem's eye at this promise, which he knew would be strictly kept. The Peccary continued—

"The Papazos chiefs are sad; their hearts are swollen by the thought of losing their father: they fear lest his death may be the cause of great disorder in their confederation, and injure the success of the war which had scarce begun."

"I belong to my sons till the last moment of my existence; what can I do for them?"

"My father can do a great deal," the chief answered.

"My ears are open; I am waiting for my son to explain himself."

"The chiefs," continued Peccary, "and the great braves of the confederation, assembled at sunrise round the council fire: they desire, in order that no discord may spring up among them, that our father, the great sachem, should himself appoint his successor; for they feel persuaded that our father's choice will fall on a brave and wise chief, worthy to command men."

The sachem reflected for a moment.

"Be it so," he said at length; "the determination of the sachems is wise, and I approve of it. Sparrowhawk will command in my place when I am called away by the Great Spirit; no one is more worthy to be the first sachem of the nation."

Sparrowhawk quitted the ranks, stepped forward, and bowed respectfully to the dying man.

"I thank my father," he said, "for the signal honour he has done me; but I am very young to command chiefs and renowned warriors, and I fear that I shall break down in the heavy task imposed on me. My father leaves a son; Stronghand is one of the great braves of our nation, and his wisdom is renowned."

"My son is a paleface; he does not know the wants of the Papazos so well as Sparrowhawk. Sparrowhawk will command."

"I obey my father since he insists; but Stronghand will ever be one of the great chiefs of my nation."

A flattering murmur greeted these clever remarks.

"I thank my son Sparrowhawk in the name of Stronghand. Modesty becomes a chief so celebrated as is my son," the sachem continued; "the Great Spirit will inspire him, and he will do great things. I have spoken. Do the chiefs approve my choice?"

"We could not have chosen better," Peccary answered. "We sincerely thank our father for having anticipated our dearest wishes by choosing Sparrowhawk."

This scene so simple in its grandeur, and so truly patriarchal, affected all the spectators, who felt their hearts swollen by sorrow. The sachem continued—

"I feel my strength rapidly leaving me, and life is abandoning me; the Great Spirit will soon call me to Him. My sons will carry me beneath a tent of my nation, in order that I may breathe my last sigh in their midst."

Stronghand, the Marquis, Peccary, and Sparrowhawk gently lifted the wounded man on their shoulders, and carried him to the front yard of the hacienda, followed by all the rest, who walked silently and thoughtfully in the rear. A lodge, formed of stakes covered with buffalo hides, had been prepared to receive the great chief; the bed on which he was lying was softly put down, and the chief's eyes were turned toward the setting sun. Then all the warriors and their squaws, whom messengers had informed of the sachem's wound, and who had hurried to the hacienda, surrounded the tent. The Mexicans themselves mingled with the crowd, and a deadly silence brooded over the hacienda, in which, however, more than six thousand persons were assembled at this moment.

All eyes were turned toward the dying sachem, by whose side were standing the members of his family, Padre Serapio, and the principal chiefs of the Papazos. Now and then the aged man uttered a few words, which he addressed at times to the monk, at others to his brother, or to the Indian chiefs. When the sun was beginning to sink on the horizon, the wounded man's breathing began to grow panting, his eyes gradually became covered by a mist, and he did not speak; but he tightly grasped his son's and wife's hands in his right hand, and Sparrowhawk's in his left.

All at once a nervous tremor passed over the dying man's body; his cheeks were tinged; his half closed eyes opened again; he sat up without any extraneous help, and shouted, in a strong, clear voice, which was heard by all—"I come, Lord! Papazos, farewell! Esperanza! Esperanza! We shall meet again!"

His eyes closed; a livid pallor spread over his face; his limbs stiffened, and he fell back heavily as he exhaled his last sigh. He was dead. His last thought was for his wife, whom he had so dearly loved. The sobs, hitherto restrained, burst forth suddenly and violently among the crowd.

"Our father is dead!" Sparrowhawk shouted, in a thundering voice.

"Vengeance!" the Redskins yelled.

In fact the murderer of the chief was still alive. The white men who did not wish to witness the horrible scene that was about to take place, withdrew. Stronghand, the colonel, Paredes, and Mariano alone remained. The body of the defunct sachem was at once surrounded by the squaws: they painted it with several bright colours, dressed it in a buffalo robe, formed his hair into a tuft as a sign of his rank, and stretched him out on a dais. The assassin, who was pale but resolute, was then brought up.

Sparrowhawk placed himself at the head of the corpse, and began a long funeral oration, which was frequently interrupted by the sobs of his audience; then, pointing with an expressive gesture to the murderer, who was still standing motionless in the midst of the Indians who guarded him, he said—

"Commence the punishment."

We will not describe the frightful punishment which was inflicted on the senator; such horrible details are repulsive to our pen. We will restrict ourselves to stating that he was flayed alive, and that all his joints were cut in succession. He suffered indescribable agony for three long hours ere he died. Night had set in during this interval. When the wretched assassin was dead, chosen warriors took their chief's body on their shoulders, and proceeded by the light of torches to the huerta, at the spot where the hacienda hung over the precipice. On reaching this spot the chief's magnificent steed was brought up. On his back his master's corpse was securely tied with deerskin thongs, holding his totem in one hand and his gun in the other; the scalps of his foes were fastened to his saddle-bow, and on his neck and arms were his bead necklaces and copper ornaments. Then, amid the sobs of the squaws, the horse was led to the plateau, where the Papago warriors, mounted and dressed in their war paint, formed a semicircle, whose ends reached the precipice.

Then took place a scene whose savage grandeur could only be compared to the funeral rites performed at the death of the barbarous chiefs during those great national migrations which produced the overthrow of the Roman Empire. By the glare of the torches—whose flames, agitated by the wind, imparted a fantastic aspect to the gloomy and stern landscape in this part of the huerta—the horse was placed in the midst of the semicircle, and the horsemen, brandishing their weapons, struck up their war song with a savage energy. The startled horse bounded on to the plateau, bearing the corpse, to which each of its bounds imparted such an oscillating movement that the rider appeared to be restored to life. On reaching the brink of the precipice the horse recoiled with terror, with flaming nostrils; then, suddenly turning round, it tried to burst the living rampart, which was constantly contracted behind it. Several times the animal renewed the same exertions; but at last, attacked by a paroxysm of terror, pursued by the yells of the Indians, and wounded by their long lances, it rose on its hind legs, uttered a terrible snort, and leaped into the gulf with its burden. At the same moment all the torches were extinguished, the tumult was followed by a mournful silence, and the warriors retired.

On the morrow, at sunrise, the Redskins left the hacienda, to which they did not once return during the whole of the war, which lasted three years. We may possibly some day tell what was the termination of this grand uprising of the Indians, who on several occasions all but deprived the Mexican republic of its finest and richest, provinces.